Witches' Brew

By Terry Brooks
PUBLISHED BY BALLANTINE BOOKS

THE SWORD OF SHANNARA

THE ELFSTONES OF SHANNARA

THE WISHSONG OF SHANNARA

The Heritage of Shannara

THE SCIONS OF SHANNARA

THE DRUID OF SHANNARA

THE ELF QUEEN OF SHANNARA

THE TALISMANS OF SHANNARA

The Magic Kingdom of Landover

MAGIC KINGDOM FOR SALE—SOLD!

THE BLACK UNICORN

WIZARD AT LARGE

THE TANGLE BOX

WITCHES' BREW

Witches' Brew

A Magic Kingdom of Landover Novel

TERRY BROOKS

A Del Rey® Book

BALLANTINE BOOKS ▪ NEW YORK

Bro

A Del Rey® Book
Published by Ballantine Books

Copyright © 1995 by Terry Brooks

All rights reserved under International and Pan-American Copyright
Conventions. Published in the United States by Ballantine Books, a
division of Random House, Inc., New York, and simultaneously in Canada
by Random House of Canada Limited, Toronto.

Library of Congress Cataloging-in-Publication Data
Brooks, Terry.
  Witches' brew / Terry Brooks.
    p.   cm.—(A Magic Kingdom of Landover novel)
  "A Del Rey book."
  ISBN 0-345-38701-5
  I. Title. II. Series.
PS3552.R6596W53   1995
813'.54—dc20   94-29441
                                                        CIP

Manufactured in the United States of America

First Edition: April 1995

10   9   8   7   6   5   4   3   2   1

To Lisa.
For always being there.
&
To Jill.
Because you must never give up
on yourself.

All children, except one, grow up. They soon know that they will grow up, and the way Wendy knew was this. One day when she was two years old she was playing in a garden, and she plucked another flower and ran with it to her mother. I suppose she must have looked rather delightful, for Mrs. Darling put her hand to her heart and cried, "Oh, why can't you remain like this for ever!" This was all that passed between them on the subject, but henceforth Wendy knew that she must grow up. You always know after you are two. Two is the beginning of the end.

J. M. Barrie, *Peter Pan*

Contents

Witches' Brew

Mistaya

The crow with the red eyes sat on a branch in the towering old white oak where the leafy boughs were thickest and stared down at the people gathered for their picnic in the sunny clearing below. That was what Holiday called it, a picnic. A brightly colored cloth was spread out on the lush spring grass, and the contents of several baskets of food were being emptied onto it. The food, if you were human and possessed of an appetite, would have pleased and delighted, the crow supposed. There were platters of meats and cheeses, bowls of salad and fruit, loaves of bread, and flasks of ale and chilled water. There were plates and napkins set around for each participant and cups for drinking and utensils for eating. A vase of wildflowers had been placed at the center of the feast.

Willow was doing most of the work, the sylph with the emerald tresses and small, lithe form. She was animated, laughing and talking with the others as she worked. The dog and the kobold helped her: Abernathy, who was Landover's Court Scribe, and Parsnip, who did most of the castle's cooking. Questor Thews, the ragtag white-bearded wizard, wandered about looking in amazement at sprigs of new growth and strange wildflowers. Bunion, the other kobold, the dangerous one, the one who could spy out almost anything, patrolled the clearing's perimeter, ever watchful.

The King sat alone at one end of the bright cloth. Ben

Holiday, High Lord of Landover. He was staring out into the trees, lost in thought. The picnic was his invention, something they did in the world from which he came. He was introducing it to the others, giving them a new experience. They seemed to be enjoying it more than he was.

The crow with the red eyes sat perfectly still within the concealment of the branches of the old oak, cognizant of the adults but really interested only in the child. Other birds, some more dazzling in their plumage, some more sweet with their song, darted through the surrounding woods, flitting from here to there and back again, mindless and carefree. They were bold and heedless; the crow was purposefully invisible. No eye but the child's would be cast; no attention but the child's would be drawn. The crow had been waiting more than an hour for the child to notice it, for its unspoken summons to be heeded, for its silent command to be obeyed, and for the brilliant green eyes to be drawn upward into the leafy shadows. The child was walking about, playing at this and that, seemingly aimless but already searching.

Patience, then, the crow with the red eyes admonished. As with so much in life, patience.

Then the child was directly below, the small face lifting, the dazzling green eyes seeking and abruptly finding. The child's eyes locked on the crow's, emerald to crimson, human to bird. Words passed between them that did not need speaking, a silent exchange of thoughts on being and having, on want and loss, on the power of knowledge and the inexorable need to grow. The child stood as still as stone, staring up, and knew there was something vast and wondrous to be learned if the proper teacher could be found.

The crow with the red eyes intended to be that teacher.

The crow was the witch Nightshade.

Ben Holiday leaned back on his elbows and let the smells of the picnic lunch bring a growl to his empty stomach.

Breakfast had been hours ago, and he had been careful to re-frain from eating anything since. Thank goodness the wait was almost over. Willow was unpacking the containers and setting them out, aided by Abernathy and Parsnip. Soon it would be time to eat. It was a perfect summer day for a picnic, the sky clear and blue, the sun warming the earth and the new grasses, chasing memories of winter's chill into the past once more. Flowers were blooming, and leaves were thick again in the trees. The days were stretching out farther as midsummer neared, and Landover's colored moons were chasing each other for increasingly shorter periods of time across the darkened heavens.

Willow caught his eye and smiled at him, and he was in-stantly in love with her all over again, as if it were the first time. As if they were meeting in the midnight waters of the Irrylyn and she was telling him how they were meant for each other.

"You might lend a hand, wizard," Abernathy snapped at Questor Thews, interrupting Ben's thoughts, obviously peeved that the other was doing none of the work in setting out the lunch.

"Hmmm?" Questor looked up from a strange purple and yellow wildflower, oblivious. The wizard always looked as if he were oblivious, whether in fact he was or not.

"Lend a hand!" Abernathy repeated sharply. "Those who don't do the work don't eat the food—isn't that how the fable goes?"

"Well, no need to get huffy about it!" Questor Thews abandoned his study for the more pressing need of appeasing his friend. "Here, that's not the way to do that! Let me show you."

They went back and forth for a few more moments, then Willow intervened, and they settled down. Ben shook his head. How many years now had they been going at each other like that? Ever since the wizard had changed the scribe into a dog? Even before? Ben wasn't sure, in part because he was the newcomer to the group and the history wasn't entirely clear even now and in part because time had lost meaning for him since his arrival from Earth. Assuming a separateness of Landover from Earth, he amended, an assumption that was perhaps more theoretical than factual. How, after all, did you define a boundary that was marked not by geographical landmarks or proper surveys but by fairy mists? How did you differentiate between soils that could be crossed in a single step, but not without words or talismans of magic? Landover was here and Earth there, pointing right and left, but that didn't begin to explain the distance between them.

Ben Holiday had come into Landover when his hopes and dreams for a life in his old world had dried to dust, and reason had given way to desperation. Purchase a magic kingdom and find a new life, the ad in Rosen's Christmas catalogue had promised. Make yourself King of a land where the stories of childhood are real. The idea was unbelievable and at the same time irresistible. It called for a supreme act of faith, and Ben had heeded that call in the manner of a drowning man reaching for a lifeline. He had made the purchase and crossed into the unknown. He had come to a place that couldn't possibly exist and had found that it did. Landover had been everything and nothing like what he had expected. It had challenged him as he had not thought anything could. But ultimately it had given him what he needed: a new beginning, a new chance, a new life. It had captured his imagination. It had transformed him completely.

It continued to baffle him, though. He was still trying to understand its nuances. Like this business of time's passage. It was different here from his old world; he knew that from having crossed back and forth on more than one occasion and finding seasons out of synch. He knew it, too, from the effect it had on him—or the lack thereof. Something was different in the way he aged over here. It was not a progressive process, a steady rate of change, minute by minute, hour by hour, and so forth. It was difficult to believe, but sometimes he did not age at all. He had only suspected that before, but he was certain of it now. This was a deduction arrived at not from observing his own rate of growth, which was not easily measured because he lacked objectivity and distance.

No, it was from observing Mistaya.

He looked over for her. She stood in front of a massive old white oak, staring upward into its branches, her gaze intense. His brow furrowed as he watched her. If there was one word he would use to describe his daughter, that was probably it. "Intense." She approached everything with the single-mindedness of a hawk in search of prey. No lapses in concentration or distractions were allowed. When she focused on something, she gave it her complete attention. Her memory was prodigious and perhaps required that she study a thing until it was hers. It was strange behavior in a small child. But then, Mistaya herself was strange.

There was the question of her age. It was from this, from his study of her rate of growth, that Ben was able to see more clearly that his suspicions about himself were not unfounded. Mistaya had been born two years ago, measured by the passing of Landover's seasons, the same four seasons that Earth saw in a year's time. That should have made her two years old. But it didn't. Because she wasn't anywhere close to two years old. She seemed almost ten. She had been two years old when she was two *months* old. She was growing quite literally by leaps and bounds. In only months she grew years. And she didn't do it in a logically progressive fashion, either. For a time she would not grow at all—at least, not noticeably. Then, she would age months or even an entire year overnight. She would grow physically, mentally, socially, emotionally, in every measurable way. Not altogether or even at the same rate, but on a general scale one characteristic would eventually catch up with the others. She seemed to mature mentally first; yes, he was convinced of that much. She had been talking, after all, when she was three. That was months, not years. Talking as if she were maybe eight or nine. Now, at two years or ten years or whatever standard of reference you cared to use, she was talking as if she were twenty-five.

Mistaya. The name had been Willow's choice. Ben had liked it right from the first. Mistaya. Misty Holiday. He thought it a nice play on words. It suggested sweetness and nostalgia and pleasant memories. It fit the way she had looked when he had first seen her. He had just escaped from the Tangle Box; she and her mother had escaped from the Deep Fell, where Mistaya had been born. Willow would not talk about the birthing at first, but then, they had both harbored secrets that needed revealing if they were to stay true to each other, and in the end they had both confessed. He had told her of Nightshade as the Lady; she had told him of Mistaya. It had been difficult but healing. Willow had dealt better with Ben's truth than he had with hers. Mistaya might have been anything, given the nature of her birth. Born of a tree as a seedling, nourished by soils from Earth, Landover, and the fairy mists, come into being in the dank, misty deadness of the Deep Fell, Mistaya was an amalgam of worlds, magics, and bloods. But there she was that first time he had seen her, lying in the makeshift coverings, a perfect, beautiful baby girl. Dazzling green eyes that cut to your soul, clear pink skin, honey-blond hair, and features that were an instantly recognizable mix of Ben's and Willow's own.

Ben had thought from the first that it was all too good to be true. He began to discover soon enough that he was right.

He watched Mistaya shoot through infancy in a matter of several months. He watched her take her first steps and learn to swim in the same week. She began talking and running at the same time. She mastered reading and elementary math before she was a year old. By then his mind was reeling at the prospect of being parent to a phenomenally advanced child, a genius the like of which no one in his old world had ever seen. But even that didn't turn out the way he had expected. She matured, but never as rapidly in any one direction as he anticipated. She would advance to a certain point and then simply stop growing. For instance, after she mastered rudimentary math, she lost interest entirely in the subject. She learned to read and write but never did anything more with either. She seemed to delight in hopping from one new thing to the next, and there was never any rational explanation for why she progressed as far as she did and no farther.

She evidenced no interest in childish pursuits, not once, not from day one. Playing with dolls or toys, throwing and catching a ball, and jumping rope were for other children. Mistaya wanted to know how things worked, why they happened, and what they meant. Nature fascinated her. She took long walks, much longer than Ben would have thought physically possible for a child so young, all the time studying everything around her, asking questions about this and that, storing everything away in the drawers and closets of her mind. Once, when she was very young, only a few months old and just learning to talk, he found her with a rag doll. He thought for just an instant that she might be playing with it, but then she looked at him and asked in that serious voice and with those intense eyes why the maker of the doll had chosen a particular stitching to secure its limbs.

That was Mistaya. Right to the point and dead serious. She called him "Father" when she addressed him. Never "Dad" or "Daddy" or some such. "Father." Or "Mother." Polite but formal. The questions she asked were serious, important ones in her mind, and she did not treat them lightly. Ben learned not to do so, either. When once he laughed at

something she had said that struck him funny, she gave him
a look that suggested that he ought to grow up. It wasn't that
she couldn't laugh or find humor in her life; it was that she
was very particular about what she found funny and what
not. Abernathy made her laugh frequently. She teased him
unmercifully, always quite serious as if not intending to put
him on at all, then breaking into a sudden grin just as he
caught on to what was happening. He bore this with surprisingly good humor. When she was very small, she used to
ride him about and tug on his ears. She was not mean about
it, only playful. Abernathy would not have tolerated this
from another living soul. With Mistaya, he actually seemed
to enjoy it.

For the most part, however, she found grown-ups dull
and restrictive. She did not appreciate their efforts to govern
and protect her. She did not respond well to the word "no"
or to the limitations that her parents and advisors placed on
her. Abernathy was her tutor, but he confessed in private that
his prize student was frequently bored by her lessons. Bunion
was her protector, but after she learned to walk he was hard
pressed to keep her in sight much of the time. She loved
and was affectionate toward Ben and Willow, though in
that strange, reserved way she cultivated. At the same time
she clearly thought them mired in conventions and atti-
tudes that had no place in her life. She had a way of looking
at them when they were offering an explanation that suggested quite clearly that they didn't understand the first thing
about her, because if they did, they wouldn't be wasting their
time.

Adults were a necessary evil in her young life, she seemed
to believe, and the sooner she was fully grown, the better.
That might explain why she had aged ten years in two, Ben
often thought. It might explain why, almost from the time she
began to talk, she addressed all adults in an adult manner, using
complete sentences and proper grammar. She could pick up a

speech pattern and memorize it in a single sitting. Now, when Ben conversed with her, it was like carrying on a conversation with himself. She spoke to him in exactly the same way he spoke to her. He quickly abandoned any attempt at addressing her as he might a normal child or—God forbid—talking down to her as if she might not otherwise pay attention. If you talked down to Mistaya, she talked down to you right back. With his daughter there was a serious question as to who was the adult and who the child.

The one exception to all this child and adult business was Questor Thews. The relationship she shared with the wizard was entirely different from the ones she shared with other adults, her parents included. With Questor, Mistaya seemed quite content to be a child. She did not talk to him as she did to Ben, for instance. She listened carefully to everything he said, paid close attention to everything he did, and in general seemed content with the idea that he was in some way her superior. They shared the kind of relationship granddaughters and grandfathers sometimes share. Ben thought it was mostly the wizard's magic that bound the two. Mistaya was fascinated by it even when it didn't work the way in which Questor intended, which was all too frequently. Questor was always showing her some little bit of sorcery, trying out something new, experimenting with this and that. He was careful not to try anything dangerous when Mistaya was around: Even so, she would follow him about or sit with him for hours on the chance that he might give her a little glimpse of the power he possessed.

At first Ben worried. Mistaya's interest in magic seemed very akin to a child's early fascination with fire, and he did not want her to get burned. But she did not ask to try out spells or runes, did not beg to know how a bit of magic worked, and she listened respectfully and uncomplainingly to Questor's admonitions concerning the dangers of unskilled practice. It was as if she had no need to try. She simply found Questor an amazing curiosity, something to study but not emulate. It was odd, but it was no stranger than anything else about Mistaya. Certainly her affinity for magic was consistent with her background, a child born of magic, with an ancestry of magic, with magic in her blood.

So what would come of all this? Ben wondered. Time passed, and he found himself waiting for the other shoe to drop. Mistaya was not the child he had envisioned when Willow had told him that he was going to be a father. She was nothing like any child he had ever encountered. She was very much an enigma. He loved her, found her intriguing and wondrous, and could not imagine life without her. She redefined for him the terms "child" and "parent" and made him rethink daily the direction his life was taking.

But she frightened him as well—not for who and what she was at present, but for what she might someday be. Her future was a vast, uncharted journey over which he feared he might have absolutely no control. What could he do to make certain that her passage went smoothly?

Willow did not seem bothered by any of this. But then, Willow took the same approach to child rearing that she did to everything else. Life presented you with choices to make, opportunities to take, and obstacles to overcome, and it presented them to you when it was good and ready and not one moment before. There was no sense in worrying about something over which you had no control. Each day with Mistaya was a challenge to be dealt with and a joy to be savored. Willow gave what she could to her daughter and took what was offered in return, and she was grateful. She would tell Ben over and over that Mistaya was special, a child of different worlds and different races, of fairies and humans, of Kings and wielders of magic. Fate had marked her. She would do something wondrous in time. They must give her the opportunity to do so. They must let her grow as she chose.

Yes, all very well and good, Ben thought ruefully. But it was more easily said than done.

He watched his daughter as she stood staring up into the branches of that great oak and wondered what more he should be doing. He felt inadequate to the task of raising her. He felt overwhelmed by who and what she was.

"Ben, it is time to eat," Willow announced, her voice a gentle interruption. "Call Mistaya."

He pushed himself to his feet, brushing the troubling thoughts from his mind. "Misty!" he called. She did not look at him, her gaze fixed on the tree. "Mistaya!"

Nothing. She was a statue.

Questor Thews came up beside him. "Lost in her own little world again, it seems, High Lord." He gave Ben a wink, then cupped his hands about his mouth. "Mistaya, come now!" he ordered, his reedy voice almost frail.

She turned, hesitated a moment, then hurried over, her long, blond hair shimmering in the sunlight, her emerald eyes bright and eager. She gave Questor Thews a brief smile as she darted past him.

She barely seemed to see Ben.

Nightshade watched the child move away from the oak to rejoin the others. She kept still within the concealing branches in case one among them should think to take a closer look. None did. They gathered about the food and drink, laughing and talking, heedless of what had just taken place. The girl was hers now, the seeds of her taking planted deep within, needing only to be nurtured in order that she be claimed. That time would come. Soon.

Nightshade's long-anticipated plan was set in motion. When it was complete, Ben Holiday would be destroyed.

The crow with red eyes remembered—and the memories burned like fire.

Two years had passed since Nightshade's escape from the

Tangle Box. Bitter at the betrayal worked upon her by the play-King, stung by her failure to avenge herself against his wife and child, she had waited patiently for her chance to strike. Holiday had carried her down into the Tangle Box, trapped her in the misty confines of the Labyrinth, stolen her identity, stripped her of her magic, broken down her defenses, and tricked her into giving herself to him. That neither of them had known who he or she was, nor who the other was did not matter. That the magic of a powerful being had snared them both along with the dragon Strabo was of no concern. One way or the other, Holiday was responsible. Holiday had revealed her weakness. Holiday had caused her to feel for him what she had long ago sworn she would never feel for any man. That she had hated him always was even more galling. It made acceptance of what had happened impossible.

She kept her rage white-hot and close to the surface. She burned with it, and the pain kept her focused and certain of what she must do. Perhaps she would have been satisfied if she had been given the child in the Deep Fell following its birthing. Perhaps it would have been enough if she had claimed it and destroyed its mother in the bargain, leaving Holiday with that legacy as punishment for his betrayal. But the fairies had intervened and kept her from interfering, and all this time she had been forced to live with what had been done to her.

Until now. Now, when the child was old enough to be independent of humans and fairies alike, to discover truths that had not yet been revealed, and to be claimed by means other than force. Mistaya—she would be for Nightshade the balm the Witch of the Deep Fell so desperately needed to become whole again and at the same time the weapon she required to put an end to Ben Holiday.

The crow with red eyes looked down on the gathering of

family and friends and thought that this was the last happiness any of them would ever know.

Then she lifted clear of the leaf-dappling shadows and winged her way home.

Rydall of Marnhull

The next morning, the sunrise still a crescent of silver brightness on the eastern horizon and the land still cloaked in night's shadows, Willow jerked upright from her pillow with so violent a start that it woke Ben from a sound sleep. He found her rigid and shaking; the covers were thrown back, and her skin was as cold as ice. He drew her to him at once and held her close. After a moment the shaking subsided, and she allowed herself to be pulled gently down under the covers once more.

"It was a premonition," she whispered when she could speak again. She was lying close and still, as if waiting for something to strike her. He could not see her face, which was buried against his chest.

"A dream?" he asked, stroking her back, trying to calm her. The rigidity would not leave her body. "What was it?"

"Not a dream," she answered, her mouth moving against his skin. "A premonition. A sense of something about to happen. Something terrible. It was a feeling of such blackness that it washed over me like a great river, and I felt myself drowning in it. I couldn't breathe, Ben."

"It's all right now," he said quietly. "You're awake."

"No," she said at once. "It is definitely not all right. The premonition was directed at all of us—at you and me and Mistaya. But especially you, Ben. You are in great danger. I cannot be certain of the source, only the event. Something is going to happen, and if we are not prepared, we shall be . . ."

She trailed off, unwilling to say the words. Ben sighed and cradled her close. Her long emerald hair spilled over his shoulders, onto the pillow. He stared off into the still, dark room. He knew better than to question Willow when it came to dreams and premonitions. They were an integral part of the lives of the once-fairy, who relied on them as humans did on instincts. They were seldom wrong to do so. Willow was visited in dreams by fairy creatures and the dead. She was counseled and warned by them. Premonitions were less reliable and less frequently experienced, but they were no less valuable for what they were intended to accomplish. If Willow thought them in danger, then they would be wise to believe it was so.

"There was no indication as to what sort of danger?" he asked after a moment, trying to find a way to pin it down.

She shook her head no, a small movement against his body. She would not look at him. "But it is enormous. I have never felt anything so strongly, not since the time of our meeting." She paused. "What bothers me is that I do not know what summoned it. Usually there is some small event, some bit of news, some hint that precedes such visits. Dreams are sent by others to voice their thoughts, to present their counsel. But premonitions are faceless, voiceless wraiths meant only to give warning, to prepare for an uncertain future. They are drawn to us in our sleep by tiny threads of suspicion and doubt that safeguard us against the unexpected. Paths are opened to us in our sleep that remain closed while we are awake. The path this premonition traveled to reach me must have been broad and straight indeed, so monstrous was its size."

She pressed against him, trying to get closer as the memory chilled her anew.

"We haven't had anything threaten us in months," Ben said softly, thinking back. "Landover is at peace. Nightshade and Strabo are at rest. The Lords of the Greensward do not quarrel. Even the Crag Trolls haven't caused trouble in a while. There are no disturbances in the fairy mists. Nothing."

They were silent then, lying together in the great bed, watching the light creep over the windowsills and the shadows begin to fade, listening to the sounds of the day come awake. A tiny brilliant red bird flew down out of the battlements past their window and was gone.

Willow lifted her head finally and looked at him. Her flawless features were pale and frozen. "I don't know what to do," she whispered.

He kissed her nose. "We'll do whatever we have to."

He rose from the bed and padded over to the washbasin that sat on its stand by the east-facing window. He paused to look out at the new day. Overhead, the sky was clear and the light from the sunrise was a sweeping spray of brightness that was already etching out a profusion of greens and blues. Forested hills, a rough blanket across the land's still-sleeping forms, stretched away beyond the gleaming walls of Sterling Silver. Flowers were beginning to open in the meadow beyond the lake that surrounded the island castle. In the courtyard immediately below, guards were in the middle of a shift change and stable hands were moving off with feed for the stock.

Ben splashed water on his face, the water made warm by the castle for the new day. Sterling Silver was a living entity and possessed of magic that allowed her to care for the King and his court as a mother would her children. It had been a source of constant amazement to him when he had first come into Landover—to find a bath drawn and of perfect temperature on command, to have light provided wherever he wished it, to feel the stones of the castle floor warm beneath his feet on cold nights, to have food kept cooled or dried as needed— but now he was accustomed to these small miracles and did not think much on them anymore.

Although this morning, for some reason, he found himself doing so. He toweled his face dry and gazed downward into the shimmering surface of the washbowl's waters. His reflection gazed back at him, a strong, sun-browned, lean-featured visage with penetrating blue eyes, a hawk nose, and a hairline receding at the temples. The slight ripple of the water gave him wrinkles and distortions he did not have. He looked, he thought, as he had always looked since coming over from the old world. Appearances were deceiving, the saying went, but in this case he was not so sure. Magic was the cornerstone of Landover's existence, and where magic was concerned, anything was possible.

As with Mistaya, he reminded himself, who was constantly redefining that particular concept.

Willow rose from the bed and came over to him. She wore no clothes but as always seemed heedless of the fact and that made her nakedness seem natural and right. He took her in his arms and held her against him, thinking once more how lucky he was to have her, how much he loved her, how desperately he needed her. She was still the most beautiful woman he had ever seen, a prejudice he was proud to acknowledge, and he thought that her beauty came from within as much as from without. She was the great love he had lost when Annie had been killed in the old world—so long ago, it seemed, that he could barely remember the event. She was the life partner he had thought he would never find again, someone to give him strength, to infuse him with joy, to provide balance to his life.

There was a knock at the sleeping chamber door. "High Lord?" Abernathy called sharply, agitation in his voice. "Are you awake?"

"I'm awake," Ben answered, still holding Willow against him, looking past her upturned face.

"I am sorry, but I need to speak with you," Abernathy advised. "At once."

Willow eased free from Ben's arms and moved quickly to

cover herself with a long white robe. Ben waited until she was finished, then walked over to open the door. Abernathy stood there, unable to disguise with any success either his impatience or his dismay. Both registered clearly in his eyes. Dogs always imparted something of an anxious look, and Abernathy, though a dog in form only, was no exception. He held himself stiffly in his crimson and gold uniform, the robes of his office as Court Scribe, and his fingers—all that remained of his human self since his transformation into a soft-coated Wheaten Terrier—fidgeted with the engraved metal buttons as if to ascertain that they were all still in place.

"High Lord." Abernathy stepped forward and bent close to assure privacy. "I am sorry to have to start your day off like this, but there are two riders at the gates. Apparently they are here to offer some sort of challenge. They refuse to reveal themselves to anyone but you, and one has thrown down a gauntlet in the middle of the causeway. They are waiting for your response."

Ben nodded, stifling half a dozen ill-conceived responses. "I'll be right there."

He closed the door and moved quickly to dress. He told Willow what had happened. Throwing down a gauntlet in challenge sounded quaint to a man of twentieth-century Earth, but it was no laughing matter in Landover. Rules of combat were still practiced there, and when a gauntlet was cast, there was no mistaking the intent. A challenge had been issued, and a response was required. Even a King could not ignore such an act. Or perhaps, Ben thought as he pulled on his boots, *especially* a King.

He rose and buttoned his tunic. He paused to grip the medallion that hung about his neck—the symbol of his office, the talisman that protected him. If a challenge had been issued, the battle would be fought by his champion, the knight called the Paladin, who had defended every King of Landover since the beginning. The medallion summoned the Paladin, who was in fact the King's alter ego. For it was Ben himself who inhabited the body and mind of the Paladin when it fought its battles for him, becoming his own champion, losing himself for a time in the other's warrior skills and life. It had taken Ben a long time to discover the truth about the Paladin's nature. It was taking him a longer time still to come to terms with what that truth meant.

He released the medallion. There would be time enough to speculate on all that later if this challenge was to combat, if the Paladin was required, if the danger was not imagined, if, if, if . . .

He took Willow's arm and went out the door. They moved quickly down the hall and climbed a flight of stairs to the battlements overlooking the castle's main entry. On an island in a lake, Sterling Silver was connected to the mainland by a causeway Ben had built—and now rebuilt several times—to permit ready access for visitors. Landover was not at war, had not been at war since Ben had come over to assume Kingship, and he had decided a long time ago that there was no reason to isolate her ruler from her people.

Of course, her people were not in the habit of casting down gauntlets and issuing challenges.

He opened the door leading out onto the battlements and crossed to the balcony that overlooked the causeway. Questor Thews and Abernathy were already standing there, conversing in low tones. Bunion skittered along the parapets to one side, swift and agile, his kobold's claws able to grip the stone easily. Bunion could walk straight down the wall if he chose. His bright yellow eyes were menacing slits, and all his considerable teeth were showing in a parody of a smile.

Questor and Abernathy looked up hurriedly as Ben appeared with Willow and hurried over to meet him.

"High Lord, you must resolve this as you see fit," Questor said in typically succinct fashion, "but I would advise great caution. There is an aura of magic about these two that even my talents cannot seem to penetrate."

"What irrefutable proof!" Abernathy observed archly, dog's ears perked. He gave Ben a pained look. "High Lord, these are impertinent, possibly demented creatures, and offering them some time in the dungeons might be worth your consideration."

"Good morning to you, too," Ben greeted them cheerfully. "Nice day for casting down a gauntlet, isn't it?" He gave them each a wry smile as he moved toward the balcony. "Tell you what. Let's hear what they have to say before we consider solutions."

They moved in a knot onto the overlook and stopped at the railing. Ben peered down. Two black-clad riders sat on black horses in the middle of the causeway. The larger of the two was dressed in armor and wore a broadsword and a battle-ax strapped to his saddle. His visor was down. The smaller was robed and hooded and hunched over like a crone at rest, face and hands hidden. Neither moved. Neither bore any kind of insignia or carried any standard.

The armored rider's black gauntlet lay before them in the center of the bridge.

"You see what I mean," Questor whispered enigmatically.

Ben didn't, but it made no difference. Not wanting to prolong the confrontation, Ben shouted down to the two on the bridge, "I am Ben Holiday, King of Landover. What do you want with me?"

The armored rider's helmet tilted upward slightly. "Lord Holiday. I am Rydall, King of Marnhull and of all the lands east beyond the fairy mists to the Great Impassable." The man's voice was deep and booming. "I have come to seek your surrender, High Lord. I would have it peaceably but will secure it by force if I must. I wish your crown and your throne and your medallion of office. I wish your command over your subjects and your Kingdom. Am I plain enough for you?"

Ben felt the blood rush to his face. "What is plain to me, Rydall, King of Marnhull, is that you are a fool if you expect me to pay you any mind."

"And you are a fool if you fail to heed me," the other answered quickly. "Hear me out before you say anything more. My Kingdom of Marnhull lies beyond the fairy mists. All that exists on that side of the boundary belongs to me. I took it by force and strength of arms long ago, and I took it all. For years I have searched for a way to pass through the mists, but the fairy magic kept me at bay. That is no longer the case. I have breached your principal defense, Lord Holiday, and your country lies open to me at last. Yours is a small, impossibly outnumbered army. Mine, on the other hand, is vast and seasoned and would crush you in a day. It waits now at your borders for my command. If I call, it will sweep through Landover like a plague and destroy everything in its path. You lack any reasonable means of stopping it, and once it has been set in motion, it will take time to bring it under control again. I do not need to speak more explicitly, do I, High Lord?"

Ben glanced quickly at Willow and his advisors. "Have any of you ever heard of this fellow?" he asked softly. All three shook their heads.

"Holiday, will you surrender to me?" Rydall cried out again in his great voice.

Ben turned back. "I think not. Maybe another day. King Rydall, I cannot believe that you came here expecting me to do what you ask. No one has heard of you. You bring no evidence of your office or your armies. You sit there on your horse making threats and demands, and that is all you do. Two men, all alone, come out of nowhere." He paused. "What if I were to have you seized and thrown in prison?"

Rydall laughed, and his laugh was as big and deep as his voice and decidedly mean. "I would not advise you to try that, High Lord. It would not be as easy as it looks."

Holiday nodded. "Pick up your gauntlet and go home. I'm hungry for breakfast."

"No, High Lord. It is you who must pick up the gauntlet if you do not accept my demand for surrender." Rydall eased his horse forward a step. "Your land lies in the path of my army, and I cannot go around it. I will not. It will fall to me one way or another. But the blood of those who perish will not be on my hands; it will be on your own. The choice is yours, High Lord."

"I have made my choice," Ben answered.

Rydall laughed anew. "Bravely said. Well, I did not think you would give in to me easily, not without some proof of my strength, some reason to believe that your failure to do as I have commanded will cause you, and perhaps those you love, harm."

Ben flushed anew, angry now. "Making threats will not work with me, Rydall of Marnhull. Our conversation is finished."

"Wait, High Lord!" the other exclaimed hurriedly. "Do not be so quick to interrupt—"

"Go back to wherever it is you came from!" Ben snapped, already turning away.

Then he saw Mistaya. She was standing alone on the parapets several dozen feet away, staring down at Rydall. She was perfectly still, honey-blond hair streaming down her narrow shoulders, elfin face intense, emerald eyes fixed on the riders at the gate. She seemed oblivious to everything else, the whole of her concentration directed downward to where Rydall and his companion waited.

"Mistaya," Ben called softly. He did not want her there where she could be seen, did not want her so close to the edge. He felt sweat break out on his forehead. His voice rose. "Mistaya!"

She didn't hear or didn't want to hear. Ben left the others and walked to her. Wordlessly he grabbed her around the waist and lifted her away from the wall. Mistaya did not resist. She put her arms around his neck and allowed him to set her down again.

He kept his annoyance hidden as he bent close. "Go inside, please," he told her.

She looked at him curiously, as if puzzling something through, then turned obediently, went through the door, and was gone.

"High Lord Ben Holiday!" Rydall called from below.

Ben's teeth clenched as he wheeled back to the wall one final time. "I am finished with you, Rydall!" he shouted back in fury.

"Let me have him seized and brought before you!" Abernathy snapped.

"A final word!" Rydall called out. "I said I did not expect you to surrender without some form of proof that I do not lie. Would you have me provide that for you, then, High Lord? Proof that I am able to do as I have threatened?"

Ben took a deep breath. "You must do as you choose, Rydall of Marnhull. But remember this—you must answer for your choice."

There was a long silence as the two stared fixedly at each other. Despite his anger and resolve, Ben felt a chill pass through him, as if Rydall had taken better measure of him than he had of the other. It was an unsettling moment.

"Good-bye for now, High Lord Ben Holiday," Rydall said finally. "I will return in three days time. Perhaps your answer will be different then. I leave the gauntlet where it lies. No one but you will be able to pick it up. And pick it up you shall."

He wheeled about and galloped away. The other rider lingered a moment, all hunched down and still. This rider had not moved or spoken the entire time. It had shown nothing of itself. Now it turned away unhurriedly and moved after Rydall. Together they crossed the open meadow through the wildflowers and grasses, black shadows against the coming light, and disappeared into the trees beyond.

Ben Holiday and his companions watched them go until they were out of sight and did not speak a word.

Breakfast that morning was a somber affair. Ben, Willow, Questor, and Abernathy sat huddled close at one end of the long dining table, picking at their food and talking. Mistaya had been fed separately and had been sent outside to play. As an afterthought, Ben had dispatched Bunion to keep an eye on her.

"So no one has heard of Rydall?" Ben repeated once again. He kept coming back to that same question. "You're sure?"

"High Lord, this man is a stranger to Landover," Questor Thews assured him. "There is no Rydall and no Marnhull anywhere within our borders."

"Nor, for all we know, anywhere without, either!" Abernathy snapped heatedly. "Rydall claims to have come through the fairy mists, but we have only his word for that. No one can penetrate the mists, High Lord. The fairies would not permit it. Only magic allows passage, and only the fairies or their creatures possess it. Rydall does not seem one of those to me."

"Perhaps, like me, he possesses a talisman that allows passage," Ben suggested.

Questor bent forward with a frown. "What of that black-cloaked companion? I told you I sensed magic in that pair, but it was probably not Rydall's. Perhaps the other is a creature of magic, a fairy being of the same sort as the Gorse. Such a being could secure passage."

Ben thought back to the Gorse, the dark fairy that had been released and brought back into Landover at the time of Mistaya's birth. A creature of that sort was certainly capable of negotiating the fairy mists and visiting as much misery as possible on any who stood in its way.

"But why would a creature of such power serve Rydall?" he asked abruptly. "Wouldn't it be the other way around?"

"Perhaps the fairy creature is in his thrall," Willow offered quietly. "Or perhaps things are not as they appear, and it is Rydall in fact who serves."

"If the black-cloaked one has the magic, it might be so and still appear otherwise," Questor mused. "I wish I could have penetrated their disguise."

Ben leaned back in his chair. "Let's review this a moment. These two, Rydall and his companion, appear out of nowhere. One of them, or maybe both, possesses magic—considerable magic, they claim. But we don't know what that magic does. What we do know is that they want an unconditional surrender of the throne of Landover and that they seem confident that they will have it one way or the other. Why?"

"Why?" Questor Thews repeated blankly.

"Put it another way," Ben continued. He pushed back his plate and looked at the wizard. "They made a demand, offering no evidence that it should be given any serious consideration. They revealed no magic of the sort that might intimidate, and they showed nothing of their vaunted army. They simply made a demand and then rode off, giving us three days to consider. To consider what? Their demand that we have already rejected? I don't think so."

"You think they intend to offer us some demonstration of their power," Willow surmised.

Ben nodded. "I do. They haven't given us three days for nothing. And they made a fairly obvious threat on leaving. Rydall was too quick to back away from his demand for immediate surrender. Why make it if you don't intend to enforce it? Some sort of game is being played here, and I don't think we know all the rules yet."

The others nodded soberly. "What should we do, High Lord?" Questor asked finally.

Ben shrugged. "I wish I knew." He thought about it for a moment. "Let's use the Landsview, Questor, to see if there is any sign of Rydall or his army in Landover. We can make a thorough search. I don't want to alarm the people by giving out word of this threat until we find out if it is real, but it might not hurt to increase our border patrols for a few days."

"It might not hurt to increase our watch here as well," Abernathy growled, straightening himself. "The threat, after all, seems directed at us."

Ben agreed. Since no one had anything further to offer, they adjourned from the table to begin the day's work, much of which was already set by an agenda that had been in place for weeks and had nothing to do with Rydall and his threats. Ben went about his business in calm, unperturbed fashion, but his apprehension about Marnhull's King remained undiminished.

When there was time, Ben went up into the castle's highest tower, a small circular chamber in which the wall opened halfway around from floor to ceiling, to look out across the land. A railing rose waist-high along the edge to guard against falls, and a silver lectern faced out from the center of the railing into the clouds. Thousands of intricately scrolled runes were carved into the metal. This was the Landsview. He closed the door to the room and locked it, then pulled a worn map of Landover from a chest and crossed to the lectern. He spread the map across its reading surface and fastened it in place with clips.

Then he placed himself directly before the lectern, gripped the guardrail, and focused his attention on the map. A warm vibrancy began to emanate from beneath his hands. He centered his concentration on the lake country, for that was where he wished to begin his search.

Seconds later the walls of the tower fell away, and he was flying across Landover with nothing but the guardrail for support. It was an illusion, he knew by now, for he was still within the castle and only his mind was free to roam Landover, but the illusion created by the Landsview's magic was powerful. He sped across the lake country's forests, rivers, lakes, and swamps, all the details of the land revealed to him, his eyes as sharp as an eagle's at hunt. The search revealed nothing. There was no sign of Rydall or his black-cloaked companion or their army. The borders to the fairy mists were quiet.

Ben was still brooding over the matter at midday when Willow took him aside. They walked out into a private garden that opened just off the ground-floor rooms Willow kept for herself and Mistaya. Mistaya was not there. She was eating with Parsnip in the kitchen.

"I want to send Mistaya away," Willow announced without preamble, her eyes fixing on him. "Tomorrow."

Ben was silent for a moment, staring back at her. "Your premonition?"

She nodded. "It was too strong to ignore. Perhaps Rydall's coming was its cause. Perhaps not. But I would feel better if Mistaya was somewhere else for a while. It may be difficult enough protecting ourselves."

They walked down a winding pathway into a stand of rhododendrons and stopped. Ben breathed in the fragrance. He was remembering Rydall's veiled threat about harm coming to those he loved. And Rydall had seen Mistaya on the wall.

Ben folded his arms and looked off into the distance. "You are probably right. But where could we send her that would be safer than inside these walls?"

Willow took his hand. "To my father. To the River Master. I know how difficult he has been in the past, how opposed to us at times. I do not defend him. But he loves his granddaughter and will see that she is well cared for. He can protect her better than we. No one can come into the country of the once-fairy if they are not invited. Their magic, for all that it has been diminished by their leaving the mists, is still powerful. Mistaya would be safe."

She was right, of course. The River Master and his people possessed considerable magic, and their country was secure from those who were not welcome. Finding the way in without a guide was all but impossible; finding the way out again was harder still. But Ben was not convinced. The River Master and his daughter were not close, and while the Ruler of the lake-country people had been pleased by the birth of Mistaya and had journeyed to Landover to visit her, he was still as aloof and independent as he had ever been. He accepted Ben as King of Landover grudgingly and without conviction that the monarchy served any real purpose in the lives of the once-fairy. He had obstructed and refused Ben on more than one occasion, and he made no effort to hide his own ambitions to extend his rule.

Still, Ben was as worried as Willow that Mistaya would not be safe at Sterling Silver. He had been thinking about it ever since he had taken his daughter down off that battlement. If Willow's premonition was correct—and there was no reason to think it wasn't—then the real danger was here, since the threat that faced the family was principally to him. It made sense to remove Mistaya to another place, and there was no safer place in Landover than the lake country.

"All right," he agreed. "Will you go with her?"

Willow shook her head slowly. "No, Ben. My life is with you. I will remain here. If I can, I will help protect you. Perhaps I will have another sensing."

"Willow . . ." he began.

"No, Ben. Don't ask it of me. I have left you before when I did not want to, and each time I almost lost you. This time I will not go. My father will take good care of Mistaya." Her eyes made it clear that the matter was settled. "Send another instead to see her safely on her journey. Send Questor or Abernathy."

Ben gripped her hand. "I'll do better than that. I'll send them both. Questor will keep Mistaya in line, and Abernathy will counsel Questor against any rash use of his magic. And I'll send an escort of King's Guards to keep them all safe."

Willow pressed herself against him wordlessly, and Ben hugged her back. They stood holding each other in the midday sunlight. "I have to tell you that I don't like letting her go," Ben murmured finally.

"Nor I," Willow whispered back. He could feel her heart beat against his chest. "I spoke with Mistaya earlier. I asked her what she was doing on the wall, staring down at Rydall." She paused. "Mistaya said that she knows him."

Ben stiffened. "Knows him?"

"I asked her how, but she said she wasn't sure." Willow shook her head. "I think she was as confused as we are."

They were quiet then, still holding each other, staring off into the gardens, listening to the sounds of the insects and the birds against the more distant backdrop of the castle's bustle. A connection between Mistaya and Rydall? Ben felt something cold settle into the pit of his stomach.

"We'll send her away at first light," he whispered, and felt Willow's arms tighten about him in response.

Haltwhistle

Mistaya's parents told her that evening that they had decided she should visit her grandfather in the lake country and would be leaving in the morning. In typically straightforward fashion she asked if anything was wrong, and they said no. But the way they said it told her there most definitely was.

Still, she was astute enough in the ways of parents to know better than to contradict them by asking what it was—even though she was quite certain it had something to do with the man who had come to the gates that morning—and she was content to let the matter lie until she could speak to one or the other of them alone. It would be her mother most likely, because her mother was more honest with her than her father was. It wasn't that her father wanted to deceive her. It was that he persisted in viewing her as a child and sought continually to protect her from what he considered life's harsh realities. It was an annoying habit, but Mistaya tolerated it as best she could. Her father had trouble understanding her in any event, certainly more than her mother did. He measured her against a standard with which she was not familiar, a standard conceived and developed in his old world, the world called Earth, where magic was practically unheard of and fairy creatures were considered a myth. He loved her, of course, and he would do anything for her. But love and understanding did not necessarily go hand in hand in real life, and such was the case here.

Her father was not alone in his puzzlement. Most of those who lived in the castle found her a bit odd for one reason or another. She had been aware of it almost from the beginning, but it did not bother her. Her confidence and self-reliance were such that what others thought mattered almost not at all. Her mother was comfortable with her, and her father, if bewildered, was supportive. Abernathy let her do things to him that would have cost another child a quick trip to its room for prolonged consideration of what good manners entailed. Bunion and Parsnip were as odd as she, all ears and teeth and bristly hair, chittering their mysterious language that they thought she couldn't really understand when, of course, she could.

Best of all, there was Questor Thews. She loved that old man the way a child does a special grandparent or a favorite aunt or uncle, the two of them mysteriously linked as if born into the world with a shared view of life. Questor never talked down to her. He never begrudged her a question or opinion. He listened when she talked and answered her right back. He was distracted, and he fumbled a bit when showing her his magic, but that seemed to make him all the more endearing. She sensed that Questor truly found her to be a wondrous person—a *person*, not a child—and that he believed she was capable of anything. Oh, he chided and corrected her now and then, but he did it in such a way that she was never offended; she was touched by his concern. He lacked her mother's fierce love and her father's iron determination and probably their sense of commitment to her as well, but he made up for it with his friendship, the kind you find only rarely in life.

Mistaya was pleased to hear that Questor would be her guardian on her journey south. She was pleased to have Abernathy come along as well, but she was especially happy about Questor. The journey itself would be a delight. She had not been away from the castle since she was a baby, barely able to walk, and then only for day trips. Picnics and horseback rides didn't count. This was an adventure, a journey to a place she had never been. Discoveries would be plentiful, and she would have Questor there to share them with her. It would be great fun.

She had to admit, considering the matter further, that part of the attraction was the prospect of getting away from her parents. When her parents were around, she was always watched more closely and restricted more severely. Don't do this. Don't touch that. Stay close. Keep away. And the lessons they insisted on teaching her were interminable and mostly superfluous to what really mattered. It was when she was alone with Questor that she felt her horizons expand and the possibilities begin to open up. Much of her enthusiasm had to do with the wizard's use of magic, which was a truly fascinating and important pursuit. Mistaya loved to watch what Questor could do with his spells and conjurings, even when he didn't get them right. She thought that someday she could learn to use magic as he did. She was certain of it.

Secretly she tried a spell or two, a conjuring here and there, and found she could almost make them work.

She kept it to herself, of course. Everyone, Questor Thews included, told her that using magic was extremely dangerous. Everyone told her not to even think of trying. She promised faithfully each time the admonition was given but kept her options open.

Magic, she knew, even if they didn't, was an integral part of her life. Her mother had told her early on of her birthright. She was the child of a human and a once-fairy. She was the child of three worlds, birthed out of three soils. She had been born in a witch's lair, the hollow they called the Deep Fell, the haven of Nightshade. All that was in her blood was laced with magic. That was why, unlike other children, she had grown to the age of ten in only two years. That was why she grew in spurts. How she grew was still something of a mystery to her, but she understood it better than her parents did. Her intelligence always grew first, and her emotions and body followed. She could neither predict nor govern the when and how of it, but she was aware of a definite progression.

She also believed that being a child was not particularly desirable or important, that basically it was a necessary step toward becoming an adult, which was what she really wanted. Children were one rung up the ladder from house pets; they were cared for, fed regularly, frequently sent outside to play, and not allowed to do much of anything else. Adults could do whatever they chose if they were willing to accept the consequences. Mistaya had mastered an understanding of the dynamics of growing up right from the beginning, and she was anxious to get through the preliminaries and try out the real thing. She chaffed and tugged at the restrictions placed on her both by her physiology and by her parents, unable to exert much control over either. A trip to the lake country and her grandfather came as a welcome respite.

So she dutifully acknowledged her parents' wishes in the matter, secretly rejoiced at her good fortune, and began making her plans. No time limit seemed to have been placed yet on this visit, which meant it might last for weeks. That was fine with Mistaya. All spring or even all summer in the lake country with the once-fairy was an exciting prospect. She liked her grandfather, although she had met him only once. He had come to the castle to see her when she had been very young, only a few months old. The River Master was a tall, spare-featured, stern man, a water sprite with silver skin and thick black hair that grew down the nape of his neck and forearms. He was tight-lipped and cool in his approach, as if disdaining to know her too well, as if suspicious about who and what she might be. She gave no quarter in their meeting. Disregarding his aloofness, she marched right up to him and said,

"Hello, Grandfather. I am very pleased to meet you. We shall be good friends, I hope."

Boldness and candor did the trick. Her grandfather warmed to her immediately, impressed that so small a child could be so forthcoming, pleased that she should seek his friendship. He took her for a walk, talked with her at length, and ended up inviting her to come visit him. He remained only a day, then went away again. Her mother said that he did not like to sleep indoors and that castles in particular bothered him. She said he was a woods creature and seldom ventured far from his home. That he had come to see her at all was a great compliment. Mistaya, pleased, had asked when she could go visit him, but the request had been filed away and seemingly forgotten. She had not seen him since. It would be interesting to discover what he thought of her now.

Following dinner she was kept busy packing for her trip and did not get a chance to ask either her mother or her father about the men at the gates. She slept restlessly that night and was awake before sunrise. With hugs and kisses from her parents to remind her of their devotion, she set out with her escort at first light: Questor Thews, Abernathy, and a dozen of the King's Guards. She rode her favorite pony, Lightfoot, and watched the sun chase the shadows back across the meadows and hills and into the dark woods as the new day began. Six Guards rode in front of her, and six behind. Questor was at her side atop an old paint improbably called Owl. Abernathy, who detested horses, rode inside the carriage that bore her clothing and personal effects. A driver nudged the team that pulled the carriage along the grassy trail they followed south.

Mistaya waited until Sterling Silver was safely out of sight, then eased Lightfoot close to Questor and asked, "Who was the man at the gates, Questor—the one Father didn't want to see me?"

Questor Thews snorted. "A troublemaker named Rydall. Claimed he was King of some country called Marnhull that none of us have ever heard about. Claimed it lies on the other side of the fairy mists, but we both know how unlikely that is."

"Is he the reason I'm being sent to see my grandfather?"

"Yes."

"Why?"

The wizard shrugged. "He might be more dangerous than he looks. He made some threats."

"What sort of threats?"

The shaggy white brows knitted together fiercely. "Hard to say; they were rather vague. Rydall wants your father to hand over the crown and let him be King instead. Pure nonsense. But he suggested it might be safer to do as he asked. Your father is looking into it."

Mistaya was quiet for a moment, thinking. "Who was the other one, the one in the black robes?"

"I don't know."

"A magician?"

Questor looked at her, surprise showing on his narrow face. "Yes, perhaps. There was magic there. Did you sense it, too?"

She nodded. "I think I know one of them."

Surprise turned to astonishment. "You do? How could you?"

She frowned. "I don't know. I just felt it while standing there on the wall." She paused. "I thought at first it was the big man, Rydall. But now I'm not sure. It might have been the other." She shrugged, her interest in the matter fading. "Do you think we will see any bog wumps on the way, Questor?"

They traveled steadily all day, stopping several times to rest the horses and once for lunch, and by sundown they had reached the south end of the Irrylyn. There they set up camp for the night. Mistaya went swimming in the warm waters of the lake, then fished with Abernathy and a couple of the King's Guards for their dinner. They caught several dozen fish in almost no time, causing Mistaya to complain to the scribe that it was all too easy. While the Guards carried their catch back to the camp to clean and cook, the girl and the dog sat alone on the shores of the lake and looked out across the silver waters as the sun sank in a shimmer of red and pink behind the distant horizon.

"Do you think Mother and Father are in danger, Abernathy?" she asked him when they were alone, her face and voice impossibly serious.

Abernathy considered a moment, then shook his shaggy head. "No, Mistaya, I do not. And even if they are, it will not be the first time. When you are a King and Queen, there is always danger. When you wield power of any kind, for that matter, there is always danger. But your parents are very resourceful people and have survived a good many things. I would not worry for them if I were you."

She liked his answer and nodded agreeably. "All right, I won't. Are you and Questor staying with me once we reach Elderew?"

"Only for a day or so. Then we must go back. Your father will have need of us. We cannot be away for very long."

"No, of course not," she agreed, rather pleased that she would be on her own. Her grandfather knew magic as well. She wondered what he could be persuaded to teach her. She wondered if he would let her experiment a bit.

A shadowy form crept out of the trees to one side and melted into some bushes that ran along the edge of the lake. Mistaya and Abernathy were seated on a cluster of flat rocks elevated above the bushes and could see anything trying to approach. Neither missed the furtive movement.

"Bog wump?" she asked in an excited whisper.

Abernathy shook his head. "Some sort of wight. Neither very old nor very bright, judging from its lack of circumspection."

She nudged the scribe lightly. "Bark at him, will you, Abernathy? A good, loud bark?"

"Mistaya . . ."

"Please? I'll not pull your ears for the rest of the trip."

The dog sighed. "Thank you so much."

"Will you?" she pressed. "Just once? I want to see it jump."

Abernathy's jaws worked. "Humph."

Then he barked, a quick, sharp explosion that shattered the twilight silence. Below, the wight jumped straight out of the bushes in which it was hiding and streaked back into the forest as if launched from a catapult.

Mistaya was in stitches. "That was wonderful! That was so funny! I love it when you do that, Abernathy! It just makes me laugh!"

She gave him a big hug and pulled lightly on his ears. "You make me laugh, you old woolly."

"Humph," Abernathy repeated. But he was clearly pleased nevertheless.

The fish cooked up nicely, and dinner was delicious. The members of the little caravan ate together, and everything was quickly consumed. It was better than a picnic, Mistaya concluded. She stayed up late swapping stories with the King's Guards despite Abernathy's clear disapproval, and when she finally rolled into her blankets—refusing the down-filled pad brought along for her personal comfort (the King's Guards, after all, didn't use them)—she was asleep in moments.

Without knowing why, she woke when it was still dark. Everyone around her was sound asleep, most of them, notably Questor Thews, emitting snores that sounded like rusty gates. She blinked, sat up, and looked about.

A pair of eyes stared back at her from only a few feet away, reflecting bright yellow in the last of the dying firelight.

Mistaya squinted, unafraid. The eyes belonged to a mud puppy. She had never seen one, but she knew what they looked like from the descriptions given by Abernathy in his endless lessons on Landover's native species. She waited a moment for her vision to sharpen to make sure. The mud puppy waited with her. When she could see clearly, she found herself face to face with an odd creature possessed of a long body colored various shades of brown, short legs with webbed feet, a vaguely rodent sort of face, great floppy dog ears, and a lizard's smooth, slender tail. Sure enough, a mud puppy, she thought.

She pursed her lips and kissed at it. The mud puppy blinked.

She remembered suddenly that mud puppies were supposed to be fairy creatures. They were rarely seen anywhere in Landover and almost never outside the lake country.

"You are very cute," she whispered.

The mud puppy wagged its tail in response. It moved off a few paces, then turned back, waiting. Mistaya rose from her blankets. The mud puppy started off again. No mistaking what it wanted, the girl thought. What luck! An adventure already! She pulled on her boots and crept through the sleeping camp in pursuit of her new companion. The mud puppy made certain never to get too far ahead, deliberately leading her on.

She remembered too late that there was a sentry on watch at either end of the camp, and she was on top of one before she could stop herself. But the sentry did not seem to see her. He was staring out into the night, oblivious. First the mud puppy and then Mistaya walked right past him.

Magic! the girl thought, and was excited anew.

The mud puppy took her away from the Irrylyn and into the surrounding woods. They walked quite a long way, navigating a maze of tightly packed trees and thickets, fording streams, descending ravines, and climbing hills. The night was warm and still, and the air was heavy with the smell of pine and jasmine. Crickets chirped, and small rodents scurried about in the brush. Mistaya studied everything, listened to everything, letting nothing escape her. She had no idea where she was going but was not worried about finding her way back. She was thinking that the mud puppy was taking her to someone, and she was hoping that it was a creature of magic.

Finally they reached a clearing in which a broad swath of moonlight glimmered off a grassy stretch of marsh that marked the end of a stream's downhill run from some distant spring. The water was choked with grasses and night-blooming lilies and was as smooth as glass. The mud puppy moved to within a few feet of its edge and sat down. Mistaya walked up beside him and waited.

The wait was a short one. Almost immediately the waters of the marsh stirred, then parted as something beneath their surface began to lift into view. It was a woman formed all of mud, slick and smooth and dark as she took shape. She rose to tower over Mistaya, much larger than any woman the girl had ever seen, her lush form shimmering with dampness in the moonlight. She stood on the waters of the pond as if they were solid ground, and her eyes opened and found Mistaya's own.

"Hello, Mistaya," she greeted in a soft, rich voice that whispered of damp earth and cool shadows.

"Hello," Mistaya replied.

"I am the Earth Mother," the woman said. "I am a friend of your mother. Has she told you of me?"

Mistaya nodded. "You were her best friend when she was a little girl. You told her about my father before he came into Landover. You help take care of the land and the things that live on it. You can do magic."

The Earth Mother laughed softly. "Some little magic. Most of what I do is simply hard work. Do you like magic, then?"

"Yes, very much. But I am not allowed to use it."

"Because it is dangerous for you."

"Yes."

"But you don't believe that?"

Mistaya hesitated. "It is not so much that I don't believe it. It is more that I don't see how I can learn to protect myself from its dangers if I never get to use it."

The eyes gleamed like silver pools. "A good answer. Ignorance does not protect; knowledge protects. Did you know, Mistaya, that I helped your mother prepare for your birth? I gave her the task of gathering the soils out of which you were born. I did that because I knew something about you that your mother did not. I knew that magic would be a very important part of your life and that you could not protect yourself from its effects if its elements did not constitute a part of your body. You required earth from the fairy mists as well as from your father's and mother's lands."

"Am I a fairy creature?" Mistaya asked quickly.

The Earth Mother shook her head. "You are not so easily defined, child," she answered. "You are not simply one thing or the other but a mix of several. You are special. There is no one like you in all of Landover. What do you think of that?"

Mistaya thought. "I suppose I shall have to get used to it."

"That will not be so easy to do," the Earth Mother continued. "There will be obstacles for you to overcome at every turn. You may think that growing up has been difficult, but it will become more difficult still. There are hard lessons ahead for you. There are trials that may undo you if you are not careful. Experience is the necessary teacher for all children growing to adulthood, filled with revelations and discoveries, with disappointments and rewards, and with successes and failures. The trick is in finding a balance to it all and then surviving to turn knowledge into wisdom. This will be doubly hard for you, Mistaya, because yours will be the lessons and trials of three worlds, and you must be especially careful how you go."

"I am not afraid," Mistaya said bravely.

"I can tell this is so."

Mistaya frowned thoughtfully. "Earth Mother, can you see what lies ahead for me? Can you see the future?"

The Earth Mother's silver eyes closed and opened slowly like a cat's. "Oh, child, I wish I could. How easy life would be. But I cannot. What I see are possibilities. The future may be this or that. Usually it may be a handful of things. I see glimpses of dark clouds and rainbows in the lives of those who inhabit my land, and sometimes I can forestall or alter what might be. The future is never fixed, Mistaya. For each of us it is an empty canvas on which we must paint our lives."

"Mother and Father believe we are in danger," the girl said. "Is it true?"

"It is," the Earth Mother answered. "One of those dark clouds of which I spoke comes toward you. It will test your resolve and challenge your insight. It looks to be a very black cloud indeed, and you must be wary of it. It is for this reason I brought you here to me tonight."

"To warn me?"

"More than that, Mistaya. You have already been warned, and my own warning adds nothing." The Earth Mother shimmered as one arm rose to point. "The mud puppy who brought you to me is called Haltwhistle. He has served me long and well. Your mother has known him since she was a child. Haltwhistle is a fairy creature, come from the mists once upon a time to be my companion. Mud puppies are able to live both in and out of the mists and serve who they choose. They are independent in making their choice and loyal ever after. They have a very powerful form of fairy magic at their command. It is a good magic, a magic of healing. It counteracts magics that are used to harm or destroy. It cannot protect against them completely, but it can alter their effects so that they are not so severe. Haltwhistle's magic does this for those he serves and sometimes for their friends."

Mistaya glanced down at Haltwhistle, who was looking

up at her with great, soulful eyes. "He seems very nice," she said.

"He is yours now," the Earth Mother said gently. "I give him to you for the time it takes for you to grow to womanhood. While you grow, Haltwhistle will be your companion and protector. He will keep you safe from some of the harm that might be done by those dark clouds that come into your life."

Her arm fell away in a shimmer of moonlight. "But understand this, Mistaya. Haltwhistle cannot protect you against everything. No one can do that. If dark magic is used to harm you, he can become your shield. But if the dark magic is your own, he can do nothing to help you. What you choose to do with your life must be your responsibility. The consequences of your acts and decisions must be your own. You will make mistakes and engage in foolish behavior, and Haltwhistle will not be able to stop you. These are the lessons of growing up that you must endure."

Mistaya's brow furrowed, and her mouth tightened. "I shall not make mistakes or behave foolishly if I can help it," she insisted. "I shall be careful of my choices, Earth Mother."

The other's strange eyes seemed suddenly sad. "You will do the best you can, child. Do not expect more."

Mistaya thought. "Have I magic that will help me?" she asked impulsively. "Magic of my own?"

"Yes, Mistaya, you do. And perhaps it will help you. But it may also cause you harm. You are at some risk should you choose to use it."

"But I don't even know what it is. How can I use it? How can it hurt me?"

"In time," the Earth Mother said, "you will learn."

Mistaya sighed impatiently. "Now you sound like Father."

"It is time for you to go back," the Earth Mother advised, ignoring her complaint. "Before you do, there are a few things you must know about Haltwhistle. He will always be with you, but you will not always see him. He keeps watch over you as he deems best, so do not despair if from time to time you cannot find him. Also, you must never try to touch him. Mud puppies are not meant to be touched. Be warned. Finally, remember this. Haltwhistle requires neither food nor water from you. He will look after himself. But you must speak his name at least once each day. It may be spoken in any way you choose, but you must say it. If you fail to do so, you risk losing him. If he does not feel needed, he will leave you and come back to me. Do you understand all this?"

Mistaya nodded firmly. "I do, Earth Mother. Haltwhistle will be well cared for." She caught herself. "Earth Mother, I am traveling to see my grandfather in the lake country. What if he will not allow Haltwhistle into his home? He is a very stern man and quite strict about some things."

"Do not worry, child," the Earth Mother assured her. "Mud puppies are fairy creatures. They come and go when and where they choose. They cannot be kept out of any place they wish to visit unless powerful magic is used. Haltwhistle will be with you wherever you go."

Mistaya glanced down at the mud puppy and smiled. "Thank you, Earth Mother. Thank you for Haltwhistle. I love him already."

"Good-bye, Mistaya." The Earth Mother began to sink back down into the ooze. "Remember what I have told you, child."

"I will," Mistaya called back. "Good-bye." Then she shouted, "Wait! When will I see you again?"

But the elemental was already gone, disappeared into the earth. The marsh shimmered faintly with small ripples in the moonlight where she had stood. The clearing was empty and silent.

Mistaya was suddenly sleepy again. It had been a wonderful adventure, and she was looking forward to more. She yawned and stretched, then smiled down at Haltwhistle. "Are

you tired, too?" she asked softly. Haltwhistle stared at her.
"Let's go back to sleep. Okay, boy?"

Haltwhistle wagged his tail tentatively. He didn't seem all
that sure it was.

But Mistaya was already walking away, so the mud puppy
dutifully followed after. Together, they went back through the
woods toward the camp and the fate that was waiting for
them.

Spell Cast

The crow with the red eyes, who in human form was Nightshade, sat high in the branches of a shagbark hickory and watched Mistaya return out of the nighttime woods. The girl materialized abruptly, a silent, stealthy shadow. Made blind to her presence by the Earth Mother's magic, the sentries did not spy her, staring right through her as she passed, as if there were nothing to see. The girl moved quickly to her blanket, wrapped it about herself, lay down, and closed her eyes. In seconds she was asleep.

The crow cast a sharp eye across the clearing and into the woods beyond. There was no sign of the mud puppy. Well and good.

The presence of the mud puppy had upset Nightshade's plans. She had not anticipated its appearance and still did not know its particular purpose. She was aware that it served the Earth Mother, of course, but that did not explain what had brought it to the girl. A summons from the Earth Mother? Possibly. Probably, as a matter of fact. But why had the Earth Mother summoned the girl this night? Did she know of Nightshade's intent? Had she warned the girl in some way? None of this seemed likely. Just as Nightshade could not penetrate the Earth Mother's magic to discover why she had dispatched the mud puppy, neither could the Earth Mother penetrate Nightshade's magic to reveal what lay in store for the girl. Either could gain a *sense* of what the other was about, but no more than that. It was a stalemate of sorts. So any attempt to follow the mud puppy and the girl in an effort to discover what the Earth Mother intended would have been quickly thwarted. Worse, it would have revealed Nightshade's presence in the lake country, and that could easily have ruined everything.

In any case, the girl had returned alone, so the Earth Mother must have finished with her. The fact that she had returned at all strongly suggested that she knew nothing of Nightshade's plans, so there was probably no reason to worry. Not that the Witch of the Deep Fell would have worried much in any event. Had the Earth Mother or her four-legged messenger chosen to interfere, Nightshade would have found a way to make them regret the decision for a long time to come. The witch's magic was much stronger than the Earth Mother's, and she could have sent the elemental scurrying for cover in a hurry.

The crow with the red eyes blinked contentedly. All was as it should be. The Earth Mother had probably summoned the girl to pay her respects as a longtime friend and protector of her mother. Now the girl was right back where Nightshade wanted her, sleeping amid her decidedly ineffectual protectors, blissfully unaware of how her life was about to change.

Nightshade had known that Holiday would send his daughter away when Rydall made his threat against their family. She had known exactly what Holiday would do. The sylph's premonition—the one Nightshade had dispatched to her in her sleep, as black and terrifying as the witch could make it—had planted the seed for the idea. Rydall's appearance had brought the seed to flower. Whatever else might happen, Holiday and the sylph would take no chances with their beloved daughter. Nightshade hadn't known where the girl would be sent, although the lake country and the once-fairy had been her first guess, but in truth it didn't matter. Wherever Mistaya might have gone, Nightshade would have been waiting.

And now it was time.

Using not just vision but instinct as well, the red eyes made a final sweep of the clearing and the woods surrounding it, a final search of the shadows and the dark where something might hide. Nothing revealed itself. The red eyes gleamed. Nightshade smiled inwardly. The sleeping men and the girl belonged to her now.

The crow took wing, lifting away from the branch on which it had kept watch, soaring momentarily skyward, circling the clearing, then dropping down again in a slow spiral. They were in the last few hours of the waning night, the ones leading into the new day, the ones during which sleep is deepest and dreams hold sway. Darkness and silence cloaked the men and the girl and their animals, and none sensed the presence of the descending crow. It passed over their heads unseen and unheard. It swept across them twice to make certain, but even the sentries, watchful once more now that the girl had returned and the Earth Mother's vision spell had been lifted, saw nothing.

The crow banked slowly left across Mistaya, then flew back again, its shadow passing over the small, still form like the comforting touch of a mother's hand. On each pass a strange green dust that winked and spun in the moonlight was released from the crow's dark wings like pollen from a flower and floated earthward to settle over the sleeping girl. Four passes the crow made, and on each the greenish dust fell like a mossy veil. Mistaya breathed it in as she slept, smiled at its fragrance, and pulled her blanket tighter for comfort. Slowly her sleep deepened, and she drifted farther from consciousness. Dreams claimed her, a conjuring of her most vivid imaginings, and she was carried swiftly away into their light.

The crow rose skyward again and circled back into the shelter of the trees. Now the girl would sleep until Nightshade was ready for her to wake. She would sleep and be no part of what was to happen next.

Descending by hops from branch to branch, the crow passed downward through the concealing limbs until it was only a few feet above the ground. Then it transformed into Nightshade, the witch rising out of feathers and wings in a swirl of dark robes to stand again on the earth in the night shadows. Tall and regal, her beauty as dazzling and cold as newly fallen snow, her black hair with its single white streak swept back from her aquiline face, her smile as hard as stone, she gathered her magic about her and stepped out from the trees and into the moonlit clearing.

In her dreams Mistaya was a bird with snow-white feathers flying across a land of bright colors. There were forests of emerald green, fields of butter yellow and spring mint, mountains of licorice and chocolate, hills of crimson and violet, lakes of azure, and rivers of silver and gold. Everywhere wildflowers bloomed, sprinkled across the land like fairy dust.

A bird with black feathers flew next to her, leading the way, showing her the miracle that lay below. The other bird said nothing; it had no need for words. Its thoughts and feelings buoyed Mistaya's small feathered body. She was borne as if on a wind, sailing down their currents, riding atop their gusts, stretching out to soar along their slides. It was wondrous, and it gave her an intoxicating sense of having the entire world at her wing tips.

The flight wore on, and they passed over people looking up from down below. The people craned their necks and pointed. Some called out to her and beckoned. They were people she had known in another life, in another form, and had left behind. They might have loved and cared for her once; they might even have helped nurture her when she was a fledgling. Now they were trying to lure her back to them, to draw her down so that they could cage her. They begrudged her the freedom she had found. They resented the fact that they no longer controlled her destiny. There was anger and disappointment and envy in their voices as they called out, and she found herself eager to get far away from them. She flew on without slowing, without looking back. She flew on toward her future.

Beside her the bird with black feathers turned to look at her, and she could see its red eyes glimmer with approval.

Having come completely clear of her shadowy concealment within the trees, Nightshade turned her attention first to the two sentries who kept watch at either end of the little clearing. She let them see her, all cloaked and hooded, a tall black shape as menacing as death. When they turned their weapons toward her, knowing instinctively that she was trouble, she brought up her hands and sent her magic lancing into them in twin flashes of wicked green fire. The sentries were engulfed before they could cry out, and when the fire died, they had been transformed into rocks the size of bread loaves, rocks that steamed and spit like live coals.

The Witch of the Deep Fell came forward another few steps. She pointed at the line that tethered the caravan's animals, and it flared and turned to ash. The horses, Lightfoot and Owl among them, bolted away. Nightshade gestured almost casually at the camp's cook fire, now no more than a clump of dying embers, and it flared alive, rising upward toward the heavens as if it had become some fiery phantasm risen from the earth. A moment later Mistaya's carriage burst into flames as well.

Now the remaining members of the King's Guards woke, blinking against the sudden light, scrambling clear of their blankets, and reaching instinctively for their weapons. They were pitifully slow. Nightshade transformed five of them before they even knew what was happening, catching them up in her magic, turning them to stones. The others were quicker, a few even swift enough to leap up and start toward her. But she pointed at them one after the other, a dark angel of destruction, and they were struck down. In seconds the last of them were gone.

Now the clearing was empty of everyone but Nightshade, the sleeping girl, and the astonished and confused Questor Thews and Abernathy. The latter two stood in front of Mistaya to protect her from harm. Everything had happened so quickly, they had barely had time to wake and come to her side. Questor Thews was weaving some sort of protective spell, his hands, as old and dry as twigs, making shadow pictures in the glare of the revived fire. Nightshade collapsed the spell before it could form and came forward to stand within the light. She swept back her hood and revealed herself.

"Don't bother, Questor Thews," she advised as he prepared to try again. "No magic will save you this time."

The old man stared at her, trembling with rage and indignation. "Nightshade, what have you done?" he exclaimed in a hoarse whisper.

"Done?" she repeated, indignant. "Nothing that I did not intend, wizard. Nothing that I have not planned for two long years. Do you begin to see now how hopeless things are for you?"

Abernathy was edging away, searching for a weapon to use against her. She made a sharp gesture, and he froze in his tracks.

"Better, scribe, if you stay where you are." She smiled at him, contented by the feeling of power that washed through her.

Questor Thews straightened himself, attempting as he did so to regain his dignity. "You overreach yourself, Nightshade," he declared bravely. "The High Lord will not tolerate this."

"The High Lord will have his hands full just trying to stay alive, I think," she replied, her smile growing broader. "Oh, I think he will have them quite full. Too bad you won't be there to help him. Either of you."

Questor Thews saw the truth of things then. "You have come for the girl, haven't you? For Mistaya?"

"She belongs to me," said the witch. "She has always belonged to me! She was born out of my soil, in my haven, from my magic! She should have been given to me then, but the fairies intervened. But not this time, wizard. This time I will have her. And when I am finished, she will not ever wish to leave me."

The fire roared and crackled in the night's deep silence, an enthusiastic accomplice to the witch's scheme. Questor Thews and Abernathy were scarecrow figures trapped within its light, helpless to escape. But they refused to crumble.

"Holiday will come for her," the old man insisted stubbornly, "even if we are gone."

Nightshade laughed. "You do not listen very well, Questor Thews. Holiday must deal with Rydall first, and Rydall will see him destroyed. I have planned it, and I will see it come to pass. The King of Marnhull is my creature, and he will bring about Holiday's destruction as surely as the sun will rise on the new day. Holiday will struggle against his fate, and that will give me great pleasure to watch, but in the end he will succumb. Stripped of his child, his friends, and eventually his wife as well, he will die all alone and forsaken. Nothing less will satisfy me. Nothing less will serve to repay me for what I have been made to suffer."

"Rydall is your doing?" the wizard whispered in shock.

"All of it is my doing—all that has come about and all that will be. I have made it my life's work to see the play-King reduced to nothing, and I will not be disappointed."

Abernathy edged forward a step. "Nightshade, you cannot do this. Let Mistaya go. She is only a child."

"Only a child?" The smile fled from Nightshade's face. "No, scribe, that is exactly what she is not. That is where you have all been so mistaken. I should know. I see myself in her. I see what I was. I see what she can be. I will give her the knowledge that you would keep hidden. I will shape her as she was meant to be shaped. She harbors within her soul demons waiting to be unleashed; I will help her set them free. She has the power of a child's imagination, and I will use that. Let this be your final thought. When I am done with her, she will become for me the instrument of the play-King's destruction! One more time will he see her, will he clasp her to him, a snake to his breast, and on that day he will breathe his last!"

She saw the hopelessness in their eyes as she finished and waited for them to react. Questor Thews was already trying furtively to gather back his scattered magic in a spell of protection, his gnarled fingers working in the shadow of his skinny body. She smiled at the futility of his effort.

None of them saw Haltwhistle edge out of the forest shadows to stand just within the clearing far to one side, splayed feet padding gingerly, sad eyes watchful.

"What do you intend to do to us?" Abernathy demanded, risking a quick glance over his shoulder at Mistaya. He was wondering why she did not wake up.

"Yes, Nightshade, what?" Questor Thews pressed. He was trying to give them more time so that he could complete the forming of his spell, not realizing that he was already far too late. "Would you turn us into rocks as well?"

Nightshade smiled. "No, wizard, I would not bother with anything so prosaic where you are concerned. Nor you, scribe. You have been a constant source of irritation to me, but you have interfered for the last time. Your lives end here. No one will ever see either of you again."

There was a moment in which time froze, the witch's words drifting away on the crackle of the fire. Then Questor Thews's hands came up, magic flaring in a wide arc before him. Abernathy turned swiftly toward Mistaya and reached down in an attempt to snatch her up. Nightshade laughed. Her arms extended, green fire exploded from her fingertips, and her magic rushed forward in a surge of energy and dark intent to engulf her victims.

As all this was happening, Haltwhistle's head drooped, his body slumped, the hackles on the back of his neck rose, and something akin to a mix of moonlight and frost rose off his cringing form and rocketed across the clearing. An instant before Nightshade's magic struck Questor Thews and Abernathy, smashing the wizard's flimsy shield to smithereens, the moon/frost reached them first.

Then the witch fire consumed them, and they were gone in an instant's time. Nothing remained but smoke and the stench of something charred and ruined.

Nightshade wheeled about. What was it she had seen? That odd glow come out of nowhere? Her eyes swept the clearing quickly, then reached into the woods beyond. Nothing. She narrowed her gaze. There had been something, hadn't there? She lifted her hands and sent witch light deep into the trees, seeking out any living thing concealed there. Small rodents, insects, and a handful of ground birds scattered before her power. But there was nothing else.

She turned back finally, vaguely dissatisfied. The clearing was empty of everyone save herself and the girl. The King's Guards had been turned to stones. The wizard and the dog were gone, never to be seen again. Everything had happened as she had intended. She was free to continue with her plans.

Still . . .

She brushed aside her misgivings in annoyance, walked over to the sleeping girl, and stared down at her. So much to be done with you, little one, she thought in satisfaction. So many lessons to be taught, so many secrets to be revealed, so many tricks to be played. Can you hear what I am thinking?

The girl stirred within her blankets, dreaming.

Yes, sleep on, the Witch of the Deep Fell urged silently. Tomorrow your new life begins.

She bent down then and lifted the girl into the cradle of her arms. Light, like a feather quilt, she was. Nightshade stared down at her new child and smiled.

Then she turned the air about them to icy mist. A moment later the clearing was deserted.

Challenge

Exactly three days after his first appearance Rydall of Marnhull returned to Sterling Silver. This time Ben Holiday was waiting.

Ben never doubted that Rydall would come to make good on his promise. The only unanswered question was, What form of coercion would Marnhull's King employ to persuade Ben to accede to his ludicrous demands? Awake before sunrise, Ben had thought to take a run in an effort to clear his mind. A carryover from his boxing days, he still trained regularly, a regimen of running, weights, and workouts on the light and heavy bags. Sometimes he boxed with members of the King's Guards, but there was no one sufficiently skilled at the sport to give him much competition. Or maybe they thought it better for him to think as much. So mostly he trained alone. This morning he prepared to run, then lost interest. Instead, he climbed atop the battlements with Willow and Bunion to watch for the sunrise and Rydall.

The night had been chilly, and when the darkness began to ease to the west and the east to brighten, he found that during the night a low fog had moved out of the trees and down into the meadow fronting the castle. It lay across the damp grasses in a thick gray smudge that ran from the woods all the way to the waters of the lake. When the sun broke against the eastern horizon in a silvery splash, the fog inched back from the water's edge where the causeway bridged to the castle, and there was Rydall. He sat atop his charger, all armored and bristling with weapons, his silent black-cloaked companion hunched atop his own dark steed, the two of them looking just as before, just as if they had never left.

Ben stared down from the castle walls without speaking, waiting them out. The gauntlet cast down by Rydall three days earlier still lay in the center of the causeway. Ben had ordered it removed, but no one had been able to comply with his demand. It was as if the gauntlet had been nailed to the bridge. No one could lift it; no one could budge it, for that matter—not even Questor Thews. Some form of magic held it in place, and nothing short of tearing up the bridge was going to get it out of there. Ben was not that desperate, so the gauntlet had stayed where it was.

It lay there now, gleaming faintly with the damp, a reminder of what Marnhull's King had promised.

"Holiday!" Rydall called out sharply. No use of "King" or "High Lord" this time. No pretense of respect. "Have you given further thought to my demand?"

"My answer is the same!" Ben shouted back. He felt Willow move in close beside him. "You knew it would be!"

Rydall's horse stamped impatiently. Rydall's hand lifted in a dismissive gesture. "Then I must ask you to change it. Rather, I must insist. You no longer have a choice. Things have changed since we last spoke. I have your daughter."

There was a long silence. Willow's hands fastened tightly on Ben's arm, and he heard her sharp intake of breath. Ben's throat constricted in response to the words. *I have your daughter.* But Mistaya was safe. She was two days gone into the lake country with her grandfather, safely beyond Rydall's reach.

Wasn't she?

"I told you I would find a way to convince you to listen to me," Rydall continued, breaking the momentary silence. "I think now that you must. Your daughter is important to you, I assume."

Ben was trembling with rage. "This is another of your games, Rydall! I have had just about all of you I can stand!"

The dismissive gesture came again. "That remains to be seen. I don't expect you to take my word for what I tell you, in any case. Not you, Holiday. You are the sort of man who demands proof even when the truth is staring him in the face. Very well, then."

He whistled, and a pair of horses appeared from out of the blanket of low-lying fog. Ben felt his heart sink as they came closer. One was Lightfoot, and the other Owl. There was no mistaking their markings. They came past Rydall and started across the bridge.

"Send someone down and have them bring you what they find tied to the pony's saddle," Rydall called up once more.

Ben looked over at Bunion. The kobold raced away instantly, a dark blur against the castle stone. Unable to speak, burning with anger, Ben stood with Willow pressed close against him. A moment later Bunion was back. There was no expression on his strange, wizened face. He handed Ben a necklace and a scarf. Ben studied them closely and sick at heart, handed them to Willow. They belonged to Mistaya. She had been wearing them when she had left for the lake country.

"Oh, Ben," Willow whispered softly.

"Where are Questor Thews and Abernathy?" Ben shouted down to Rydall. "Where are the men of their escort?"

"Safely tucked away," Rydall answered. "Are you ready to hear my demands now, High Lord of Landover?"

Ben choked back the emotions that threatened to steal away his good sense. He put his arm around Willow as much to steady himself as to steady her. He was still not willing to

accept what he was being told. It was not conceivable that
Rydall could have taken Mistaya so easily. How had he man-
aged it? How could he have overcome her escort? Questor
Thews and Abernathy would have died before giving her up.

"Rydall!" he called down suddenly, shocking himself
with the strength he found in his voice. "I will not surrender
Landover's throne or her people for any reason. I will not be
blackmailed. You seem comfortable with preying on small
children, and that makes me doubt your claims of conquest
with armies numbering in the thousands. I think you are a
coward."

Rydall laughed. "Brave words for a man in your position.
But I do not begrudge them. Nor, in fact, do I expect you to
hand over the throne now any more than I did before. I took
your daughter not to blackmail you into accepting my demands but to persuade you to hear me out. You would not do
so before. You must now. Listen well, then. You can ill afford
not to, I think."

Rydall pointed to the gauntlet. "The challenge I offer is
not the one you have anticipated. As I said, I do not expect
you to hand over your throne. I made the demand because, of
course, I must. A King must always try what is easiest first. It
is in the nature of conquest. Sometimes an opponent will accede. I did not think you would be one who would, but it was
necessary to find out. Now we are past that, past game playing,
past negotiation, and are face to face with reality. I have your
daughter and your friends. You have my kingdom. One of us
must give something up. Which of us is it to be?"

Rydall brought his horse forward onto the edge of the
causeway. "I think it must be you, King of Landover, but I am
willing to settle the matter in an honorable way. A challenge,
then, as I have said. The challenge is this. I will send seven
champions to face you. Each will come at a time of my choosing. Each will be of a different form. All will come to kill you.

If you prevent them from doing so, if you are able to kill them first, all seven of them, then I will free your daughter and friends and abandon my claim to Landover. But if any of them succeeds, then your kingdom will be forfeit and your family will be sent into exile for all time. Do you accept? If you do, walk out upon the causeway and pick up my gauntlet."

Ben stared down at the other in disbelief. "He's crazy," he whispered to Willow, who nodded wordlessly.

"You have a champion of your own to defend you," Rydall continued. "Everyone knows of the Paladin, the King's knight-errant and protector. You shall have some form of defense against the creatures I send." Creatures now, Ben thought. Not champions. "I understand that no one has ever defeated the Paladin. That means you have a more than reasonable chance of winning, doesn't it? Do you accept?"

Still Ben did not respond, his mind racing as he considered the proposal. It was ridiculous, but it was the only chance he had to get Mistaya back. It gave him time to find out where she was and perhaps rescue her. And Questor Thews, Abernathy, and his soldiers. But the bargain itself was insane! His life measured against Rydall's seven killers? If he accepted this challenge, if he went down on the causeway and picked up that gauntlet, he would be bound as surely as by his most sacred oath. There were witnesses to this—members of his castle staff, King's Guards and retainers—and Landover's laws would not allow him to forsake his word once it was given. He might kill Rydall and be relieved of it, but the options offered were extreme and narrowly drawn.

"If you do not accept," Rydall shouted out suddenly, "I shall have your daughter and your friends tied to horses and set before my armies as we sweep into your kingdom. They shall die first, before any of my men. I would regret this, but it would be necessary if I were to ask my men to give up their lives as the price of your stubbornness. I told you once before,

I prefer to gain your kingdom without bloodshed. You might prefer the same—if for different reasons. My challenge gives you that chance. Do you accept?"

Ben was thinking now that if he did, he must also accept the fact that he would be required to become the Paladin in order to stay alive—not once or twice but seven times. It was his worst fear. He struggled constantly with what giving himself over to his alter ego meant. Each time it became increasingly more difficult to keep from losing his own identity. Becoming the Paladin meant complete submersion into the other's being. Each time it was a little harder coming back out of the armored shell, out of the memories, out of the life that was his champion's. If he accepted Rydall's challenge, he would be facing the prospect not only of being killed in combat but of being transformed forever into his darker half.

"High Lord, do you accept?" Rydall demanded again.

"No, do not!" Willow exclaimed suddenly, seizing his arm. "There is more to this than what you are being told! There is something hidden behind Rydall's words! I can sense it, Ben!" She moved in front of him. There were tears in her eyes. Her voice was so quiet, he could barely hear her speak. "Even if we must lose Mistaya, do not accept."

What it must have cost her to say this, Ben could not begin to guess. She was fiercely protective of Mistaya. She would do anything to keep her safe. But she was giving him a chance to save himself anyway. She loved him that much.

He folded her into his arms and held her close. "I have to try," he told her softly. "If I don't, how will I live with myself afterward?"

He kissed her, then turned away. Beckoning Bunion to follow, he crossed the parapets to the stairway leading down. "Wait for me here," he called back to Willow.

He went down the stairway thinking of what he must do once he picked up the gauntlet. His options were few. He must find Mistaya, Questor, Abernathy, and his Guards and set them free. That was first. Then he must persuade Rydall to withdraw his challenge and his threat to Landover. Or, if he was unable to do that, kill him. The alternative was to face Rydall's seven challengers and hope that he killed them before they killed him. Or was he required to kill them? Perhaps he could simply defeat them. But Rydall had not made it seem as if that were an option. "Creatures" Rydall had called them the second time. Ben found himself wondering what sort of creatures they would be.

He crossed the courtyard to the main gates, Bunion a step behind, the kobold's teeth clenched in a frightening grimace. It was clear what he was thinking. "Let them be, Bunion," Ben cautioned softly. "We need Mistaya and the others back first."

The kobold grunted something in response, and Ben hoped it was the answer he was seeking.

He walked through the main gates and out onto the causeway. The day was brightening, the sky clear and blue, the last of the fog dissipating on the meadow fronting the castle's lake. Rydall and his silent companion sat atop their horses and waited. Ben moved out onto the causeway, alert for any treachery, his anger growing with every step he took. Perhaps Bunion had the right idea. How hard would it be to summon the Paladin and put an end to Rydall once and for all? Easy enough if he chose to do it, he thought. But where would that leave Mistaya?

He wondered suddenly if this was all an elaborate trick, if the horses, the necklace, and the scarf were lures to bring him out into the open. He wondered if Rydall really did have Mistaya and her escort as his prisoners. He surmised that it could all be a clever lie.

But he knew in his heart it wasn't.

He reached the far end of the causeway and stopped. The riders stared down at him from atop their chargers. Wordlessly Ben reached down for the gauntlet. It came away from the bridge easily, as if nothing more than force of will had held it in place those three days past. Ben straightened and looked directly at Rydall. Marnhull's King was much bigger than he had first thought, a man of surprising size and undoubted strength. His black-cloaked companion, on the other hand, seemed smaller. The faces of both were carefully hidden beneath helmet and hood, respectively.

Ben flung the gauntlet back at Rydall. The big man caught it easily and waved it in mock salute.

"Do not mistake this for anything but what it is, Rydall," Ben said quietly. "And know this. If anything happens to Mistaya or Questor Thews or Abernathy or one of my Guards, I will hunt you down even if I am required to descend into the fires of Abaddon!"

Rydall bent forward. "You will never have to search that far for me, Holiday. Nor think for one moment that I would be afraid of you if you did." He tightened his reins and swung his horse about. "Three days, High Lord of Landover. The first of my creatures comes for you then. If I were you, I would start thinking about how to stay alive."

He kicked his mount sharply, and the warhorse leapt away. Once again his black-cloaked companion lingered. Ben could feel eyes studying him from within the hood's deep shadows, as if trying to discover something. Fear, perhaps? Ben held his ground, staring back determinedly. Then Bunion was beside him, hissing furiously at the rider, all teeth and claws as he advanced.

The second rider wheeled away then and galloped after Rydall across the meadow. Ben stood with his kobold protector and watched until they had disappeared into the trees.

Safely back within the forest shadows where even the new light had not yet penetrated, the riders reined to a halt and dismounted. Nightshade threw off the cloak that had concealed her and, discarding the cramped and hunched form she had assumed as her disguise, restored her body to its normal shape. Her hands lifted then to form a brief spell of invisibility, protection against the unlikely event that someone would stumble across them. When the spell was in place, she used her magic a second time to change the horses back into tiny green and black striped lizards that quickly skittered up her arm and into the folds of her robes.

Rydall stood watching, his visor still lowered. "He does not seem afraid," he offered petulantly.

Nightshade laughed. "No, not yet. His anger shields him for the moment. He still doubts that we really have his daughter. He will need to make certain of that before fear can take hold. Then my creatures will come for him, one after the other, and the fear will build. He will begin to imagine all sorts of things coming to pass, none of them good. He will search for us and fail to find even the smallest trace. He will despair of hope. Then, I promise, the fear will have him."

"He has the sylph for support, don't forget."

There was a flash of anger in Nightshade's red eyes. "Do not mock me, King Rydall, who never was Rydall or King. You serve at my pleasure; do not forget that."

The other stood motionless before her and said nothing, a wall of iron. But she could sense his hesitation and was satisfied. "He has her for now, yes," she admitted. "But in the end I'll see her stripped from him as well. In the end he will be left alone."

Rydall shifted impatiently. "I would feel better about this if I knew the whole of your plan. What if something goes wrong?"

She straightened so that she seemed to grow before his eyes. "Nothing will go wrong. I have planned too carefully for that. As for knowing what I intend, it is better for now that I keep some things to myself. You know as much as you need to know." She gave him a coldly appraising look. "I'll send you back now. Tend to your affairs and await my summons."

Rydall looked away, his armor creaking. "I could have killed him on the bridge and the matter would have been finished then and there. You should have let me."

"And spoil what I have worked and planned for these two years past?" Nightshade was incredulous. "I think not. Besides, I am not so sure you are his better. You have never given proof of it."

He started to object, a grunt of anger rising from his throat, but she cut him off with a wave of her hand. "Stay silent. You will do as I say. Holiday's demise is to be left to me. Your part in this is settled. I want no dispute. You are not trying to dispute me, are you?"

There was a long silence from the other. "No," he replied finally.

"Good. If you want Holiday dead, and I know you do, then leave it to me to arrange. Now go."

She wove her hands through the air before her, and Rydall disappeared in a rising column of mist. She waited until she was sure he had been dispatched back to where he had come from. She neither liked nor trusted him, but he was useful in this matter and would do as a cat's-paw until she was finished. Until Holiday was dead.

She closed her eyes in pleasure as she envisioned the play-King's final moments. She had pictured it over and over again in her mind, shaping it, honing it, polishing it until it was perfect. She could see every detail of it. She could see him breathing for the final time, see the look in his eyes as he realized what had been done to him, hear the despair in his voice as he tried to cry out.

Oh, it would happen. It most definitely would. For now, however, there were other matters that needed her attention.

She brought up her hands one final time. A rush of dark mist engulfed her, and she was gone.

Ben Holiday was already thinking furiously as he walked back across the causeway and reentered Sterling Silver. Willow had come down from the battlements and was waiting for him. She rushed up, and he held her close in an effort to still the trembling inside them both.

"We'll get her back," he whispered, feeling her fists tighten against his back. "I promise."

Then he turned to Bunion, who was trailing behind. "Leave for the lake country right away," he ordered the kobold. "Tell the River Master that his granddaughter has been kidnapped by Rydall of Marnhull and ask for his help in searching for her. Tell him any assistance he chooses to give will be greatly appreciated. Be sure he understands that she was traveling to his country for safekeeping when she was taken. Keep an eye out for any sign of what might have happened on your journey down. And Bunion," he added, "be careful yourself. Don't take any chances. I've already lost Questor and Abernathy. I don't want to lose you as well."

The kobold grinned and showed his teeth. It wasn't likely that anything would happen to a creature that could dispatch a cave wight or a bog wump without breaking a sweat, but Ben was spooked by how easily Rydall had overcome those he had sent to protect Mistaya. If that was what had really happened, of course. He still wasn't sure, but he had to assume the worst. Bunion's visit to the River Master was necessary.

Bunion turned and was gone so swiftly that Ben had to remind himself why he had dispatched his royal messenger in the first place. Kobolds were the fastest creatures alive. A trip to the lake country would take a kobold barely a day. They were strange beings, their bodies all gnarled and bristly, their legs bowed and their arms crooked, their faces monkeylike, and their teeth as numerous and sharp as an alligator's, an amalgam of bizarre and diverse features. But kobolds had served the Kings of Landover for many years, and they were loyal and tough. Ben knew he could depend on Bunion.

He started across the entry court, Willow at his side. "I'm going up to use the Landsview. Maybe I can find some trace of Misty. Will you cancel all my appointments for the day? I'll be down as soon as I can."

He climbed to the castle's highest tower and boarded the Landsview, the magical instrument that allowed its user to travel from one end of Landover to the other without leaving Sterling Silver. He invoked the magic, rose out of the tower as if actually flying, and in his mind's eye scanned the whole of the countryside without finding his daughter or his friends or any indication of what had happened to them. He made a quick visit to Elderew, the home of the River Master, but there was nothing to show that the once-fairy were aware that anything had happened.

He went from there to the eastern borders, searching the fringes of the fairy mists from the Fire Springs south, but there was no sign of Rydall or Mistaya or anything that would have led him to either. He looked for Strabo, but the dragon was not to be found. Probably sleeping in one of the fire pits it called home. He moved on to the Melchor north and finally to the Deep Fell, whose hollows were the one place he could not enter from the Landsview. Nightshade's magic would not permit it. He paused momentarily, thinking that those he searched for could easily be hidden there and he would never know. But it was reaching to imagine that Nightshade was in-volved in any of this. As much as she hated him, she hated outsiders more. She would never conspire with anyone who intended to invade Landover. Besides, no one had even seen her in months. Ben moved on.

He spent the whole of the morning searching the coun-tryside for Mistaya and his friends and found not a single trace of any of them. It was as if they had disappeared off the face of the earth. When he finally came back into the chamber and stepped down off the lectern, he was exhausted. Use of the

Landsview's magic had worn him out, and he had nothing to show for it. He was discouraged and frightened. He went down to his bedchamber and fell asleep.

When he woke, Willow was seated next to him, anxious for any news. But he had none to give her. They spent the remainder of the day going over the agenda of meetings and appointments for the week and ended up canceling most. Some had to be kept because there were obligations that could not wait. But it was a desultory effort at best, and Ben could think of little besides his missing daughter and friends. He did not know what to do next. It seemed there was nothing he could do other than wait on Rydall's challengers. Three days he had been given. Then the first would appear. He did not speak of it with Willow, but he could see in her eyes and hear in her voice that she was thinking of it, too. A battle to the death seven times over if he was to survive. A use seven times of the Paladin's armored body and battle skills. A giving over of himself seven times to the life and memories of a being whose only purpose was to destroy the King's enemies. It was a thoroughly terrifying prospect.

They slept poorly that night, waking often to hold each other, lying close in the silence and thinking of what the days ahead promised. Ben had never felt so empty. It seemed on reflection that he had betrayed Mistaya by sending her away, that he should have kept her close beside him. Perhaps that way he could have protected her better from Rydall. He did not say so to Willow, of course. It was easy to engage in second-guessing now, when it was too late to matter, when things were over and done. There was nothing to be gained by rehashing the "what ifs" of the situation. All that remained was to try to find some way to make things right again. But how was he to do that? What was left to try?

By noon of the following day Bunion was back. He had met with the River Master. Mistaya and the others had never reached Elderew. No one among the once-fairy had any idea what had happened to them. There was no sign they had ever passed that way.

Ben Holiday and Willow exchanged a long, helpless look and tried to hide their despair.

Seduction

Mistaya woke to find herself shrouded in hazy light and deep silence. She lay upon the ground, still wrapped in her blanket but far from the place where she had fallen asleep. She knew that instinctively. She knew as well that she had slept for a long time. She was still drowsy, her limbs were stiff, her eyes were blurry, and her entire body was filled with the sort of heaviness that comes only after a deep sleep. Something had happened to her. Something unexpected.

She rose to a sitting position and looked around. She was alone. There was no sign of Questor, Abernathy, or the King's Guards. There was no trace of Haltwhistle. The animals were gone, and her baggage and carriage were missing. She was not surprised. She had been taken away from all that while she slept. She did not think she was even in the lake country anymore. The look of things was all wrong. She glanced skyward. There was no sky to be seen. There were trees all about, but they were ancient and webbed with vines and moss. The light was gray and thick with mist. It smelled and tasted of damp earth and decay. Strangely enough, it seemed familiar.

She stood up and brushed herself off. She was not afraid. She should have been, she supposed, but she was not. At least not yet. There was a strangeness to things that she could not explain, but she had not been harmed in any way. She wondered what had happened to her friends, but she was not yet ready to conclude that she was in any danger.

She peered about carefully, turning a full circle to spy out anything that might be spied, and discovered nothing but the old-growth trees and the misty silence.

When she had completed her circle, she found herself face to face with a tall, regal woman.

"Welcome, Mistaya," the woman said, smiling. A cold smile.

"Where am I?" Mistaya asked, thinking as she did, *I know this woman. I know her. But how?*

"You are in the Deep Fell," the woman answered, calm and still against the half-light. She was cloaked in black. Her hair was black with a single white streak down the middle. Her skin was alabaster white. Her eyes . . .

"You remember me, don't you?" the woman said, making it more a statement of fact than a question.

"Yes," Mistaya answered, certain now that she did, yet unable to remember why. This was the Deep Fell, the woman had said, and only one person lived in the Deep Fell. "You are Nightshade."

"I am," Nightshade answered, pleased. The eyes, silver before, turned suddenly red.

"You are the bird, the crow," the girl said suddenly. "From the picnic. You were watching me."

Nightshade's smile broadened. "I was. And you were watching me, weren't you? Your memory is excellent."

Mistaya looked about uncertainly. "What am I doing here? Did you bring me?"

The witch nodded. "I did. You were asleep when your camp was attacked by those in service to King Rydall of Marnhull, the man who came recently to your father's castle. Do you remember him?"

Mistaya nodded.

"The attack was sudden and unexpected. It was made in

an effort to kidnap you. If you were in Rydall's power, then he might force your father to do as he seeks—to relinquish the crown of Landover and go into exile. Your parents thought Rydall would not know of your journey to the lake country and your grandfather, but he is more dangerous than they suspected. It was fortunate that I was keeping an eye out for you, that I was concerned for your safety. I was able to spirit you away before you were taken. I brought you here, to the Deep Fell, to be with me."

Mistaya said nothing, but her eyes gave her away.

"You do not believe me, do you?" Nightshade said.

Mistaya's lips compressed into a tight line. "My father would not want me here," she said quietly.

"Because we are not friends and he does not trust me," the witch acknowledged with a shrug. "That is true. But the fact of the matter is that he knows you are here and can do what he chooses with the information."

Mistaya frowned. "He knows?"

"Of course. I have already sent word. Secretly, of course, so that Rydall will not know. I was forced to act swiftly when the attack came, so I could not leave word with your friends. I think they are well, but I could not stay to make certain. Questor Thews seemed to be holding his own, and I suspect that with you gone, the attack would have been withdrawn rather quickly. After all, there was no point in continuing it."

"Because I was with you."

"Exactly. But Rydall does not know that. He thinks you are returned to Sterling Silver or gone on to Elderew to be with your grandfather. Neither place is safe, of course. He will be looking for you there. He will not think to look for you here. You are better off with me until this matter is resolved. Your father will agree with that once he thinks it through."

Mistaya shuffled her feet, thinking hard. None of this seemed right to her. "How do you know about Rydall? Why have you been watching me?"

"I am interested in you, Mistaya," Nightshade answered slowly. "I know things about you that even you do not know. I wanted to tell them to you, but I wasn't sure how to do so. I was following you, waiting for a chance. I know how your father and mother feel about me. We have not always been on good terms. At times we have fought. But we share a common interest in you." She paused. "Do you know, Mistaya, that you were born in the Deep Fell?"

Mistaya's brow furrowed. "I was?"

"Your mother didn't tell you, did she? I thought not." Nightshade moved to one side. She seemed unconcerned with everything as she gazed off into the trees. "Did she tell you that you can do magic?"

Mistaya's mouth dropped. Interest flickered in her emerald eyes. "I can? Real magic?"

"Of course. Every witch can do magic." Nightshade glanced over, and her red eyes glittered. "You knew you were a witch, didn't you?"

Mistaya took a very deep breath before answering. "No, I didn't. Are you lying to me?"

Nightshade gave no answer. Instead, she gestured vaguely at the air before her, and a table and two chairs appeared. The table was covered with a scarlet cloth and laden with fruit, nuts, bread, cheese, and cider. "Sit down," said the witch. "We shall have something to eat while we talk."

Mistaya hesitated, but hunger won out over reticence, and she took the chair opposite Nightshade. Still cautious, she tried a nut and then a slice of cheese. Both tasted wonderful, so she went on to the rest of the foodstuffs and a cup of the cider. Nightshade sat opposite her and chewed absently on a slice of bread.

"I will tell you something, Mistaya," she said. "I brought you here because the opportunity presented itself, and I was afraid it would not come again. It was chance, of course. If I had waited for you to come on your own or for your parents to send you—if I had been bold enough to make the request, for there would have been no offer from them—you probably would not have come at all. I do not begrudge that. I under-stand the way of things. I am not well thought of in many quarters and by many people. I am sure you have heard bad things about me."

Mistaya glanced up from her eating, a flicker of concern in her green eyes. But there was no threat in the witch's voice and none mirrored on her face.

"You needn't be afraid of me," Nightshade assured her. "You are here to be kept safe, not to be harmed. You are free to leave whenever you wish. But I would like you to hear me out first. Will you agree to that?"

Mistaya thought it over, chewing on a handful of nuts, then nodded.

"Good. You are perceptive. I meant what I said about you being safer here than with your family." Nightshade made a dismissive gesture with her hand. "Rydall is an outsider, a pretender to the throne, a conqueror of lesser lands who would add Landover to his holdings. Whatever differences your father and I have shared, we agree on one thing. Land-over should not be ruled by Rydall. I am a witch, Mistaya, and witches know things that others do not. They hear of them first and comprehend them more fully. Rydall was known to me the moment he crossed out of the mists with his black-cloaked companion. His wizard, I discovered. A very powerful being, one who is, perhaps, as powerful as me. I knew of them and shadowed them on their visit to your home. I heard their demands. I knew what they would do. When they came for you, I was waiting."

She looked off into the trees again, contemplative. "But I had other reasons for intervening at the time I chose. I wanted to bring you here. I wanted you to spend time with me in the Deep Fell. The chance would not come again, I felt. So I was anxious to take advantage of it. I think it is important that you hear the truth about yourself—important to you and to me."

"To you?" Mistaya looked doubtful.

"Yes, Mistaya." Nightshade's hands caressed each other like small white mice. "I am the Witch of the Deep Fell, the only witch in all of Landover, and I have waited a long time for there to be another. I want to reveal what I know. I want to talk with someone who shares my passion for magic. You are that person."

Mistaya had stopped eating. She was staring at Nightshade, entranced. "I thought I might have magic," she said quietly, hesitantly, thinking of the Earth Mother. "Sometimes I could almost feel it. But I wasn't sure."

"You are unschooled in its use, untrained in its calling, and the truth of its existence has been kept from you. But the magic is yours," Nightshade said. "It has always been yours."

"Why wasn't I told?" Mistaya was still not convinced, but she was beginning to explore the possibilities. "Why did my parents and even Questor tell me that use of the magic—of any magic—was dangerous? Are you saying they lied to me?"

Nightshade shook her head. "Of course not. They would never do that. They simply kept from you what they felt you were not yet ready to know. In time they would have told you everything. I think they were mistaken in keeping it from you for as long as they did, of course. But now there are other reasons to tell you, ones that have nothing to do with a difference of opinion between your parents and me, ones that have everything to do with the coming of Rydall and the danger he poses to your father."

"What danger?" Mistaya asked at once. "Tell me."

But Nightshade shook her head and held up one slim hand. "Patience, Mistaya. Let me tell you things in my own way. You can make up your mind when I am finished."

She rose again, and Mistaya rose with her. Nightshade

gestured briefly, and the table with its food and drink disappeared. The clearing in which they stood was empty again, save for them. Nightshade smiled at Mistaya. The same cold smile. But it seemed more comforting to the girl this time, more acceptable. She found herself smiling back almost without being aware of it.

"We shall be friends, you and I," the witch said, arching one eyebrow toward the beginning of the white streak in her black hair. "We shall tell each other all our secrets. Come with me."

She moved across the clearing and into the woods without looking back. Mistaya followed, curious now, anxious to hear more of what the other would tell her. She was no longer thinking of the circumstances that had brought her to the Deep Fell. She was not even thinking of her parents or Questor Thews or Abernathy. She was thinking instead of her magic, the magic she had always known she possessed, the magic she had so desperately coveted. Now, at last, it was going to be revealed to her. She could sense it in the tall woman's words.

When they had gone a short distance into the trees, back where the haze was thick enough to cut and the light was drawn thin, Nightshade stopped and turned to face the girl.

"You are not easily frightened, are you, Mistaya?" she asked. Mistaya shook her head. "You do not find the use of magic a cause for tears and huddling under covers as some children do when a storm comes with its lightning and thunder?"

Mistaya shook her head again, this time looking absolutely defiant. "I am not frightened of anything!" she said bravely, and almost meant it.

Nightshade nodded, eyes silver and serene once more. "I brought you here to the Deep Fell because you are a witch. A witch," she repeated emphatically, "like me. You were born in

the Deep Fell, born of soil which has been consecrated time
and again by my magic, born of a heritage of fairy blood, born
into a world in which the strong and the certain are blessed
with the use of power. You are something of an enigma to
your parents because of this. An enigma. Do you know the
word?"

Mistaya nodded. "A mystery."

"Yes, a mystery. Because there is not another like you in
all of Landover. You have abilities they do not even suspect.
You have magic that only I can comprehend. I can teach you
to harness your power and use it well. No one else can do for
you what I can. Not your parents. Not Questor Thews. Not
anyone. None of them share in being what we are—witches—
and so none of them can give you what you need. Yes, use of
the magic can be very dangerous indeed. There is no secret in
that. But the danger comes in not understanding what it is the
magic can do and in making certain that you always know
how to control it. Do you see?"

Mistaya nodded once more, eager now, excited by the
implicit promise of the other's words.

"Good. Here, then." Nightshade bent down and plucked
a wildflower with its buds still unopened. She held it up before
Mistaya. Then she lifted one finger and caressed a tiny bud.
The bud shuddered and blossomed into a crimson flower.
"See? Magic brought it to life. Now you try."

She handed the stalk with its multiple buds and single
open flower to Mistaya, who took it tentatively and held it before her as if it were made of glass.

"Concentrate on one bud," the Witch of the Deep Fell
said. "Concentrate on how it will look as it opens into a
flower. Bring the feeling of its coming to life deep within
your body, deep down where there is only darkness and the
pictures we form in our imaginations. Concentrate on the
flower you would make and then reach up slowly and touch
the bud."

Mistaya did as she was told, focusing every ounce of energy on a mental picture of the bud opening into a flower. She reached up and touched the bud gently, hesitantly.

The bud opened halfway and stopped.

"Very good, Mistaya," Nightshade offered, taking the stalk from her hand and casting it aside. "Was that so hard?"

Mistaya shook her head quickly. Her mouth was dry, and her heart was pounding. She had actually performed magic. She had felt the bud respond to her touch, had watched it shudder slightly, just as it had for Nightshade. But there had been more. There had been a ripple of something smooth and silvery deep down inside her that caressed like a cat and left her warm and anxious for more.

Nightshade's slender hand brushed her own. Mistaya did not mind the touch. It seemed familiar and therefore comfortable. "Try this," the witch said.

She reached down and picked up a black and orange striped caterpillar. The caterpillar rolled into a ball in the palm of her hand, then unrolled again after a moment and began to inch its way to safety. The witch reached down and touched the caterpillar, and it was turned instantly to gold.

"Now you change it back again," she instructed, holding out her open palm with the caterpillar to Mistaya. "Concentrate. Picture in your mind what it is you intend to do. Reach down inside yourself for the feeling of it happening."

Mistaya wet her lips, then compressed them. She focused as hard as she could on the caterpillar, envisioning it alive, seeing it turn from metal to organic matter. She saw it in her mind, then felt it in her heart. She reached down and touched the caterpillar.

The caterpillar turned orange and black once more and began to crawl away.

"I did it!" she breathed excitedly. "Did you see? I did it! I used magic!"

She forgot everything in that instant: her doubts, her

questions, her parents, and her friends. Nightshade brushed the caterpillar away and bent down quickly in front of the girl, her eyes as sharp as cut glass.

"Now you understand, Mistaya. Now you see the truth of what you can do. But that was nothing, that little bit of magic you just performed. That was only the beginning of what you can accomplish. But you must listen to what I tell you. You must study the lessons I give you. You must practice what I show you. You must work very hard. Are you willing to do that?"

Mistaya nodded eagerly, blond hair shimmering with the jungle damp, eyes as bright as a cat's in a cave. "Yes, I am. But . . ." She stopped then, catching herself as she remembered anew the circumstances of her being in the Deep Fell. "My father . . ."

"Your father knows you are here and will come for you if he feels you should not stay," Nightshade answered smoothly, quickly. "The question you must answer is whether or not *you* wish to stay. The choice is really yours now. But before you make that choice, there is something else you must know. Remember I told you there was another reason for your being here with me, for being told of your potential, for exploring your magic?"

She waited expectantly. Mistaya hesitated, then nodded. "I remember. You said you would tell me later."

Nightshade smiled. "Close enough. In my own time and way, I said. So listen carefully now. Rydall of Marnhull has come to your father again since your leaving. He has told your father that he will use the magic of his wizard to destroy him. Questor Thews will try to protect your father, but he lacks sufficient power to do so. Rydall's wizard is much more powerful."

She raised one slender finger and touched Mistaya gently on the tip of her nose. Like a snake's kiss. "But you have the potential, Mistaya, to be even more powerful. You have the magic, still latent but undeniably contained within you, to defeat Rydall and his wizard and save your father. I sense that power, and it is for this reason that I thought it right to bring you here and prepare you for your destiny. For you will be a witch of no small consequence, and a King's daughter as well, and your mastery of your heritage as both will determine the course of your life."

Mistaya stared openmouthed. "I will be able to save my father? My magic will be that strong?"

"As strong as any you could possibly imagine." The witch paused, smiling anew, suddenly intense. "Didn't the Earth Mother tell you any of this?"

"Yes, she . . ." Mistaya hesitated, thinking all at once that she should not reveal everything to someone who already knew so much. Her meeting with the Earth Mother, after all, was supposed to be a secret. "She told me something of my heritage but left me to discover for myself the nature of any magic I possessed or for my parents to tell me of it when they were ready."

She wondered suddenly about Haltwhistle. Where was the mud puppy? Had he, too, been left behind in the attack when Nightshade had brought her to the Deep Fell? She wanted to ask the witch, but once more something kept her from speaking. Nightshade had not mentioned Haltwhistle when she spoke of the others. Perhaps she did not know of the mud puppy.

"The Earth Mother is your friend, as she was your mother's," Nightshade continued. "A good friend, I expect, isn't she?" Mistaya nodded. "She brought you to her just before the attack. I was watching. Did she warn you it was coming?"

"No," Mistaya answered, again thinking, *Why doesn't she know this?*

"What was it that she wanted with you, then?" the other softly asked. "Tell me."

Mistaya shrugged, a reflex pure and simple. She was outwardly calm, inwardly cold. Something was happening here that she didn't understand. She managed a small smile. "She warned me that there would be danger ahead and that I must be wary of it. She said I would need to keep my wits about me."

She waited, the smile frozen on her face as the witch stared deep into her eyes. She doesn't believe me! she was thinking, and wondered all at once why that mattered and what it was that frightened her so.

Then Nightshade's eyes lowered, and she rose. Her slim white hands came to rest on Mistaya's small shoulders. "Do you want to stay with me in the Deep Fell, Mistaya? Do you want to study magic with me?"

Mistaya was soothed by the touch, encouraged by the words, and reassured as swiftly as she had been made to doubt. "How long would I stay?" she asked tentatively, still thinking of her father.

"As long as you wish. You may leave at any time. But," the witch said, and bent down again, her face close, "once you leave to go back to your home, you leave for good. That is the way of things. Once you begin your training, you must remain until it is completed or give it up entirely."

"But if my father comes for me, then what?"

"Then we will speak with him, and a decision will be reached," the other answered. "But Mistaya, you must understand this. Magic is a fragile vessel, one that carries great power but can shatter like glass. It cannot be left untended once it is brought out into the open. So if we are to begin your lessons, you must agree to see them through to their completion. Can you do that?"

Mistaya thought of the way the bud had flowered and the caterpillar had come to life. She thought of the feeling of the magic simmering inside her, smooth and silky. Her misgivings about her circumstances in coming to the Deep Fell seemed inconsequential compared to that.

"I can," she answered firmly.

"So you agree to stay?"

Mistaya nodded, a child's determined affirmation. "I do."

Nightshade smiled down at her benevolently. "Then we shall begin at once. Come with me." She turned away and started back toward the clearing. "Now, there are rules to be heeded, Mistaya," she said as they walked through the haze. "You must listen to me and do as I say. You must never use your magic without me. You must use your magic in the ways I tell you even when you do not understand what it is that I am trying to teach. And—"

She glanced back to make certain Mistaya's eyes found her own. "You must never leave the Deep Fell without me." She let the words sink in. "Because Rydall will be looking for you, and I would never forgive myself if you were to fall into his hands through my carelessness. So we shall stay close to each other while you remain in my charge. Never leave the hollow. Do you understand?"

Mistaya nodded. She did.

The witch turned away, and although Mistaya could not see, there was a satisfied smile on her smooth, cold face. There was triumph in her red-tinged eyes.

They spent all that day working on Nightshade's lessons. Some were incomprehensible to Mistaya, just as the witch had warned. Some were exercises that lacked any discernible purpose. Some were charged with power that Mistaya could feel flowing out of her like the pulse through her body when she ran. Some were so gentle and serene that they lacked any feeling at all and were only words or small gestures on the air.

When the day ended, Mistaya was left with mixed feelings about what she had accomplished. On the one hand, she had felt and seen the magic that lay buried within her, a strange, ephemeral creature that stirred to life and flashed brief glimpses of its visage as she sought to lure it from its den. On the other hand, the ways in which it appeared and was used were enigmatic and unrevealing. Nightshade seemed satisfied, but Mistaya was left confused.

Once, for instance, they had worked at creating a monster. The monster had been one of Mistaya's own choosing, the girl urged on in her creativity by her new mentor, encouraged to make her creature as invulnerable as she could imagine it. Nightshade had been particularly pleased with her efforts there. She had said it was very good. She had said they would try another tomorrow.

Monsters? Mistaya did not understand, but then, she had been told she would not at times, hadn't she?

Rolled up in the blanket by the fire that the witch had allowed her for warmth—Nightshade herself seemed to need no nurturing of that sort—she stared out into the darkness of the Deep Fell, out into the silent gloom, and wondered if she was doing the right thing. Discovering the magic she possessed was exciting, but there was a forbidden quality to its study that she could not ignore. Would her father really approve? He must, if he did not come for her. But then, perhaps he did not know what it was that she was doing with Nightshade. If he did and wanted her to stop, what would she do? She wasn't sure. It was true that she was safer here than in places where Rydall would know to look for her. It was also true that it was much more interesting here. Nightshade was fascinating, filled with strange knowledge, possessed of exotic lore. Although she was clearly the teacher, she treated Mistaya as an equal in their studies, and Mistaya liked that. She coveted the respect she was accorded here, something that had been denied her at home.

She would stay awhile, she decided. Long enough to see what would happen. She could always leave, after all. Nightshade had said so. She could leave whenever she wished if she was willing to pay the penalty of losing her instruction.

Yes, she would stay on a bit longer.

She thought again of Haltwhistle. He would always be with her, the Earth Mother had promised. Was that so? He did not require food or drink or looking after. Mistaya needed only to say his name at least once each day to keep him close.

Her hand came up to her mouth. She had not done that. She had not said his name even once. She had not thought to do so.

She opened her mouth and stopped. Nightshade did not know of the mud puppy. What would she say? Would she send Haltwhistle away? And Mistaya as well?

Mistaya's mouth tightened. Well, it didn't make any difference if the mud puppy wasn't there. She might as well find out before she worried about any of the rest of it.

"Haltwhistle," she said softly, almost inaudibly.

Instantly the mud puppy was next to her, staring down at her from out of the darkness with those great, soulful eyes. Elated, she started to reach for him and stopped. You must never touch a mud puppy, the Earth Mother had warned. Never.

"Hey, boy," she whispered, smiling. Haltwhistle thumped his odd tail in response.

"Did you call, Mistaya?" Nightshade said from out of the darkness in front of her, and Mistaya's head jerked up sharply. Abruptly, the Witch of the Deep Fell appeared, bending over her. "Did you say something?"

Mistaya blinked and looked down for Haltwhistle. The mud puppy had disappeared. "No, nothing. I must have been talking in my sleep."

"Good night, then," the witch said, and slipped away again.

"Good night," Mistaya said.

She took a deep breath and let it out slowly. She looked again for Haltwhistle. The mud puppy appeared anew, materializing out of the night. She watched him for a moment, smiling. Then she closed her eyes and was asleep.

Bumbershoot

The instant Nightshade's witch fire enveloped them, Landover disappeared and time stopped. Soft, gauzy light cocooned Abernathy, and he lost sight of Questor Thews completely. He drifted, suspended in the light, wrapped in silence and consumed by a numbness that emptied him of all feeling. He did not know what was happening to him. He supposed that he was dead and that this was what dying felt like, but he wasn't sure. He tried to move and couldn't. He tried to see beyond the white brightness surrounding him and couldn't do that, either. He could barely manage to form a coherent thought. He didn't even know if he was breathing.

Then the light disappeared in a sudden rush of wind and brilliant colors, and the sights, sounds, tastes, and smells of life rushed back into focus with brilliant clarity. The lake country was gone. He was pretty sure that Landover itself was gone, as well. He was sitting on a grassy flat that spread all around a great stone basin. A fountain at the center of the basin spouted a plume of water that arched high into the air in a feathery spray. Light caught the water and created small, shimmering rainbows. People were seated all across the lawn and at the edge of the fountain. Children played in the fountain, having ventured down into the shallow stone bowl, darting in and out of the spray, laughing and teasing one another. It was summer, and the day was sunny and hot.

Abernathy sat up straight and looked about. There were people everywhere. It was some sort of festival, and everyone was celebrating. Across the way were a pair of jugglers. A clown walked by on stilts. At a nearby table a small boy was having his face painted. Walkways bordered the lawn, the one nearest him packed end to end with makeshift booths selling the works of artisans and craftsmen: glass prisms, wood carvings, metal sculptures, and clothing of all sorts. Other walkways were jammed with carts and stands selling food and drink. Garish signs proclaimed the types of edibles and libations offered. Abernathy did not recognize the names.

But he could read the signs. If he was not in Landover, he should not have been able to do that.

His first thought was, Where am I, then?

His second was, Why aren't I dead?

A man with long, tangled black hair and a full beard streaked with purple dye stood next to a woman with her hair braided in tight beaded rows tipped with tiny bells. Both wore gold earrings and neck chains and sported matching face-painted roses framed in red hearts. They were staring at Abernathy in disbelief.

"Hey, man, that was awesome!" the man declared reverently. "How did you do that?"

"Was it some sort of magic?" the woman asked.

Abernathy had no idea what they were talking about. But he could understand them, and that was as mystifying as being able to read the signs. He looked around in confusion. Music rose from all about, mingling with shouts and laughter. The walkways ran past large stone buildings and pavilions jammed with people. The buildings did not look familiar—and yet they did. The music was of all sorts, none of it immediately recognizable. It was loud and decidedly discordant. One group of musicians occupied a stage that had been erected across the pavilion on the far side of the fountain. The music they played

was raucous and amplified so that it sounded as if it were coming out of the air itself. Flags and pennants and streamers flew
at every turn. People were dancing and singing. There was
something going on everywhere you looked.

"Hey, that's not your whole act, is it?" the man with the
purple-streaked beard was asking.

"C'mon, do something more!" his companion pressed.

Abernathy smiled and shrugged, wishing the man and
woman would go away. What was going on here, anyway? He
wasn't dead, obviously. So what had happened to him? He ran
his hands over his body experimentally, checking for damage.
Nothing seemed out of place. Two arms, two legs, a body, fingers, and toes—he could feel them inside his boots. All present
and accounted for. He ran his fingers through his hair,
smoothing it back. He rubbed his chin and found that he
could use a shave. He adjusted his glasses on his nose. He
seemed to be all right.

He turned the other way then and found himself face to
face with Questor Thews. The wizard was staring at him. He
was staring at him as if he had never seen him before in
his life.

"Questor Thews, are you all right?" he asked anxiously.
"Whatever in the world is going on?"

Questor's mouth opened, but no words came out.

Abernathy was immediately irritated. "Wizard, what is
the matter with you? Has the witch's magic rendered you
speechless? Stop looking at me like that!"

The other's gaunt arm lifted as if to ward off a ghost.
"Abernathy?" he asked in obvious disbelief.

"Yes, of course. Who else?" Abernathy snapped. Then he
realized that something was seriously wrong with the other
man. It was in his eyes, the sound of his voice, the way he
seemed unable to accept the obvious, not even recognizing his
oldest friend, for goodness' sake. Shock, perhaps. "Questor

Thews, would you like to lie down for a moment?" he asked gently. "Would you like me to bring you some water or a glass of ale?"

The wizard stared a moment longer, then quickly shook his head. "No, it's not . . . it's . . . I'm all right, really, but you . . ." He stopped, clearly perplexed. "Abernathy," he said quietly. "What has happened to you?"

Now it was Abernathy's turn to stare. Happened to him? He looked down at himself once more. Same body, arms, legs, familiar clothing, everything in place. He looked back at the other, shaking his head in confusion. "What are you talking about?" He had to speak loudly to be heard over the music.

The gaunt, white-bearded face underwent a truly incredible series of contortions. "You've . . . you've changed back! Look at yourself! You're not a dog anymore!"

Not a dog . . . Abernathy started to laugh, then stopped, remembering. That was right—he *was* a dog! He was a soft-coated Wheaten Terrier, made so by Questor Thews when the old King's spiteful son, Michel Ard Rhi, had sought to do him serious harm, then left that way because Questor could not change him back again.

Yes, a dog.

Except, he realized suddenly, shockingly, he wasn't a dog anymore. He was a man again!

"Oh, goodness!" he breathed softly, unable to believe it. "It can't be! My heart and soul . . . !"

He reached down hurriedly and examined himself all over. Yes, those were arms and legs and fingers and toes. His body was back! His human body! He patted wildly at himself, reaching inside his clothing. No fur, but skin, like any normal man! He was beginning to cry now, tears running down his cheeks. He scrambled for something to look into, finally grasping one of the silver buttons that fastened his ornate tunic. He peered down into its tiny, carved surface, and his breath caught in his throat.

It was his human face he found staring back at him, the face he had not seen in more than thirty years.

"It's me!" he whispered, swallowing. "Look, Questor Thews, it's really me! After all this time!"

He was crying so hard and at the same time laughing that he thought he might simply collapse. But Questor Thews reached forward and braced him with hands on both shoulders. "My old friend," he declared in delight, and he was crying, too. "You're back!"

Then, in a spontaneous and quite out of character display of affection, they were hugging and clapping each other on the back, rendered unable for the moment to speak a word.

The audience that had gathered while all this was going on watched uncertainly. It was sizable by now, drawn initially by the odd costumes and the obvious interest of the man and woman who had first approached, then held there by what everyone presumed was a drama of some sort being played out as open-air theater. Really, they were thinking, it was quite good, if somewhat inappropriate for the occasion.

There was a scattering of polite applause.

Abernathy continued to cling to Questor Thews, as if letting go would change him back again. He could feel the air and the sun's warmth, and he could smell the food and hear the music as if he had never been able to do any of those things before in his life. If he could be born again, he thought, it would feel like this!

"What's happened to us?" he managed finally, drawing away from the other's grasp. "How did I change? How did it happen?"

Questor released him reluctantly, then shook his head, wispy hair sticking out all over the place, the result of his enthusiastic embrace. "I don't know," he declared wonderingly. "I don't understand any of it. I thought we were dead!"

The crowd applauded some more. Abernathy became aware of them now, three and four deep all around the wizard and himself. He was startled in spite of himself—and deeply embarrassed. "Questor Thews, do something!" he demanded heatedly, gesturing at the knot of people ringing them.

The wizard glanced about in surprise but somehow managed to maintain his equanimity. "Hello, there!" he greeted. "Can anyone tell us where we are?"

There was laughter from the crowd.

"Bumbershoot," came a tall, lanky boy's quick answer.

"Bumbershoot?" repeated Questor Thews doubtfully.

"Sure. You know, Bumbershoot, festival of the arts." The boy grinned. He was enjoying whatever game it was they were playing.

"No, no, he means the city," a burly fellow said. He was enjoying the game, too. "You're in Seattle, Washington, fellows."

"United States of America," another voice added.

Other names and places were shouted out, spectators now having decided that this was an audience participation performance. Everyone was quite enthusiastic, and the crowd grew larger still.

"Questor!" Abernathy said sharply. "Do you realize where we are? We're in the High Lord's old world! We've been transported through the fairy mists once again!"

The wizard's jaw dropped. "But how could that have happened? Nightshade meant to destroy us! What are we doing here?"

"Ask Scotty to beam you up!" someone shouted.

"Are they Trekkies?" someone else asked hopefully.

The crowd howled with laughter and engaged in some rhythmic clapping to urge the two on. The music from the pavilion had ceased momentarily, and it seemed as if everyone at the festival had suddenly converged on them, anxious for a new show. Belatedly, Abernathy realized that their unexpected appearance had been the trigger for all this attention, materializing as they had out of nowhere as if . . . well, as if by magic—which was exactly how they *had* gotten there, of course, but that was beside the point. This was Earth, the High Lord's old world, and magic was not practiced here. Not tolerated, really. Not even believed in for the most part. The crowd thought the two were part of the festival, like the jugglers and the stilt walkers and what have you. Whatever magic they possessed was illusion. It was meant to entertain.

"We have to extricate ourselves from this situation right now!" Abernathy insisted in an anxious covert whisper. "These people think we are offering them some sort of performance!"

He scrambled quickly to his feet, looking down at himself as he did so, at his human self, wondering in amazement that he was there, restored once more, miraculously, impossibly. His voice caught in his throat. "We have to talk this out . . . this whole business! But alone, Questor Thews!"

The wizard nodded in emphatic agreement, rising with him. They were both dressed in Landover clothing, looking very out of place unless you accepted their appointed roles as entertainers. The wizard quickly decided that it was better to go along with perceptions than to try to argue or explain them away. He was as confused as Abernathy about what had happened and just as anxious to sit down in a quiet spot and attempt to reason it all out.

"Ahem! Ladies and gentlemen! Could I have your attention, please." He addressed the crowd in his most authoritative voice, lifting his arms in an encompassing gesture to gain their undivided attention. They quieted at once. "My colleague and I require a few moments of preparation before we can proceed with the next act. So if you will just go about your business— enjoy the rest of the festival—we will see you back here in, oh, perhaps an hour. Or not," he added under his breath. "Thank you, thank you very much."

He lowered his arms and turned away. The crowd did not move. No one was prepared to leave just yet, not prepared in some cases to believe that they were even supposed to. This might all be part of the act. Two strangers from another world come mysteriously into this one—it was intriguing. What might happen next? No one wanted to miss out. There was some shuffling of feet but not much lateral movement.

"This isn't working!" Abernathy complained, irritated, confused, and overwhelmed by the entire business. "Confound it, wizard, get us out of here!"

Questor Thews sighed, not at all sure how to do that, then scrunched up his face with determination, took Abernathy by the arm, and marched him directly through the crowd. "Please excuse us, thank you, yes, that's very kind of you, excuse us, please." The crowd parted, polite if somewhat disappointed. Questor Thews and Abernathy escaped untouched and moved swiftly away across the festival green toward a clump of buildings and food stands.

"Where are we going?" Abernathy asked, not daring to look over his shoulder to see if anyone was following.

"Wherever we can, I suppose," Questor answered with a shrug. "Since we have no idea where anything is."

They moved down onto a walkway, past the face painter, past a fellow spinning tops, past several carts selling food and drink, and onto a square of grass fronting a cavernous glass and metal structure out of which rolled a particularly vile-sounding form of music.

"What is that noise?" Questor demanded, shaking his head in dismay.

"Rock and roll," Abernathy answered absently. "I heard a good deal of it the last time I was here." Memories were triggered in his mind, but he brushed them aside. He turned, grabbed Questor by the shoulders, and brought him about so that they were face to face. "Wizard, what is going on? Look at me! I don't know whether to laugh or cry! I'm a man again, for goodness' sake! How did that happen? Surely Nightshade didn't intend it! She was trying to kill us! Why aren't we dead? Why are we here?"

Questor's mouth tightened, and he blinked rapidly. "Well, either something went wrong with her magic or another magic intervened and changed the intended result. I favor the latter." Questor reached up and touched the other's face. His hand was shaking. "Goodness gracious, here's something new! Abernathy, are you aware of the fact that you haven't aged a day from the moment I transformed you from a man into a dog all those years ago?"

"That isn't possible!" Abernathy exclaimed in disbelief. "Not a day? No, I must have aged! Why wouldn't I have aged? It must be the magic, mustn't it? The one that you think intervened? It changed me back again not only to a man but to the man I once was. Questor, why? Why would it do that?"

They stared at each other in confused silence, the sound of the music in the hall washing over them, the laughter and gaiety of the festival rising up all around, outworlders in a foreign land, exiles by means they could not fathom. Oh, but I am a man again! Abernathy thought in joy and with a smidgen of terror. Whatever else, I am changed back to who I was and want always to be!

Questor Thews shook his head. "I don't mind telling you that this is all very strange," he declared solemnly.

"Excuse me?"

They turned on hearing the girl's voice and found her standing a few feet away, staring at them. She was somewhere in her middle teens, Abernathy guessed, rather small, with curly blond hair and a scattering of freckles across her nose. She was wearing short tan pants, a rather tight sky-blue blouse with some writing on it, and sandals. She looked perplexed.

"I was in the crowd a moment ago," she said, studying them intently, particularly Abernathy. "I followed you after-

ward because your voice . . . I know this sounds silly, but because . . . you remind me of someone . . ."

She stopped, and her brow furrowed. She looked suddenly at Questor Thews. "I do remember you. I'm sure of it
now. Your name is Questor Thews."

Questor and Abernathy exchanged a quick glance. "She
overheard us talking," Abernathy said at once.

"No, I didn't." She shook her head emphatically and
came forward a step. "Abernathy, that's you, isn't it? You're not
a dog anymore! That's why I was confused. But your voice is
the same. And your eyes. Don't you remember me? I'm Elizabeth Marshall." She smiled helpfully. "I'm Elizabeth."

He remembered then. Elizabeth, twelve years old when
he had last seen her, a child wandering the halls of Graum
Wythe, the castle fortress of Michel Ard Rhi, once a Prince of
Landover and son of the old King in the days before Ben Holiday. Abernathy had been dispatched to Earth through another
of Questor's inept spells, consigned to the trophy room of his
worst enemy, and fated for a swift end when Elizabeth had
found him and saved his life. Together they had struggled to
conceal Abernathy's presence from Michel and help the scribe
find a way back into Landover. Elizabeth had stuck with him
every step of the way. Even when she was discovered and her
own safety was threatened, she had refused to betray her
friend.

"I never thought I'd see you again," she said softly, as if
still not certain it was really him.

"Nor I," he breathed in disbelief.

She came forward quickly then and hugged him. "I can't
believe this," she said into his shoulder, holding him tightly
against her. "This is just too weird."

"Well, yes," he agreed, speechless, and hugged her back.

She broke the embrace. There were tears in her eyes.
"Look at me, crying like some little kid." She brushed the
tears away. "When I saw you, the two of you, surrounded by

all those people, I didn't see how it could be true. I mean . . ." She broke off, shaking her head. "Abernathy, what are you doing here?"

He shrugged, embarrassed. "I'm really not sure. We were just trying to figure that out. We don't quite know how we got here. It is rather a long story." He stared at her. "You've grown up."

She laughed. "Well, not all the way, but some from the last time you saw me. I'll be sixteen in a few months. So hello. And hello to you, too, Questor Thews."

"Very nice to see you again," Questor replied. He cleared his throat. "Ah, I wonder, Elizabeth, if we could impose on you—"

"You don't have anywhere to stay, do you?" she declared before he could finish. "Of course you don't. Did you just arrive? Well, you have to have somewhere to stay while you're here. How long will that be?"

Questor sighed, "That is a matter of some speculation at present."

"It doesn't matter; you can stay with me. I still live out in Woodinville, but not at Graum Wythe anymore. We have a house, my dad and me, down the road a short distance. Dad still looks after the estate and manages the castle. But he's away until late next week, so we have the place to ourselves. Except for Mrs. Ambaum. She's the housekeeper. My keeper, too." She giggled. "I'll tell you later. Abernathy, I just can't believe this. Look at you!"

Abernathy turned red. "Well," he managed.

"Maybe we should go now," Questor advised. "To your house, Elizabeth. We really need to sit down and talk."

"Sure," Elizabeth quickly agreed. "Let me tell my friends I'm leaving. I rode down here on the bus, so we'll have to take the bus home. I've got enough money for the three of us, I think. Hope so, because I bet you don't have any. Boy, this sure is strange, isn't it, meeting again like this?"

Questor Thews nodded, looking around absently at the crowds and the festival. Music rolled across the open spaces between buildings. Flags and balloons floated in the warm breeze. Cooking smells filled the air. Laughter and singing rose from every quarter. Bumbershoot, festival of the arts. Seattle, Washington, United States. The High Lord's old world. Now Elizabeth. It was strange, all right. It was also the most colossal coincidence he had ever encountered—or it was something far more complicated. He didn't say so, but he favored the latter interpretation.

He thought they might do well to figure it all out before anything else happened.

Graum Wythe Redux

After Elizabeth had made excuses to her friends, she guided Abernathy and Questor Thews through the Bumbershoot crowds past a building called the Center House, a collection of mechanical rides filled with screaming children, and a series of food stands to a platform that serviced a monorail—which was something new to Questor, who hadn't spent as much time in the High Lord's old world as Abernathy. After a brief wait they boarded the monorail and rode downtown. Abernathy took great delight in his familiarity with things, his spirits further buoyed by the incredible fact of his transformation. As they sat in the monorail and passed down the track toward the tall buildings of the city, he kept looking at his reflection in the glass window next to him, not yet quite able to believe that it was true, worried deep inside that he might change back again at any moment.

But it was true, and there was no indication that he was going to revert. He was himself once more, a whole man, the exact same man, in fact, he had been when Questor had first changed him into a dog, rather average-looking, medium height and weight, hair dark and lank where it framed his bookish face. His rimless glasses sat comfortably upon his nose, fitting him perfectly, as if it made no difference whether he was a man or a dog. His eyes were wide-set and brown in color. His mouth was full, and his chin firm. An average face, certainly, but still and all a good one.

And it was his. Looking at it in the window glass, he felt as if a huge weight had been lifted from his shoulders. The last time he had passed into Ben Holiday's world, he had been forced to pretend he really was a dog to avoid a good many unpleasantnesses. Magic was not accepted here. Talking dogs were unheard of. Abernathy had been an oddity of monumental importance, and there had been more than one attempt to exploit the fact. So he had crept about like a thief in the night, playing at being something he wasn't, embarrassed and frightened. Now he could walk about like everyone else because he looked like everyone else. He fit comfortably in place. Well, more so than he would have if he had still been a dog. This was, after all, not his own country. But when he finally got back to Landover . . .

It made him smile to think about it.

"How does it feel?" Elizabeth asked him suddenly. She had been watching him. "Being a man again?"

Abernathy had the decency to blush. "I can't seem to stop looking at myself. I apologize. But it does feel wonderful. I can't tell you how wonderful. It has been a very long time, Elizabeth, since I was . . ." He trailed off. "I . . . I'm very happy."

She grinned in response. "Do you know something? You are quite handsome."

His mouth gaped. He could feel his cheeks burn.

"No, really," she insisted. "You are."

He expected at that point to hear a snide comment from Questor Thews, but the wizard was not paying attention to the conversation, his gaze turned away as he stared off into space, lost in thought. Abernathy muttered something unintelligible to Elizabeth and looked out the window at the passing buildings. Enough of admiring himself. He should be thinking, too. He should be trying to figure out what was going on. What was it that had brought them to this place and time, changed him back into a man, and linked him up once again with Elizabeth? Like Questor, he thought it an awfully large coincidence. He had the sense that there was machinery at work that he didn't understand and probably should. But for the moment he was so caught up in his transformation that he could not bring himself to think of anything else.

He looked at himself in the window one more time and almost started to cry. He was entitled to enjoy this feeling for a few moments more, wasn't he? After all, he had waited so long!

At the end of the monorail line they departed their car and entered a tall building set among other tall buildings, the whole of it very imposing, almost overwhelming, and from there they followed stairs, some of them actually moving, to an underground station, where they boarded a bus. Questor didn't know about buses, either, so Abernathy took a moment to explain how they worked and got it wrong. Elizabeth giggled and set them both straight. By now they were far enough removed from Bumbershoot that people were beginning to take notice of their somewhat odd clothing—Questor in his gray, patched robe with its brightly colored sashes and Abernathy in his crimson-lined, silver-trimmed riding cloak— but no one was rude enough to say anything. The bus took them underground for a ways, stopping twice, and then exited from a tunnel back into the sunshine of the late afternoon. They were on a roadway packed with other vehicles spread out in lanes that stretched away into the distance. No one was moving very fast. They sat at the back of the bus and stared out the windows, and for a time no one said much of anything.

"Are Ben Holiday and Willow well?" Elizabeth asked finally, speaking to Abernathy.

He said they were. He told her then about Mistaya. One thing led to another. When Questor didn't give him a pointed

look or offer a word of caution, he went on to tell her about
Nightshade and the attack on the caravan that had been taking
the little girl to stay with her grandfather. He kept his voice
low so that no one sitting close could hear. Not that there was
much chance of that happening, what with all the noise the
bus made. He told her how they had thought themselves finished once Nightshade had summoned her formidable magic
but then had inexplicably found themselves in the High Lord's
old world, in Seattle, at Bumbershoot. She was aware of
the rest.

"It's all very strange," she said when he was done. "I
wonder why you ended up back here."

"Indeed," Questor Thews said without looking over.

"I would like to live in your world," she offered suddenly.
"There's always so much happening."

Abernathy looked at her in surprise, then looked quickly
away.

They rode the bus to a stop in Woodinville, then got off
and walked rather a long way out into the country. Houses
and traffic faded away, the day cooled, and the sun dropped toward the mountains that framed the horizon. The land was
forested and rolling about them, filled with pungent smells and
birdsong. The road they followed ran straight and unhindered
into the distance, empty of life.

"I should tell you about Mrs. Ambaum," Elizabeth said
after a while. She had her face scrunched up, the way she always did when she was addressing a doubtful subject. "She's
the housekeeper. She lives with us. Dad's away a lot, and she
looks after me while he's gone. She's pretty nice, but she
thinks all kids—that's me and anyone else under twenty-five
or so—can't stay out of trouble. It's not that she thinks we go
looking for it; it's that she thinks we can't avoid it. So she
spends a lot of time trying to keep me tucked safely away in
the house. She had a fit when I told her I was going by bus
to Bumbershoot, but Dad had told her it was all right, so

there wasn't much she could do. Anyway, we had better come up with a story that will satisfy her about where you came from or there will be trouble for sure."

"The truth wouldn't work, I suppose?" Questor asked.

Elizabeth grinned. "The truth would blow her mind."

"We could stay somewhere else if we are going to be too much trouble," Abernathy offered.

"Yes, we could stay in a barn or out in a field, perhaps," Questor declared, giving him a reproachful glance. "Really, Abernathy."

"No, no, you have stay with me," Elizabeth insisted quickly. "We have plenty of space. But we need a story for Mrs. Ambaum. How about this? Abernathy, you can be my uncle, visiting from Chicago. And Questor Thews is your friend, a professor of . . . geology. You're fossil hunting. No, you're participating in a forum on extinct species at the university, and you dropped by to see Dad, not knowing he was out of town, so I asked you to stay with us. There, that should work."

"We shall rely on you," Questor Thews announced. He smiled bravely. "With luck, our visit should only be a short one."

"I wouldn't bet on it," Elizabeth said, and neither of her companions presumed to disagree.

They arrived shortly afterward at a two-story home set back from the road in a grove of spruce and dogwood, the foundation bordered by flower beds, the walkway lined with petunias, and the yard dotted with rhododendrons. The building was wood sided and painted white with deep blue trim. Window boxes filled with flowers decorated its front, and a covered porch with a swing and rockers ran its length. Dormers jutted out from the sloping roof, the windows brightly curtained, and massive stone chimneys bracketed the walls at either end. Sunlight streaked the house and yard through gaps in the trees, and an orange and white cat stalked into view and disappeared into a wall of bushes. Elizabeth took them up the walk to the door and rang the bell. There was no answer. Mrs. Ambaum had gone out, it appeared. Elizabeth fished in her pocket for a key, unlocked the door, and took them inside.

"We'll have to come up with an explanation for your not having any luggage, too," she declared once she had made certain that Mrs. Ambaum was indeed out. "This might be harder than I thought."

She showed them the second-story bedroom where they would be staying, then brought them some of her father's clothing, most of which fit after a fashion and was certainly less attention-getting than their own. When they were dressed, she guided them downstairs to the kitchen, sat them at the breakfast table, and set about making sandwiches. In short order they were eating. Both Albernathy and Questor found that they were hungrier than they had thought and quickly consumed everything they were given.

When they were finished, the daylight fading rapidly now to dusk, they began to talk about what had happened. They remained at the table, drawn up close in their chairs, arms and elbows resting on the polished wooden surface, hands locked before them or cupping their chins, a thoughtful if somewhat perplexed threesome.

"Well, we can be certain of this much, I think," Questor Thews declared, opening the discussion. "Nightshade intended to see us destroyed, not transported to this world. We are here, therefore, in spite of her efforts and not because of them."

"Well, yes, of course," Abernathy agreed impatiently. "That much we have already established, wizard. Tell us something new. What about me, for instance?"

"You were changed at the same time. Transformed back into a man, then sent here, with me." Questor rubbed his whiskers, his brow furrowing deeply. "It is all tied together somehow, don't you think?"

"I don't know what to think," Abernathy admitted. "What do you mean, tied together?"

Questor steepled his fingers before his face. "We must assume, as I said earlier, that magic intervened to prevent the witch from destroying us. Whose magic, then? It could have come from the once-fairy, perhaps from the River Master himself, sent in an effort to save his granddaughter. It could have come from the Earth Mother; she has always been close to Willow and would have reason to want to protect her friend's child."

Abernathy frowned. "Neither sounds exactly right. If the River Master or the Earth Mother had been watching out for Mistaya, how could Nightshade have gotten so close in the first place? Anyway, I saw nothing that would indicate Mistaya was about to be saved once we were dispatched."

"True, it doesn't fit, does it?" Questor agreed.

Elizabeth, who had been listening intently but saying nothing, now said, "Could it have been Mistaya herself who saved you? Does she have magic she can use?"

They both looked at her at once, considering the possibility. "An excellent idea, Elizabeth," Questor said after a moment. "But Mistaya is untrained in the use of whatever magic she possesses, and the magic that was used to deflect or alter Nightshade's was both sophisticated and well practiced."

"Besides," Abernathy interjected, "Mistaya was still sleeping. I saw her when I looked to see if she had been harmed. She was sleeping as if nothing had happened. I think the witch might have cast a spell on her to prevent her from waking."

"Entirely possible," Questor agreed. He leaned back and pursed his lips. "Well, then. Some other magic intervened and saved our lives. It sent us to the High Lord's old world, trans-

formed Abernathy, and gave us the ability to speak and understand the language. But—and this is significant—it sent us
here, to the very place we last appeared, where Abernathy was
inadvertently exchanged for the Darkling, to the site of Graum
Wythe, to what was once the home of Michel Ard Rhi. And,"
he said, nodding meaningfully at Elizabeth, "to within a few
feet of you."

Abernathy stared. "Wait one minute, Questor Thews.
What is it you are saying here?"

"What we all have said at one point or another since
meeting up at the Bumbershoot festival: that ending up back
here, close to Graum Wythe and practically in the arms of
Elizabeth, is rather too large a coincidence to be swallowed in
one bite. I would be willing to bet that there is a reason for
everything that has happened to us. Whoever or whatever
saved our lives did not do so haphazardly. It did so with fore-
sight and purpose. We were saved for a reason. We were sent
here, to the High Lord's old world, but here to the site of
Graum Wythe specifically, quite deliberately."

He paused, considering. "Elizabeth, didn't you say that
Graum Wythe is still here?"

"Come look," she offered, getting up from the table.

She took them from the kitchen through a curtained
door and out into the backyard, a well-tended lawn that spread
away through a scattering of spruce to a split-rail fence. She
took them midway to the fence, to where the trees opened up,
then stopped and pointed right. There, silhouetted against the
skyline by the fading light of the sun, stood Graum Wythe.
The castle sat alone on a rise, ringed by its walls and warded
by its towers. It sat solitary and immutable, black and brooding
as the night swept toward it.

Elizabeth lowered her arm. Specks of sunlight flashed in
her curly hair. "Still there, right where you left it. Remember,
Abernathy?"

Abernathy shivered. "I could do without the reminder. It

is as forbidding as ever, I must say." A sudden thought chilled him further. "Michel Ard Rhi hasn't come back by any chance, has he?"

"Oh, no, of course not." Elizabeth laughed disarmingly. "He moved down to Oregon, several hundred miles away. He gave Graum Wythe to the state as a museum. A trust fund administers the estate. My father is the chief trustee. He oversees everything. No, don't worry. Michel is long gone."

"My magic made certain of that," Questor Thews added pointedly.

"I certainly hope so," Abernathy muttered, thinking as he said it that Questor Thews's magic had never been very reliable.

They went back inside and resumed their places at the table. Darkness had fallen, and the last of the daylight had faded. Elizabeth poured them tall glasses of cold milk and produced a plate of cookies. Questor helped himself eagerly, but Abernathy found that he had lost his appetite.

"So none of this is coincidence; all of it is part of some mysterious plan," the scribe summed up doubtfully. "What plan?"

Questor regarded him as he might an inattentive child, eyebrows lifting. "Well, I don't know the answer to that, of course. If I did, we wouldn't need to have this discussion, now, would we?"

Abernathy ignored him. "An intervening magic saved us from Nightshade and sent us to the High Lord's old world, to Earth, but in particular to Graum Wythe and Elizabeth." He looked at Elizabeth. Then he looked at Questor. "I still don't understand."

"I'm not sure I do, either," Questor Thews admitted. "But assume for a moment that whoever or whatever helped us did so to help Mistaya as well. As far as we know, no one is aware of what happened to the child except for us. We know Nightshade took her. We know that the witch intends to use the child to gain revenge against the High Lord and that Rydall of Marnhull is part of her scheme. If we can get word to Ben Holiday, then he might be able to do something to disrupt the witch's plans. Perhaps that is what we are meant to do. We are alive and here for a specific reason, Abernathy. What better reason than to discover a way to stop Nightshade before she carries out her scheme?"

"Saved to fight another day, is that it?" Abernathy asked, scratching his head with his fingers instead of his hind leg and not thinking twice about it. "Maybe we were sent here simply to get us out of the way. Maybe our rescuer then saved Mistaya as well."

But Questor Thews shook his head emphatically. "No. No, I'm quite certain it didn't happen that way. In the first place, if our rescuer was there all along, keeping watch for just this, as must have been the case given the quick response, why not save Mistaya early on? Why wait until the last moment? If our rescuer was looking simply to get us out of the way, as you put it, why send us all the way here? Why not send us back to Sterling Silver or some such? No, Abernathy, we are here for a reason, and it has something to do with saving Mistaya from the witch."

"You think the answer to all this lies in Graum Wythe, don't you?" Elizabeth declared, making the jump in logic first.

"I do," Questor Thews replied. "Graum Wythe is a vast repository for artifacts of magic, some quite powerful. One of those artifacts could provide a way back into Landover. Or provide us with a means to foil the witch. The fact remains that without magic of some sort, we are trapped here and helpless to aid the High Lord or Mistaya. We do not have a way to pass through the fairy mists. No one knows where we are. No one will come for us. I think we are meant to find our own way home. I think we *must* if Ben Holiday and Mistaya are to be saved."

The three stared at each other, weighing the import of the wizard's words.

"Maybe," Abernathy agreed finally.

"There is no 'maybe' about it. Graum Wythe holds the answer to our dilemma," Questor Thews continued solemnly. "But the key to Graum Wythe is you, Elizabeth. We were sent to you because your father is administrator of the castle and all its treasures. You have lived in the castle and are familiar with its holdings. You have access to places where others are not permitted. What we require is somewhere in that castle. I'm certain of it. We simply have to search it out."

"We can start tomorrow morning when the castle opens," Elizabeth promised. "That's the easy part. The hard part will be finding what it is you need when you don't know what it is you're looking for."

"True," Questor Thews admitted with a slight shrug.

"But what does all this have to do with my being changed from a dog back into a man?" Abernathy asked once more.

He was still waiting for an answer to his question when there was the sound of a key turning in the front door lock and of the door opening. Three heads turned as one.

"Elizabeth, are you home?" a woman's voice called.

"Mrs. Ambaum!" Elizabeth announced, making a face.

For the moment at least, Abernathy's question was left unanswered.

Mrs. Ambaum proved to be less formidable than anticipated. She was a large, straight backed woman with graying hair, a bluff face, and a suspicious mind, but she was not a villainous sort. Elizabeth offered her explanation of how Abernathy and Questor had come to visit and had been invited to stay, and Mrs. Ambaum, after a few perfunctory questions and a general disclaimer of responsibility, accepted their presence without further argument, retiring to her room at the back of the house for some herbal tea and television. Questor and Abernathy went to bed much relieved.

They were up early the next morning and came down to breakfast to find Mrs. Ambaum already gone to her sister's for the day. They ate hurriedly, anxious to get under way with their search of Graum Wythe, then cleared off their dishes and, with Elizabeth leading the way, headed out the door.

It was a beautiful, cloudless, sun-filled day. Birds sang from the trees, and the air was fragrant with the smell of flowers and spruce. The company of three smiled agreeably as they departed the house, came down the walkway to the edge of the yard, turned left, and began following the road toward the castle.

Elizabeth linked arms with Abernathy, grinning conspiratorially. Abernathy felt stiff and uncomfortable. "You look very nice in Dad's clothes," she told him. "Very distinguished. You should dress like this all the time."

"He should smile more, too," Questor Thews added before he could think better of it.

"This is so incredible, Abernathy, you being here again," the girl continued, hugging his arm affectionately. "Look at you, just look! Who would believe what's happened? Isn't it wonderful? Aren't you happy?"

"Very," Abernathy acknowledged, putting on his best face, though in truth he was still wondering what the price would be for his remarkable but still unexplained transformation. There was always a price for those things. He thought back to the mind's eye crystals of Horris Kew. Always a price.

Elizabeth was wearing a powder-blue sweatshirt that said something about Seattle grunge, a pair of jeans, and worn sneakers. Her hair was tousled artfully, and she was wearing violet eye shadow and dark magenta lipstick. Abernathy thought she had grown up awfully fast, but he kept it to himself.

"Do you have family?" she asked him suddenly. "A wife and children?"

He shook his head, a tad downcast.

"Father and mother?"

"Not for many years." He could barely remember them.

"Brothers and sisters?"

"No, I'm afraid not."

"Hmmm. That's rather sad, don't you think? Maybe I should adopt you!" She grinned brightly. "Just kidding. But you really could be part of my family, since it's rather small and could use another member or two. What do you say? An unofficial adoption, okay?"

"Thank you, Elizabeth," he replied, and was really quite touched.

They strolled up the road, the older man with the electric white hair and beard, the younger man with the rimless glasses and the pensive face, and the curly-haired girl who seemed in charge of them both, closing on Graum Wythe like Dorothy and her companions at the Emerald City of Oz. Except, of course, that Graum Wythe, though castlelike and imposing, was in no other way anything at all like the Emerald City. It was not green or bright but stone-gray and dreary. No yellow brick road led to its entry, just blacktop. No fields of poppies surrounded its walls, although its working vineyards still showed touches of green. It was medieval and fortresslike with no pennants flying from its parapets, only the flags of the United States and the state of Washington to announce its entrance.

Not that either Abernathy or Quester Thews knew anything about Oz or the Emerald City. Had they given the matter any consideration, they probably would have contrasted the drabness of Graum Wythe to the brightness of

Sterling Silver, for instance. They were thinking, in fact, of very different things entirely. Abernathy was trying to conceive of what his life would be like now that he was no longer a man in dog form but a man for real. He was trying to picture himself in his new role in various situations. Questor Thews, on the other hand, was recalling his friend's question of the previous night concerning what his change from dog back to man had to do with their coming to the High Lord's world and hoping that his suspicions, unvoiced as yet, would be proved wrong.

The little company came to the low stone wall that encircled the castle and passed through the open iron gates to the drawbridge. Graum Wythe loomed before them, a massive cluster of towers and parapets. The drawbridge was down and the portcullis up, so they moved into the shadow of the castle wall, through the gate entry, and out to the castle's parking lot. Graum Wythe seemed empty of life. A single car was parked in the rear of its visitors' lot. The souvenir stand, ensconced in what used to be a guardhouse, was closed and shuttered. Graum Wythe seemed deserted.

"It's all right," Elizabeth assured her companions. "The museum hasn't opened to the public yet, but we can get in."

She took them across the parking lot and up the steps to the iron-bound front doors. She rapped the heavy knocker on its plate and waited. A moment later the door opened, and a man she greeted as Harvey smiled in recognition and let them inside. They entered the same foyer where several years earlier Ben, Willow, and Miles Bennett—Ben's old law partner, pressed into service for the occasion—all three dressed for Halloween night, had engineered Abernathy's escape from Michel Ard Rhi's dungeons. Abernathy looked around with foreboding, but the menace of Michel and his guards was long absent and the foyer itself had been redecorated with bright tapestries, pamphlet stands, and an admission desk where Harvey held forth. After giving the same explanation about Questor and Abernathy that she had given Mrs. Ambaum, and exchanging a few pleasantries with Harvey, Elizabeth led the wizard and the scribe into the bowels of the castle.

They spent the rest of the day searching. Their search was confined at first to the corridors and rooms left open for the public and to the artifacts and collectibles on display. Most of the items Questor Thews recognized for what they were. Almost all possessed no inherent magic. But a few did, and once or twice the wizard felt obliged to comment on an item that really had no business being exposed to the public, so dangerous was its potential for misuse.

Nowhere, however, did he find the elusive and still unidentified item he was looking for.

Midday passed without result. They ate lunch in the little sandwich shop situated in what used to be the castle kitchen. Visitors were arriving by the carload now, and there were buses filled with touring groups. Business was picking up. To avoid the crowds, Elizabeth took them into the back rooms and storage areas of the castle, those kept closed to the public, looking at the things either deemed unworthy or unready for display. Crates were stacked everywhere, but they managed to get most down for a look inside. Cabinets were filled with odd rocks and minerals, carvings and sculptures, paintings and crafts of all sorts, and none of them were of any recognizable use.

An hour after the castle closed Harvey advised them that they would have to leave and come back tomorrow. Reluctantly they trudged homeward with nothing to show for their efforts. Questor Thews was particularly frustrated.

"It's there, I know it," he muttered, shaking his ragged white head. "I cannot be wrong about this. It's there, but I'm not seeing it, that's all. We'll just have to come back and try again tomorrow. Drat!"

Abernathy and Elizabeth exchanged a quick glance. Neither of them was bothered by the prospect of the hunt going on another day. If Questor had been paying attention, he would have noticed that Elizabeth was holding Abernathy's hand. If he had been paying attention, he would have noticed that Abernathy no longer seemed to mind.

What You See

The first of Rydall of Marnhull's champions appeared exactly as promised three days after Ben Holiday had accepted the King's challenge.

By the time the sun rose, it was waiting outside the gates of Sterling Silver, a strong, solitary figure standing at the far end of the causeway, looking over at the castle. It was a man of great size and obvious strength. In a land where warriors often reached seven feet, this man was easily eight. A giant of massive girth, broad shoulders, and tree trunk legs, he wore animal skins tied with leather thongs about his muscular body. Boots linked to greaves ran to midthigh, and iron-studded wrist guards laced into leather gloves. A black beard and coarse, thick hair obscured most of his face, but his eyes could be seen to glint brightly in the rise of the morning sun.

He bore but a single weapon, a battle-scarred wooden club bound with strips of hammered iron.

Ben Holiday stood with Willow and Bunion on the ramparts of the castle and stared down at Rydall's champion. His coming was no surprise, of course. Ever since Mistaya had disappeared along with Questor Thews and Abernathy, Ben had been convinced that Rydall was for real. The fact that no one had ever heard of him or of Marnhull, or could begin to discover where he came from or where he had gone to, or, more important, what he had done with Ben's daughter and friends

115

did nothing to lessen the certainty of his threat. Using the Landsview, Ben had scoured Landover from end to end for all three days given to him after Rydall's departure and had found exactly nothing. There was no trace of Rydall, no sign of his passing, and no clue as to where he had gone to earth. Bunion had searched as well, using his kobold speed and extraordinary tracking powers. He, too, had failed. In the end the only conclusion left, however improbable, was that somehow Marnhull's King indeed had managed to penetrate the fairy mists from a land without. Having done so, he had snatched away Mistaya and her guards, Abernathy and Questor included, and had gone back the way he had come, leaving Ben Holiday to face the challenge he had issued, to stand alone against the seven he would send to destroy him.

Ben shook his head resignedly. He had been awake since shortly after midnight, anticipating the arrival of this first destroyer. He was not tired, not even weary, only sad. He would be forced to fight this creature, whoever and whatever it was, and probably would destroy it. He would do so as his alter ego, the Paladin, but it wouldn't change the fact that he would still be the one doing the fighting and perhaps the killing. It wouldn't change the necessity of his transformation into the iron-clad warrior who protected the Kings of Landover, a transformation he feared and despised, because each time it happened a little more of him slipped away into the abyss of dark madness that shrouded the life of the Paladin. Warrior and knight-errant, protector and champion, the Paladin was before all things a destroyer to which no sane man could ever wish to be joined. But Ben Holiday was. And would forever be from now until the end.

But I made that choice when I gave up my old life for this new one, he chided himself. The decision was mine.

"Perhaps we can simply ignore him," Willow said quietly. Ben looked over at her, but she kept her eyes focused on the giant. "If we keep him locked outside the gates, what can he do? He might grow weary of his vigil. Time favors you, Ben. Let him be."

Ben thought it over. He could do that. He could leave the giant where he was and see what happened. It wasn't a bad idea, though it would inconvenience those who might wish to enter or leave the castle. But it did nothing to enhance his image as King. It left him a prisoner in his own palace.

"He has made no demands?" Ben asked Bunion, still weighing the possibilities.

The kobold chittered softly. No, the giant had not spoken.

"Well." Ben tightened his mouth. "We'll let him wait a bit. A little breakfast first, now that we know he's here. Then we'll see."

He started to turn away, and abruptly the giant's arm lifted and pointed directly at him. There was no mistaking the gesture. Do not turn away, it said. Do not turn your back on me.

Ben wheeled about and came back to the wall. The giant's arm lowered, and he resumed waiting, one hand resting on his belted waist, the other on the butt of his massive club. The strange eyes glinted. The huge figure looked to be carved of stone.

"It appears he does not approve of your idea, Willow," Ben murmured, feeling her hand close over his. He could tell what she was thinking: Be careful. Do not rise to his goading. Do not be drawn into this fight until you are ready.

She did not say to him, "Do not go." She knew he must. She knew he could not avoid this confrontation or any of those which must follow if they were to see Mistaya alive again. She hated the situation as much as he did, but they had understood from the moment of Rydall's coming with the news of their missing daughter that they were trapped in this deadly game and that somehow they must find a way to win.

"What is his strength?" she asked suddenly, indicating the

giant with an irritated wave of her hand. "He is large and strong, but he is no match for the Paladin. Why has he been sent?"

Ben had been wondering that, too. The Paladin was better armed and protected. How could the giant hope to defeat him?

At his side Bunion chittered softly. He wanted to go down and test the giant's strength, to see what his edge might be, to probe for his weakness. Ben shook his head. He would risk no one but himself in this struggle with Rydall. Not when the lives of Mistaya, Abernathy, and Questor were at risk already.

"He forbids us to leave the wall," he said finally. "What will happen if we disobey? Perhaps we should see. Bunion, stay put and keep watch for us."

Keeping tight hold of Willow's hand, he turned from the wall and walked over to the open stairs that wound downward about the watch house to the courtyard below. He was barely to the first step when he heard Bunion hiss in warning.

The giant was beginning to shimmer like a mirage in the midday summer heat. The air all about it was as damp as liquid, rainbow colors sliding across its surface like autumn leaves across glass.

Ben hesitated, waiting. Then Bunion started and looked quickly over.

The giant had disappeared!

Ben stared at the kobold, undecided about what to do, then started toward him once more, needing to see for himself. At the same moment he heard Willow gasp. He wheeled back, following her gaze to the courtyard below. Soldiers and retainers had scattered as light filled the yard's center in a blaze of shimmering color.

The giant reappeared, come out of the ether, come now into the walls of the castle itself. It rose up out of nothingness, huge and dark. The massive club was shouldered, and there was a new menace about it. A squad of soldiers approached it warily, placing themselves between the giant and their King. In a moment the battle would be joined.

But Ben already knew he could not let that happen.

"Stand where you are!" he called down.

The soldiers looked up at him expectantly. The giant's gaze lifted as well.

Ben felt Willow release his hand, but he could not bring himself to look at her. He reached into his tunic and withdrew the medallion of Landover's Kings, the talisman that warded them from danger. Holding it forth so that it caught the morning sun, he reluctantly summoned the Paladin.

Brilliant white light flared instantly at the foot of the gatehouse stairs, and from out of its brightness the Paladin appeared. He was afoot and armed with his unsheathed broadsword and an iron-tipped mace strapped to his waist. He was armored in silver, shining with the intensity of the sun at midday.

Ben instantly felt a connection between them, locks snapping into place, a picture forming in his mind, a strange combination of fire and ice mixing into something else altogether. Tendrils of feeling and thought began to link them, to join them as one. He was carried out of his body and into the Paladin's armor on a wave of light. He was clasped to the other as if by dozens of hands, wrapped about and encased in the iron, and made one with his protector's weapons. He was submerged in memories of battles fought and won over a thousand lifetimes. He was joined with times and places long past and all but forgotten. He was made over into his other self, and that other self rose up in fury and blood lust to confront Rydall's giant.

They came together in a rush, weapons clashing and grating as metal and iron-bound wood caught, held momentarily, then slid away. They parted grunting, then clashed again. The giant was powerful and determined, using leverage and his awesome strength in an effort to overpower his quarry. But the Paladin was too battle-tested to be taken down so easily. A moment later he had thrust the giant aside, knocked the club from his hands, and thrown him to the earth.

The giant struck heavily, rolled free of the sword blade that hovered over him, and came back to his feet, club in hand once more, unharmed. He came at the Paladin instantly. The Paladin parried another monstrous blow and struck the giant alongside the head. The giant went down, tumbling away, blood smearing the dusty earth where he struck.

Then he was back on his feet yet again, the blood drying and the wound closing. For the first time the Paladin hesitated. The giant should be hurt, but its wounds had healed immediately. Either blow should have slowed or weakened him; neither had.

The giant attacked anew, stronger now than before, thrusting into the Paladin with such force that the King's champion was driven backward to the castle wall. The giant pinned him there, wresting away his sword and bringing the massive club up under his chin to break his neck. The Paladin tried to twist free of the killing hold and could not. The giant grunted with the effort of pushing forward against the Paladin's neck. The dark eyes glinted. The great body heaved mightily. The Paladin's breath was cut off. He could not break loose.

In desperation he hammered both iron-gloved fists into the giant's midsection. The giant grunted in pain. The Paladin struck at him again, this time where his ribs joined. The giant fell back, clutching himself, the club falling away. The Paladin struck him once more, this time squarely between the eyes. The giant reeled backward and collapsed.

But then, impossibly, he came to his feet again, righted as if he had never fallen, his club hefted eagerly as he advanced anew. The Paladin had lost his sword, and now he freed the mace he wore tied to his belt. It was shorter than the giant's club, though just as deadly. Still, there was no weapon to match the speed of the giant's recovery each time he was felled. It was as if the blows gave him new strength.

The giant attacked the Paladin again, hammering at his armored body with blows so powerful that they knocked the mace aside as if it were a toy. The Paladin grappled with his adversary, leaping inside the killing arc of the club. With his arms locked about the great body, he heaved upward to throw the giant down. The giant roared in dismay. Something about this attack clearly bothered him. The Paladin pressed forward. Together, the combatants staggered across the courtyard, grunting and straining from the effort of their struggle. The giant was trying to break free, the club abandoned, both massive arms hammering down on the Paladin's armored body. But the Paladin had discovered something useful. When he lifted upward on his adversary, the giant weakened noticeably. He lost the fury and intensity of his effort. He howled in obvious frustration. He wanted to be put down again, and so the Paladin fought to hold him aloft, to break his connection to the earth, for it was from the earth, it now appeared, that the giant gained his strength.

Finally the Paladin brought the giant to the steps of the watchtower and threw him down upon the stone. The giant kicked and fought to roll from the steps to the earth of the courtyard, but the Paladin would not let him break free. The giant roared anew, and now there was blood spurting from his nostrils and mouth, leaking from his wounds at every turn. The Paladin thrust his adversary farther up the steps, farther from the courtyard dirt, and the giant fell back with a sudden convulsive gasp. Up another few steps the Paladin heaved the great body, and now the giant could no longer breathe. His arms fell back, and his legs sprawled askew on the steps.

The Paladin held him there, pinned and helpless, until he was dead. When his life departed, the giant turned to dust.

Afterward, when the Paladin had vanished and Ben had come back to himself, he wondered if he could have saved the giant's life. It was not a simple matter to resolve. There was the question of whether the Paladin would have permitted it, for when Ben was the Paladin, he was subject to the knight's ethics and life rules, and they were far different from his own. The Paladin had no interest in saving the life of an enemy. Enemies were to be killed swiftly and remorselessly. Ben was not certain he could exercise sufficient control over his alter ego to permit even a small consideration for the sparing of a life. There was also the question of whether the giant would have cooperated or whether he would have disdained compassion as thoroughly as the Paladin had and gone on fighting until he was killed. There was the question finally of whether the giant was even real. It had turned to dust on dying, and creatures of flesh and blood did not do that so swiftly. It seemed probable that the giant was a thing of magic and that its destruction was inevitable in the face of a stronger magic.

All of which did nothing to make Ben feel any better about what he had been put through. The impact of having killed the giant was not lessened by the fact that the giant might not have been a mortal man. His dying had been real enough, and it had come at Ben's hand. He could still feel the giant's struggles weakening as he held him pinned fast on the tower steps. He would remember for as long as he lived the other's eyes as the life went out of them.

He went back to his bedchamber with Willow and slept for a time, seeking escape from the experience. She stayed with him while he rested, lying close beside him on the bed, her cool hands running across his chest and arms, her voice whispering to him compassionately, soothingly. He did not know how he could live without her, so close was she, so much a part of him. If the Paladin was his dark side, then she most certainly was his light. He took heart from her radiance and drifted in warmth and peace.

When he awoke, it was midday. He ate then, hungry again and anxious to get on with matters that required his attention. He did not speak to Willow of what had happened. He had never told her—never told anyone, for that matter—the truth about the Paladin. No one knew that Landover's King and her champion were one and the same, joined by the magic of the medallion, bound irrevocably in the defense of the realm. No one knew that when the latter surfaced, the former was submerged, one supplanting and repressing the other, one dominant. But it was becoming increasingly difficult for Ben to keep this secret from his wife. The strain of holding himself together after each transformation, of keeping whole when bits and pieces of himself were being ripped away, was beginning to tell. He could not avoid the fact that when he was the Paladin, he gloried in the power of the magic that transformed him and did not want to change back again. One day, he feared, he would succumb to its lure.

Visitors to the castle included officials of the land reformation committee he had appointed to oversee changes in the application of agricultural techniques and irrigation in various parts of the kingdom, particularly the arid Eastern Wastelands, and he met with them at length to discuss their progress in convincing the Lords of the Greensward to commit manpower and materials to his project. The meeting produced mixed results but encouraged him sufficiently to plan a visit to a few of those who remained recalcitrant, notably but not surprisingly Kallendbor of Rhyndweir. Kallendbor resisted everything Ben proposed and two years ago had been persuaded to rise up against him in rebellion through the machinations of a dark fairy called the Gorse. Kallendbor had been all too willing to participate, so Ben Holiday had punished him severely. One year in exile and the loss of certain titles and land had been the punishment decreed. Kallendbor had accepted the verdict without complaint, recognizing perhaps that his punishment could—and some said should—have been much worse. His year in exile had been served, and some of his land and titles had been restored. But he continued to be obstreperous and challenging at every turn, and it was clear to Ben that for all Kallendbor had suffered, he had learned almost nothing.

Ben moved from the committee meeting to a reception with several of his judicial representatives that lasted only a short time, then on to a perusing of law documents concerning disputes over property. Having to deal with those matters without Abernathy's able assistance made him think again on the kidnapping of Mistaya. He pondered anew the inadequacy of his efforts to find her, warding off the despair he felt every time he envisioned losing her. His already white-hot hatred of Rydall grew measurably. That Marnhull's King should use such despicable tactics to force him to play this ridiculous game of pitting Kings' champions against each other was unforgivable. But it was puzzling as well. It lacked balance somehow; it lacked good sense. Something about it suggested that there was more to the puzzle than Ben was seeing.

He would have considered the matter further perhaps, but Bunion arrived in a rush to announce that another of Rydall's champions had appeared.

Ben was stunned. A second, so soon? He had barely bested the first! It seemed that Rydall was determined to have the matter of Landover's Kingship resolved quickly.

Ben headed for the battlements, Bunion scurrying ahead. Guards stepped aside with his passing, uttering words of encouragement and disdain for this latest challenge. By now everyone realized what was happening, knew that an unknown outside force was attempting to wrest control of the throne. There had been peace in Landover since the defeat of the Gorse two years earlier, but now here was a new threat. Ben acknowledged the kind words with a nod and an occasional word of encouragement back. He was joined by Willow, emerald hair streaming out behind her, beautiful face hardened by

her iron will, as he mounted the watchtower steps. King's
Guards were assembling in force in the courtyard, readying to
march forth. Retainers were bringing up a line of warhorses.
Everyone was preparing for battle.

Ben climbed to the top of the wall overlooking the drawbridge, Willow and Bunion at his side, and stopped dead.

Armored all in silver, its lance tilted upward in salute, a
solitary knight waited at the far end of the causeway. It was instantly recognizable even from this distance. Ben Holiday
found himself looking at the Paladin.

He stared in speechless shock, unable to believe what he
was seeing. The Paladin? Here, unsummoned? Had it come to
do battle with its master? Had Rydall somehow subverted it?

"This can't be possible," he muttered.

"That isn't the Paladin." Willow was the first to say it. "It
can't be. You haven't summoned it, and no one else can. This
knight is a fraud, a pretender."

But a realistic-looking one for all that, Ben thought
darkly. Well, there was no help for it. He was faced with the
same dilemma that he had confronted when the giant had appeared. Waiting was pointless. If he refused to meet the knight
without, he would all too soon find it within.

Ben put his hands on the stones of the castle wall and
tried to decide if he was strong enough to do battle again so
soon. For while his transformation into the Paladin required
little of him physically, it was excessively demanding mentally
and emotionally. When the battle was finished and another
challenger lay dead, it was his psyche that the shards of battle
would have damaged. He stared down grim-faced at this newest threat from Rydall. This one, at least, was faceless, but the
prospect of doing battle with himself—or a part of himself—
was unnerving, even if it wasn't really a part but only something that seemed to be . . .

He gave up on his ruminations. Too much of that could
be deadly. There was no choice offered him in this matter. If

Rydall sent three champions this day, he would still have to fight them all.

"Ben," Willow said softly, her arm linking into his.

He nodded. "I know; you don't have to say it. But I can't make that thing down there go away by ignoring it."

"There will be another trick to winning," she said, "just as there was with the giant."

She released him reluctantly then, and he brought forth the medallion. A moment later he summoned the Paladin. He felt a measure of relief when it appeared in a flare of light from out of the forest at the edge of the meadow; now he could be certain that it was not the real Paladin who served Rydall. His protector wheeled toward the pretender, lance lowered for the attack. Ben felt himself transported once more, flowing easily with the change this time, used to it since this morning, almost welcoming it. The Paladin's armor closed about him, its memories stirred in his blood, and the expectation of battle was a rush of heat that flooded through bone and muscle and into the iron of his weapons.

The Paladin kicked his warhorse in the flanks, and the beast surged forward to the attack. Ahead, the false knight turned and spurred toward him in response. Lances lowered, they raced across the grassy stretch of the meadow in a thunder of hooves and met with a clash of iron and splintered oak as both lances shattered into pieces.

Still mounted, shields cracked and scarred, the combatants wheeled back toward each other, battle-axes in hand. They rushed together a second time, weapons swinging. The Paladin deflected the other knight's heavy blade, and his adversary did the same with his. A second blow got through, but so did one of his adversary's. The knights hammered at each other, and then both axes snapped at the hilt and fell away, broken and useless.

Reining their warhorses about savagely to get into position, the combatants reached for their broadswords.

A third time they came together, the blades of their broadswords striking fire in the late afternoon sun, sparks exploding from their weapons and armor. Their horses were weakening, snorting and huffing from the strain of bearing their armored riders and absorbing the shock of the blows dealt. Finally both went down together, throwing their riders free, rising shakily, and standing with heads lowered and blood on their muzzles, unable to continue.

The twin Paladins rose as well, broadswords still in hand, and advanced to the attack on foot. If they were tired, they did not show it. They went at each other with single-minded determination, and it was clear to everyone watching that neither would give quarter until the other was down for good.

Atop the castle wall Willow observed the struggle with growing apprehension. For every blow landed, a matching one was dealt. The Paladins were exact duplicates of each other, wheeling and charging, striking and blocking, moving with synchronized movements in a bizarre dance of destruction. Soon it became impossible for her to tell which was which. The real Paladin should have been able to distinguish itself from the pretender through its experience and battle skill, but it did not seem able to do so. The longer the struggle went on, the more impossible it became to tell one from the other. They attacked and defended exactly the same—blow for blow, wound for wound, damage for damage—no difference in their looks, no variation in their strategies, no counters that were not instantly imitated. Something was wrong with the way in which the struggle was progressing, and she realized soon enough what it was. The Paladin could not gain an edge in this battle because it was fighting itself. It was like watching yourself in a mirror, seeing your image reflected back at you, seeing everything you did imitated exactly. Your reflection never tired and never slowed sooner than you did. While you stood before the mirror, you could never escape it . . .

She caught herself. She realized the secret of Rydall's

champion then. She recognized, too, how it could be defeated.

"Ben!" she shouted above the clash of armor and weapons. She clutched at him, but there was no response. He stood beside her, looking out at the battle, motionless, voiceless, seemingly entranced. "Ben!" she shouted again, shaking him harder.

He turned toward her, a barely perceptible movement. He seemed to be looking at her from a great distance off.

"Ben, send the Paladin back!" she cried out. "Send him away! Rydall's champion is stealing his strength. He's using him up! Listen to me, Ben! If you send the Paladin away, Rydall's champion will disappear, too!"

From somewhere in the back of his mind Ben heard the plea. But he was too far away to respond, trapped in the Paladin's body, caught up in the terrible struggle with his twin, an adversary that seemed to know his every move, to anticipate his every attempt at surprise, to counter his every strategy.

Ben! he heard the voice call frantically. *Ben, listen to me!*

The Paladin brushed aside the plea and renewed his attack. He thought he sensed a weakening in his enemy. He refused to accept that it reflected his own.

In desperation, Willow released her grip on the unresponsive Ben and went down off the wall in a rush. Ben did not seem to be able to act; something was happening with him that she did not understand. Since he could not respond to the Paladin's need, it was left to her to do so. She gained the courtyard below, snatched a spear from a weapons rack, crossed to where a knot of King's Guards stood before the open gates watching the struggle taking place beyond the castle walls, vaulted onto the back of the closest warhorse, and, heedless of the cries that immediately sprang up around her, kicked the horse forward and went out through the gates.

She thundered across the drawbridge and onto the grasslands beyond, heading for the combatants. Shouts of alarm trailed after her, but she was heedless of them. She knew what was needed. The Paladin and Rydall's champion were locked in a battle of twins that was intended to destroy them both. The only thing that would save the Paladin was a disruption of the magic Rydall's champion relied on. This time it was not the earth that sustained it, as had been the case with the giant, but the Paladin's own strength and skill. Rydall's champion was a form of succubus, a reflection in the mirror that fed off its original, imitating it, copying its every move, draining it of its life.

But if the mirror were darkened . . .

She reached the combatants and swept by them without slowing, her lowered spear raking their armored bodies. It was enough to get their attention. They turned as one, seeing her for the first time. She reined in her horse and swung the beast about, spear lowered in challenge, preparing to charge again. Confusion was evident in both Paladins, an uncertainty over what her presence meant. She had to hope that this was disruption enough of the magic that bound them, that Ben somehow could communicate still with the Paladin, and that his protector would find a way to act on the plea.

"Withdraw!" she shrieked in fury, and flung the lance at them.

The closest of the two brushed the weapon aside as it flew past, swatting at it as if it were nothing more than a fly. The other, standing a few paces behind, pointlessly mimicked the action.

There, she thought triumphantly, that one is Rydall's creature!

She spurred as close as she dared to the real Paladin and reined in once more. The meadow had gone quiet.

She looked down at the Paladin. "Sheathe your sword and withdraw!" she said. "Only then can you win!"

There was a long moment of silence and uncertainty, of confrontation between the sylph and the two armored knights.

Then, abruptly, the true Paladin sheathed his great broad-sword. A motion of one metal-gloved hand brought his exhausted warhorse to him. He looked back at Willow momentarily and then mounted.

Sunlight flared off the silver armor as he wheeled toward Sterling Silver. A sliver of brightness lanced away toward the castle battlements and reflected off the medallion that hung from Ben Holiday's neck, turning it molten.

Then horse and rider disappeared in a flash of light, and the Paladin was gone.

Willow turned quickly to the other knight, held her breath, and waited.

Rydall's creature stood staring at the air into which the Paladin had faded. With its enemy gone, its purpose in life was finished. Bound by the dictates of the magic that had created it, it mimicked its original one last time. Sheathing its sword, it walked to its warhorse and mounted. But there was no provision for its leaving. There was no magic to sustain it beyond this moment. And so it simply fell apart, collapsing in a veil of windblown ash.

Willow stood alone in the meadow. She had guessed right. Once the Paladin had gone, whatever the reason, Rydall's champion could not survive. Permitting herself a smile of satisfaction and relief, she rode slowly back toward the castle and to Ben.

Ardsheal

It was still light, the sun hovering at the horizon's crest in the shadow of the mountains to the west, when the River Master's messenger appeared to Ben and Willow at the door of their bedchamber. They had retired to wash and dress for dinner, physically exhausted from the day's events but mentally and emotionally on edge and unable to contemplate rest until after they had calmed down. How the creature knew where to find them or got as far as it did without being seen was a matter best left for the speculation of others. Ben knew by now that the once-fairy, Willow among them, could pass almost anywhere among humans without being seen.

The messenger knocked softly, and when Willow opened the door, he was standing there, stone-faced and motionless. He was a wood sprite, as lean and gnarled as a fence post and with eyes as bright as gemstones in a face almost devoid of any other features. He bowed respectfully to Willow and waited for Ben to join her at the door.

"High Lord," he greeted, and gave a second bow. "My Lord the River Master asks that his daughter and her husband come at once to Elderew to speak with him. He would hear more of his missing granddaughter and would give counsel and assistance to her parents. Will you come?"

Ben and Willow exchanged a brief glance. Neither felt much like going anywhere at present, but both recognized instantly that there were reasons to accept the invitation. If they stayed where they were, they would soon enough receive a visit from another of Rydall's champions. Perhaps by being somewhere else they could forestall that visit. Buying time in their search for Mistaya and for a solution to Rydall's challenge was one of the few options left to them. It might also be that the River Master, a creature of great magic, meant to offer them a talisman or spell to use for their protection. At least he might have news of his granddaughter, for he had learned of her abduction some days ago and by now must have scoured the lake country and beyond for some sign of her.

No words passed between them, but Ben and Willow frequently communicated on another level, and words were not always necessary.

"Tell the River Master we will come," Ben told the messenger.

The sprite nodded, bowed once more, and was gone. He went down the hallway into the growing twilight shadows and simply disappeared.

They took dinner in their room, preferring to be alone and in as much seclusion as they could manage. The castle still bustled with King's Guards set to watch and preparing to go out on patrol. Two attacks in the same day was unheard of. Even Bunion was out tracking, trying to trace the origins of Rydall's defunct champions, though it was a good bet that there was nothing to be found. Appointments had been canceled for the next few days, and the entire castle garrison was on alert. No one would be allowed in or out of the castle without first being thoroughly checked.

Such precautions were of marginal value, however, where the use of magic was concerned, as the unorthodox appearance of the River Master's messenger had made clear. There was no doubt in Ben's mind that Rydall commanded significant magic of his own, and it would probably allow his champions to circumvent the usual precautions that might be laid to stop them. Probably it was Rydall's black-cloaked companion who wielded that magic and Rydall himself who commanded its use, but just who did what made no difference. The first two champions sent to destroy him had possessed magic, and it was a safe bet that the five yet to come would possess stronger magic still.

So Ben and Willow talked out their situation during dinner and reasoned anew that it would be best for all if they traveled to the lake country for a few days. Maybe Rydall would have trouble finding them. Maybe their movement would cause some disruption in his plans. Staying where they were, waiting helplessly, would play right into his hands. Besides, there was little chance of finding Mistaya or Questor and Abernathy without aid from another source. Use of the Landsview had failed repeatedly. All efforts at searching the countryside had failed as well. But there was always the chance that someone they hadn't thought to talk with yet knew something. Or that someone with powers greater than their own and resources denied to them, such as the River Master, might have knowledge to impart.

They chose to go that night, to leave under cover of darkness and before the coming daybreak. They hoped to leave unseen, without having to encounter another of Rydall's champions. Ben particularly was suffering from the day's encounters. Willow could not determine the reason. Ben was still closemouthed about what had happened during that second struggle, why he hadn't responded to her pleas, why he had seemed so removed from what was happening yet so exhausted by it afterward. He had thanked her for her help, not rebuked her in any way for going out onto the battlefield, and then had dropped the matter abruptly, retreating somewhere deep inside himself until the messenger from the River Master appeared. Willow, for her part, had not pressed him. It was apparent that this was something he would talk about when he was ready, and she was satisfied with having helped defeat

Rydall's creature. She was worried, though, about what would happen the next time. She did not like the way he had behaved during the Paladin's battle. She did not like not knowing what was wrong.

They waited for Bunion to return, cautious enough to decide to take the kobold with them for added protection. Leaving instructions with a chosen few as to what should be done in their absence, canceling all remaining appointments into the next week, and declaring the King to be on holiday, Ben and Willow departed from a side door on the east, took the lake skimmer across to the far shore, and met Bunion, who was already in place with Ben's bay gelding, Jurisdiction, and Willow's white-faced sorrel mare, Crane. With Bunion afoot and leading the way, they mounted their horses and trotted off into the night.

They journeyed until it was almost dawn. By then they were well away from Sterling Silver and closing on the lake country. Some miles short of the Irrylyn they turned into a heavy grove of ash and hickory, dismounted, tethered their horses, rolled into light blankets, and fell asleep. While the seemingly tireless Bunion maintained watch, they rested until midmorning of the following day. When they awoke, Willow unpacked the cheese, bread, fruit, and ale she had brought for them, and they consumed it in a sunny space at the base of a gnarled old shagbark. Bunion appeared momentarily to snatch a few bites, then set out again, anxious to let the people of the lake country know they were coming. Once they were within the lake country, they all agreed, Rydall would have a hard time reaching them.

When Ben and Willow had finished eating, they rode out again to the south. Bunion would find them along the way. The morning was sultry and still, and the sun's heat beat down on the forestland like a blacksmith's hammer. No breeze came to cool them in their travels, and when they reached the Irrylyn, Willow pulled Crane into the shelter of a cove along the lake shore, dismounted, tied her horse to a tree, stripped off her clothing, and walked into the water. Ben followed. They swam in the lake for a time, floating on their backs, looking up at the tree limbs and the sky, not saying anything. Ben was reminded anew of how impetuous Willow was. He remembered the first time he had met her, here in the waters of this lake just after sunset, waiting for him without knowing who he would be. *You are for me,* she had told him. *It was foretold at the time of my conception. I knew you would come.*

She swam over to him now, embraced him, kissed him, and said, "I love you." Then she swam away again.

They emerged from the lake cool and refreshed, dressed anew, remounted, and started out again. They rode until after midday, when they were closing on the old growth that marked the boundary of Elderew and the country of the once-fairy. Bunion was waiting where the trail began to melt away into weeds. The River Master was expecting them, he reported. Guides would meet and escort them into the city a little farther on.

They left the trail where it ended and began to snake their way through monstrous fir and spruce, shagbark hickory and white oak, red elm and ash. The trees towered overhead, shutting out the sky, closing off the light. It was dark and chilly in spots, some of which never saw the sun. It was still, as if nothing lived in these woods. But already Ben could feel the eyes watching.

When the ground turned soft and the air began to smell of swamp and bog, the guides they had been promised appeared, creatures with green hair trailing off their heads and limbs like tree silk, lean, wiry figures that blended with the forest and could ease through any opening, no matter how narrow and obstructed. Their guides took them on a lengthy circuitous path through the great trees and across uncertain ground. To either side faces appeared out of newly formed mist, eyes bright and curious, there one moment and gone the next. Swamp closed about to either side, and water creatures lifted from the mire and out of the grasses to watch them pass.

Time ebbed. Elderew lay deep within the old growth, warded by elements of nature and magic, and no one passed within unless invited. The once-fairy were a secretive people, suspicious of the world without, cautious of the creatures who inhabited it. Ben had gone a long way toward removing that suspicion and fear, and the people of the lake country now traveled forth into other parts of Landover and on occasion brought outlanders back. But old habits and deep-rooted doubts died hard, and it would be some time yet before the barriers came down completely.

Ben could have found his way to Elderew using Willow or Bunion, but it would have been rude to ignore tradition and hospitality. The River Master's guides were a courtesy extended to those who were welcome. Ben forced himself to be patient. Soon the swamp areas were behind them, and they were climbing back toward solid ground. The trees were larger here, older and more established, hardwoods that had been alive for two hundred years and more. The air turned fresh and warm with the smell of sun and wildflowers. A scattering of people appeared. A few offered shy greetings. Children were among them, darting boldly between the horses, laughing and teasing. The trail reappeared, starting up again out of nowhere, well worn and broad where the trees opened up for it. Ahead, the city of Elderew came into view, a marvel of engineering and ingenuity that never failed to impress Ben.

The city was situated in a stand of massive old hardwoods that were even larger than the redwoods of California. The boughs of these trees were interlocked to form pathways above the earth, and the city rose in levels from the ground to the middle branches of the old growth, cradled like a series of toys in a child's arms. Homes and shops lined roads and tree lanes, an intricate webwork of pathways. Sunlight spilled through the canopy of limbs in long streamers that dappled the shadows and lit the natural gloom brightly. People scurried everywhere, the once-fairy an industrious folk who understood the importance of hard work. Much of that work was with small magics, their stock-in-trade. Much of it dealt with healing and sustaining their forest world. It was intriguing to discover how many aspects of their life they could affect with their efforts. Ben Holiday, as Landover's King, was still just beginning to learn.

Willow gave Ben a reassuring smile, her promise that her home city was still a friend to them. They rode on in silence, Bunion afoot before them with their guides, watching Elderew's complexity unfold as the trees spread wider and the city levels grew more visible. Ahead, the amphitheater that served as the site for the many celebrations of the once-fairy opened out to them in greeting. Formed of trees interlaced in a vast horseshoe, with seats on branches that started high up and ran downward to the arena floor, the amphitheater was as impressive as the city it served.

The River Master was waiting for them at its entry, standing amid his retainers, dressed in simple, nondescript clothing. If you did not know who he was, you would not have been able to pick him out by what he wore. You might have done so by his bearing, however. He was a tall, slender, impressive-looking man, a water sprite with silvery skin so grainy that it resembled fish scales, with thick black hair that, like Willow's, ran down the underside of his forearms and the back of his calves, and with features so stark and sharp that they might have been hewn from stone. His face was an expressionless mask, but his eyes were bright and quick, and Ben had learned to read the River Master's thoughts from what he found there.

The River Master came up to them as they slowed and dismounted, moving at once to Willow, embracing her stiffly, whispering to her that he was glad she had come. Willow embraced him back, equally uncomfortable with the greeting.

Their relationship remained an uneasy one, distant and mired in mistrust. Willow's mother was a wood nymph so wild that she could not survive anywhere but in the forest, and Willow's father had never gotten over her refusal to live with him. Willow had been a constant reminder to him while she was growing of the woman he had loved and had not been able to hold for more than a single night. He had resented his daughter for what she represented, abandoning her emotionally from childhood on, leaving her to grow up alone. Even after she was grown, he found her a source of disappointment. He had not approved of her marriage to Ben, a human and an outlander despite being named Landover's newest King. Willow, he thought, had betrayed her people. It had taken time for him to accept her decision. He was less cool and aloof toward her these days than he had once been, but the old memories died hard for both.

Yet the River Master genuinely cared for Mistaya, the differences between father and daughter somehow bypassed in his bonding with his granddaughter. If there was anything he could do to help the little girl, it was certain he would spare no effort. It was for this reason that Ben and Willow had agreed to come to Elderew.

The River Master turned from his daughter and gave Ben a formal bow. It was as much as Ben could expect. He nodded back.

"There will be a dinner in your honor tonight," the River Master advised, surprising them both. "While preparations are being made, come speak with me a bit."

He led them from the arena, where tables and benches were being set up and colored cloths laid out, to the park that fronted Elderew and ran back to the city's closest buildings. Children raced past them as they walked, heedless of the adults who called after them in admonishment. It reminded Ben of other times and places, of Annie and the children they might have had, of Chicago parks in the summertime, of dreams long since abandoned. But the memory lingered only a moment. He thought seldom of his old world these days. He had little reason to do so.

They passed through the play area to a walkway that followed along a stream, weaving and dodging through shaggy conifers as if looking to stay out from underfoot. The children and their guardians faded behind, reduced to distant shouts and laughter. The three walked alone now, though it was certain that the River Master's guards kept pace somewhere in the trees, silent and unseen. When they reached a deserted glade where a pair of benches faced each other across a pond rimmed with flower beds, the River Master beckoned them to take seats. Ben and Willow sat on one bench, and the River Master automatically moved to the other.

"We will not be disturbed here," he advised, his strange eyes giving a cursory glance about at the sun-filled clearing. He looked back at them. When he spoke, his tone was accusatory. "You should have told me you were sending Mistaya here. I would have sent an escort to protect her."

"There wasn't time," Ben responded calmly, cutting short the retort he was tempted to make. "I thought Questor Thews and a dozen King's Guards sufficient protection. I hoped Rydall would be concentrating on me."

"Mistaya is his tool now to use against you," the River Master declared bitterly.

"Have you learned anything?" Willow asked in an attempt to deflect his anger.

The River Master shook his head. "This is what I know. I was able to discover the place where the attack took place. There was a significant amount of magic used in Mistaya's taking. Traces of it still lingered several days after. I could not determine their source. There were no signs of attackers or defenders. There were no footprints leading away from the battle site."

Ben did not miss the other's choice of words. Battle site.

He forced his thoughts away. "No footprints. How could that be?"

The River Master's chiseled features tilted into shadow. "Either everyone was destroyed or travel by foot wasn't necessary for the survivors." He paused. "As I said, there was significant magic employed in the attack."

"Have you discovered anything since?"

The River Master shook his head. "I have never heard of Rydall or Marnhull. They do not exist within Landover's boundaries. Marnhull must lie somewhere without. I have tried to trace Rydall and his black-cloaked companion without success. I have watched for them; I have laid traps. They are nowhere to be found."

"Nor Mistaya and her escort?"

"No."

Ben nodded. He looked at Willow and read the disappointment in her eyes. She had been hoping that some small bit of good news might be waiting for them.

"So we are no closer to finding Mistaya than before," he finished, trying not to sound bitter. "Why did you summon us, then?"

The River Master sat delicately poised on the edge of his bench, staring over at them with no expression visible on his face and no emotion revealed in his eyes. "I *requested* your presence," he corrected, his voice flat and calm. "I wish to offer my help in returning Mistaya to her home. It is true that I have not been able to do much as yet, but perhaps I can make up for that now."

He paused, waiting for their response. Ben nodded in acquiescence. "Any help you might give would be greatly appreciated," he said.

It seemed to reassure the River Master. There was a barely perceptible relaxing of his shoulders. "I know we have not been friends," he said quietly. "I know our relationship has not been a warm one." He looked from Ben to Willow, in-

cluding them both in this assessment. "This does not mean I
wish you any harm. I do not. You know as well how strongly
I feel about Mistaya. Nothing must be allowed to happen
to her."

"No," Ben agreed.

"Can you find her?" Willow asked suddenly.

The River Master hesitated. "Perhaps." He gave her an
appraising look. "I would not discount too quickly the possibility that you will find her yourself. Nor would I discount the
possibility that she will find a way to get free on her own. She
is a very resourceful child. And very powerful. She has great
magic, Willow. Did you know that?"

Willow and Ben exchanged another glance, one of surprise. They shook their heads in unison.

"I sensed it the moment we met," the River Master
advised. "Her power is latent but definitely there. She is a
once-fairy of extraordinary potential, and once she discovers
her talent, the possibilities are limitless."

Ben stared, trying to decide if this was good. He had
never considered seriously that Mistaya might have the use of
magic. It seemed ridiculous to him now that he hadn't. Her
heritage allowed for it, and her odd growth pattern certainly
suggested it. But she was his daughter, and the fact remained
that he had never wanted to believe that she might be anything different from what he expected.

"You did not tell her?" Willow asked quietly.

The River Master shook his head. "It was not my place.
I understand that much about being a grandfather."

"Will Rydall sense her potential for magic?" Ben asked
suddenly.

The River Master considered. "If he is a creature of
magic himself, as he appears to be—if he is one of us, for instance, a once-fairy, a being who wields magic—then I would
have to say that he will recognize her power."

"But *she* doesn't know, so having the use of magic won't

help her," Ben reasoned. "Unless Rydall reveals the truth to her. Or unless she discovers it on her own."

The River Master shrugged. "I only tell you of her magic so you will understand that she is not entirely helpless in this situation. She is a resourceful and independent child in any case. She may find a way to save herself."

"But you will continue your own search for her," Willow pressed. "You will not abandon your efforts to help her."

The River Master nodded. "I will not stop looking for her until she is found. I will leave nothing to chance, Willow. You know me better than that." He sounded rebuked. "But the immediate help I can offer is not to her but to you. Or, more correctly," he amended, looking at Ben, "to you."

A small yellow-and-black speckled bird flew down out of the trees and landed at the far edge of the pond. It regarded them solemnly, bright-eyed and watchful, then stopped quickly to drink. It bobbed up and down a few times, then took wing and was gone. The River Master watched after it thoughtfully.

"The danger is to you, High Lord," he advised, returning his gaze to Ben. "Rydall, whoever he is and wherever he comes from, is looking to destroy you. He uses Mistaya to this end, and whoever stoops to using a child to devise the death of an enemy is dangerous indeed. I heard about the attacks of yesterday. The risk to you is great, and it will not lessen until Mistaya is recovered and Rydall defeated. But this may take time. It will not come easily. Meanwhile, we must find a way to keep you alive."

Ben was forced to smile. "I'm doing the best I can, I promise you."

The River Master nodded. "I am quite certain. The problem is, you lack sufficient resources. You have no magic to ward against Rydall's, save that of the Paladin. Rydall knows this; I expect he is counting on it. Something is strange about this challenge he has set you. Seven champions sent to destroy the Paladin, and if one succeeds, you agree to abdicate. Why? Why play this game? Why not simply order you from the throne now or kill your daughter?"

"I have wondered about that as well," Ben acknowledged.

"Then you will appreciate it when I tell you that there is more to this game than is being revealed. Rydall is keeping something important from you. He is hiding a surprise." The River Master looked away. "So perhaps you should have a surprise for him."

He stood up abruptly. "I have one I think you might appreciate. Come with me."

Ben and Willow rose, and the three of them walked from the glade farther into the forest. They went only a short distance, weaving down a small pathway that led back into a thickly grown mass of spruce and fir. The ground was carpeted with needles, and the air was heavy with their scent. It was exceptionally quiet within those trees, sounds cushioned by the forest floor and the heavy green boughs that swept downward about them.

The sun was sinking to the west into the trees, a red orb in a purple haze. Twilight filled the woodlands with long shadows and cool places that whispered of night's coming.

They reached a second clearing. A figure stood there waiting, cloaked and hooded. It did not move as they came into view. It stayed perfectly still.

The River Master took them to within six feet of the figure and stopped. He lifted his arm and beckoned. The figure raised its hands in response and lowered the hood. It was a creature of indeterminate sex and origin, its skin wood-color, its mouth, nose, and eyes slits on its flat, nearly featureless face. There was a glimmer of light behind the eyes but nothing more. It was of average size and build, but its body was all smooth and lean and sleek and hard beneath the cloak.

Ben glanced at Willow. There was recognition in her eyes and something he hadn't seen for a long time. There was fear.

"This is an Ardsheal," the River Master said to Ben. "It is an elemental. It does not need food or drink or sleep. It requires nothing to survive. It was created by the magic of the once-fairy for a single purpose: to protect you. Willow knows. An Ardsheal is a match for anything alive. Nothing is more dangerous."

Ben nodded in response, not certain what to say. He was not expecting this gift. He was not certain he wanted it. He glanced at the Ardsheal. It made no response. It seemed comatose. "This creature will protect me?" he repeated.

"To the death," the River Master said.

"An Ardsheal is very dangerous, Father," Willow observed softly.

"Only to its enemies. Not to you. Not to the High Lord. It will serve as it is directed. In the absence of specific direction, it will do the one thing it has been set to do—it will protect you." He looked at Willow curiously. "You are frightened of them still?"

She nodded, a strange look on her face. "Yes."

Ben was thinking and missed the look. "Why have you chosen to give me this?" he asked finally. "I mean, the Ardsheal as opposed to another form of magic?"

"A good question." The River Master turned to face him, the Ardsheal now become his shadow. "Rydall expects the Paladin to defend you. He must have reason to believe that at some point it will fail to do so adequately. Perhaps that will happen. The Ardsheal will be there if it does. You defend yourself against an enemy you neither know nor understand. You require a defense your enemy does not expect in return. The Ardsheal will be that defense. Take it. It will give you a measure of reassurance. It will give you time to look for Mistaya, time for all of us to look."

He came forward a step, chiseled face bent close. "You are needed alive, High Lord Ben Holiday. If you die, there is a good chance your daughter will die with you. She serves only a single purpose: to draw you on. Once that purpose is served, what reason do you have for believing that she will be allowed to go on living? Consider carefully for a moment the nature of your enemy."

Ben held the River Master's gaze and did as he was bidden.

"He is right," Willow said quietly, almost reluctantly.

Ben found himself in immediate agreement. It did not require a great deal of thought to recognize the value of a second protector. Perhaps it would give him an edge against Rydall's creatures. If it saved him even once from having to call up the Paladin, it would have served a valuable purpose.

"I will accept your gift," he said finally. "Thank you."

The River Master nodded in satisfaction. "A good decision. Now come to dinner."

The feast was a sumptuous, extravagant affair, very much in keeping with the nature of celebrations among the once-fairy. There were tables laden with food, pitchers of iced ale, garlands of flowers, children and adults dressed in bright clothing, and music and dancing everywhere. The River Master placed Ben and Willow at the head of his table, announced their presence to those assembled, welcomed them to the lake country, and toasted them on behalf of the once-fairy. All evening, while the celebration wore on, the people of Elderew came up to greet them personally, some bearing small gifts, some offering good wishes. It made Ben and Willow smile and helped them relax. For a few hours they forgot about Rydall of Marnhull and the misery he had caused them. They ate and drank and laughed with the once-fairy, caught up in the merriment and feasting, soothed by the cool breezes that blew out of the trees and by the warmth of the people surrounding them.

At midnight they retired to a small guest house provided for their lodging. They fell into bed, exhausted but smiling, lying together, holding each other against a return of the fears and doubts they had managed to put aside, falling asleep finally as exhaustion overtook them.

Sometime afterward, several hours before morning, Ben woke, extracted himself from Willow's arms, rose, and walked to the window. The world without was lit by a single half-moon and stars that peeked down through a scattering of low-slung clouds and interlocked tree limbs. He stared out into the darkness, looking for the Ardsheal, wondering if it was there. He had not seen it since the River Master had presented it to him. It had been real enough then but now seemed somehow to be an imagining conjured in a dream.

An Ardsheal is very dangerous, Father, Willow had said.

He saw it then, back within the trees, another of the night's shadows. He would not have seen it at all except that it moved just enough when he was looking so that he would know it was there, standing guard, keeping watch.

Why was Willow so frightened of it? Was that a good thing or bad, given its purpose?

He didn't know. He put both questions in the cupboard in his mind that held all his unanswered questions and went back to bed. Tomorrow he would try to find out. He pressed himself tight against Willow's body, wrapped his arms around her, and lay awake holding her for a very long time before he slept.

Nightshade's Tale

Mistaya's days in the Deep Fell slipped by so quickly that she was barely aware of their passing. Enthralled by her lessons on the use of magic, caught up in the exploration of her newly revealed powers, and consumed by the intensity of Nightshade's demands, she gave little notice to any expenditure of time. It might have been only days since she had arrived; it might have been weeks. In truth, it didn't matter. What mattered was what she was doing and the progress she was making in doing it. In that she was delighted, if never satisfied. She had learned a great deal; she had not yet learned enough.

She almost never thought of her parents and home. They were an extraneous and inconsequential consideration for her. Once she had determined that they knew where she was and that therefore she had no need to worry, she had dismissed them completely. Her growing trust in Nightshade and her enthusiasm for her studies made it easy for her to do so. In the beginning she had not been sure that it was all right for her to be here. She had not been sure her parents really did know where she was. But Nightshade's reassurances and her own desire to believe soon convinced her that her fears were misplaced and that all was well. Nightshade had said she could leave when she wished, so it was easy enough to discover whether the witch was lying. That was proof enough for

Mistaya that she was being told the truth. Besides, her growing mastery of her magic would help her father in his battle against Rydall, and that provided an extra incentive for her to stay. Her father needed her; she must not fail him.

Time's passage was also affected by where she was. The Deep Fell had a tendency to blur day into night, light into darkness, then into now, making all seem very much alike. The Deep Fell's thick jungle canopy kept everything beneath it gray and misty. Sunlight did not penetrate. The moon and stars were never seen. Temperatures seldom changed more than marginally, and the look of Mistaya's surroundings was constant and unremarkable. What color and brightness were to be found came solely from her magic, from the wonders she performed and the marvels she uncovered. Nightshade gave her new insight with each lesson, turning the focus of Mistaya's attention inward so that she saw only what she created and almost nothing of the world about.

Nightshade was an effective teacher, endlessly patient with her pupil, praising and correcting by turns, offering small insights where needed, never disparaging or condemning a failed effort. It seemed to Mistaya that in the beginning Nightshade was interested primarily in results, but as her involvement in uncovering the girl's latent magic increased, the witch became more and more caught up in the mechanics of how the magic was performed. It seemed to surprise the witch as much as the girl; it also served to draw them closer.

And they were remarkably close by now, so close that Mistaya was beginning to think of Nightshade as a second mother. This did not seem odd to her. No one would ever replace her real mother, of course, but there was no reason why she could not have more than one, each fulfilling certain functions in her life. Nightshade was a strong presence, and her command of magic and revelation of its secrets were powerful inducements to the girl. Mistaya was very young and easily impressed. Nightshade had rescued her from Rydall. She had brought her to the Deep Fell to keep her safe. She was training her in the magic arts so that she could help her father. She was proving herself a good friend and a wise counselor. Mistaya could not have asked for more.

Yet there were still times when she experienced small twinges of doubt. Most of them were inspired by the appearance of Haltwhistle, who came to her in secret each night. While she no longer agonized over her parents or even Questor Thews and Abernathy, she was reminded by the continued presence of the mud puppy that there was another life waiting for her beyond the confines of the Deep Fell. Try though she might, she could not make the memories of that life go away, and while Haltwhistle never said or did anything to interfere, she knew somehow that he was there to make certain she did not forget. It was disconcerting to have to endure this, but she was mindful of the Earth Mother's warning of the dangers she would face and the promise given that the mud puppy would help protect her if she kept him by her side by remembering to call him once each day. So she conducted a balancing act, immersing herself in Nightshade's teachings by day while each night suffering small glimpses of what she had left behind.

Haltwhistle never gave her away. It was a risky thing she was doing, keeping the mud puppy's presence a secret. Nightshade would not approve, though was it really the witch's place to give that approval? Now and again Mistaya thought she could see Haltwhistle watching her while she worked, concealed by the mist and gray, hidden back in the jungle. Small bits and pieces of him would appear: eyes one time, feet the next, ears or nose another. At night he came at her smallest whisper, sitting just out of reach in the misty dark, barely more substantial than the haze out of which he materialized. Good old Haltwhistle, she would say. And smile when his tail thumped.

Doubt surfaced at other times as well, though, when its coming had nothing to do with Haltwhistle. The most troublesome was Nightshade's insistence on creating monsters. At first there were only the two, and Mistaya accepted the task as a natural part of her learning experience. After all, creating the unusual was at the heart of her endeavors. Together the girl and the witch had turned stones to liquid metal, flowers to butterflies, and dust motes to rainbows. They had made tiny insects speak and mice fly. Mistaya had even discovered a way to sing so that the sound of her voice filled the air with colors. Creating monsters wasn't all that different, she decided. She had been told she would be asked to do things she did not understand and to accept it without question. So she did. Try to imagine things against which there is no defense, Nightshade encouraged. Mistaya began with creatures she had read about in a book her father had brought with him from his old world, a book she had found tucked back in his personal library, all but forgotten. The title was something about mythology or myths or some such. The book was intriguing for its subject matter and the strangeness of its language, and Mistaya had mastered it quickly and then had set it aside. But her memory of its creatures had remained with her. The giant who took his power from the earth. The changeling who could duplicate anyone or anything. She built her first two monsters based on those. They were not even monsters, really, only things that evidenced inhuman powers.

Nightshade had seemed happy enough with her efforts until today. Today she announced, rather abruptly, that she desired Mistaya to create a third monster, this one less human and more powerful than the original two. For the first time since she had arrived, Mistaya questioned a command. What was the purpose of creating a third monster? What was the reason for this exercise, since she had performed it twice already? For just a moment she thought that Nightshade was going to be angry. There was a darkening of her strange eyes and a tightening of the tendons along her slender neck. Then she turned away momentarily, her face lost from view, and just as quickly turned back again.

"Mistaya, listen to me," she said. She was calm, poised, still. "I hoped to spare you this, but it seems I cannot. Your father is already under attack from Rydall and his wizard. Creatures are being sent against him, and he is being forced to use the magic of Questor Thews and the Paladin to survive. Thus far he has been successful. But Rydall's wizard will summon ever greater forces. Eventually your father may not be able to defend himself. Then it will be up to you. The best defense against one monster is another. That is the purpose of this exercise."

Nightshade's logic won out over Mistaya's doubt. So the girl worked hard at her creation all that day. Sunset approached, and she was exhausted. Nightshade's coaching had taken her far in the use of her magic, and some of what she did frightened her. Some of what she envisioned and brought to life was truly terrifying. But Nightshade was quick to sweep it all up, to gather it into the closet of first efforts, and to close it safely away. Mistaya was relieved. She did not want to see any of it again.

Now she sat alone in front of a small cooking fire—the only light the Witch of the Deep Fell permitted after dark—rolling dough into bread to fry with vegetables. Parsnip had taught her how. She cooked mostly for herself since Nightshade ate less than Haltwhistle. In truth, Nightshade rarely lingered once the day's lessons were complete, disappearing back into whatever place she occupied when she wanted to be alone. Sometimes she stayed close, just out of sight; Mistaya could feel her presence when she did that. The closer they became, the more aware the girl was of the witch. It was as if something in their shared use of magic brought them closer physically as well as emotionally, as if ties were being formed that allowed the girl to know more of what the other was about. She could not read Nightshade's thoughts or know her mind, but she could sense her presence and movements. Mistaya wondered if it was the same for Nightshade, and knew somehow it was not.

On this night the witch did not retire as usual, but came instead to sit with Mistaya before the fire. In silence she watched the girl work, watched her knead and roll the dough, form it into patties, wash and peel the vegetables, and place all of it in a pan with oil to cook. She continued to watch after Mistaya removed the meal from the fire and ate it. She sat as still as stone, looking over as if what she was observing were the most interesting thing she had ever seen. Mistaya let her sit. She knew that when Nightshade was ready to speak, she would do so. She knew as well that Nightshade had something to say.

It wasn't until the pan and dishes were washed and put away in the large wooden chest that sat out in the middle of the clearing as if it belonged there that the witch finally said, "I am pleased with you, Mistaya. I am encouraged by your progress."

The girl looked up. "Thank you."

"Today's effort was especially good. What you created was quite wonderful. Are you as satisfied with it as I am?"

"Yes," Mistaya lied.

Nightshade's cold white face lifted to the haze as if searching for stars and then lowered again to the fire. "I will tell you the truth. I was not certain you were equal to the task I set for you. I was afraid that you might not be able to master the magic."

Her eyes shifted, fixing on the girl. "It was clear to me from the first that your magic was strong. It was clear that your potential for using it was virtually limitless. But possession of the magic is never enough. There are intangibles that limit the user's success. Desire is one. Determination. Focus and a sense of purpose. Magic is like a great cat. You can harness and direct its energy, but you must never look away, and you must never let it see fear in your eyes."

"I am not afraid of the magic," Mistaya declared firmly. "It belongs to me. It feels like an old friend."

Nightshade gave her a brief, small smile. "Yes, I can see that. You treat it as you might a friend. You are comfortable with it yet do not regard it lightly. Your sense of balance is very good." She paused. "You remind me of myself when I was your age."

Mistaya blinked. "I do?"

Nightshade looked through and past her into some distant place. "Very much so. It seems odd to contemplate now, but I was your age once. I was a girl discovering her latent talents. I was a novice in search of a life, in quest of my limits as a witch. I was younger than you when I first discovered I possessed magic. It was a long time ago."

She trailed off, still looking away into the darkness. Mistaya shifted closer. "Tell me about it," she encouraged.

Nightshade shrugged. "The past is gone."

"But I would like to hear. I want to know how you felt. It might help me understand myself. Please, tell me."

The strange red eyes shifted back into the present, fixing on the girl. They penetrated with such ferocity that for a moment Mistaya was frightened. Then the glare changed to something worn and faded.

"I was born in the fairy mists," the Witch of the Deep Fell began, her tall, spare form as still as moon shadows on a windless night. She brushed at her raven hair with her slender fingers. "Like you, I inherited the blood of more than one world. Like you, I inherited the gift. My mother was a sorceress come out of one of the worlds that border on Landover, a world where magic is feared. She was very powerful, and she could cross back and forth between worlds through the mists. She was not a fairy creature, but she could walk among them comfortably. One day, while she was crossing between worlds, she met my father. My father was a changeling, a creature who had no true form but adopted whatever form he chose to suit his needs. He saw my mother and fell in love with her. He made himself into something that attracted her. A wolf, all black hair and teeth. In the end he seduced her and made her his own."

Her voice was flat and devoid of emotion, but there was an edge to it that Mistaya did not miss. "He kept her with him for a time, then abandoned her and went on to other interests. He was a fickle and irresponsible creature, like all of the fairy folk, unable to comprehend the demands and responsibilities of love. I was born of that union, conceived in the madness of spring light when the second cycle rounds and the shards of winter spill into melting ice."

Her gaze went away again. Her words, though poetic and lyrical, were nevertheless incomprehensible to the girl.

"My father took the shape of a wolf when he conceived me with my mother. My mother embraced him as a beast and was, I think, his equal in fury and passion." She blinked once, dismissing some picture that formed in her mind. "I took from their coupling a part of each, beast and madwoman, fairy and human, magic of one world and magic of the other. I was born with eyes that could freeze you alive. I was born with the ability to transform myself into a beast. I was born with disdain for life and death."

She looked at Mistaya. "I was a child still, and I was soon alone. My father was gone before I came into the world. My mother gave birth to me, but then she was taken away."

She trailed off, the echo of her words lacing the silence with bitterness. Mistaya waited, knowing better than to speak.

"The fairies condemned her for her efforts to become one of them. She had mated with a fairy and conceived a child, and that was not allowed. She was an outcast for this. She was sent from the mists and forbidden to return. She begged the fairies to reconsider. She wanted me to have the training and experience that only they could offer. She wanted me to have my father's life as well as hers. She wanted everything for me. But she was turned away. She was sent back into her own world. It was a death sentence. She had been able for too long to travel the mists, to cross from one world to another, to fly where she chose. Confinement in one world was unbearable. She bore it as long as she could. Then she threw caution to the winds and tried crossing once more through the mists. She went in, and she never came out. She disappeared like smoke on the wind."

Nightshade's gaze was gathering focus once more. The force of her words was palpable. "Do you see how alike we are? Like you, it was left for me to discover on my own who I was. Like you, the truth of my birthright was hidden from me. I was given over to other people to raise, a man and a woman who did not understand my needs, who did not recognize the magic growing within me. They kept me for as long as I would let them, and then I ran away. I had begun to sense my power, but I did not yet comprehend its uses. There were stirrings, but I could give them no voice. Like you, I grew in the fairy way, in spurts that eclipsed human measure. The man and the woman were frightened of me. If I had stayed, they might have killed me."

"Like you," she was on the verge of saying, but did not. Nevertheless, Mistaya could hear the whisper of the words in the silence, and she was startled by them. She was not like Nightshade, of course. Not in that way, at least. She could see it quite plainly. Yet Nightshade felt an overwhelming need to believe that they shared more than they did. There was something happening here that the girl did not understand, and it made her uneasy and cautious.

Nightshade's eyes glittered in the firelight. "I escaped into a forest that bordered on the fairy mists, a shelter for those who were part of both worlds and accepted in neither. I found companions there, some of one species, some of another. We were not friends, but we had much in common. We were outlaws without reason; we were condemned for who we were. We taught each other what we knew and learned what we could. We explored our talents. We uncovered the secrets hidden within us. It was dangerous to do so, for we were unskilled, and some of our secrets could kill. More than a few of us died. Some went mad. I was fortunate to escape both fates and emerge the mistress of my talent. I came away a full-grown woman and a witch of great power. I found and mastered knowledge."

Wood from the fire crackled suddenly, sending sparks flying into the air. Mistaya started, but Nightshade did not move. She stayed frozen against the firelight, rigid with concentration.

Her eyes fixed on Mistaya. "I was younger than you when I learned of my power. I was alone. I did not have another to guide me, as you have me. But we are alike, Mistaya. I was hard inside, and nothing could break me. I was stone. I would not be lied to. I would not be cheated or tricked. I understood what I wanted, and I set about finding ways to obtain it. I see all that in you. I see such determination. You will do whatever you set your mind to, and you will not be deterred. You will listen to reason but will not necessarily be dissuaded from a course of action because of it, not if what you covet is important to you."

Mistaya nodded not so much in agreement, for she was not at all sure she agreed with this assessment, as in encouragement. She wanted to hear more. She was fascinated.

"After a time," Nightshade said slowly, "I determined that I would go into the fairy mists. I had been banished, but that was before I had discovered the extent of my powers. Now, I felt, things were different. I belonged among the fairies. It was my right to travel between worlds as my mother had once done. I went to the edge of the mists and called. I did so for a very long time. No answer came. Finally, I simply entered the mists, determined that I would confront those who had banished me. They found me at once. They gave me no hearing. They refused me out of hand. I was cast out, unable to prevent it despite my magic."

Her mouth had grown tight and hard. "I did not give up. I went back again and again, unwilling to accede to their wishes, determined in the end that I would die first. Years passed. I lived several human lifetimes but did not age. I was impervious to time's dictates. I was more fairy than human. I belonged in the mists. Still, I was not allowed to enter.

"Then I found a rift that let me come into the mists unseen. I changed shape to disguise myself, to keep from being discovered. I entered the mist and hid among its lesser creatures. No one recognized me. I stayed first as one thing, then as another, always keeping carefully back from the light of discovery. I became accepted. I found I could pass freely among the fairies. I began to use magic as they did. I worked my spells and performed my conjuring, and I lived as they did. My deception had worked. I was one of them."

She smiled, cynical and bitter. "And then, like my mother, I fell in love." Her voice was suddenly very small and brittle. "I found a creature so beautiful, so desirable, that I could not help myself. I had to have him. I was desperate to be his. I followed him, befriended him, companioned with him, and in the end gave myself to him completely. To achieve this, I was forced to reveal myself. When I did so, he spurned me instantly. He betrayed me. He exposed my presence. The fairies were not kind. I was banished out of hand. Because I fell in love. Because I used poor judgment."

One eyebrow arched in bitter reflection. "Like my mother."

She was almost crying, Mistaya realized suddenly. There were no tears, but the girl could feel the knife edge of the witch's pain, sharp and close against her skin.

"I was sent here," Nightshade finished. "To the Deep Fell. Banished from the fairy mists, banished from my homeland. Banished to Landover to live out my life. I had used my magic and left my mark upon their world, and I wasn't one of them. I had transgressed. So I was punished. I was placed at the gateway of all the worlds I could never enter. I was placed at the edge of the mists I could never pass through." Her hands clasped, and her fingers tightened into knots. Her head shook slowly from side to side. "No, the fairies were not kind."

"It seems very unfair," Mistaya offered quietly.

Nightshade laughed. "The word has no meaning for the fairy people. They have no conception of it. There is only what is allowed and what isn't. If you think about it, the whole idea of fairness is a fool's fiction. Look at our world, here in Landover. Fairness is determined by those who wield the power to deny it. Invocation of its use is a beggar's plea for help when all else fails. 'Be fair with me!' How pitiful and hopeless!"

She spit out the words in disgust. Then she bent forward with sudden intent. "I learned something from what was done to me, Mistaya. I learned never to beg, never to expect kindness, never to rely on chance or good fortune. My magic sustains me. My power gives me strength. Rely on these and you will be protected."

"And do not fall in love," Mistaya added solemnly.

"No," the witch agreed, and there was such fury in her face that she was momentarily unrecognizable, a beast of the sort into which she claimed she could transform herself. "No," she repeated, the word bound in iron, and Mistaya knew she was thinking of someone in particular, of a time and place quite close, of an event that still burned inside her with a white-hot heat. "No, never again."

Mistaya sat motionless in the dwindling firelight and let Nightshade's rage drain away, willing herself to be little more than another shadow in the dark, nonthreatening and inconsequential. Had she revealed herself to be anything else, it seemed that the witch's rage might have swallowed her whole.

Nightshade looked at her as if reading her mind, then gave her a disarming smile. "We are alike," she said once more, as if needing to reassure herself. "You and I, Mistaya. The magic binds us, witches first and always, born with power that others can only covet and never possess. It is our blessing and curse to live apart. It is our fate."

Her hand lifted and filled the air with emerald light, a dust that spread against the darkness and fell away like glitter.

Later, when she rolled herself into her blankets, Mistaya was still thinking of what Nightshade had revealed to her. So much misery, bitterness, and solitude in the other's dark life. So much anger. *Like me*, the witch had repeated over and over again. *You and I.*

Mistaya's uncertainty grew as she pondered the words. Perhaps there was more truth to their claim than she was willing to allow. She had not thought so, but she was beginning to wonder. Since she was a witch, too, perhaps she belonged here with Nightshade.

She was so troubled by the possibility that she only just remembered to call Haltwhistle before she fell asleep.

Juggernaut

Dawn brought a change in the weather in the lake country, and when Ben and Willow awoke, a slow, steady rain was falling. They dressed; ate a light breakfast of fruit, bread and jam, and goat's milk; wrapped themselves in their travel cloaks; and went out to find the River Master. Elderew was misty and shadowed beneath a ceiling of dark clouds, and the city's canopy of rain-drenched boughs shed chilly droplets on them as they moved along the deserted trail toward the city. They did not hurry. The River Master would have been advised by now that they were awake. He would come to meet them before they were required to ask for him, because that was the way he was.

Ben glanced about surreptitiously for the Ardsheal but did not see it. He could feel its presence, though. He could sense it watching from the gloom.

The River Master appeared as they neared the city center, standing alone in a clearing through which the trail passed. He greeted Ben with a nod and Willow with a brief embrace, neither gesture offering much in the way of warmth, and advised them that their horses were waiting. He did not ask if they would like to stay longer. Now that he had given them the Ardsheal, he expected them to continue the search for Mistaya. He elicited their promise to keep him advised on their progress. Bunion appeared with Jurisdiction and Crane,

160

his gnarled body hunched and dripping in the gloom, eyes narrowed to yellow slits. As Ben and Willow mounted, the River Master put aside his reserve long enough to declare that if he was needed in the effort to reclaim his granddaughter, they had only to send for him and he would come at once. It was an unexpected deviation from his deliberate distancing of himself from them. Ben and Willow were surprised but did not show it. They took him at his word and rode out.

Wood sprites met them at the edge of the old growth leading down from Elderew to guide them back through the swamp and timber mass that warded the city. Rain continued to fall, a drizzle that turned the ground beneath their horses' hooves sodden and slick. When their guides had returned them to the more lightly forested country below Elderew, they paused to rest before continuing on.

"Have you seen it yet this morning?" Ben asked Willow as they passed an ale skin back and forth while standing down from their horses beneath the canopy of the trees.

"No," she replied. "But Bunion has. He said it is tracking us back in the shadows, keeping pace. Bunion doesn't like having it along any better than I do."

Ben glanced over. Bunion was crouched to one side in a covering of trees, looking disgruntled. "He certainly appears unhappy, even for him."

"He considers himself your bodyguard. The presence of the Ardsheal suggests that he isn't capable of doing his job."

Ben looked at her. "You don't think the Ardsheal should be here, either, do you?"

"As a matter of fact, that isn't what I think at all. I think the Ardsheal will do a better job of protecting you than anyone." She gave him a long, cool look. "That doesn't mean I like having it along, though."

He nodded. "You said as much last night. Why is that?"

She hesitated. "I will tell you later. Tonight." She was silent for a moment. "I told Bunion that the Ardsheal was a gift from my father and that it would have been impolite and possibly dangerous to refuse it. Bunion accepted that."

Ben looked at the kobold again. It was staring back at him, yellow eyes glittering. When it saw Ben looking, it smiled like a hungry alligator.

"Well, I hope you're right," he said absently. His gaze shifted to meet hers. "I've been thinking. Should we try to contact the Earth Mother? She always seems to know what is happening in Landover. Perhaps she could give us some insight into what's become of Mistaya and the others. Perhaps she knows something of Rydall."

Rain dripped off the edge of Willow's hood onto her nose, and she pulled the hood forward for better protection. "I gave thought to that. But the Earth Mother would have come to me by now in my dreams if she had any help to give. Mistaya is important to her, a promise of some special fulfillment. She would not let her be harmed if there was anything she could do to prevent it."

Ben prodded a bit of rotting wood with his boot. "I wish some of these people would be more consistent with their help," he muttered sourly.

She gave him a small smile. "Help is a gift that one must never grow to expect. Now, where do we go from here?"

He shrugged and looked off into the trees again. He hated that he couldn't see the Ardsheal. It was bad enough being shadowed by his enemies. Did he have to put up with being shadowed by his protector as well?

He sighed. "Well, I can't see any reason to go back to Sterling Silver. If we do, Rydall will just send another monster. And we won't be any closer to finding Mistaya." He frowned as if questioning his own reasoning. "I thought we might go into the Greensward. Kallendbor knows every adversary Landover has ever faced. He has fought against most of them. Perhaps he will know something of Rydall and Marnhull. Perhaps he will have heard something that will help us find Mistaya."

"Kallendbor isn't to be trusted," she advised him quietly.

He nodded. "True. But he has no reason to favor an invading army. Besides, he owes me for sparing him worse punishment than I gave when he sided with the Gorse. And he knows it. I think it's worth a try."

"Perhaps." She did not look convinced. "But you should be especially careful where he is concerned."

"I will," he assured her, wondering how much more careful he needed to be now that he had the Paladin, Bunion, and the Ardsheal all standing guard over him.

They remounted and rode on. Bunion, advised of their new destination, scurried ahead through the trees, scouting the land they would pass through, leaving them to the temporary care of their invisible bodyguard. The Ardsheal, however, stayed hidden. The day stretched away with languid slowness, morning turning into midday, midday into afternoon. Still the rain continued. They moved northeast toward the Greensward, the trees thinning as the lake country gave way to the hills below Sterling Silver. They stopped for lunch at a stream, where they took shelter beneath an old cedar. Rain dripped off the sagging limbs, a steady patter on the muddied ground. The world around them was cool and damp and still. When the meal was finished, they rode on. They didn't see another traveler all day.

Nightfall brought them to the edge of the Greensward, where the grasslands spread away through the provinces of Landover's lesser Lords to the Melchor. Sunset was an iron-gray glimmer in the west above the distant mountains, its light hammered tin reflecting off the advancing night. Ben and Willow made camp in a grove of cherry and Bonnie Blues on a rise that overlooked the plains. Bunion returned to share dinner, a cold meal prepared without the benefit of a fire, and then he was gone again. The Ardsheal did not appear at all.

When night had fallen and they were alone in its deep silence, the rains having abated to a damp mist that floated across the grasslands like ghost robes, Ben put his arms around Willow, pulled her back against him so that they were both staring out at the gloom, and said, "Tell me about the Ardsheal."

She did not say anything at first, resting rigid and unmoving against him as his arms cradled her. He could feel her breathing, the rise and fall of her breast, the small whisper of air from her lips. He waited patiently, looking past the veil of her hair to the thickening roil of mist beyond.

"There have always been Ardsheals," she said finally. "They were created to protect the once-fairy after they left the mists and came into the world of humans. The Ardsheals were an old magic, one born of earth lore, and because they were elementals, they could be summoned from anywhere. The once-fairy used them only rarely, for they were destroyers, cast of harsh purpose and desperate need. When the threat was so great that the once-fairy feared there would be loss of life among their people, the Ardsheals were called in. A few were usually all it took. In years long past, before the old King, when Landover was newly conceived and birthing yet its lands and peoples, there were wars between humans and once-fairy. Humans occupied Landover first; the once-fairy came after and were regarded as invaders. In the battles fought, Ardsheals were summoned to do battle against creatures conjured by wizards who served the humans."

She stopped, gathering her thoughts. "That was a long time ago. Since then, Ardsheals have been used only rarely. The last time was not long ago. It happened when one of Abbadon's demons penetrated the wards of Elderew disguised as a once-fairy. It was a sorcerous being, a changeling who sought entry for its fellows through the heart of the lake country. The magic harbored there, it reasoned, would then belong to them. So it disguised itself and came into the city, and it tried to kill my father."

"Because he was the River Master?" Ben asked softly.

"Yes, because of that. Because he was the leader of his people." Willow's words were almost inaudible. "The demon tried and failed. But in its attempt to kill my father, it destroyed a handful of others, including several children. The demon escaped. There was terrible panic among the once-fairy. And rage. My father and the elders summoned five of the Ardsheals and sent them in search of the demon. The Ardsheals tracked the creature from house to house, caught it at last in one of its many disguises, and killed it."

She took a deep breath. "It was my house it was hiding in when they found it. It had disguised itself as one of my sisters. It was very clever. It had worked its way back to the one place it thought it might be safe: the River Master's own house. But the Ardsheals were relentless. They could track by touch, smell, taste, the smallest sound, even by a change of heat caused by the casting of a shadow. Nevertheless, they were not infallible. Not this day. They had been conjured quickly and imperfectly. Haste led to carelessness. The demon took several shapes before he took the one in which they caught him. The one he took before that was of my sister Kaijelln. The Ardsheals were closing on it by then, and when they came into our house, bursting through the entry, tearing apart the doors as if they were cloth, they thought the demon was Kaijelln still.

"And so," she whispered, her voice shaking now, "they killed her without taking time to discover the truth. They acted on instinct. They killed her right in front of me."

Ben swallowed against the dryness in his throat. "Your father couldn't stop them?"

Willow shook her head. "They were too quick. Too powerful. An Ardsheal, when it attacks, is unstoppable. It was so that day with Kaijelln. She was gone in the blink of an eye."

They were silent for a long time then, Ben holding the

sylph tight against him, neither of them moving, eyes staring
out into the darkness. Somewhere a night bird called, and another responded. Water dripped from leaves in the stillness.

"We should have left it behind," Ben said finally. "We
should have refused it."

"No!" Willow's voice was hard and certain this time.
"Nothing can stand against an Ardsheal. Nothing! You need it
to protect you against whatever else Rydall chooses to send.
Besides, my father will have taken great pains to make certain
that this one does what it is supposed to do and nothing
more."

She twisted suddenly in his arms and looked directly at
him. "Don't you see? It doesn't matter that I am afraid of it.
It only matters that it will keep you alive." She leaned forward
until her face was only inches away. "I love you that much,
Ben Holiday."

Then she kissed him and went on kissing him until he
forgot about everything else.

At dawn they rode out once more. The day was gray
and misty, but the rains had moved on. Bunion had come back
during the night and this time traveled with them as they
moved out onto the open grasslands, the kobold skittering
ahead eagerly to lead the way. The Ardsheal appeared as well,
emerging from the forest to take up a position some twenty
yards to their rear. It stayed there as they journeyed, attached
to them like a shadow. They watched it for a while, glancing
back over their shoulders, marveling at the easy, fluid motion
of its stride. It wore nothing, and its body was virtually
featureless—arms, legs, feet, hands, torso, and head smooth
and slick with the damp, skin stretched seamless and taut, eyes
black holes boring straight ahead into the gloom. It did not
acknowledge them as it traveled; it never spoke. It stopped
when they did, waited patiently for them to begin moving
again, then resumed its steady pace.

By midmorning they quit looking for it. By midday they stopped thinking about it completely.

The grasslands were carpeted thickly with mist, and the towns and farms of the people of the Greensward and the castle fortresses of the Lords materialized with ghostly abruptness before them. They skirted all, intent on reaching Rhyndweir and Kallendbor by nightfall. They bought hot soup from a vendor at a market on the edge of a small town and sipped it from tin cups while they rode. Bunion finished his in the blink of an eye and was off. The Ardsheal stayed back in the gloom and ate nothing.

Ben and Willow traveled in silence, riding side by side, content to be company for each other, not needing to speak. Ben spent much of the day thinking on the tale of the Ardsheal and Kaijelln. He found himself comparing the Ardsheal to the Paladin, both destroyers, both perfect fighting machines, both in his service and therefore his responsibility for whatever damage they might do. The comparison bothered him more than he could say. It made him ponder anew what his transformation into the Paladin was doing to his psyche. Would he someday reach the point where the difference between them was no longer discernible? Would he then become like the Ardsheal, a passionless, remorseless killing machine, a creature without a conscience, serving only its master? He found himself thinking about how he had felt when, as the Paladin, he had been trapped within the Tangle Box, how he had lacked identity beyond his role as King's champion, how he had been lost to everything but his skills as a warrior. The thoughts spun and twisted together with insidious intent, making him question anew his strength of purpose in the battle with Rydall's monsters. He struggled with his thoughts but kept the struggle carefully to himself.

By late afternoon they had come in sight of Rhyndweir. The castle of Kallendbor rose on a bluff at the juncture of the Anhalt and Piercenal rivers, walls, parapets, and towers lifting darkly above the grasslands. A town lay below the castle gates, bustling and crowded, filled with buyers and sellers of goods: tradesmen, farmers, trappers, and craftsmen of all sorts. Rain had begun falling again, a gray drizzle that mingled with the mist and shrouded buildings and people alike, turning them to dark, uncertain images in the gloom.

Ben and Willow had come with no fanfare, no escort, and no advance notice. There was no one expecting them and no one to guide them to the palace. But this fit with Ben's intent. He wanted to surprise Kallendbor, to catch Rhyndweir's Lord unprepared so that he would be forced to improvise a response to Ben's coming. There was a better chance of enlisting his cooperation if he was not given time to weigh the gain and loss.

Ben slowed when they reached the Anhalt and the bridge that spanned it to the castle. He called Bunion back to him, then turned to the Ardsheal and beckoned it close. To his surprise, it did as it was asked. It came to stand directly next to him, face flat and expressionless, eyes staring straight ahead. Ben arched his eyebrow at Willow, told them all to stay close, and nudged Jurisdiction forward.

They crossed the bridge and entered the town, riding through the people and rain as the afternoon light faded toward murky dark. People were hurrying home now, so few paid much attention to the riders and their footmen. Those who did looked quickly away. An Ardsheal and a kobold were not something they wished to ask questions about.

The little company reached the castle gates and was quickly halted by the guards. There were wide eyes and protestations of all sorts, but Ben simply ordered the nearest functionary to guide them to the palace. Word would be sent ahead in any event, and he did not care to wait for its arrival. One commander, braver than his companions, questioned the presence of the Ardsheal and was silenced by Ben's curt reply. The Ardsheal was the High Lord's personal guard. Where the

High Lord went—or his Queen—so went the Ardsheal. The commander gave ground, and they were allowed to enter.

They rode through gateways and cobblestone passages, up several levels of defenses, and past quarters for the soldiers who served Kallendbor to the grassy flats on which the palace sat. Their guide tried to slow the pace to give time for word to reach his Lord and for his Lord to prepare, but Ben pushed Jurisdiction ahead and almost rode the lagging functionary down. In minutes they were before the palace entrance and dismounting.

To his credit, Kallendbor came out immediately to greet them. He was alone save for the doorman who stood waiting nervously at the entrance; apparently there had been no time to summon retainers. The Lord of Rhyndweir was a tall, raw-boned man with fiery red hair and a temper to match. Battle scars crisscrossed his hands and forearms and marred an otherwise handsome face. He wore a broadsword strapped to his waist as if it were a natural part of his dress. He was flushed as he approached and his eyes were angry, but he gave his guests a deep, respectful bow.

"Had I known you were coming, High Lord, I would have prepared a better welcome," he added, almost hiding his petulance. He took in Bunion with a glance and then for the first time saw the Ardsheal. "What is the meaning of this?" he snapped, and now his anger was obvious. "Why do you bring this creature here?"

Ben glanced at the Ardsheal as if he had forgotten it was there. "It was a gift from the River Master. It serves as my protector. Shall we go inside where it's dry and talk it over?"

Kallendbor hesitated and looked as if he might object, then apparently thought better of it. He led them out of the rain into the front hall and then down a long corridor to a sitting room dominated by a vast stone fireplace that rose from floor to ceiling. The blaze from the logs burning in the hearth threw heat and light from wall to wall and made their shadows

dance as they crossed to chairs to sit before it. Bunion had remained to see to the horses. The Ardsheal stopped by the door
and merged with the shadows that crowded forward from
the hall.

Kallendbor seated himself across from Ben and Willow.
His anger had not abated. "Ardsheals have been the enemy of
the people of the Greensward for centuries, High Lord. They
are not welcome here. Surely you must know that."

"Times change." Ben looked at the empty glasses set next
to the decanter of amber liquid on the table between them and
waited for Kallendbor to fill two and pass them to himself and
Willow. The Lord of Rhyndweir's lips were set in a tight line,
and his great hands were knotted into fists.

"Are you quite settled now, High Lord?" he snapped.

Ben nodded. "Thank you, yes." He ignored the other's
curt tone. "I apologize for bringing the Ardsheal into Rhyndweir, but circumstances dictate unusual caution just now. I assume you have heard of the threat against my life."

Kallendbor brushed at the air dismissively. "By Rydall of
Marnhull? I have heard. Has he pressed the matter?"

"Two attacks so far."

Kallendbor studied him. "Two. With five more promised,
I understand. But nothing can stand against the Paladin. And
now you have an Ardsheal as well. They should keep you safe
enough."

Ben leaned forward. "Will you be terribly disappointed if
they do?"

For the first time Kallendbor smiled, a bitter and sardonic
grimace. "We are not good friends, High Lord. I have no particular reason to wish you well. But Rydall of Marnhull is no
friend, either."

"Do you know him, then?" Ben pressed.

Kallendbor shook his head. "I know nothing of him. He
must come from somewhere outside Landover."

"But if so, how did he cross through the fairy mists?"

"As you did, I suppose." Kallendbor shrugged. "He used magic."

Ben sipped at his drink. A rather sweet wine. He would not have expected it of Kallendbor. At his side Willow stirred, impatient with the conversation, anxious to be finished with it. She did not like Kallendbor or Rhyndweir or much of anything about the Greensward. She was a once-fairy, and the Lords of the Greensward had never been their friends.

Ben looked over at the fire momentarily, then back at Kallendbor. "This is a brief visit. One night to dry out from the rains, and then we will be on our way. We will take our meals in our rooms, so you won't have to trouble yourself with entertaining us. The Ardsheal will stay close to us and out of sight. Bunion can join us as well."

Kallendbor nodded, and there was a look of obvious relief on his face. "Whatever pleases you, High Lord. I'll send hot water for baths."

Ben nodded. "There is one thing." He leaned forward so that the full weight of his gaze was resting on Kallendbor. "If I thought for one minute that you knew anything of Rydall and were keeping it from me, I would have you in chains."

Kallendbor stiffened, and his face went hot with rage. "High Lord, I do not have to—"

"Because I am reminded of how you sided with the Gorse against me not so very long ago," Ben continued, cutting him short. "I had every cause to have you exiled for life and stripped of your holdings. I had cause to have you put to death. But you are a strong leader and a man who can bring considerable weight to bear among your peers, and I value your service to the throne. I did not want the Greensward to lose you. Besides, I believe you were misguided in that matter. All of us were to some extent."

He paused. "But if it were to happen again, I would not hesitate to rethink my position where you are concerned, Lord Kallendbor. I want you to remember that."

Kallendbor gave a curt, barely perceptible nod. He could barely bring himself to speak. "Is that all, High Lord?"

"No." Ben held his gaze. "Rydall has taken our daughter. Your spies may not have told you that. She is a hostage until the Paladin either defeats or is defeated by the creatures he sends to do battle. I search for her now. But there is no sign of Rydall or Marnhull. No one seems able to help, yourself included. I am determined to get my daughter back, Kallendbor. If you can help, it would be wise for you to do so."

He waited. Kallendbor was silent for a moment. "I do not need to take children as hostages to do battle with my enemies," he managed finally.

He seemed to have trouble speaking the words. Ben wondered why. "Then you will send for me if you hear anything that will help me find Mistaya?" he pressed.

Kallendbor's face closed down, flat and expressionless. There was a hard look in his eyes. "You have my word that I will do whatever I can to see your daughter safely home. I can promise no more."

Ben nodded slowly. "I will take you at your word."

There was a long, harsh silence. Then Kallendbor shifted uncomfortably in his seat and said, "If you are ready, I will show you to your rooms."

For the moment at least they had each had enough of the other.

Midnight came and went. Rain poured down out of the heavens, brought to the grasslands by thunderheads that had broken free of the barrier of the mountains and had crossed in the dark. Lightning seared the black skies in white-hot streaks that dazzled and stunned. Below Rhyndweir's walls the turgid waters of the Anhalt and the Piercenal churned against their banks, swollen and clogged with debris.

Ben Holiday slept uneasily. Twice already he had awakened and risen to look about. Silence had woken him the first time, the storm's fury the second. Both times he had crossed to the doorway and stood listening, then had walked to the windows of the bedchamber tower and looked down. They were housed in the west tower in rooms reserved for important visitors, high up in the palace, away from the household staff and other guests. From their windows it was well over a hundred feet to the rocks of the bluff and the waters of the Anhalt. From their door it was a long climb down a winding set of stairs past several other floors and unoccupied rooms to the hall that led back to the main part of the castle. As was the custom, the rooms selected for the High Lord of Landover were separate and secure, offering but a single approach.

On this night, however, Ben could not stop thinking that they also offered only one way out.

Still, he was safe here. Bunion kept watch just outside the door, and the Ardsheal roamed the stairs and hall below. Without, lightning flashed, thunder boomed, and the wind howled across the plains, a vast immutable force. But the storm did not penetrate to where Ben and Willow slept, save for the sound of its passing, and there was nothing else to make the High Lord wakeful.

Yet he was.

And when the heavy thudding came from the stairs and Bunion shrieked in warning, he was already awake and sitting up in the bed. Willow lifted herself beside him instantly, her face stricken, her eyes wide. The iron-bound oak door flew inward, splintered into shards that barely managed to hang together from the shattered bindings. Something huge and dark filled the doorway, tearing at the stone walls that hindered its passage. Bunion clung to the thing, ripping at it with teeth and claws, but it didn't even seem to notice the kobold. Into the bedchamber it came, hammering apart stone and mortar, shredding the lintels and the last of the mangled door. Lightning flashed and lit up the monstrous apparition as Ben and Willow stared in disbelief.

It was a giant encased in metal from head to foot.

My God, Ben thought in stunned surprise, it's a robot!

Iron creaked and groaned as it swung toward them, arms lifting, fingers grasping. The creature was formed of metal plates and fastenings. A robot! But there were no robots in Landover, no mechanical men of any kind! No one here had ever even heard of such a thing!

Willow screamed and tumbled from the bed, looking for room to maneuver. Ben scrambled back, slipped on the bedding, and fell. His head cracked hard on the wooden headboard, and his eyes were filled with bright lights and tears. *"Ben!"* he heard Willow scream, but he could not make himself respond. He knew he should do something, but the blow to his head had shaken him so that he could not think what it was.

A weapon! He needed a weapon!

Through the blur of his tears he saw the robot fling Bunion away as if the kobold were made of paper. Massive iron feet thudded in heavy cadence as the monster closed on the bed, reached down for the footboard, and tore it away. The bed dropped with a lurch, and Ben rolled free, trying to gain his feet. Bunion attacked again, and this time the robot slapped him away so hard that the kobold struck the wall with an audible crunch, crumpled to the floor, and lay still.

"Ben, call the Paladin!" Willow cried out, throwing loose bedding and broken pieces of wood at the monster in a futile effort to slow it.

Then the Ardsheal appeared, flying through the doorway out of the darkness beyond, slamming into their attacker from behind. The force of the blow caused the robot to sway momentarily before turning back. The Ardsheal closed fearlessly with the giant, grappling with it in an effort to bring it down.

Lightning flashed once more, outlining the combatants as they fought for footing across the chamber floor. Willow darted past them, trying to reach Ben. Ben was on his feet, leaning dazedly against the far wall. Blood ran down his temple. He groped for the medallion so that he could summon the Paladin, but to his horror he couldn't find it. The medallion and the chain that had bound it about his neck were gone!

Back against the stone wall crashed the robot and the Ardsheal, locked together in mortal combat, caught up in their terrible struggle like great bears. The Ardsheal fastened its hands on one of the robot's great metal forearms and wrenched at it with terrific force. There was a frightening screech of metal giving way, and suddenly the lower arm and hand separated and fell to the floor with a crash. Instantly the robot wrapped both arms about the Ardsheal, locked its good hand to the remnants of its shattered arm, and tightened its arms in a crushing grip. The Ardsheal stiffened and threw back its head. Something inside it broke with an audible series of snaps.

Willow grabbed up a piece of the shattered door, charged forward with a cry, and slammed the makeshift club across the robot's face. The robot did not seem to notice, still concentrating all its efforts on the Ardsheal. Able to see again, Ben surged forward, his head clear. He pulled Willow away, snatched up a large piece of the bedding, threw it over the robot's head, and yanked back on the ends. The metal giant twisted its head, then started to swing about, still grasping the stricken Ardsheal.

But one boot caught on the bedding, and it tripped. To regain its balance, it was forced to release its grip.

Instantly, the Ardsheal broke free. A dark liquid ran from its mouth and nose, and its joints looked to have come loose from their pinnings. Yet it did not seem to feel its injuries. It attacked anew, hammering into the robot with both fists and knocking it backward toward the open windows. As the robot reeled away, the Ardsheal catapulted into it with a ferocious charge that carried both combatants into the metal-barred opening. Stone and mortar gave way beneath their combined weight, and the iron bars broke loose. The window frame and part of the surrounding wall shattered.

Then the Ardsheal locked itself about the robot, drove it through the opening, and both creatures tumbled out into the night.

Ben and Willow reached the rain-swept opening a moment later, too late to see them fall but in time to hear them smash against the rocks below and tumble into the river. Rain drenched their faces and shoulders as they leaned out into the dark, peering down. Lightning flashed, revealing the water-slick castle walls, the empty rocks, and the surging river. Nothing moved on the rocks. Nothing could be seen in the river.

Ben drew Willow back into the room and hugged her close. She buried her face in his shoulder, and he could feel her drawing in great gulps of air.

“Damn Rydall!” he swore in her ear, trying to keep from shaking.

Her fingers dug into his arm as she nodded in fierce, voiceless agreement.

Dragon Sight

It was afterward that Ben discovered he was still wearing the medallion. He looked down and there it was, hanging by its chain from his neck. For a moment he couldn't believe it. He held it up and stared at it. The familiar graven image of the Paladin riding out of Sterling Silver at sunrise glimmered back. He had been so certain he had lost it. He had looked for it, and it wasn't there.

"Ben, what's wrong?" Willow asked quickly, seeing the look on his face.

He shook his head, letting the medallion fall back into place. "Nothing. I was just . . ."

He trailed off, confused. The blow on the head when he had stumbled must have stunned him worse than he thought. But he had been so sure! He had reached for the medallion, and it hadn't been there!

Willow let the matter drop, moved to the clothes chest, and brought out clean robes. Seconds later a contingent of palace guards came charging up the stairs, weapons at the ready, responding finally to the attack. Ben and Willow were working on Bunion by then and ignored them. The kobold was banged up considerably but otherwise appeared to be all right. Kobolds are tough little fellows, Ben thought admiringly, relieved that his friend had not been seriously injured, thinking that almost anyone else would have been killed.

177

The palace guards poked around the room, stared out through the gap in the wall into the rain-streaked night, and mostly looked uncomfortable with the fact that they were forced to be there at all. It was a reflection on them that the attack had almost succeeded, and they were wary of both the High Lord's and Kallendbor's reactions to their failure to prevent it.

Ben, for his part, was too preoccupied to concern himself with casting blame; he was still mulling over the suddenness of the assault and the circumstances that had surrounded it. But Kallendbor, bare-chested and broadsword in hand when he burst into the room, was less charitable. After hearing a shortened version of the attack from Ben, he berated everyone within shouting distance. Then he dispatched one search party to the riverbanks below to discover if any trace of the Ardsheal or Rydall's monster could be found. Others he sent throughout the castle to make certain nothing else threatened. Ben, Willow, and Bunion were moved to other rooms, and guards were ordered to keep close watch over them for the remainder of the night. Obviously ill at ease with what had happened and anxious to avoid staying longer in their company, Kallendbor bid them a gruff good night and went off to sleep.

An exhausted Willow and Bunion were quick to follow.

Ben, however, stayed awake for a long time thinking about this latest monster. Two things bothered him, and he could reconcile neither.

The first was how the creature had gotten into the castle in the first place. How had it managed to slip past Kallendbor's guards and the Ardsheal as well? Something that big and cumbersome should never have been able to do so. It should not even have gotten past the front gates. Unless, of course, it hadn't come through them in the first place but had gotten into the palace by use of magic, which was the only conclusion that made any sense. And that made him wonder— although admittedly this was more of a stretch—if magic had

also been used during the attack to make him think the medallion was lost. Otherwise, why hadn't he been able to find
it—even stunned by the blow to his head, even in the frenzy
of the moment—when it was hanging right there around
his neck?

The second thing bothering him was that something was
vaguely familiar about that robot, and he didn't see how that
could be. There weren't any robots in Landover or even, so far
as he knew, any idea of what robots were. So he must have
seen it in his old world in a movie or a comic or some such,
since even there robots were still mostly conceptual. He raked
through his memories in an effort to recall where, but nothing
came to mind.

When he finally fell asleep close to morning, he was still
trying unsuccessfully to place it.

Willow woke him sometime around midmorning. The
skies were clear again; the rains had moved east. He lay quietly
for a moment, watching her sitting next to him, looking
down, smiling in that particularly wonderful way, and he made
an impulsive decision. Willow was suffering from Mistaya's loss
and Rydall's threat as much as he was. It was wrong to keep
his thinking to himself. So he told her all of it, even part of
what he had never revealed before to anyone: that the medallion and the Paladin were linked, that the one summoned the
other to the defense of the High Lord. They were alone in the
room, Bunion having gone off much earlier on business of his
own, the nature of which he had not disclosed. Willow listened carefully to everything Ben had to say, then took his
hands and held them.

"If the medallion was tampered with," she said quietly,
sitting close on the bed beside him, "then whoever did so
would have to know that it provides your link to the Paladin."
She stared at him steadily a moment. "Who, besides me,
would know that?"

The answer was no one. Not even Questor Thews, and

after Ben he knew more than anyone about the medallion. Most knew that it marked and belonged to whoever ruled Landover as High Lord. A few knew that it allowed its wearer passage through the fairy mists. Only Ben, and now Willow, knew that it summoned the Paladin.

He was almost persuaded at that moment to tell her everything about the medallion, the last of his secrets, the whole of the truth. He had told her how it linked him to the Paladin, how it allowed him to summon the High Lord's champion. Why not tell her as well how the Paladin and he were joined, how the Paladin was another side of himself, a darker side that took form when he was brought to combat? He had thought to tell her several times now. It was the last secret he kept from her about the magic, and the burden of it suddenly seemed almost unbearable.

Yet he kept silent. He was not ready. He was not certain. The immensity of such a revelation could have unexpected results. He did not want to test Willow's commitment to him by giving up so terrible a truth. He was afraid even now, even after so long, that he might lose her.

"Where do we go now, Ben?" she asked suddenly, interrupting his thinking. "You do not intend to remain here longer, do you?"

"No," he replied, relieved to be able to move on to another subject. "Kallendbor does not appear to have any help to give us, so there's no reason to linger. We'll leave as soon as I dress and we have something to eat. Where's Bunion, anyway?"

The kobold returned to the bedchamber just as Ben finished washing and putting on his clothes. Willow's bandage from the previous night, which had been applied to the worst of his injuries, a severe head cut, was gone. Bunion had been able to retain a strong scent from the robot, and he had gone down the stairway, backtracking its progress from the previous night. It had been a short trip. Much of the scent had been obliterated by the trampling of guards up and down the stairs, but there was enough left to determine that Rydall's monster had materialized out of nowhere on the landing of the floor just below their own. Ben looked at Willow, then back at Bunion. They all knew what that meant.

Bunion also advised them that a thorough search of the Anhalt and its banks by Kallendbor's soldiers had revealed no trace of either their attacker or the Ardsheal.

They summoned breakfast and ate it in their room, then had their belongings gathered and went down to the main hall. Kallendbor met them there, stern-faced and subdued from the previous night's events. Ben advised him that they were leaving, and there was veiled relief in the other's eyes. Ben had expected as much, since they were hardly friends under the best of circumstances. He offered his thanks for the other's hospitality and made him promise anew that he would send word if he learned anything of Mistaya or Rydall. Kallendbor walked them to the palace doors, where their horses were already saddled and waiting. Ben smiled to himself. Kallendbor would never make a good poker player.

They mounted and rode out the fortress gates and back through the town. They crossed the bridge over the Anhalt and headed southwest, retracing their steps in the direction of Sterling Silver. Willow gave Ben a questioning look, wondering anew at his plans, but he just cocked an eyebrow and said nothing. It was not until they were well beyond the castle and deep into the grasslands beyond that he swung Jurisdiction about and stopped.

"I didn't want Kallendbor to see where we were really going," he offered by way of explanation.

"Which is?"

"East, to the Wastelands, to the one other creature who might know something of Mistaya."

"I see," Willow replied quietly, way ahead of him by now.

"He'll talk to you. He likes you."

She nodded. "He might."

They worked their way back toward the Anhalt and fol-lowed it for the remainder of the day. By nightfall they had reached the beginning of the Wastelands. They camped there, taking shelter in a grove of ash on a hill that provided a good view in all directions of the surrounding countryside. They ate dinner cold. Bunion offered to stand watch for the entire night, but Ben would not hear of it. The kobold needed his rest as well, particularly if he was to be of any use when the next attack came—and there was no longer any pretense that it wouldn't. Since they were all dependent on one another, they would share the responsibility, he insisted.

There were no monsters this night, and Ben slept undis-turbed. By morning he was feeling revitalized. Willow seemed rested, too. All three were anticipating what lay ahead. Even Bunion had figured it out. He went on ahead to scout while Ben and Willow followed at a more leisurely pace. They left the Greensward behind and entered the Wastelands. The day was cloudy and gray once again, but there did not appear to be any immediate threat of rain. Even without sunshine the air was hot and dry, the ground parched and cracked, and the country about them empty of life and as still as death.

By midday they were deep into the Wastelands, and Bun-ion came back to report that the Fire Springs were directly ahead and that Strabo the dragon was at home.

"If anyone knows of Rydall, it will be Strabo," Ben said to Willow as they rode into the craggy hills surrounding the Springs. "Strabo can go anywhere he wishes, and he may have flown through the fairy mists into Marnhull at some point. It's worth asking, in any case. As long as you're the one who does the asking."

Strabo did not much care for Holiday, although they were somewhat closer now after their shared experience in the Tan-gle Box. But the dragon genuinely liked Willow. He was fond of declaring that dragons had always had a soft spot for beautiful maidens, even though from time to time he thought that he was mistaken in this and that it was eating them that dragons really enjoyed. Too vain to admit his confusion, he had allowed himself to be charmed by the sylph on several occasions. Still, each visit to the Fire Springs was a new and uncertain experience, and Strabo the dragon was nothing if not temperamental.

When they were close enough to feel the heat of the pits, long after they had spied the smoke and inhaled the smell, they dismounted, tethered the horses, and proceeded on foot. It was a difficult walk over rugged, barren hills and across rock-strewn gullies. Bunion led the way as always, but he stayed close to them now. They had gone on for some minutes when they heard the crunching of bones. Bunion glanced over his shoulder and showed all his teeth in a humorless smile.

The dragon was feeding.

Then they crested a ridge, and there it was.

Strabo lay coiled about the mouth of one of the Springs, his forty-foot bulk as black as ink, all studded with spines and spikes, his sinewy body gnarled and sleek by turns. He was lunching on the remains of what appeared to have been a cow, although it was hard to tell since the dragon had reduced the carcass to legs and part of one haunch. Wicked blackened teeth glimmered as it gnawed on a large bone, stripping it of a few last shreds of flesh. Yellow eyes hooded by strange reddish lids focused on the bone, but as the newcomers topped the rise and came into view, its massive horned head lifted and swung about.

"Company?" it hissed none too pleasantly. The yellow eyes widened and blinked. "Oh, Holiday, it's only you. How boring. What do you want?" The voice was low and guttural, marked by a sibilant hiss. "Wait, don't tell me, let me guess. You want to know about this cow. You've come all the way from the comforts of your shiny little castle to reprimand me about this cow. Well, save your breath. The cow was a stray. It wandered into the Wastelands, and that made it mine. So no lectures, please."

It always surprised Ben that the dragon could talk. It went counter to everything life experience had taught him in his old world. But then, there were no dragons in his old world, either.

"I don't care about the cow," Ben advised. He had made Strabo promise once upon a time that he would give up stealing livestock.

The dragon's maw split wide, and it laughed after a fashion. "No? Well, in that case I'll confess that perhaps it wasn't quite inside the boundaries of the Wasteland when I took it. There, I feel much better. The truth shall set you free." The eyes narrowed again. "Well, well. Is that the pretty sylph with you, Holiday?" He never called Ben "High Lord." "Have you brought her to me for a visit? No, you would never be that considerate. You must be here for some other reason. What is it?"

Ben sighed. "We've come to ask—"

"Wait, you're interrupting my dinner." The dragon's nostrils steamed, and it gave a rough cough. "Politeness in all things. Please take a seat until I've finished. Then I'll hear what you have to say. If you keep it brief."

Ben looked at Willow, and reluctantly they sat down on the knoll with Bunion and waited for Strabo to complete his dinner. The dragon took his time, crunching up every single bone and devouring every last shred of flesh until nothing remained but hooves and horns. He made a deliberate production out of it, smacking his lips and grunting his approval with every bite. It was an endless performance, and it produced the intended effect. Ben was so impatient by the time the dragon had finished that he could barely contain his temper.

Strabo tossed away a stray hoof and looked up at them expectantly. "Now, then, let's hear what you have to say."

Ben tried to refrain from gritting his teeth. "We have

come to ask your help with something," he began, and got no further.

"Save your breath, Holiday," the dragon interrupted with a curt wave of one foreleg. "I've already given you all the help you're getting in this lifetime—more help, in point of fact, then you ever deserved."

"Hear me out at least," Ben urged irritably.

"Must I?" The dragon shifted as if trying to get comfortable. "Well, for the sake of the lovely young lady, I will."

Ben decided to cut to the chase. "Mistaya is missing. We think she has been taken prisoner by King Rydall of Marnhull. At least he claims to have her. We are trying to get her back."

Strabo stared at him without speaking for a moment. "Am I supposed to know what you're talking about? Mistaya? Rydall of Marnhull? Who are these people?"

"Mistaya is our daughter," Willow said quickly, interceding before Ben lost his temper completely. "You helped Ben find us when I was carrying her out of the Deep Fell."

"Ah, yes, I remember." The dragon beamed. "Good of me, wasn't it? And you've named her Mistaya? Very pretty. I like the name. It sings with the promise of your own beauty."

Gag me with a spoon, Ben thought blackly, but kept his mouth shut.

"She is a beautiful child," Willow agreed, keeping the dragon's attention focused on her. "I love her very much, and I am determined to see her safely home again."

"Of course you are," Strabo affirmed indignantly. "Who is this King Rydall who's taken her?"

"We don't know. We were hoping you could help." Willow waited.

Strabo shook his horn-crusted head slowly. "No. No, I don't think so. I've never heard of him. Another in a long line of lesser Kings, I expect. There's literally hundreds of them, all parading about, all posturing as if anyone of note could ever for a minute be impressed." He gave Holiday a meaningful glance. "Anyway, whoever he is, I don't know him. And he's from some place called Marnhull? Really? Marnhull? Sounds like what's left after you crack a nut open."

The dragon laughed uproariously, the laughter culminating in a choked gasp as he fell backward into one of the Fire Springs, sending ashes and shattered rock flying everywhere. He hauled himself upright with an effort. "Marnhull! Ridiculous!"

"So you've never heard of either?" Ben pressed, unable to keep silent any longer.

"Never." Strabo snorted dirt and steam from his nostrils. "They don't exist, either of them."

"Not outside Landover, beyond the fairy mists, perhaps?" Ben pressed, disbelieving. "Not even there?"

The great black head swung sharply about. "Holiday, pay attention here. I have traveled all the lands that ever were and a few that weren't. I have been to all those that surround the mists. I have been well beyond. I have been alive a long time, and travel has always agreed with me—especially when I find places where I am not welcome and can feed on the inhabitants."

The yellow eyes lidded. "So. If a land called Marnhull existed, I would have found it. If a King named Rydall existed, I would have heard of him. I haven't. So they don't."

"Well someone calling himself King Rydall exists, because he's come to Sterling Silver twice now to threaten me, claims he's taken Mistaya, and promises to send monsters to try to kill me!" Ben's patience was at an end. "Mistaya's disappeared, and I've been attacked three times already! Something's happening, wouldn't you say?"

"I wouldn't," the dragon declared with studied disinterest, "since I don't know what you are talking about. I have better things to do than to keep up on the local gossip. If you've been attacked, it's news to me. Rather unimportant news, I might add."

Willow took Ben's arm and gently pulled him back, then stepped forward to face the dragon. "Strabo, listen to me, please. I realize what we are telling you is of little personal interest. You are involved in much larger concerns than ours. And if you say you have never heard of Rydall or Marnhull, then it must be so. Everyone knows that dragons never lie."

This was the first time Ben had heard of that, but it appeared to please Strabo, who gave a courtly nod in response.

"Now, I must ask you as someone who has been my friend," Willow continued, "to consider helping me find my daughter. She has disappeared, and we have searched the whole of Landover for her without success. We have spoken with everyone we could think of in an effort to discover where she is. No one can help. You are our last hope. We thought that if anyone would know of Rydall or Marnhull, it would be you. Please, is there anything you could tell us, anything at all that might be of help? Is there anyone you know who might be Rydall? Or any place that might be Marnhull?"

The dragon was silent for a long time. All about him the Fire Springs belched and coughed, spewing forth ashes and smoke. The grayness of the day deepened as the sun drifted west, and the clouds locked together in the skies overhead to form a solid covering. Below the clouds and smoke the landscape stretched away in numbing solitude, bleak and desolate.

"I treasure my privacy," Strabo said finally. "That's why I live out here, you know."

"I know," Willow acknowledged.

The dragon sighed. "Very well. Tell me more of Rydall. Tell me whatever you either know or suspect."

Willow did so, leaving out nothing but the information about the medallion. When she was finished, Strabo thought some more.

"Well, Holiday," he advised softly, "it appears I must help

you once again, even though it is against my better judgment. Such help as you receive, however, is due entirely to my considerable affection for the lovely sylph."

He cleared his throat. "Nothing passes through the fairy mists without my knowing. That is simply the way of things. Dragons have excellent hearing and eyesight, and nothing escapes their attention." He paused, considering. "If they deem it worthy of their attention, that is." He appeared to remember his earlier disclaimer of any knowledge about what had been taking place at Sterling Silver. "The point is, no one has come through the mists recently. But even if I were mistaken in this—and a lapse in my attention span could have occurred just as Rydall or whoever was passing through, I suppose— there would still be a discoverable trace of that passing. In short, I could find out anyway."

He gave them a broad smile and added, "If I were to choose to do so." He cocked his ugly head at Willow. "I wonder, my Lady, if you would favor me with one of your exquisite songs. I do miss the sound of a maiden's voice now and then."

It was his favorite thing in all the world, and although once it would have embarrassed him to ask, he seemed to have gotten over his discomfort. Willow had been expecting this. Her success in charming him before had been due in large part to her singing, so she did not hesitate now to do so again. There was an unspoken bargain being made, and the price the dragon was asking for his help was certainly small enough. Willow sang of meadows and wildflowers filled with dancing maidens and of a dragon who was lord over all. Ben had never heard the song and found it more than a little saccharine, but Strabo lay his horn-crusted head on the rim of one of the springs and got very dreamy-eyed.

By the time she had finished he was almost reduced to the limpness of a noodle. Tears leaked from his lantern eyes.

"When you return from your search," she called over to

him, reminding him of his end of the bargain, "I will sing one more song for you as a further reward."

Strabo's head lifted slowly from its resting place, and his teeth showed in a pathetically futile attempt at a smile. *"Je t'adore,"* he advised softly.

Without another word great wings spread from his serpent's body and lifted him skyward, circling up and away until he was lost from view.

They waited through the remainder of the day and all night for his return. Bunion went back for their blankets, and all three took turns standing watch, settled down on the windward side of the Fire Springs so they would not have to breathe the smoke and soot. Flames licked out of the craters, and molten rock belched forth at regular intervals, effectively disrupting attempts to sleep. The heat was intense at times, relieved only when a small breeze blew across them on its way to a better place. But they were safe enough, for nothing would dare to venture into the dragon's lair.

It was nearing dawn when Strabo returned. He came out of a sky in which Landover's moons were already down and the stars were fading into a faintly brightening east, his bulk a massive dark shadow that might have been a chunk of sky unexpectedly broken away. He settled earthward as smoothly and delicately as a great butterfly, without sound, without effort, belying his monstrous bulk.

"Lady," he greeted Willow in his deep, raspy voice. There was weariness and regret in that single word. "I have flown the four borders of the land, from Fire Springs to Melchor, from Greensward to lake country, from one range of mountains and mists to the other. I have searched the whole of the boundaries that mark the passage from Landover to the fairy worlds. I have smelled all tracks, studied all markings, and hunted for the smallest sign. There is no trace of Rydall of Marnhull. There is no trace of your child."

"None?" Willow asked quietly, as if perhaps he might reconsider his answer.

The dragon's gnarled head swung away. "No one has passed through the mists in recent days. No one." He yawned, showing row upon row of blackened, crooked teeth. "Now, if you will excuse me, I need to get some sleep. I am sorry, but I can do nothing more. I release you from your pledge to sing further. I regret to say I am too tired to listen. Good-bye to you. Good-bye, Holiday. Come again sometime, but not for a while, hmmm?"

He crawled off through the rocks, snaked his way down between the simmering craters, curled up amid the debris, and promptly began to snore.

Ben and Willow stared at each other. "I don't understand it," Ben said finally. "How can there be no sign at all?"

Willow's face was pale and drawn. "If Rydall did not come through the mists, where did he come from? Where is he now? What has he done with Mistaya?"

Ben shook his head slowly. "I don't know." He reached down for his blanket and began to fold it up. "What I do know is that something about all this isn't right, and one way or another I'm going to get to the bottom of it."

Taking Willow's hand in his own and with Bunion leading the way, he turned disconsolately from the Fire Springs and the sleeping dragon and started back toward their horses.

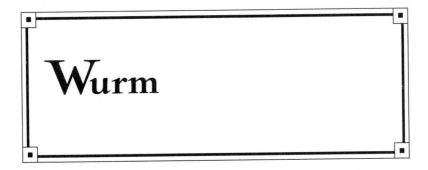

Wurm

They rode out from the Fire Springs and back into the Wastelands, heading west. The sun crested the horizon behind them in a hazy white ball, obscured by mist and clouds and the thickness of heat on the summer air. Already it was hot and threatening to grow hotter. Clouds rolled in from the west, beginning to build on one another, promising rain before the day was done. Ahead, the land stretched away, stark and unchanging.

Ben rode in silence, his mood as bleak and despairing as the land he traveled. He was putting up a brave front, but he knew he had run out of options. Strabo had been his last chance. Since the dragon couldn't tell him how to find Rydall, he was faced with the unpleasant possibility that no one could. And if he couldn't find Rydall, he couldn't find Mistaya or Questor Thews or Abernathy. If he couldn't find his daughter and his friends, he would have no other choice but to return to Sterling Silver and sit around waiting for the rest of Rydall's monsters to come for him. Three down and four to go; it was not a comforting thought. They had almost had him several times already—almost had the Paladin, he corrected, but it was the same thing. He didn't think he could survive four more, and if he did, he didn't really believe he would get Mistaya back, anyway.

It was a terrible thought, and he cursed himself silently

for thinking it. But it was true. It was what he believed. Rydall wasn't the sort to keep a bargain, not this man who devoured countries, who sent monsters to kill their Kings, and who kidnapped children and used them as hostages. No, Rydall played games with his victims, and when you played games of his sort, you made up the rules as you went along so that you didn't lose. It didn't matter if the Paladin survived all seven challengers or not. Mistaya wasn't coming back.

Unless Ben found her and brought her back himself.

Which at the moment he didn't seem to have the slightest hope of doing.

He thought about what Strabo had told him. There was no sign of Rydall's passage through the fairy mists now or any time in the recent past. There was no sign of Mistaya. So what did that tell him? That Rydall was lying? That Strabo had missed something? But Rydall had said he had come through the fairy mists. He had said his army was prepared to follow. Through the mists. Maybe, Ben thought suddenly, Rydall's black-cloaked companion had magic that facilitated this and left no trail. Maybe the magic was such that it could conceal the point of passage. But wouldn't Strabo have found some trace of that magic? Nothing escaped the dragon. Had Rydall been able to do what no one else could and deceive the beast?

Then it occurred to Ben that there was another way into Landover, a way he had forgotten about—through the demon world of Abbadon. Could it be that Rydall had gained entry from there? But in order to do so he would have had to bypass the demons. Or win their support, as the Gorse had done, promising them something in return. Could Marnhull's King have done that? It didn't feel right. The demons hated humans; they never made bargains with them unless they were forced to. It was one thing to ally themselves with the Gorse, itself a creature of dark magic. It was another to join forces with someone like Rydall. Besides, Rydall had said that he

had come through the mists, and that was not the same thing
as coming out of Abaddon.

Jurisdiction was proceeding at a walk, picking his way
carefully over the rocky ground, moving so slowly that they
were barely making any progress at all. Ben was oblivious, lost
in thought. Willow rode next to him, watching his face, not
wanting to distract him. Bunion walked beside them, bright
eyes shifting from one to the other, then back to the barren
land ahead. It was no concern of his. Behind them the Fire
Springs had disappeared into the curve of the horizon, leaving
little more than a dark smudge of smoke and ash against
the sky.

A crow with red eyes appeared out of the retreating night
to the west and circled lazily overhead, unseen.

What was it he was missing? Ben wondered. Surely there
was something he had overlooked, or mistaken, or failed to
recognize—something that would lead him to Rydall. Maybe
he was going about this the wrong way. Assume for the moment that Rydall was lying about who and what he was and
where he came from. It was a fair enough assumption given
Rydall's disposition toward game playing. Invent the rules of a
game, put them in play, and wait to see what would happen—
that seemed to fit with what he knew of Rydall. The question
he had asked himself earlier and then not gotten back to for an
answer was, Why was Rydall doing all this? It had been the
River Master's question as well. Why was Marnhull's King
sending monsters to challenge Ben instead of simply demanding his life in exchange for Mistaya's? Why was he spending so
much time challenging the Paladin to individual duels when
he could just as easily have marched his army into Landover
and taken it by force? To avoid bloodshed and loss of life? That
didn't seem likely.

In fact—and admittedly this was a stretch—Ben was beginning to question if Rydall had any real interest in Landover
at all.

Because the truth was that this entire business was beginning to feel very personal. Ben couldn't put his finger on why, but he definitely sensed it. It was something about those monsters, the nature of their magic, and the manner of their attack. Something. The confrontation between Rydall and himself looked to have more to do with the two of them than with Landover. Landover seemed almost an excuse, a pawn to be played and then discarded. Rydall didn't appear to be in any hurry to complete his conquest. No time limits had been imposed regarding the passing of the throne, and no mention had been made of when a transition was expected to take place. All that seemed to matter was the contest.

Why was Rydall wasting so much time if all he wanted was to persuade Ben to give up the throne? Wouldn't Ben do that anyway if it meant getting Mistaya back safely?

Wouldn't he?

He looked quickly at Willow, a pang of guilt lancing through him as he hesitated with his answer. She was staring back at him, but no condemnation or suspicion registered in her green eyes, only concern and sadness and, behind it all, unfailing love. He was suddenly ashamed. He knew the answer, didn't he? When his wife in his old world, Annie, and their unborn child had died, he had thought he would never recover; they were gone, and he could not get them back again. Now he had Willow and Mistaya, and he could not bear losing them as well. He would give up anything to keep them.

Midmorning had arrived, and the Wastelands were hazy—bright and sweltering.

Ben turned to Willow. "Another mile or so and we'll stop and rest," he told her. "And we'll talk things out a bit."

She nodded and said nothing. They rode slowly on.

Overhead, the crow with red eyes wheeled back the way it had come and was gone.

Nightshade flew quickly to the draw through which Holiday and his companions would pass, holding the struggling wurm firmly in her beak. She could barely keep her rage in check. She had waited all night for him to come to her, believing he must, certain that the dragon would offer no help and send him away. Instead, the beast had gone hunting for him—hunting, like some tame dog!—and Holiday had not come back as expected but had camped within the confines of the Fire Springs, a place she could not safely penetrate even with her formidable magic. So she had been forced to wait, to spend the entire night in the Wastelands keeping watch over her prize.

As if in response to her anger, the wurm wrapped itself around her beak and tried to bite her.

She laughed to herself as she watched its tiny teeth gnash. It had been a regular earthworm once, fat and sleek and indolent. Now it was her creature and would undertake the task she had set for it, becoming Rydall's fourth monster.

She was still dismayed that there had been a need for a fourth. The robot should have been enough, would have been enough if not for the Ardsheal. That the River Master should intercede on Holiday's behalf as well, granddaughter or no, was infuriating. Holiday and he were no more friends than Holiday and the dragon. Why did these obvious enemies keep offering to help the play-King and interfering with her plans? What madness was this?

On the other hand, she thought, trying to put matters in a better light, it had been her intention from the beginning that Holiday survive until the particular end she had devised for him, the end that would come at Mistaya's hands. It would be less enjoyable if he was to die before then. And the appearance of the Ardsheal had provided her with fresh inspiration for playing with Landover's beleaguered High Lord. So nothing had been lost, after all, had it?

She swooped down onto the flats and glided into the shadow of a draw that opened between two massive hills that blocked passage to the west and east. Holiday and his companions had come through the draw on the way to the dragon; the hoofprints of the horses made that plain enough. They would return the same way. But this time she would have the wurm waiting for them. She hopped across the ground on her bird feet to the tiny puddle of seepage water that sat back in the shadow of the rocks and had not yet evaporated with the heat of the day. A little water was all it took; a little would be more than enough.

She held the wurm over the water, watching it struggle to get free. She was tired of holding it. It was bad enough that she'd been forced to travel all the way to the Wastelands in nonhuman form, not daring to use her magic for fear it would reveal her presence and give the game away. But having to keep a secure grip on the little monster for so long was really too much. She had been able to put it down last night, safely up in the rocks where the ground was dry and hard and offered the creature no escape. Now she was ready to release it for good. She was thinking that she would like to stay around to see what would happen when she did, but she had been gone from the Deep Fell for a long time now, and she didn't like leaving the girl alone. Mistaya was growing impatient with the direction and limitation of her lessons. In fact, the wurm had been Nightshade's idea, devised when the girl had failed to come up with anything new. She was still obedient, but there were signs that the girl might test the rules Nightshade had imposed on her. Mistaya was incredibly gifted, both with imagination and with talent, and under the witch's tutelage her skills at applying her magic had grown formidable. If she ever chose to challenge Nightshade . . .

The witch brushed the idea aside with a sneer. She was not frightened of Mistaya. She wasn't frightened of anyone.

But it didn't hurt to be cautious.

She made up her mind. It was best that she return to the Deep Fell as quickly as she could. It was best that she make certain Mistaya did not step out of line.

She dropped the wurm into the puddle of water and watched it sink. Then she flew swiftly away.

Ben Holiday peered into the distance, catching sight of the draw that led through the rugged Wasteland hills to the flats beyond. The light was so poor this day, its clarity so diluted by heat and mist, that everything appeared fuzzy and distorted. Even the horizon shimmered as if it were a mirage in danger of disappearing altogether. Ahead, the draw was a mass of impenetrable shadows.

He guided Jurisdiction toward the opening, his mind on other things.

He was thinking again about that robot. Why was it so familiar? Where had he seen it? He was absolutely certain by now that he had, and it was maddening that he could not remember from where. Complicating matters was his growing suspicion that he had seen Rydall's other monsters, as well. And he was now willing to bet, having given the matter considerable thought, that he had seen them since coming into Landover. Yet how could that be? They couldn't have been alive; he would have remembered that. Had Questor or Abernathy told him about them? Had someone described them to him? Had he seen a drawing or a picture?

They reached the edge of the shadows that marked the entrance to the draw. Ahead, the passageway was dark and empty. Ben nudged Jurisdiction forward, his stomach grumbling softly as he savored the prospect of lunch.

Suddenly Bunion chittered in warning. Ben glanced down at the kobold, who was looking back from where they had come. Ben followed his gaze, shading his eyes against the glare of the sun. At first he saw nothing. Then he caught sight of a tiny black speck hanging low against the horizon. The speck seemed to be growing larger.

Ben blinked uncertainly. "What in the heck is—"

That was all he got out before the ground in front of them erupted in a shower of earth and rock and something huge and dark rose out of the draw's deep shadows. Bunion catapulted over Crane, snatching Willow from the saddle an instant before the horse was swallowed whole by the thing before it. There was a terrified scream and the crunching of bones. Dust and heat filled the air. Jurisdiction leapt away in panic, barely avoiding the massive jaws that reached now for him, sweeping past Ben's head with ferocious purpose. Ben hung on as his horse bolted, catching just a glimpse of the thing attacking them—a monstrous snake of some sort, faceless, eyeless, all teeth and maw, its purplish body smooth and ringed like . . .

Like a worm's, for goodness' sake!

Ben reached instinctively for the medallion, but Jurisdiction was shying so badly—skittering up the slope of a steep rise, twisting and bucking in terror—that he had to abandon the attempt and grasp the saddle and reins with both hands to avoid being thrown. He saw Bunion and Willow scrambling up the far side of the draw and into the rocks. The monster dove downward suddenly into the earth, wriggling underground, its great bulk disappearing in the manner of a whale's beneath the surface of an ocean. It burrowed down, the earth rising above it as it tunneled, and the line of the tunnel moved directly toward Ben.

Ben kicked Jurisdiction frantically, trying to make the horse come down off the rise. But Jurisdiction was panicked beyond all reason and could think only to climb higher. It was a losing battle, the horse's hooves slipping badly on the loose rock and earth, its progress stalled. Ben wrenched the horse's head about and sent him scrambling along the side of the slope parallel to the crest, still hoping to turn him downward. Behind them the earth buckled and lifted, the monster turning to follow.

The gap between them closed.

In desperation Ben released his grip on the saddle and tried to reach inside his tunic for the medallion. But the instant he did so Jurisdiction stumbled and went down, throwing him head over heels into the scrub. The terrified horse came back to his feet at once and this time bolted down the slope to safety. Ben was not so fortunate. Dazed and bloodied from his spill, he scrambled up and began racing ahead without any idea what it was he was racing toward, aware only that the subterranean horror was almost on top of him. Rocks and earth split and rumbled as the creature's huge bulk tunneled deliberately in pursuit. Ben groped for the medallion, feeling its hardness through the fabric of his tunic, unable to work it free from where it lodged in the folds. Sweat and blood ran down into his eyes, blinding him. Any moment now his attacker would surface. Any moment it would have him. He could feel the medallion's smooth edge, could touch its engraved surface through the tunic cloth. *Another moment! Just one more . . . !*

Then earth and rock exploded skyward, knocking Ben off his feet and sending him tumbling away. He lost his grip on the medallion and landed on his back with a sharp grunt, the wind knocked from his lungs. The worm-thing towered over him, earth-encrusted body arching forward, jaws opening, mouth reaching down.

Ben twisted wildly in an effort to escape, knowing he was too late, knowing he could not. *The medallion!* he thought. *Have to . . . !*

Then something bigger and blacker and more ferocious than his attacker hurtled out of the sky. Claws fastened on the monster's body, snatching it backward and away. Huge jaws snapped down, severing the sightless head. The head, its maw still gaping, fell away in a gush of ichor, but the body continued to squirm madly. The jaws snapped down again and yet again, and the monster at last fell lifeless.

Strabo dropped what was left, fanned the air once with his great wings, and settled slowly earthward. Willow and Bunion were already running over from the far side of the draw.

"You really are a great deal of trouble, Holiday," the dragon hissed. The great head swung about, and the lantern eyes fastened on him. "A great deal."

"I know," Ben managed, gasping for breath as he pulled himself back to his feet. "But thanks, anyway."

Willow reached him in a rush and threw her arms around him. "Thank you, Strabo," she echoed, releasing her grip on Ben just enough to turn toward the dragon. "You know how much he means to me. Thank you very much."

Strabo sniffed. "Well, if I've given you reason to smile, fair enough," he declared, a hint of pleasure in his rough voice.

"How did you know to come?" Ben asked. "When we left, you were asleep."

The dragon folded his wings against his body, and his eyes lidded. "The Wastelands are mine, Holiday. They belong to me. They are all I have left of what once was unending. Therefore, they are ruled as I determine they should be. No magic is allowed here but my own. If another intrudes, I am warned at once. Even asleep, my senses tell me. I knew of this creature the moment it took shape." He paused. "Do you know what this is?"

Both Ben and Willow shook their heads.

"This is a wurm. W–U–R–M. An ordinary worm turned predator by magic. Expose it to water, and it grows to the size you see now." Strabo glanced down at the severed parts and spit in distaste. "Pathetic excuse for disturbing my rest."

"Rydall again," Ben said quietly.

Strabo's head swung back. "I don't know about Rydall,"

he hissed softly, "but I do know about witches. Wurms are a particular favorite of witches."

Ben stared. "Nightshade?" he said finally.

The dragon's head lifted. "Among others." He yawned and looked to the east. "Time to be getting back to bed. Try to stay alive long enough to get out of the Wastelands, Holiday. After that you won't be my responsibility anymore."

Without another word he spread his wings, lifted away, and flew out of sight. Ben and Willow watched him go. Bunion stood with them a moment, then left at Ben's direction to hunt for Jurisdiction.

Willow wiped blood from Ben's face with a strip of cloth torn from her shirt. After a moment she said, "Could Nightshade be involved in this?"

Ben shook his head. "With Rydall? Why would she do that?"

Willow's smile was hard and bitter. "She hates you. That's reason enough."

Ben stared off into the empty hills, into the glare of the sun, looking at nothing. Willow finished cleaning off his face and kissed him lightly. "She hates all of us."

Ben nodded. He was thinking suddenly of something else. "Willow," he said, "I remember now where I've seen Rydall's monsters—all three of them."

The sylph stepped back from him. "Where?"

He looked back at her, and there was wonder in his eyes. "In a book."

Poggwydd

Mistaya woke early that same morning and found herself alone for the first time since she had arrived in the Deep Fell. Her reaction was disbelief; Nightshade never left her alone. She rose in the gray, misted dawn and looked about expectantly, waiting for the mistress of the hollow to present herself. When she failed to appear, Mistaya called for her. When she still didn't show, the girl walked all about the edges of the clearing, searching. There was no sign of Nightshade.

Unexpectedly, Mistaya found herself relieved.

There had been considerable changes of late, and chief among them was her relationship with the witch. In the beginning Nightshade had been a willing, enthusiastic teacher, a companion in the magic arts, anxious to share her knowledge, a secret friend who could instruct Mistaya in the uses of her mysterious, intriguing power. Mistaya was there to discover the truth about her birthright, Nightshade had said. She was there to find ways to help her father in his struggle against Rydall of Marnhull. There was good to be achieved from the skills they would uncover. But somehow all that had gotten lost along the way. There was no longer any mention of Rydall or of her birthright. There was barely any mention of the world outside the hollow. All that seemed to matter now was how swift and compliant Mistaya could be in carrying out the witch's instructions. Patience, once so much in evidence, had dropped by the wayside. Diversity and exploration had been abandoned entirely. For days now all they had done was use the magic for a single purpose: to create monsters. Or if they weren't actually creating monsters, they were talking about it. In the process the student-teacher relationship had suffered drastically. Instead of continuing to grow closer to each other, it seemed to Mistaya that they were now growing farther apart. Praise and encouragement had been replaced with criticism and disgust. Accusations flew. Mistaya wasn't trying hard enough. She wasn't concentrating. She wasn't thinking. She seemed to have reached a point where she couldn't do anything right.

When Mistaya had devised the robot, another of the creatures she had seen in her father's old book, Nightshade had pronounced it wonderful. Then, barely two days later, she had dismissed it as a failure. It wasn't good enough; she wanted something better. Mistaya tried to think of a new monster, but under the intense pressure of the witch's demands and her own growing disinterest in the project, she had been unable to come up with anything. In exasperation, Nightshade had devised a creature of her own—a wurm, she called it—which together they had changed from a harmless crawler to a dangerous predator. This time Mistaya had balked openly, saying that she was tired of monsters, weary of this particular use of the magic, and anxious to try something new. Nightshade had dismissed her complaint with a scathing look and a reminder of the girl's promise to do as she was told in exchange for the privilege of being taught. Mistaya was tempted to remark that the exchange had grown decidedly one-sided, but she held her tongue.

In truth, she didn't understand what was happening. Their differences notwithstanding, she still looked upon Nightshade as her friend. There was a closeness between them that transcended even her present dissatisfaction, but she was discovering that it was grounded in the reality of shared pow-

ers and bordered more and more on an increasingly intense
form of competition, as if somehow both of them knew that
rather than be friends, they were fated to be rivals. Each day
there was more tugging and pulling against than with each
other, and the breach between them continued to widen inex-
orably. Mistaya did not want this to happen, but she found
herself powerless to prevent it. Nightshade would not listen to
her; she would not make any effort to compromise or concil-
iate. She wanted Mistaya to do as she was told, to not ask
questions, and to repress any and all objections. More and
more Mistaya found she could not do that.

So this morning she was alone, and she breathed the air
as if it were new and fresh. Wary about her unexpected freedom, she cast a simple spell to be certain that Nightshade was
not attempting some sort of deception. But no trace of the
witch revealed itself, so she called for Haltwhistle. The mud
puppy appeared immediately, materializing out of the gloom,
eyes soulful, ears cocked slightly, tail wagging.

"Good old Haltwhistle," she greeted him with a smile.
"Good morning to you."

Haltwhistle sat back on his haunches and thumped the
ground with his tail.

"Shall we do something, you and I?" she asked her four-
legged friend. "Just the two of us?"

She looked around the clearing as if expecting the answer
to present itself. The familiar misty haze cloaked everything.
Trees and brush were shrouded in gloom, the sky was invisible,
and the world was a cocoon of silence. She was tired of being
confined in so small a space; she wanted to see farther than the
edge of the mist. She remembered the world without, and she
wanted to look upon it again—on sunlight, green grass, blue
skies, lakes, forests, mountains, and living things. She had been
thinking about her parents lately, something she hadn't done
for a while. She was wondering why they hadn't come to see

her or written her or sent word of some sort asking how she was. And what about her friends at Sterling Silver? Why hadn't she at least heard from Questor Thews? They were best friends. What had happened to everybody?

She had not asked this of Nightshade. She knew what the witch would say. They were being careful because Rydall was searching for her. They were making sure she stayed safe. But the answer didn't satisfy her the way it should have. It seemed inadequate somehow. There should have been a way for her parents and friends to contact her, even here. Like it or not, Mistaya was becoming homesick.

"Well," she declared impulsively. "Enough standing about. Let's go for a walk."

She started out resolutely and without further considera- tion of her decision. She was about to take a big chance, and she knew it. She intended to walk out to where she could see for more than fifty feet at a time, where there was light and warmth, where there were living things. She intended to go outside the Deep Fell, and that meant breaking Nightshade's rules.

Oddly enough, she didn't much care.

She conjured up a stalk of Bonnie Blue to chew on, anx- ious for something she hadn't seen for a while. Travel was easy. Once she would not have been able to find her way out of the Deep Fell. Now she employed her magic with barely a thought and was at the base of the slope leading up to the rim in no time at all. She found a pathway and climbed toward the light. Haltwhistle plodded steadfastly along behind her.

Moments later she emerged from the murky haze into a day filled with sunshine and summer smells. She smiled as the light fell across her face and arms. She blinked away its bright- ness as she looked first left into forested hills with their deep green shadows and then right across a valley of blue and yellow wildflowers. Purple-shadowed mountains rose on the distant horizon, clouds scraping across their peaks. Birds flew in the trees close by, and a woodland rabbit darted away through the long grasses of the valley.

"Well, which way shall we go?" she asked Haltwhistle with a bright, determined smile.

Since the mud puppy didn't seem to have a preference, Mistaya made the choice for them. They struck out east into the trees, winding their way through glens and clearings, seeking out small streams and quiet ponds, watching for forest creatures, and smelling out nuts and berries. Mistaya meandered without concern for where she was going, knowing her magic would allow her to find her way back again when she was ready. She gave Rydall a passing thought, then dismissed him. Her wards were up, the magic lines that kept her alert to anyone who might approach so that she would be warned well in advance of discovery. She did not think Rydall would find her out here in any event. She did not think anyone would.

She was surprised when, in the middle of skipping stones across a small pond, she sensed somebody just a short distance off. She stopped what she was doing and stood perfectly still, using her magic to send out feelers. Nightshade had taught her a lot. She found the other without difficulty. One man, all alone. She sensed no danger from him. She debated what to do, then decided it might be fun to speak with someone. After all, she hadn't talked with anyone besides the witch in weeks. She would have a look at him, and if he seemed safe, she would show herself.

With Haltwhistle in tow, she slipped through the trees, treading soundlessly, cloaking herself in her magic. She found her quarry sitting cross-legged in a clearing before a tiny fire, chewing on the remains of some small animal he had cooked. He was an odd-looking fellow, small-limbed, round-bodied, and hairy all over. He had whiskers that stuck out from his face like the bristles of a brush and tiny pointed ears that were ragged at the ends. His clothes were badly sewn, ill fitting, and frayed from wear. He wore a gold ring in one ear with a dilapidated feather hanging off it. He was encrusted in dirt and grime from his bare feet to his bare head.

She searched her memory in an effort to identify what sort of creature he was and decided finally that he was a G'home Gnome.

Safe enough to talk to, she believed, and she strolled bravely out into the clearing.

"Good morning," she greeted him.

The fellow at the fire started so that he dropped the bone he was gnawing into the dirt. "Jumping junipers, don't do that!" he exclaimed irritably. "Give a person some warning, will you? Where did you come from, anyway?" He reached down hurriedly to pick up the bone, wiping it off with his fingers.

"Sorry," she apologized. "I didn't mean to scare you."

"Didn't scare me! Didn't scare me one bit! No sir!" He was instantly defensive. "Startled me was all. Thought I was alone out here. Had every reason to feel that way, too. No one comes to these woods, you know. Say, who are you, anyway?"

She hesitated. "Misty," she said, no fonder of the name now than before but opting for caution over pride. "What's yours?"

"Poggwydd. That your pet, cute little fellow behind you?" His eyes were suddenly sharp. "What is he?"

She came all the way over and stood looking down at him. Haltwhistle followed. "What are you eating?" she asked in return.

"Eating? Oh, uh, a rabbit, yes, a rabbit. Caught it myself."

"It has a rather long tail for a rabbit, doesn't it?" She indicated the leavings of his meal piled next to him in a bedraggled heap.

Poggwydd frowned petulantly. "Well, I forget. Maybe it's

not a rabbit. Maybe it's something else. What difference does it make?"

"It looks like a cat."

"It might be. So what?"

Mistaya shrugged and sat down across from him. "I just didn't want you to get any ideas about Haltwhistle, that's all." She indicated the mud puppy, who was sniffing at the ground. "You're a G'home Gnome, aren't you?"

"Proud to be so," he announced with uncharacteristic boldness for one of Landover's most despised peoples.

"Well, everyone knows G'home Gnomes eat pets."

Poggwydd threw down his bone in disgust. "That's a lie! An outright lie! G'home Gnomes eat creatures of nature and the wild, not those of house and hearth! Now and then a stray gets eaten, but that's its own fault! See here, little girl, we must have an understanding if we're to continue this conversation. I will not be maligned. I will not be reviled. I will not sit here and defend myself. I was here first, so if you feel compelled to impugn the integrity and character of G'home Gnomes, you must leave now!"

Mistaya wrinkled her brow. "You seem awfully grouchy."

"You'd be grouchy, too, if you had to spend your whole life bearing up under the abuse of others. G'home Gnomes have been wrongfully accused since the dawn of time for crimes of which they were not guilty. They have been scorned and ridiculed with never a thought given to the harm that was done. Innocent little girls like you should know better than to follow in the ways of your ignorant, prejudiced elders. Not everything you hear is true, you know."

"All right," Mistaya acknowledged. "I'm sorry for being suspicious. But there are lots of stories about you."

Poggwydd screwed up his whiskered face in distaste. "Humph! Stories, indeed!" He glanced again at Haltwhistle. "So what is he, anyway?"

"A mud puppy."

"Never heard of it," Poggwydd held out one grimy hand. "Come over here, Haltwhistle. Come here, boy. Let old Poggwydd give you a pet."

"You do not pet mud puppies," Mistaya declared quickly. "You never touch them."

Poggwydd looked at her suspiciously. "Why not?"

"You just don't. It's dangerous."

"Dangerous?" Poggwydd looked back at the mud puppy. "He doesn't look dangerous. He looks rather silly."

"Well, you mustn't touch him."

"Suit yourself." The G'home Gnome shrugged. He looked down at the bones gathered in his lap. "Want something to eat?"

Mistaya shook her head. "No, thank you. What are you doing out here?"

Poggwydd ate a sliver of meat off a bone. His teeth looked sharp. "Traveling." He shrugged. "Enjoying my own company for a while, getting away from the noise and bustle of home, escaping from this and that."

"Are you in trouble?"

"No, I'm not in trouble!" He gave her a peevish look. "Do I look like I'm in trouble? Do I? Say, what about you? Little girl wandering around out here in the middle of nowhere. Are you in trouble?"

She thought about it a moment. She was in trouble, she supposed. Not that she was going to tell him. "No," she lied.

"No, huh? What are you doing out here, then, all by yourself? Taking a long walk, maybe? Are you lost?"

Her jaw tightened defensively. "I'm not lost. I'm visiting."

"Hah!" Poggwydd made a face. "Visiting who? The witch, maybe? That's who you're visiting?" The look on her face brought him up short. "Now, now, I was only teasing; no need to be frightened," he reassured her hastily, misreading the look. "But she's right over there, you know. Just a mile or so off in the Deep Fell. You don't want to be wandering about

down there. Just remember that." He cleared his throat and
tossed away the last of the bones. "So who are you visiting
way out here?"

She smiled coyly. "You."

"Me? Ho, ho! That's a good one! Visiting me, are you?"
He rocked with laughter. "You must lack much in the way of
choices, then. Visiting me! As if that were something a little
girl would do!"

"Well, I am."

"Am what?"

"Visiting you. Sitting here having this conversation is
visiting, isn't it?"

He gave her a sharp look. "You are too smart by half, little girl. Misty, is it? You tell me now, if we're really friends—
who are you?"

She tried her best to look confused. "I already told you
that."

"So you did. Misty, out for a walk in the middle of nowhere. Come to visit a new friend she didn't know she had
until just now." Poggwydd shook his whiskered face at her.
"Well, you look like trouble to me, so I don't think I want to
talk with you anymore. I don't need any more trouble in my
life. G'home Gnomes have enough as it is. Good-bye."

He rose and brushed himself off, sending dust and
crumbs flying. She stared at him in disbelief. He really meant
it. She scrambled up with him.

"I don't see what difference it makes who I am," she declared angrily. "Why can't we just talk?"

He shrugged. "Because I don't like little girls who play
games, and you're playing one with me, aren't you? You know
who I am, but I don't know who you are. I don't like that. It
isn't fair."

"Isn't fair?" she exclaimed.

"Not a bit."

She watched him begin to gather up his few belongings.

"But I don't really know who you are, either," she pointed out quickly. "I don't know any more about you than you know about me. Except your name. And you know mine, so we're even."

He stopped what he was doing and looked at her. "Well, now, I suppose that's right. Yes, I suppose it is."

He put down his pack with a small clatter of implements and sat down again. Mistaya sat with him.

"I'll make you a deal," he said, holding up a single grimy finger for emphasis. "You tell me something about you, and I'll tell you something about me. How about that?"

She held out her finger and touched it to his, binding the agreement. "You first."

Poggwydd frowned, shrugged, and rocked back. "Humph. Let me see." He looked marginally thoughtful. "Very well. I'll tell you what I'm doing out here. I'm a treasure hunter for the King, for the High Lord himself." He gave her a con-spiratorial look. "I'm on a special mission, looking for a very valuable chest of gold that's hidden somewhere in these woods."

She arched one eyebrow. "You are not."

"I am so!" He was immediately indignant. "How would you know, anyway?"

"Because I just do." She was grinning in spite of herself. Poggwydd made her laugh almost as much as Abernathy did.

"Well, you don't know anything!" He dismissed her with a wave of his hand. "I have been a treasure hunter for the King for years! I have found a good many valuable things in my travels, I can tell you! I know more about treasure hunting than anyone, and the High Lord appreciates that. That's why he employs me."

"I bet he doesn't even know you," she persisted, enjoying the game. It was the most fun she'd had in some time. "I bet he has never seen you before in his entire life."

Poggwydd was beside himself. "He has so! I happen to

know him quite well! I even know his family. I know the Queen! And the little girl, the one who's missing! Why, I might even find her while I'm looking for that chest of gold!"

She stared at him. *Missing?* She kept her lips tightly together. "You don't know her. You're making this all up."

"I am not! I'll tell you something, since you seem so intent on being rude. The High Lord's little girl is a whole lot nicer than you!"

"She is not!"

"Hah! Fly doodles! How would you know?"

"Because I'm her!"

It was out before she could help herself. She said it in a rush of indignation and pride, but she supposed that she would have said it anyway because this was a game, and he wouldn't know whether to believe it. Besides, she wanted to see the look on his face when she said it.

The look was worth it. He gaped in undisguised amazement, sputtered something unintelligible, and then finished with a monstrous snort. "Pfah! What nonsense! What a heap of horse hunks! Now who's telling tall tales?"

"And I'm not missing, either!" she added firmly. "I'm right here with you!"

"You're not the High Lord's daughter!" he exclaimed vehemently. "You can't be!"

"How would you know?" she mimicked. Then she put her hands to her face and feigned shock. "Oh, excuse me, I forgot! You're the King's personal treasure hunter and know the whole family!"

Poggwydd scowled. He hunched forward, his round body rocking on its stubby, gnarled legs as if in danger of tipping over completely.

"Look here," he said carefully. "Enough foolishness. It's one thing to play at being someone where the playing is harmless but another altogether to make light of misfortune. I know you are just a little girl, but you're a smart little girl and old enough to appreciate the difference."

"What are you talking about!" she snapped, furious at being lectured like this.

"The High Lord's daughter!" he snapped back. "That's what I'm talking about! Don't tell me you don't know." He stopped short. "Well, now, maybe you don't—little girl all alone out here in the woods, bumping up against a fellow like me. Who are you, anyway? You never did say. Are you one of those fairies, come out from the mists for a visit? Are you a sprite or some such from the lake country? We don't see many up this way. Not us G'home Gnomes, anyway."

He paused, collecting his thoughts. "Well, here's what's happened, if you don't already know. The High Lord's daughter is missing, and everyone is looking for her. She's been missing for days, weeks perhaps, but gone for sure, and there were search parties hunting for her from one end of Landover to the other."

He bent close, lowering his voice as if he might be heard. "Word is, King Rydall has her. He's from someplace called Marnhull. He has her. Won't give her back, either. He's making the King's champion do battle with some monsters. I don't know that for a fact, but that's what I've heard. In any case, she's missing, and you shouldn't make fun of her."

Mistaya was dumbfounded. "But I am her!" she insisted, hands on hips. "I really am!"

There was movement in the trees to one side. She caught just a glimpse of it and whirled about, poised to flee, her heart in her throat, her stomach turned to ice. The movement turned to color, a rush of wicked greenish light that filled the shadowed spaces between the trunks and limbs. The color tightened and took shape, coalescing into human form, lean and dark and certain.

Nightshade had returned.

The witch stepped out of the shadows, silent as a ghost.

Her bloodred eyes fixed on Mistaya. "You were told not to leave the Deep Fell," she said softly.

Mistaya froze. For a moment her thoughts were so scattered that she couldn't think. Then she managed a small nod in response. "I'm sorry," she whispered. "I wanted to see the sun again."

"Come stand over here," the witch ordered. "By me."

"It was just for the day," Mistaya tried to explain, frightened now of what might happen to her, terrified by the look on the other's face. "I was all alone, and I didn't think—"

"Come here, Mistaya!" Nightshade snapped, cutting her short.

Mistaya crossed the clearing slowly, head lowered. She managed a quick glance back at Poggwydd. He was standing in front of his fire, eyes wide and staring. Mistaya felt sorry for him. This was her fault.

"I am waiting, Mistaya," Nightshade warned.

Mistaya's gaze swung back again toward the witch. She realized suddenly that Haltwhistle was missing. He had been right beside her while she had been talking with Poggwydd. Where had he gone?

She reached Nightshade and stopped, dreading what might happen next. Nightshade forced a smile, but there was no warmth in it. "I am very disappointed in you," she whispered.

Mistaya nodded, ashamed without being quite sure why. "I won't do it again," she promised. She remembered Poggwydd. "It wasn't his fault," she said quickly, looking back over her shoulder at the unfortunate G'home Gnome. "It was mine. He didn't even want to talk to me." She hesitated. "You won't hurt him, will you?"

Nightshade reached out and placed her hands on the girl's shoulders. Gently but firmly she moved her aside. "Of course not. He is nothing but a silly Gnome. I'll just speed him on his way."

"Excuse me?" Poggwydd ventured, his voice small and thin. "I don't need to be here anymore, do I? Any longer, I mean? I . . . I can just pick up my things, and I can—"

Nightshade's hands came up, and green fire blazed sharply to life at her fingertips. Poggwydd squeaked and cringed back in terror. Nightshade let the fire build, then gathered it in her palms and caressed it lovingly as she watched the Gnome. Mistaya tried to speak and found she couldn't. She turned to Nightshade, pleading with her eyes, suddenly certain that the witch meant to harm Poggwydd, after all.

Then she saw Haltwhistle. The mud puppy was crouched at the edge of the trees just out of Nightshade's field of vision. His hackles were standing on end, and his head drooped forward as if he were concentrating. Something white and frosty-looking was rising off his back.

What was he doing?

Abruptly Nightshade sent the green fire hurtling into Poggwydd. But Haltwhistle's moon/frost reached him first. Mistaya screamed at the sound of the impact. The fire and the frost exploded together, and Poggwydd disappeared. All that remained was the Gnome's discarded pack and the smell of ashes and smoke.

"What was that?" Nightshade exclaimed instantly, eyes raking the clearing from end to end. She wheeled on Mistaya. "Did you see it? Did you?"

Mistaya blinked. Her breath came in little gasps. The moon/frost. She *had* seen it, of course. But she would never admit it to the witch. Not after what had happened to Poggwydd. At least Haltwhistle had escaped. There wasn't a trace of him to be seen.

She faced Nightshade down, her voice shaking. "What did you do to Poggwydd? I asked you not to hurt him!"

The witch was nonplussed by the girl's vehemence. "Calm yourself," she soothed. Her eyes were still skittering about uneasily. "Nothing has happened to him. I sent him home, back to his people, away from where he doesn't belong."

Mistaya would not be placated. "I don't believe you! I don't believe anything you say anymore! I want to go home right now!"

Nightshade gave her a cool and dispassionate look. "Very well, Mistaya," she said quietly. "But first listen to what I have to say. You can do that for me, can't you?"

Mistaya nodded, tight-lipped.

"Your friend *wasn't* harmed," the witch emphasized. "But he couldn't be allowed to remain here. What he told you was true, so far as he knew. Everyone thinks that Rydall has you. Your father arranged for them to think that. He started the rumor when Rydall first tried to kidnap you. He even organized a search for you to make the claim seem true. He did this to confuse Rydall and whoever might be trying to find you on his behalf. This way it seemed that no one knew where you were."

She gave Mistaya a sympathetic smile. "But now the little Gnome knows the truth. Suppose he tells someone what you said? Suppose he tells them where he saw you? What if word of this gets back to Rydall's spies? The risk is too great. So I returned him to where he came from, and I used my magic to erase his memory of this incident. I did it to protect you both."

"He won't remember anything?" Mistaya asked carefully.

"Nothing. So no harm is done, is it?" Nightshade bent close. "As for going home, you may do so immediately if you wish." She paused. "Or you may stay with me for three more days and then leave. If you choose to stay, I will make you a promise. I won't ask you to make any more monsters. We've done enough of that, I know. You have been more than patient, and I have been rather demanding of you. So we shall try something else. What do you think about that?"

Mistaya stared at her, surprised by this unexpected turn of

events. The witch's eyes were silver again, soft and compelling. Mistaya remembered how things had been when they had first met, how eager Nightshade had been to teach, how anxious she had been to learn. She remembered how excited she had been the first time she had used her magic. She felt a little of the anger and mistrust drop away. She would like to continue the lessons, she supposed. She would like to stay. She didn't have to go home right this instant, not if Poggwydd was really safe and she didn't have to make any more monsters.

"Are my parents all right?" she asked suddenly.

Nightshade looked shocked. "Of course they are. Where do you think I was this morning? I changed form and went to Sterling Silver to make certain. Everything is fine. Your father and mother are well. Questor Thews protects them from Rydall, so we have time to finish your training in the use of magic. Then you will be ready to help protect them as well."

Mistaya stared at the witch without speaking. Nightshade seemed to be telling the truth. And Poggwydd hadn't said anything about her parents being in any danger or having come to any harm. Of course, it was hard to know whether anything the Gnome said was true, she supposed.

She was suddenly very confused. She sighed and looked away from the witch. The clearing was silent and empty save for them. Overhead, the sun brightened the skies and streamed down through the trees. She could almost believe that Poggwydd had never been there at all.

"Well," she said finally, "I guess I could stay for three more days."

"That would be very wise of you," Nightshade encouraged, and Mistaya failed to catch the hard edge that shaped the words or the way the witch's back lost a touch of its stiffness. "But you must not go out of the Deep Fell again."

Mistaya nodded. "I won't." She looked back at the witch tentatively. "What will we study now?"

Nightshade pursed her lips. "Medicine," she answered. "Healing through the use of magic."

She put her arm about Mistaya and began to walk her from the clearing back toward the hollow. "Mistaya," she said softly, "would you like to learn how to use your magic to bring something dead back to life?"

She smiled at the girl, and her eyes were lidded with pleasure.

Concealments

After three days of searching Graum Wythe and finding nothing, Questor Thews became convinced that somehow they were overlooking the obvious.

"We're wearing blinders!" he announced abruptly. He sat down on a packing crate with his chin in his hands and a frown on his face, bushy white eyebrows fiercely knit. "It's here, whatever it is, but we're simply not seeing it!"

Elizabeth and Abernathy looked over at him in voiceless contemplation. They were secluded in one of Graum Wythe's many storage rooms, deep in the bowels of the castle, a small windowless room where the sun never penetrated and the air was close and stale. They had searched the room once and were engaged at present in searching it a second time. By now, unfortunately, they had searched everywhere at least once and were growing discouraged.

"It shouldn't be taking this long," the wizard declared forcefully. "If we are meant to find it, if that is why we were brought here, then we should have stumbled on it by now."

"It would help if we knew what we were looking for," Abernathy observed glumly, lowering himself onto a second crate with a weary sigh. He was sick of poking through old boxes and dusty corners. He wanted to be outside, where the sun was shining and the air was fresh. He wanted to enjoy being who he was now that he had finally been restored to himself. All those dog years had fallen away as quickly as leaves from a tree on winter's first storm, as if none of it had ever really happened, all of it a dream from which he had finally awoken.

Elizabeth pursed her lips, causing her button nose to wrinkle. "I don't suppose you could be mistaken about what you are doing here?" she asked Questor Thews tentatively. "Is it possible that your coming was simply a fluke?" She seated herself next to Abernathy. "Or that you were dispatched here for some other reason?"

"It is possible," the wizard acknowledged charitably, "but unlikely. The consequences of magic are seldom haphazard. They almost always have a reason for turning out as they do. Nightshade would not have made the mistake of letting us live when she expected us to die. No, the conclusion is inescapable. Another magic intervened and saved us. We were sent here for a purpose, and I can think of no other purpose than to rescue Mistaya."

"Is it possible you are wrong about the magic being at Graum Wythe?" Elizabeth pressed. "Could it be somewhere else?"

Questor Thews scrunched up his face. "No. It has to be here. It has to be a magic that originally came from Landover. Nothing else makes sense!"

They stared at each other wordlessly for a moment, then looked about the room. "Could there be a second medallion?" Abernathy asked suddenly. "Another like the High Lord's?"

Questor raised a spiny eyebrow thoughtfully. It was a possibility he hadn't considered. But no; Michel Ard Rhi would have found such a talisman quickly enough and would not have gone to such great lengths to force Abernathy to give up the High Lord's when the scribe had been his prisoner at Graum Wythe those several years back.

The wizard shook his head. "No, it is something else, something that Michel would not have recognized. Something, at least, he could not find a way to use." He rubbed at his bearded chin thoughtfully. "This is exceedingly frustrating, I must say."

"Maybe we should have some lunch," Elizabeth suggested, nudging Abernathy playfully. "We might think better on full stomachs."

"We might think better after a short nap," Abernathy observed, nudging her back.

Questor Thews watched them wordlessly. He didn't like what he was seeing. Abernathy was growing complacent in his new life. He was altogether too satisfied with himself, as if getting back to Landover didn't mean anything to him now that he was a man again. He was forgetting his responsibilities. The High Lord and his family still depended on them, and Questor was afraid Abernathy was losing sight of that. He knew he shouldn't judge, but what was happening was obvious. Abernathy was rediscovering himself, and in the process of doing so he was making over his life to fit his new circumstances. It was a dangerous indulgence.

He cleared his throat sharply, causing both of them to jump. "Before we eat or nap, perhaps we could talk this business through one more time." He offered a smile to soften the force of his words. "Just for a few more moments, if you would. I admit to being rather desperate just about now."

Elizabeth smiled back reassuringly. "Don't worry, Questor. You'll find it sooner or later, whatever it is." She ran her fingers through her curly hair. "Even if you don't, this isn't a bad place to be trapped in, is it?"

She sounded altogether too hopeful. Questor did not dare say what he was thinking. "We have to get back to Landover," he insisted quietly. "We have to find the magic that will allow it."

Elizabeth sighed. "I know." She didn't sound convinced. "This magic, whatever it is, has to be something you'll recognize when you see it, doesn't it? If it's really here?"

"We've seen everything at least once already," Abernathy countered, pushing back his glasses on his nose.

"Maybe we're not looking at it the right way," Questor Thews mulled aloud.

Elizabeth swung her feet away from the crate and studied her sneakers. They were silent again, considering.

"Wait a minute," Abernathy said suddenly. "Maybe what we're looking for isn't a thing at all. Maybe that's why we're not seeing it. It was a spell that brought us here, magic conjured out of words. What if a spell is needed to take us back again?"

Questor's eyes widened, and he jumped up instantly from the packing crate. "Abernathy, you are an absolute genius! Of course that's what it is! A spell! We're not looking for a talisman at all! We're looking for a book of spells!"

Abernathy and Elizabeth rose as well, looking decidedly less certain of the matter. "But wouldn't Michel have recognized a book of that sort?" Abernathy asked doubtfully. "Wouldn't he have used it to get back into Landover there at the end, when he wanted to regain the throne? Or wouldn't your brother have searched it out when Holiday defied him? I know it was my idea, but on thinking it through, it doesn't make much sense. If there is a spell that allows passage back into Landover, why didn't one of them use it?"

"Perhaps because they couldn't," the wizard offered, stalking first to one side of the cluttered room, then back again to the other, head lowered, hands swinging animatedly. "Because the spell wouldn't work for them, maybe. I don't know. But I think you have stumbled on something nevertheless. A spell brought us over. It would make sense that a spell would take us back. A reversal of the magic that brought us here. A reworking of the words . . ."

A nasty suspicion crossed his mind, one that had occurred to him earlier in Elizabeth's kitchen when they had been discussing the reasons for what had happened to them. He had discarded it then, refusing to consider it too closely, unable to contemplate the possibility. Now it was back again, looking all too possible to be ignored.

He stopped his pacing and looked at Abernathy with haunted eyes. "Abernathy, this is difficult for me to suggest, but what if . . ."

He never finished. Light flared in the shadows at the far side of the storage room, and all three turned abruptly to face it. The light brightened sharply and then disappeared, leaving in its wake a decidedly ragged and frightened G'home Gnome sitting stunned and shivering on the concrete floor.

When he saw them staring at him, he gasped and threw up his hands defensively. "Don't hurt me!" he begged, blinking rapidly and trying to curl into a ball. "I just want to go home!"

Questor Thews exchanged a startled glance with Abernathy. A G'home Gnome? Here? What was this all about?

"Now, now, no one is going to hurt you," Questor reassured the other, starting forward, then stopping again as the Gnome started to gasp for air. "Are you all right?"

The Gnome nodded uncertainly. "If you can call being fried in witch fire 'all right,' then I suppose so."

Witch fire? Questor and Abernathy exchanged a second glance. "What's your name?" Questor pressed. The grimy little fellow was twisted down into an impossible position. "Come, now. We mean you no harm. We are all friends here."

The Gnome sniffled uncertainly, peering out from beneath crossed arms. "G'home Gnomes have precious few friends anywhere," he pointed out sullenly. He lifted his head. He was the scruffiest fellow imaginable, tattered and disheveled and in desperate need of a bath. "You tell me who you are first."

Questor sighed. "I am Questor Thews. This is Abernathy. That is Elizabeth." He pointed to each in turn. "Now, then. Who are you?"

"Poggwydd," the G'home Gnome said. He sounded proud of the fact. He lowered his arms and straightened up a bit. "Questor Thews, the Court Wizard? I heard you were Rydall's prisoner. You and the dog. Is that where we are, in Rydall's prison? Is that where the witch sent me?"

"Wait a minute." This time Questor Thews came right over and brought the Gnome firmly to his feet. "The witch, you said? Do you mean Nightshade?"

Poggwydd nodded. "Who else?" He was a little more sure of himself now. "She's the one who did this to me. Sent me here, wherever that is. Used her witch fire. Say, you didn't answer. Are we in Rydall's prison? What's going on?"

Questor Thews took Poggwydd by the elbow, marched him over to a vacant packing crate, and sat him down. The Gnome was rubbing at his wet nose and trying unsuccessfully to look brave. He kept his eyes fixed on Questor, as if by doing so he could stave off anything worse happening to him.

"Poggwydd," the wizard addressed him solemnly. "I want you to tell us everything that happened, everything you can remember, especially about Nightshade."

"I can do that, all right," the Gnome declared. He paused suspiciously. "You promise me you aren't friends with her?"

"I promise," Questor replied.

Poggwydd nodded, thought it over, then cleared his throat officiously. "Well, I thought she was going to hurt me—the witch, that is. She had that look in her eye. She was real mad at me because of the little girl. Caught me talking with her out there in a clearing about a mile from the Deep Fell. Ridiculous, really. I didn't even know her; she just showed up out of nowhere, way out in those woods, wanting to talk. So we did, and then the witch came, and the little girl asked her not to hurt me, said it wasn't my fault, but the witch didn't look like she believed her, so—"

"Whoa! Stop! Hold on!" Questor held up his hands imploringly. His brow knit furiously. "What little girl are you talking about? What did she look like? Did she tell you her name?"

Poggwydd stared, startled by the look on the other's face. He glanced past the wizard to the other two, found no help there, and looked back again. "I don't know what she looked like. Who can remember? She was . . . small. Not very old, maybe ten. Had freckles and blond hair." He frowned. "She was very clever. Played some games with me while we talked. Pretended to be . . . She said she was the High Lord's . . ." He stopped, no longer certain where to go. "She said her name was Misty."

"Mistaya," Questor breathed, backing away. "So Nightshade has her. Or had her. Did she escape, Poggwydd? Is that what happened?"

The G'home Gnome looked at him blankly. "Escape? I don't know if she did or not. I don't know where she came from. I don't even know who she is for sure. What I do know is that the witch was furious when she found me talking with her and that's why I'm here!" He paused, rubbing at his bristly chin. Bits of dirt flaked off. "Although maybe that's not right, either. You know, she asked the witch not to hurt me, the little girl did. But I don't think the witch was paying any attention to her and meant to fry me like a piece of old meat."

"But she didn't," Questor interjected, trying to hurry the story along, anxious to pin down his suspicions.

Poggwydd shook his head. "Well, there was this mud puppy, you see. I think maybe he stopped it from happening." He looked confused all over again. "Is that possible?"

Eventually they got the whole story out of him although it took a while to do so. They heard about how Mistaya had come upon his camp not far from the Deep Fell and engaged him in conversation. They heard about Haltwhistle and how he seemed to be the girl's companion. Finally, they heard about Nightshade's unexpected appearance, her anger at discovering Mistaya outside the Deep Fell, and her attack on

Poggwydd, which appeared to have been thwarted in part by the magic of the mud puppy, resulting in the Gnome's appearance at Graum Wythe.

"Just like us!" Abernathy exclaimed as the Gnome finished. He was standing next to Questor Thews by now, looking quite animated. "Questor, that must be what happened to us, too! The mud puppy intervened, changed Nightshade's magic, and sent us here! It sounds exactly the same!"

"Indeed," Questor agreed, pursing his lips, thinking hard.

"Where is here?" Poggwydd asked once again. "You haven't said yet."

"In a minute," Questor replied, turning away momentarily and then back again. "But who sent the mud puppy to Mistaya? It must have happened that night, while we slept, before the witch came. We were in the lake country, so it could have been the River Master. But the only mud puppy I ever heard of outside the fairy mists is the one who serves the Earth Mother."

"What difference does it make?" Abernathy cut him short. "What matters is that the witch has Mistaya and is using her to hurt the High Lord, just as she promised she would. You were right, Questor Thews. We are here for a purpose, and it must have something to do with helping Ben Holiday. We just have to find out what it is."

"A book of spells," Questor recalled, thinking back to where this conversation had started. "All right, then." He wheeled about, strode quickly to Poggwydd, and placed both hands firmly on the Gnome's narrow shoulders. "Where you are doesn't matter, Poggwydd. What's important is that you are in no immediate danger. But the little girl, Misty, is. We have to get out of here and back to where she is. There is something here, in this place, that can help us do that—if we can find it. That is what we intend to do right now. While we search, I want you to stay right here."

Poggwydd looked around doubtfully. "Why should I do

that? Why can't I just go home? I can find my way once I'm outside again."

Questor gave him a sympathetic look. "Not from here, you can't. You will have to trust me on this." He paused, thinking. "If you try, Poggwydd, Nightshade might get her hands on you a second time. Do you understand me?"

The Gnome nodded quickly. He understood, all right. "I'll do as you say," he agreed reluctantly. "How long do I have to wait?"

"I don't know. Maybe quite a while. You must be patient."

Poggwydd sniffled. "I don't have anything to eat. I'm hungry."

Abernathy rolled his eyes. Questor squeezed the Gnome's shoulders and released him. "I know. Be brave. We'll try to find you something to eat and bring it down. But you have to stay where you are, no matter what. This is important, Poggwydd. You must not leave this room for anything. All right?"

The Gnome rubbed at his nose and shrugged. "All right. I'll wait. But try to hurry."

"We'll be as quick as we can." Questor backed away, looking once again at Abernathy and Elizabeth. "We'll have to start over, tourists or no tourists. The common rooms first, then back into storage. But I'm willing to bet the book we need is right out there where we can see it."

"You know," Elizabeth said thoughtfully, "I think there were some books that were kept separate from the others, ones printed in a language that no one here could read. My father mentioned them once."

"Now we're getting somewhere!" Questor exclaimed in undisguised glee. "Books written in Landover's language, carried over by Michel or my brother! They would have to be the ones, wouldn't they?"

And with that, following Questor's final reassuring smile

and wave of the hand to Poggwydd, they were out the door and on their way back through the castle.

The search took them longer than they expected, however, extending well into the late afternoon, when the last of the tourists were straggling back to their buses and cars and heading home. They hunted through the rooms of the castle twice before they found what they were looking for. There were books in every room, and most of them were under lock and key. That meant keeping watch and distracting both tourists and guides while the locks were released and a quick survey made to determine if any of the books were what they were looking for. Questor used magic on the locks, which hastened the process, but checking through the books took an inordinate amount of time and for most of the day yielded absolutely nothing.

Until finally, with time running out and the castle closing down, Elizabeth remembered a massive old glass-front cabinet in an upstairs drawing room tucked away in a dormer that was not visible from the roped-off doorway. There were some books there, she thought. Just a few, but she remembered them because her father had remarked once on their covers. Following her suggestion, they hurried to the drawing room as a bell sounded closing time in the downstairs hall. While the girl and Abernathy kept watch, Questor stepped over the ropes and wormed his way through an obstacle course of furniture to the cabinet. He peered inside. Sure enough, there were the books, a dozen of them, all wrapped in dark cloth covers that concealed the titles. The cabinet latch was locked, but a whisper of magic and he was inside.

Excited now, Questor reached past a collection of amethyst glassware that fronted the books and pulled the first out. To his extreme disappointment it was written in English and had nothing at all to do with Landover. He checked another two. It was the same. Another dead end, it seemed. Hope

dwindling, he continued on more quickly. Books on garden-
ing, travel, and history.

"Questor Thews, hurry!" Abernathy hissed from the
doorway as voices from down the hall rapidly approached.

Questor opened the eighth book in the collection and his
eyebrows shot up. It was written in Ancient Landoverian
script, in a language the old wizards had commonly used. He
paged through it hurriedly to make sure, hearing the voices
more clearly: laughter, a quick greeting to Elizabeth, her response. Feverishly, he wedged himself between the wall and
the cabinet, where he was out of sight of anyone standing in
the doorway.

"Still poking about, Elizabeth?" someone asked, coming
to a stop beyond the ropes. "Aren't you getting hungry?"

"Oh, we're almost done," she replied with a nervous
laugh. "Is it all right to stay a bit longer?"

"One hour," a second voice advised. "Then *we* leave. Call
if you need anything."

The voices continued on down the hall and faded away.

"Questor!" Abernathy warned a second time, his patience obviously at an end.

Questor freed himself from his hiding place and looked
down at his discovery. Carefully he pulled back the cloth covering. There were symbols etched in gold leaf on the leather
binding that read *Gateway Mythologies*.

"Drat!" he muttered, shoved the book back into place,
and pulled out the next one. *Greensward Histories*. He reached
for the third.

Theories of Magic and Its Uses.

"Yes, yes, yes!" the wizard whispered in relief.

He could not take time to read it here, he knew. He
checked the last of the volumes and found nothing. He would
have to hope that the one in his hands held what he was
looking for. He moved quickly back across the room toward
the door.

"I've got it!" he announced triumphantly as he reached Elizabeth and Abernathy.

Abruptly an alarm went off. They all jumped, and Elizabeth gave a short cry. Questor hurriedly tucked the book into the carry bag he had brought. "What's happened?" he gasped, white hair and beard flying out in every direction. "What did I do?"

"I don't think you did anything at all!" Elizabeth grasped his arm as he whirled this way and that, casting about for imagined attackers. "It's a fire alarm! But I can't imagine what set it off!"

Questor Thews and Abernathy immediately looked at each other. "Poggwydd!" they exclaimed.

They hurried along the corridor to the stairs and started down, jostling and bumping against each other, all talking at once.

"We shouldn't have left him alone!" Questor moaned, clutching the carry bag and its precious contents close against his chest.

"We should have tied and gagged him!" Abernathy snapped. From below came the sound of shouts.

"Maybe it isn't him at all!" Elizabeth encouraged.

But it was, of course. Two security guards were hauling Poggwydd into view just as they arrived at the bottom of the stairs. The Gnome was disheveled and covered from head to foot in a coating of ash. He was struggling and moaning pathetically while the guards held him at arm's length between them, not at all certain what it was they had.

"Boy, I've seen it all!" one of them was muttering.

"Shut up and hold on to him!" the other growled irritably.

Poggwydd caught sight of Questor Thews and started to call for help, but the wizard made a quick motion with one hand and the startled G'home Gnome was rendered instantly voiceless. His mouth worked in futile desperation, but nothing came out.

"Stand back, folks," one of the guards advised as they carried the struggling Gnome past.

"What do you have there?" Questor asked, feigning ignorance.

"Don't know." The guard's attention was diverted momentarily as Poggwydd tried to bite him. "Some sort of monkey, I guess. Filthy as a pig and twice as ugly. Found him in the kitchen, trying to start a fire. It almost looked like he was trying to cook some food he'd stolen, but c'mon, he's a monkey, right? Anyway, the fire alarm went off or he might have burned the place down. Look at him fight! Mean little devil. Must have escaped from a zoo or something. How he found his way here, I'll never know."

"Well, be careful with him," Questor offered, trying to avoid Poggwydd's furious look.

"Careful as can be." The guard laughed.

"There, there, little fellow," Questor called after the struggling Gnome. "Someone will come to claim you soon!"

"Can't be soon enough for me!" the other guard called back, and the unfortunate Poggwydd was dragged kicking and writhing through the front door and out of sight.

Questor, Abernathy, and Elizabeth stood staring after the Gnome in silence for a moment. Then Questor said, "This is my fault. I completely forgot about him."

"You told him to wait where he was," Abernathy reminded him, evidencing a noticeable lack of sympathy. "He should have listened."

"Questor, what did you do to stop him from talking?" Elizabeth asked.

The wizard sighed. "Cast a small spell. I couldn't very well let him tell them who we are, and that is exactly what he was about to do. Besides, things would be much worse for Poggwydd if they found out he can talk. He is better off if they think him an animal, believe me."

"He *is* an animal," Abernathy muttered. "Stupid Gnome."

"Stupid or not, we have to help him," Elizabeth said at once.

"What we have to do," Questor announced quickly, "is to go back to the house, where I can study this book and find out if it is what we are looking for."

"It better be," Abernathy grumbled. "I have seen all I care to see of Graum Wythe!"

"Where do you think they will take him?" Elizabeth asked, her brow creased with worry.

"Wherever they think he came from, I suppose," Questor replied absently. He was peering down into the carry bag at the book.

"I just don't want us to forget about him a second time," Elizabeth insisted. They started for the entry. "He looks so helpless."

"Believe me, he is anything but," Abernathy sniffed. He was thinking about the G'home Gnomes' penchant for eating stray pets. "He does not deserve an ounce of your sympathy. He is a nuisance, plain and simple."

Elizabeth took his hand and squeezed it. "You are being difficult, Abernathy. It's not his fault he's here."

"It is not our fault, either. Nor our responsibility."

"She's right, you know," Questor Thews offered.

Abernathy gave his friend a scathing look. "I know she's right. You don't have to tell me that."

"I was just trying to point out—"

"Confound it, Questor Thews, why do you insist on belaboring—"

Still arguing between themselves while Elizabeth tried in vain to reestablish some semblance of peace, the wizard and the scribe passed down the corridor to the front door of the castle and out into the fading light.

In front of them, a King County police car was just pulling away.

After their return to Elizabeth's house, Questor Thews stayed up all night reading the purloined book. He sat curled up in an easy chair in the far corner of his bedroom with a single light illuminating the pages as he turned them one by one. He was certain early on that this book was what they had been looking for and that hidden within its text lay the answer to the riddle behind their improbable escape from Nightshade. *Theories of Magic and Its Uses.* They were right there, all the discoveries of all the wizards since the dawn of Landover, set out as postulates and axioms, theories proved and suspected, absent only the recipe and ingredients for each specific stew. They were theories, not formulas, but were quite enough to get at the essence of things. Questor even knew what to look for. He hated himself for this, but the obviousness of the truth facing him was inescapable once he accepted its possibility. He worked his way through the book tirelessly, ignoring his exhaustion, suppressing his growing fear, reading on determinedly.

Across the room from him Abernathy slept with his face turned away from the light. It was just as well. His friend didn't want to have to look at him just now.

Sometime during the long, slow hours after midnight Questor Thews discovered what he was looking for. Even so, he kept reading, not wanting to take anything for granted, not wanting to give up his search for a better answer, although he knew already that there wasn't going to be one. He read all the way through the book and back again. He studied individual passages and considered alternative possibilities until his head hurt. Then he went back to the passage he had discovered earlier and read it again slowly, carefully. There was no mistake. It was what he was looking for. It was the answer he had been seeking.

He sighed and put the book down in his lap. He looked over at Abernathy again, and tears came to his eyes. His face

crumpled, and his chest ached with need. Life was just so unfair sometimes. He wished things could be different. He
wished this could be happening to someone else. His sticklike
frame twisted into a clutter of old bones and wrinkled skin,
and his heart knotted in his chest.

Finally, exhausted of feeling, he reached up, turned out
the light, and sat motionless in the dark, waiting for morning.

Specter

"The title of the book is *Monsters of Man & Myth,*" Ben told Willow, speaking directly into her ear.

They rode double atop a still-skittish Jurisdiction, Willow in front, Ben behind. Bunion had retrieved the horse after a lengthy chase, and now they were traveling west again toward the Greensward. Ahead rose the black wall of an approaching thunderstorm. Behind lay the remains of the wurm and the sulfurous stench of ash and gases from the Fire Springs. Overhead, the sun beat down mercilessly, a blinding white-hot flame that turned the arid emptiness of the Eastern Wastelands into a furnace.

Rain will come as a welcome relief, Ben thought wearily, trying to distance himself from his growing thirst.

"And Rydall's creatures were in this book?" Willow asked in response, half turning to catch a glimpse of his face.

He nodded into her emerald hair, breathing the dusty scent of it. "A giant that gained strength from its contact with the earth, a demon that could mimic the look and abilities of whatever foe it faced, and a robotic machine man, armored and indestructible." He looked off into the sweltering distance, trying to make out the geography of the land against the blackness of the storm. "I don't remember the specific stories so much as the picture of the robot. It's right on the cover, and it's exactly the same as Rydall's. But they're all there. It's as if Rydall read the book!"

"But that isn't possible, is it?"

Ben sighed. "You wouldn't think so."

Willow looked forward again. The land shimmered with heat and dust. Bunion was out there somewhere, scouting for further dangers. If he found any, he would try to find a way around them. Another confrontation in their present condition was unthinkable.

"Where is this book?" Willow asked.

"In the library with the others," Ben answered. "It's one of several I brought over with me from my old life, books that I thought I might like to have. I remember why I picked that one in particular. I've had it since I was a boy, and it seemed to represent something of what I was hoping to find here in Landover—as if what wasn't real in my old life might be real in this one." He shook his head. "I got my wish, didn't I?"

Willow was silent for a moment. "But how would Rydall know about it?"

Ben shrugged. "I can't imagine. It doesn't make sense. Why would he know about this book as opposed to any other book? Has he read through my whole library? Does his magic enable him to search out any book at random and read through it without even being there?" He swallowed against the dryness in his throat and kept his temper tightly in check. "What I keep coming back to, Willow, is how personal this all feels. Rydall using my own things against me; striking out at my family and friends; kidnapping Mistaya, Questor, and Abernathy; attacking you and me, chasing us all over the place with this business of pitting his monsters against the Paladin; coming after me over and over again—I just don't get it. Supposedly it's about surrendering the throne to Landover, but it doesn't feel like Landover's got all that much to do with it."

Willow nodded without looking at him. "No," she agreed, and was silent again.

They rode on through the afternoon until the storm met them as they approached the edge of the Greensward. Black clouds swept past, blotting out the sun and blue sky, and a driving, blinding rain enveloped and soaked them to the skin in moments. The dust and grime of their travel were washed from their bodies, and the air about them was cooled. Jurisdiction plodded on, head lowered against the sheets of rain and swirling wind, and soon Bunion reappeared to lead them down into a grove of maple trees that provided good shelter from the damp. They dismounted, stripped off their clothing, wrung it out, and hung it to dry by a fire that Bunion had somehow managed to start. Sitting cross-legged in a soft patch of grass beneath the canopy of the trees, they watched the storm swirl around them and pass on. Darkness descended, and the world beyond their encampment disappeared. They dressed again, chewed halfheartedly on stalks of Bonnie Blue, rolled into their travel cloaks, and quickly fell asleep.

When they woke, it was raining again, a slow, persistent drizzle that fell out of low, empty leaden skies. The whole of the land about them had gone gray and misty in the early-morning light. They mounted Jurisdiction once more and rode out into the weather. Bunion went on ahead, a small, spidery figure skittering into the gloom until he was lost from view. The summer day was warm and filled with the smell of damp earth. Ahead, the Greensward stretched away in a patchwork of greens and browns, of tilled fields and grassy pastures, of mature forests and midseason plantings, all interspersed with rivers and lakes that in the rainy haze took on the look of molten metal, their surfaces stirred by the faint breezes that swept down across the flats.

By midday Bunion had returned with a second horse. He didn't offer an explanation of where he had gotten the beast, and Ben and Willow didn't ask. It was not a farm animal; it was a trained riding horse. Willow stood in front of the horse, a brown mare, and spoke to it encouragingly for a moment, then mounted smoothly and wheeled over beside Ben. She gave Bunion a smile and a wink, and the kobold was gone again.

They rode on through the rest of that day and most of the next. All the while it rained, leaving them wet clear through except for brief periods of dryness when they camped and were able to chase away the damp with the help of the fires Bunion always seemed to be able to construct. They passed Rhyndweir and several of the other castles of the Lords of the Greensward but did not stop to ask for shelter. Ben had no interest in seeing anyone, preferring to minimize the chance of further attacks from Rydall. Surprisingly, there were none. Since Rydall had found them in the Eastern Wastelands with the wurm, Ben had supposed he would be able to find them anywhere. Given the frequency and consistency of the attacks, he had expected another by now. On the other hand, Rydall had used up four of his promised seven challenges, so perhaps he was rethinking his strategy. Ben didn't consider it worth his while to ponder the matter further. He was simply grateful for the respite.

He used the time to think. With his travel cloak a shield against the elements, Willow a silent wraith riding next to him, and the rain a curtain that shrouded everything in damp, gray silence, he shut himself away from his discomfort and tedium and concentrated on the puzzle of Rydall of Marnhull. He was beginning to consider possibilities he had not considered before. Some of this was prompted by his growing sense of desperation. He could feel time running out. Sooner or later Rydall was going to send a monster from which no one could save him—not the Paladin, not Strabo, not anyone. Sooner or later his defenses were not going to be strong enough, and the struggle to survive would be over. The only thing that could prevent that from happening was uncovering the secret behind Rydall, and Ben seemed to be no closer to

doing that than ever. So he determined to quit thinking in
predictable ways, to be more innovative, more daring. He had
to stop being led around by Rydall. He had to refuse to follow
the paths Marnhull's King left open to him and start opening
a few of his own. There was a net being woven about Ben
Holiday, and he could sense it tightening with every new
strand laid out. He had to find a way to cut through the
webbing.

His thinking, however, was prompted not so much by his
desperation as by his realization that there were a few loose
threads in Rydall's carefully woven net. First, there was Ben's
growing certainty that Rydall's sending of monsters to do battle with the Paladin was part of a game that had far more to
do with Ben than with Landover's throne. Second, there was
his recognition that three of the four monsters had come from
the stories in his *Monsters of Man & Myth* book. Three created
in painstaking detail from the writer's descriptions, as if Rydall
had copied the creatures directly from the book's pages. Three,
but not the fourth. No, the fourth, a wurm, had come from
somewhere else.

A witch's favorite magic, Strabo had informed him.

In Landover that meant Nightshade.

He had given no serious consideration before to the possibility that Nightshade might be involved in this. Why would
he? Rydall was an outlander, a usurper of power, an interloper
whose goals were directly at odds with Nightshade's. On the
other hand, no one hated Ben Holiday and his family more
than the witch did. Stripped of Rydall's obvious presence, this
entire business felt very much like her work. The use of dark
magic, the attack on family and friends, and the calculated effort to destroy him all smacked of Nightshade. While he had
heard nothing from the witch in more than two years, he did
not expect that she had forgotten her promise that she would
never forgive him for what had happened to her in the Tangle

Box. For what she had been made to feel for him when they had both been stripped of their identities. For what she viewed as the loss of her dignity.

What if there was no Rydall? Oh, there might be someone masquerading as Marnhull's King, but what if Rydall himself was a fiction? No one had ever heard of Rydall or Marnhull—not the River Master, not Kallendbor, not even Strabo, who had traveled everywhere. No one could find Rydall or Marnhull. There was no trace of Mistaya, Questor Thews, or Abernathy. There was no sign of an invading army. The only physical evidence of Rydall at any time in this entire episode had been presented when Marnhull's King and his black-cloaked companion had appeared at the gates of Sterling Silver.

So, Ben mulled, what if this whole business was an elaborate charade? Where, after all, was the one place in Landover that he hadn't searched since Mistaya had disappeared? Where was the one place he had ignored because it wasn't readily accessible to him and because it didn't seem reasonable to look there? Where was the one place none of them had looked?

The Deep Fell, where Nightshade made her home.

Ben Holiday's suspicions hardened. What had begun as a consideration of possibilities rapidly evolved into a careful sifting of facts. Nightshade as Rydall; it made as much sense as anything else he had envisioned. Or Nightshade as Rydall's black-cloaked companion, he amended. He remembered the way the hooded rider had studied him when he had come down onto the causeway to pick up the gauntlet, the intensity of that veiled gaze. He remembered the way both riders had looked upon Mistaya when she had climbed onto the ramparts.

His chest tightened, and his stomach turned to ice.

It was late on the third day of their journey home when they came in sight of Sterling Silver. The castle materialized through the gloom like a vision brought to life from a child's

imagining, a gleaming, rain-streaked rise of spires and parapets
that hardened into stone and mortar, timber and metal, pennants and flags as they closed on its island surround. They
crossed the moat through a misty curtain and passed beneath
the raised portcullis. Retainers scurried to take their horses
and usher them inside out of the weather. Ben and Willow
went wordlessly to their bedchamber, stripped off their sodden
clothing, climbed into a tub of steaming water, and lay back to
soak. When some of the ache and discomfort of their travel
had been eased, they climbed out again, dried off, and dressed
in fresh clothing.

Then Ben led Willow down to the library for a close
look at his copy of *Monsters of Man & Myth.* It took only moments to locate it. It sat on the shelf exactly where he remembered leaving it. He pulled it out and looked at the cover. Sure
enough, there was Rydall's robot. He thumbed through the
pages and in short order found a drawing of the giant. Then
he found the writer's description of the demon that could
mimic any foe.

He showed the book to Willow. "You see? Exactly the
same as Rydall's monsters."

She nodded. "But how did he do it? How did he know
about this book and these particular monsters? Ben, *I* didn't
know about this book. I didn't even know it was here. We've
never talked about it, not once. How did Rydall know?"

It was true, he realized. He had never taken it down and
shown it to her before. They had never discussed it. There had
never been any reason to do so. He had carried it over with
him through the mists, unpacked it, placed it in the library,
and forgotten it.

Until now. He stood close to the sylph, staring down at
the book in silence. Without, the rain continued in dreary, unchanging monotony, the sound of its falling a soft patter on
the stone. Ben felt strangely lulled, as if he might fall asleep at
any moment. He was more tired than he wanted to admit, but

he could not afford to sleep until he had unraveled the secret of Rydall and his monsters. Not until he had found a way to bring Mistaya home.

Mistaya.

He stared at Willow in surprise. "You said you didn't know about this book. But do you know who did? Mistaya. I caught her reading it once, paging through it. I didn't say any-thing, didn't interrupt her. I don't think she even saw me watching. She was so small, and I didn't think she could even understand it . . ."

He trailed off, his mind racing. "Willow," he said quietly, "I want you to listen to something. I want you to tell me what you think."

Then he told her of his suspicion that Nightshade might be Rydall's creator and that the Witch of the Deep Fell might be behind everything that had happened to them. He gave her all his reasons, laid out all the possibilities, and provided all the underpinnings of his conjecture. Willow listened intently, not interrupting, waiting for him to finish.

"The thing is," he concluded worriedly, "Mistaya could have told Nightshade about the book, could have described the monsters, could even have drawn a picture. She's smart enough to have remembered. She probably understood a whole lot more than I gave her credit for."

"But why would she do this?" Willow wanted to know instantly. "Why would she do anything to help the witch?"

Ben shook his head. "I don't know. I'm guessing about all this. But she has seen the book, and if Nightshade is Rydall, then it was Nightshade who kidnapped her. And has her now."

Willow gave him a long, steady look as she considered the possibility. "Do you remember when we talked about who else knew of the connection between the medallion and the Paladin? Only you and I, you said. But Nightshade knows, too. She was with you in the Tangle Box when you used the medallion."

Ben took a deep breath. "You're right. I forgot about that."

"You said you believed magic was used to hide the medallion when the robot attacked at Rhyndweir. Nightshade possesses such magic." Willow's face was stricken. "Ben, we have to go to the Deep Fell."

Ben slid his book back into its slot on the shelf. "I know. We'll go tomorrow, first thing. It's too late to start out again today. We're exhausted. We need at least one night's sleep in a dry bed."

He moved over to her and put his arms about her waist. "But we're definitely going," he promised. "And if that's where Mistaya is, we'll get her back."

Willow put her arms around him in response and lay her head against his shoulder. They held each other in silence, drawing comfort and strength from their joining, hardening themselves against the feelings of fear and doubt that twisted within.

Outside, the shadows lengthened toward twilight and the rain fell harder.

They ate dinner alone in the dark silence of the eating hall, two solitary figures hunched close within the candlelight where it pushed back against the gloom. They did not speak much, too tired to attempt conversation, too immersed in their own thoughts. When they were finished, they retired to their bedchamber, climbed beneath the covers, and quickly fell asleep.

It was midnight when Ben woke. He lay quietly for a moment, trying to gain his bearings. He felt a faint burning where the medallion lay against his chest, a warning that something was wrong. He sat up slowly, his ears straining for sounds in the darkness. The rain had ceased finally, but the clouds hung across the sky like a shroud, blotting out the light of moons and stars. He could hear water dripping from the eaves and battlements, soft, small splashes in the inky night. Next to him Willow's breathing was relaxed and steady.

Then he heard something scrape against the stone outside his window, a barely discernible sound, a whisper of trouble approaching. He slipped from the bed swiftly, noiselessly, feeling the medallion burn sharply now against his skin. Panic raced through him. He knew what was coming, and he was not ready for it. It was too soon. He had convinced himself that Rydall would not strike again so quickly, that he would deliberate before sending his fifth monster.

Ben glanced about the room, looking for help. Where was Bunion? He had not seen the kobold since their return. Was he anywhere close at hand? He turned back to the bed and Willow. He had to get her out of there. He had to get her to safety, away from whatever was going to happen next.

He reached down for her shoulder and shook her gently. "Willow!" he hissed. "Wake up!"

Her eyes opened instantly, a brilliant emerald even in the near black, wide and deep and filled with understanding. "Ben," she said.

Then the room's light shifted as a shadow filled the window, and Ben wheeled back to face it. The shadow rose into the gap and perched there, hunched down against the lesser blackness of the night, lean and sinewy and somehow terribly familiar. He could not see but could feel the shadow's eyes upon him. He could feel the eyes taking his measure.

He did not move, knowing that if he did so, he would be dead before he could complete whatever effort he began. His hand was already closed about the medallion, as if by instinct it had reached for the only help left. He held the medallion within the clutch of his fingers, feeling the graven image of the knight riding out of his castle at sunrise, the Paladin from Sterling Silver off to do battle for his King. He felt the image and stared at the shadow in the window, seeing now that it wasn't all smooth and taut as he had first believed but was in fact in places ragged and broken, a creature that had suffered some catastrophic misfortune and bore the injuries because there could be no healing. Bits and pieces of the shadow hung loose, as if layers of skin had been shredded. Bone jutted in cracked shards from joints no longer whole. It made no sound, but he could hear the silent wail of its inescapable pain and despair.

Then the shadow's head shifted slightly, a tilting to one side, little more, and silver eyes gleamed catlike out of the black.

Ben's breath caught in his throat.

It was the Ardsheal, come back from the dead.

He had no time to ponder how this could be, no chance to deliberate on what it meant. His response was instinctive and eschewed reason and hope. His fingers tightened on the medallion, and the light flared outward in spears of white brightness. Willow screamed. The Ardsheal launched itself at Ben, a black panther at its prey, quicker than thought. But the Paladin was there instantly, come out of a sudden, impossibly brilliant explosion of light that erupted in the dozen yards of space between King and assailant. The knight rose up in a surge of gleaming silver armor and weaponry, catching the Ardsheal in midair and flinging it aside. The force of the collision sent the Ardsheal slamming into the stone wall and the Paladin stumbling backward into Ben. A metal-clad elbow hammered into Ben's head, and he collapsed on the bed next to Willow, so stunned that he was barely able to hold on to the medallion.

The Ardsheal was on its feet in a heartbeat, pulling itself upright with the smoothness of a snake, the ease of its recovery belying its ragged condition. Through a haze of pain and dizziness, Ben watched it rise, his vision blurred and his head aching from the blow. But he felt the pain and the dizziness from inside the Paladin's armor, where his consciousness was now irrevocably lodged, there to remain until he triumphed or died. He saw Willow embracing his corporeal body, whispering frantically in his ear. He wondered for the briefest second what she was saying, remembering that he had wanted to get her clear of the room before this battle was joined. He caught a sudden glimpse of the Ardsheal's face in the gloom, one eye gone, a gash opened from forehead to chin, skin crosshatched with cuts and lesions. He saw it tumbling out of the castle window at Rhyndweir, riding the robot to the rocks below and certain death. He wondered how it could possibly have survived.

Then the mind-set of the Paladin closed down like a visor, and all he knew were the knight's long memories of battles fought and survived. He went down into his harder-than-iron other self, the battle-tested veteran of a thousand struggles from which only he had emerged. He withdrew into his armor and his experience, locking away what life there was beyond, shutting out the man and the woman on the bed behind him, the castle in which he now battled, the world beyond, the past and the future, all things but the here and now and the enemy that sought to destroy him.

The Ardsheal feinted right to left, testing. It was a dead thing by the look of its flat silver eyes, by the broken mix of skin and bone, by the gaping wounds that marked its body. But it lived beyond death, fed by magic that wrestled through its once-lifeless tissues and demanded of it one more task before it could rest in peace. The Paladin sensed this, knowing its enemy from knowledge innate and from some spark of Ben Holiday's own reason and memory. He watched the wraith before him shift and shift again, snakelike, looking for an opening. He saw it for the danger it was, a creature created of magic to serve a single purpose; to hunt and destroy. He saw it as he saw so few others he faced—as an equal.

The Ardsheal came at him with lightning speed, so low that it would be hard to take away his legs. The Paladin dropped on the creature in an effort to pin it, his dagger digging futilely into the stone floor as the Ardsheal rolled away, ripping at the knight's visor, twisting at it wickedly. The Paladin shook off the blow and rose to face his enemy once more. Quickness and strength, cunning and experience—the Ardsheal had them all and felt nothing beyond the magic that compelled it. It would not stop; it would not quit. It would keep coming until it could come no more.

An Ardsheal is a match for anything alive. Nothing is more dangerous. The River Master's words.

In the shadows the Ardsheal crouched. The Paladin thought momentarily of drawing forth his broadsword, but the weapon was too cumbersome and unwieldy for this foe. Small weapons would be more effective, until an opportunity presented itself, as it must if he was to survive.

He shifted the dagger to his left hand, reaching with the right for his long knife, and the Ardsheal was on him in a flash, ripping and tearing and wrenching at armor and limbs. The Paladin stumbled back under the fury of the attack, hearing the shriek of fastenings as they tore loose, feeling metal plates threaten to give way. Forsaking the dagger, he jammed both armored hands against the creature's chest and again flung it away. It came back at him at once, animal-wild, crazed beyond sense, a thing insane. It was impossibly strong, and its strength was aided by its lack of feeling and the rush of magic that fed it. It fought without hindrances of any kind; it battled without the complications that emotion and reason demanded. Its efforts were pure and unrestricted, its struggle single-minded. It would win or lose and still be dead either way.

For the third time the Paladin flung it away, and this time snatched free the long knife before it could recover. When it came again, he would skewer it on the blade and rip it in two. His breathing was harsh and unsteady. Though he would not acknowledge it because he could not permit himself to do so, his strength was already beginning to fail. He could not tell if it was the number of battles fought in so short a span of time or the weakened condition of the King he served, for both could play a part in determining whether he survived. He relied on himself, but he was irrevocably attached to the man who commanded his services and lent him his strength of will. If the King failed in his resolve, so might he. But such thoughts were not permitted. So he told himself only that he should end the fight quickly and not speculate further.

The Ardsheal stalked him through the bedchamber's gloom, another of night's faint shadows sidestepping the light. It was no longer attempting a frontal attack; it was looking to do something else. The Paladin shifted, turning to follow its movements, not leaving his place before the King and Queen. His armor hung loosely from the bindings in several places. He was coming undone, as ragged as his attacker. He could feel the other's eyes studying him, searching for an opening. Beneath the armor the Paladin was vulnerable. The Ardsheal sensed this. One strike was all it would take if the strike was deep enough.

It faked a quick rush and retreated. It faked another. The Paladin stayed set, not allowing himself to be drawn out. Then, in a flash of recognition, he saw what the Ardsheal was trying to do. It was trying to pull him far enough away from the King and Queen to leave them exposed. It would kill them, sensing, perhaps even knowing, that this would mean the defeat of the Paladin as well.

As if reading his thoughts, the Ardsheal attacked anew. It came in a slashing, wild charge, so quick that it was almost past the Paladin before he could act. As it was, he barely caught the Ardsheal's arm as it reached for the Queen, snatching the creature back and flinging it aside. This time he went after it, intent on finishing the battle, but again he was too slow, and the Ardsheal was up and away again into the gloom.

Twice more the elemental tried to slip past, and both times it nearly succeeded. Only the Paladin's experience and determination kept it at bay. The Queen was crying on the bed behind him now, small sounds only, almost silent in her misery, her despair. She was strong, but her fear was immense and impossible to conceal. She was terrified of the Ardsheal. The King was awake again. He had placed himself before her, and he held the medallion out like a talisman. Too frail, the both of them, the Paladin knew, to survive if he should fall.

The thought was a mind spike he was quick to wrench free and cast away from him.

The Ardsheal faded into emptiness, leaving the Paladin searching the darkness frantically. Then it reappeared out of nowhere directly before him, a frenzied blackness whipping atop him and beating him to the floor. It sought to break past, but the Paladin collapsed and, momentarily blinded, held on to one leg and dragged it back. The Ardsheal wrenched at the fallen champion, kicked at him, struck at him, tore at his weakened armor. The Paladin felt pain. In desperation, he hauled himself to his knees through the flurry of blows, through a massive effort that came mostly from the heart, and one final time hurled the Ardsheal away.

This time when the Ardsheal came to its feet, one arm hung limp. But the Paladin was a shambles of broken armor and torn bindings, aching muscles and wearied limbs, standing upright through sheer force of will. There was blood in his mouth and on his body. He still gripped the long knife, still waited for his chance to use it. But time was fleeing quickly now. Time was racing away.

The Ardsheal moved forward, an inexorable, implacable force.

Then the door to the room flew open, and a small bristling fury hurtled into the fray. It hammered into the Ardsheal and bore it backward to the wall. All claws and teeth, Bunion appeared to have gone berserk. The Ardsheal was caught off guard, staggered by the force of the kobold's attack. It twisted wildly, trying to dislodge its assailant. The Paladin lunged forward, the chance he had been waiting for there at last. He drove the dagger through the Ardsheal's skull with such force that he buried it to the hilt. The Ardsheal arched upward, silver eyes filling with blood. It tore Bunion free and wheeled toward the Paladin. But the knight had unsheathed the great broadsword, and with every ounce of strength left to him he swung the blade crosswise and down at his enemy. The blade caught the Ardsheal between neck and shoulder and cut straight through. Down it sliced, all the way to the creature's heart.

The Ardsheal slumped into the blow. It convulsed, and in the terrible eyes there was a hint of some ancient recognition that not even the darkest magic could withstand. The eyes fixed, and the magic faded. Death stole the Ardsheal back once more.

Broken, exhausted, a ragged caricature of the silver knight he had been when the battle had begun, the Paladin freed the broadsword and turned to Landover's King where he crouched on the bed. Their eyes met and held. He had the odd sense of looking back at himself. He started to drop to one knee, but he was caught up in the light of the medallion still held outstretched in the King's hand and carried down into healing sleep.

In the silence that followed Ben and Willow could hear the rain begin to fall again.

King's Guards were summoned, and the remains of the Ardsheal were removed. The sounds of the struggle had gone unheard, an impossibility in the absence of magic deliberately employed. When the soldiers were gone and the room had been cleaned and straightened, Bunion took up watch just outside the door. The kobold blamed himself for what had happened. He had been scouting once more, just beyond the castle walls, but somehow the very enemy he had been seeking had slipped past him and entered the castle unseen. No words were spoken, but Bunion's apology was there in the squint of his eyes and the flash of his teeth.

When Ben and Willow were alone again, they clung to each other as if to the last solid grip on a crumbling rock. They did not speak. They stood pressed together in the darkness and took comfort from their closeness. Willow was shaking in the summer heat. Ben, though he appeared steady, was inwardly shattered.

They climbed back into their bed, there in the no-longer-reassuring dark, eyes wandering the room, ears pricked for the faintest of sounds. They could not sleep and did not try. Ben stilled Willow's shivering, chasing momentarily at least her fear of the thing that had come to kill them. He held her tight against him and tried to find words for what he would say, for the confession he now knew he must make if he was ever again to find peace.

Without, the rain pattered on the stone and dripped from the capping on the walls in a steady cadence.

"I have to tell you something about the Paladin," he said finally, speaking in a rush the words he could not seem to organize better. "This isn't easy to explain, but I have to try. We're the same person, Willow. Right now his pain is all through me. I can feel the ache of his body and limbs, the wear on his soul, the hurt that threatens to break him down. I feel it when he does battle, but I feel it now, as well." He took a deep breath. "It's all I can do to stand it. It seems as if it might pull me apart, break all my bones, and flatten me into the earth. Even now it's there. He's gone, but it doesn't matter."

He felt her head lift from his shoulder so that her eyes could see his face. He felt her fingers move along his chest, searching. "He is part of me, Willow. That's what I want to say. He is part of me and always has been, ever since I came into Landover and took up the medallion of Kingship. The medallion joins us, makes us one when I call him up from wherever it is he waits."

He looked at her, looked quickly away. "When the medallion summons him, the magic carries some part of me inside his armor. Not my body or my mind but my heart and will and strength of purpose—those he requires. In some way the King and the King's champion are the same. That's the real secret of the medallion. It's a secret I couldn't tell you."

Her emerald eyes were steady as she stared at him. "Why couldn't you tell me?" she asked quietly.

"Because I was afraid of what it would do to you." He forced himself to meet her gaze and hold it. "I've wanted to tell you. I've felt I should, that it was wrong not to, but I was afraid. What would it do to you to know that every time the Paladin was summoned, it was me—or at least some important, necessary part of me—that would be required to do battle. What would it mean if you knew that the Paladin's death could bring mine as well."

He shook his head, feeling adrift. "But it's worse than that. Every time I go into the Paladin and become one with him, I feel myself slipping farther away from who I really am. I become him, and each time it is harder to get back. I live in constant fear that one time I might not be able to return because I do not want to, because I have forgotten who I am, because I like what I have become. The power of the magic is so seductive! When I'm the Paladin, he's all I wish to be. If the medallion did not bring me back to myself, if it did not take the Paladin away, I do not think I could ever return of my own will. I think I might be lost forever."

The pain in her eyes was terrible to see. "You should have told me," she said quietly. He nodded, emptied of words. "Don't you understand, Ben? I gave myself to you unconditionally when I found you at the Irrylyn. I belong to you, and nothing would ever make me leave. Nothing!"

"I know," he agreed.

"No, you don't, or you would not have hesitated to tell me this." Her voice was soft, but there was iron at the core. "There is nothing you could not tell me, Ben. Not ever. We will be together always, until the end. You know how it was foretold. You know the prophecy. You should never question the strength of its truth."

"I was afraid—" he began, but she hushed him quickly.

"No, let it go for now. Let it go." She touched him gently. "Tell me again. All of his pain comes back into you? All that he bore in your defense?"

He closed his eyes. "I feel as if I am falling apart. I feel as if I'm dying, and I cannot find the wound that's killing me. It's everywhere, inside and out. I am in fragments scattered all over this room—in the air, in the sound of the rain, in my own breathing. I don't know what to do. The Paladin won, but I seem to have lost. Calling him again so soon was too much to bear. It took too much out of me, Willow. I haven't the heart for this!"

"Shhh, no more," she comforted, pressing herself against him. She kissed his mouth. "You have heart enough for all of us, Ben Holiday. It has always been your greatest strength. You survived a terrible struggle. No ordinary man could have done what you did. Do not disparage yourself. Do not demean what you have accomplished. Listen to me. The secret of the Paladin is ours now, not yours alone to bear. Its weight can be better carried by two. I will help you. I will find ways to sustain you when you are weary and sick at heart as you are now. I will help shield you from the pain. If you must go into the Paladin for our sake, I will find a way to bring you back. Always. Forever. I love you."

"I have never doubted that," he replied softly. "I would have been finished long ago if I did."

She stroked his forehead gently, kissing him once more. Gradually he felt himself relax and begin to drift. "Go to sleep," she whispered.

He nodded, his breathing growing slower and deeper. Some of the pain eased. Some of the ache lessened. The memories of his battle as the Paladin lost their hard edge, giving way to the softness of Willow's touch. Sleep would renew his strength, and with morning he would be able to go on. All that would remain was the inescapable knowledge that he must go through this again with each new transformation. And even that could be accepted, he supposed. Even that.

He stilled himself, pushed back the fear and despair. Find Mistaya, he thought. Find her safe and well, and it would all be worth it. Bring back Questor Thews and Abernathy. Put an end to Rydall of Marnhull and his insidious games.

In the inky night's stillness the words were a whisper of hope.

Seek out Nightshade in the Deep Fell. Look there for the truth.

Then he was asleep.

Dog Dreams

When Abernathy woke the next morning, having slept particularly well considering the trauma of yesterday's events, Questor Thews was sitting in a chair across from his bed, staring at him like Death's coming. It was very disconcerting. Abernathy blinked, reached for his glasses, and gave the wizard a long, slow deliberate look.

"Is something the matter?" he asked.

The wizard nodded, then shook his head, unable to decide. "We have to talk, old friend," he announced wearily.

Abernathy almost laughed at the solemnity of the declaration. Then he saw the look in the other's empty eyes and felt something cold settle into the pit of his stomach. Questor Thews was deeply troubled.

"Well," he said in reply, and went still again, as if that one word had addressed the matter and disposed of it without the need for further conversation.

He rose to a sitting position, taking a moment in spite of himself to admire the smooth line of his arms and legs, pausing then to give critical consideration to the look of his fingers and toes. His fingers were long and slim, but his toes were all scrunched up like those gummy things he had recently acquired a taste for. Elizabeth kept a bag of them down in the kitchen and was forever offering him one. He didn't care for the idea that they reminded him of his toes.

He cleared his throat. "What would you like to talk about?" he asked, hoping it was something other than Poggwydd.

Questor Thews bestirred himself sufficiently to rise from the chair and pace to the window, a tall, bent scarecrow with the stuffing coming out at the seams. He parted the curtain and looked out, squinting against the light. The day was sunny and warm, the sky cloudless, the world coming awake. "Let's go down to the yard and sit in the shade of those trees," he suggested, sounding cheerful in a forced sort of way.

Abernathy sighed. "Let's."

He showered, shaved, and dressed, and in the middle of doing so it occurred to him that what Questor Thews wanted to talk about was the book. *Theories of Magic and Its Uses.* Abernathy had forgotten about the book, all caught up in Poggwydd's unexpected appearance at Graum Wythe and resultant capture, the G'home Gnome another outcast from Landover, trapped now as he was, the difference being, of course, that Poggwydd really didn't want anything at all to do with this world, while Abernathy was growing steadily more comfortable with his exile.

Which meant, he concluded, that the book had revealed something to Questor about leaving. That was why the wizard was still awake: he had found the answer he was looking for and was trying to decide how to tell Abernathy, who he knew wasn't as keen to be getting back. Although, he argued to himself, he really was, because he understood as well as Questor that the High Lord needed them, Mistaya was in the hands of Nightshade, and something awful was going to happen if they didn't get back in time to prevent it.

But what? What was going to happen? He wished he knew. A little certainty in the matter certainly wouldn't hurt.

He finished pulling on his shoes and went out of the bathroom to stand before Questor. The wizard faced him, seemed startled by what he saw, and quickly turned away.

"Well, thank you very much, I'm sure!" Abernathy snapped. "Are my pants on backward? Are my shoes the wrong color?"

"No, no." The other put a hand to his forehead, pained. "In fact, you look quite sartorial." The wizard waved vaguely at the air. "I'm sorry to be so rude. But I've been up all night reading, and I didn't particularly care for the end of the story."

Abernathy nodded, having no idea at all what he was nodding about. "Why don't we go on down and get started with this talk," he pressed, anxious to get it over with. "We can see if Elizabeth is awake and ask her to join us."

But Questor quickly shook his head. "No, I'd rather this discussion was just between you and me." He looked down, then bit at his lower lip. "Indulge me, please."

Abernathy did. They went out the door of the bedroom, along the short hallway, and down the stairs. As they passed Elizabeth's closed door, they heard her singing inside. At least someone was feeling cheerful. They walked from the living room into the kitchen and came face to face with Mrs. Ambaum. She was standing in front of the stove making tea, bluff, hardy, watchful, and decidedly triumphant as she turned to face them.

"I spoke with Elizabeth's father last night. He doesn't recall having an Uncle Abernathy. Doesn't recall anyone by that name. What do you have to say to that?"

One hand gripped a tea strainer. Armed and dangerous if they were foolish enough to try anything.

Abernathy offered his most disarming smile. "We haven't seen each other in years. We were just boys the last time."

The corner of her mouth twitched. "He said to tell Elizabeth he's flying in tonight. He wants to have a look at you."

Abernathy blinked, conjuring up a picture of the meeting. Mrs. Ambaum cocked her head as if trying to get a look inside his.

Questor Thews quickly took charge. "Imagine that!" he

declared. He took Abernathy by the arm and steered him past the startled housekeeper and out the back door. "Don't be worried, now," he called over his shoulder. "It will all get straightened out before you know it!"

They went down the porch steps and into the yard, Abernathy working very hard at not looking back over his shoulder to see if Mrs. Ambaum was staring after them. "I don't much care for that woman," he muttered.

Questor Thews grimaced. "Fair enough. She doesn't much care for you, either."

They moved out into the backyard, well away from the house, where curious ears might pick up what they had to say. Abernathy gazed at the sky and took in the sweep of its vast blue dome. He breathed in the smell of flowers and grasses and fading damp. Mrs. Ambaum was forgotten.

They reached an old bench painted glossy white to protect the wood against weathering and seated themselves, looking west across a broad stretch of empty fields to where the Cascade Mountains rose white-peaked against the depthless sky.

After a moment's silence Abernathy looked at Questor. "Well?" he said.

The wizard sighed, folded his hands in his lap, fidgeted, and sighed again. "We have a problem," he said.

Abernathy waited until it was clear that Questor did not know what to say next. "Could you possibly speak more than one sentence at a time, Questor Thews? That way we won't waste the whole day."

"Yes, all right." The wizard was flustered. "The book. *Theories of Magic and Its Uses.* I read it last night. Read it twice, as a matter of fact. Made a very thorough study of what it had to say. I think it is what we are looking for."

Abernathy nodded. "You think? Not very encouraging for those of us expecting a definite yes or no."

"Well, it's about magic—the book, that is—and magic is never exact. As you know. And this is a book about theory, a general discussion of how various magics work, about their principles, their commonalities. So it doesn't say, for instance, 'Take the eye of a newt, mix with a frog's foot, and turn around three times left' or some such."

"I certainly hope not."

"Well, that isn't a real spell, anyway, of course. But it's an *example* of a specific spell as opposed to general theory. This book is theory, as I said, so you can't be certain about anything until you've tried it out; you can only apply the theory to the situation and be reasonably sure."

Abernathy frowned. "Why do I not feel reassured by this? I wonder. Why does this conjure up memories of other times?"

Questor Thews threw up his hands. "Drat it, Abernathy, this is serious! You are not helping matters by making flippant remarks! Please, no more attempts at humor! Just listen!"

They faced each other in stunned silence. The smile dropped from Abernathy's face. "I apologize," he said, surprised that he could even speak the words.

Questor nodded hurriedly and brushed the apology aside. Unnecessary between friends, he was saying. "Theory," he continued, picking up the thread of his conversation. "The book reveals a theory that I remember from the days I studied under my brother in the time of the old King. It goes something like this. When one magic intervenes to change the result of another, to alter that result in a substantive way, then to undo the consequences of the intervening magic, you must use a third magic to put things back exactly the way they were. So magic one is applied, magic two changes the result, and magic three puts everything back the way it was before magic two was applied."

Abernathy stared. "What about the consequences of magic one where the consequences of magic two are negated?"

"No, no, that doesn't have any bearing on things! Magic

one is already disposed of!" Questor's thin lips tightened, and his bushy eyebrows narrowed. "Are you following me on this?"

"Nightshade tried to kill us with her magic. She failed because another magic intervened, the one that belongs to the mud puppy, we think. Now we have to use a third magic to put things back the way they were. You lose me there. Put what things back?"

Questor's eyes hooded. "Wait, there's more. The second magic, in order to overcome the first and at the same time facilitate the future possibility of its own negation, must use a catalyst, a powerful hook, a peripheral consequence that can't be mistaken for anything other than what it is. This consequence facilitates the dominance of the second magic over the first. Think of it as a form of sacrifice. In some cases it actually is. One life given to save others, for instance. Pretty hard to reverse that one. Normally the consequence has no meaning in the course of events beyond providing a clear indication of what it is that needs putting back in place." He took a long breath. "I'm sorry. I know this is confusing."

But Abernathy shook his head slowly, his face suddenly gone pale. "You're talking about me, aren't you, Questor Thews? Talking about changing me back again from a man to a dog. Aren't you?"

His friend sighed and nodded. "Yes."

"You think that if magic is used to change me back again, back into a dog, then the consequences of the second magic will be undone and we will all be sent back into Landover. Don't you?"

"Yes."

"That's ridiculous."

But he didn't sound as if it were, and he didn't believe it, either. Some part of him already whispered that it was so. Some part of him had been expecting this from the first moment he had discovered his good fortune. It was an inevitability that he should not enjoy such luck without consequences, not be allowed to escape from his fate so easily. He hated himself for thinking like this, but he could not help it. Damned by fate. Consigned to purgatory. He had been given a vacation from reality, nothing more.

"You could be wrong," he pressed, trying to stay calm, feeling desperation begin to build inside already, feeling the heat of it rise along his neck and into his face.

"I could be," Questor Thews acknowledged. "But I don't think I am. We have already agreed that we were dispatched to the High Lord's old world to save our lives and because something hidden here would help us find our way back again. The magic that sent us, and whoever used it, would have provided us with the key to our prison. Everything fits into place except your transformation—unless your transformation itself is the key. There is no other reason for it to have happened. It is too dramatic a result to be simply a side effect. It must be something more, and what else is there for it to be?"

Abernathy came to his feet—his human feet—and stalked off. He stopped when he was far enough away from the wizard that he felt alone and stared out at nothing. "I am not going to do this!" he shouted.

"I'm not asking you to!" the other replied.

Abernathy threw up his hands in disgust. "Don't be ridiculous! Of course you are!"

He wheeled about in challenge. Questor Thews looked old and frail. "No, Abernathy, I'm not. How could I? I was the one who changed you in the first place. An accident, yes, but that doesn't excuse what happened. I changed you from a man into a dog, and then I couldn't change you back again. I have lived with that failing, that stupidity, every day of my life since. Now I find myself maneuvered into a position where I am expected to change you a second time. I must relive the worst moment of my life, knowing, mind you, that I still cannot undo the magic's consequences once they are in place."

There were tears in the old man's eyes, and he wiped at them savagely. "I do not mind telling you that it is almost unbearable to contemplate!"

For both of us, Abernathy thought dismally. He looked down at himself, at his real self, his restored self, and thought for a moment what it would mean to be a dog again. He pictured himself anew as the shaggy-haired, clumsy, laughable creature he had been. He imagined himself trapped inside that alien body, struggling to keep his dignity, fighting every single day of his life to convince those surrounding him that he was as human as they were. How could anyone expect him to make such a sacrifice? *This* was the trade-off for returning to Landover? But he knew it was more than that. It was the trade-off for being alive. Had the mysterious magic not intervened, he would be dead. Nightshade would have put an end to him. To the both of them. And Questor Thews was undoubtedly right, as much as it pained him to admit it. His transformation from a dog back into a man had had a purpose, and the only purpose that made any sense was the one the wizard had revealed after studying the book of magic.

So he could stay or he could go. The choice was his. Questor would not attempt to persuade him either way. The wizard had to live with his own demons in this matter. It was being left to Abernathy to decide. If he rejected the transformation, he was stuck here. Good and bad in that, he supposed. It didn't need detailing. Of course, High Lord Ben Holiday was stuck as well; there would be no help from this end. On the other hand, if he allowed Questor to invoke the magic, he would presumably return in time to help the High Lord. But would he, in fact? Was there some real purpose to be served in going back, or would matters run their course whether he returned or not? If only he knew. It was one thing if by returning he would help save the High Lord and his family from Rydall and Nightshade. It was another if his return would make no difference at all.

He glanced toward the house. Mrs. Ambaum was looking out the window at them, sipping contentedly at her tea. Retribution by nightfall, she was thinking. Still no sign of Elizabeth. Beyond, where the road curved past the front yard and disappeared over a rise, the sunlight was a hazy curtain through the trees.

He walked back to Questor Thews and stopped in front of him, eyes fixed on the worn old face. "I really don't think I can do this," he said quietly.

The wizard nodded, face scrunched into a mass of wrinkles. "I don't blame you."

Abernathy held out his hands and looked at them. He shook his head. "Do you even remember the magic you used to change me that first time?"

Questor did not look up but nodded that he did.

"After so many years. Isn't that something?" Abernathy looked down at himself. He hadn't been changed back all that long, and already he was comfortable with himself in his old skin. "I like myself as I am," he whispered.

Elizabeth appeared in the doorway. "Breakfast!"

Neither moved. Then Questor waved. "We'll be there directly!" he called. He looked at Abernathy. "I am truly sorry."

Abernathy smiled ruefully. "Of course you are."

"I would give anything not to have to tell you this, anything not to have it so." He bit at his lip.

"If it isn't so, for the sake of argument," Abernathy mused, "I will be trapped here not as a man but as a dog."

Questor Thews nodded, holding his gaze this time.

"But it is so. You're sure. As sure as you can be, aren't you?"

The wizard nodded once more, didn't speak.

"I have to make up my mind about this right away, don't I?" Abernathy pressed on reluctantly. "If we are to be of any use to the High Lord and Mistaya, we have to get back quickly. There isn't time to give this a lot of thought."

"No, I'm afraid there isn't."

"Why don't you argue the matter with me, then?"

"Argue with you?"

"Convince me, one way or the other. You choose a side. Argue both ways if you like. But give me some issues I can debate. Give me something to dispute. Give me a voice besides my own to listen to!"

"I have already explained—"

"Stop explaining!" Abernathy was suddenly livid. "Stop being rational! Stop being passive! Stop standing around waiting for me to make this decision all by myself!"

"But it is your decision to make, Abernathy—not mine. You know that."

"I know nothing of the sort! I know nothing at all! I am sick and tired of being ignorant of what is happening in my life! All I want is to be able to go back to the way things were, and I am not being allowed to do that! I am still being required to perform, just as I was when we appeared at that Bumble-whatever festival, only the audience isn't anyone we can see! Why should I agree to go along with this? It would be better just to sit down and refuse to do another thing!"

"Doing nothing is the same as doing something!" Questor was growing a bit heated himself. "A choice is made either way!"

Abernathy clenched his hands in fury. "So it still comes down to the same thing, doesn't it? A choice must be made one way or the other, even if the choice is not really a choice at all?"

"You are babbling!"

"I am trying to make sense!"

Questor Thews sighed. "Why don't we eat some breakfast and then perhaps—"

"Oh, forget it! I'm going back!"

"—things will be a little easier." The wizard caught his breath sharply. "What did you say?"

Abernathy struggled to keep his voice from breaking. "I said I am going back! I want you to use the magic to change me!" He grimaced at the look on the other's ragged face and was suddenly calm. "It isn't so difficult a decision, Questor Thews. When this matter is over and done, I have to be able to live with myself. If I am required to be a dog again, I can adjust. I can accept it knowing that I did everything I could to help the High Lord and his family. But if I stay a man and learn later that by changing to a dog I could have saved their lives . . . well, you can imagine."

He cleared his throat. "Besides, I swore an oath." For a long moment he looked to be the saddest man who ever lived. "I am Court Scribe to the throne of Landover and pledged to serve her King. I am bound to serve in whatever way I can. I might wish it otherwise just now, but I cannot change the fact of it."

Questor Thews stared. The old eyes were fierce. "You really are quite remarkable," the wizard said softly. "Really."

Impulsively, he wrapped his arms about his friend and hugged him, whiskers rubbing roughly into Abernathy's smooth skin. "Well," Abernathy said in reply, overcome by the other's response. He tried to shrug his indifference. "Really, yourself."

They went up to the house to have breakfast with Elizabeth. The three of them sat at the little kitchen table, crowded over bowls of cereal and milk. Mrs. Ambaum bustled about officiously for a few moments as if attempting to supervise in some way, then gave up trying and disappeared out the front door with a promise to be back by noon.

As soon as she was gone, Elizabeth said, "Dad is coming home tonight, flying in from New York."

"So Mrs. Ambaum informed us," Questor advised. He did not look at Abernathy. His friend was eating with his head bent close over the bowl and his hand to his forehead.

"We have to make up a new story," Elizabeth continued. Her curly hair was damp from washing, and her face was freshly scrubbed. "It won't be hard. We'll just say that Mrs. Ambaum got it wrong, and that you . . ."

But Questor was already shaking his head. "No, Elizabeth. That won't be necessary. Abernathy and I are leaving."

"Leaving? When?"

Questor smiled sadly. "Right away. As soon as we finish eating."

Disappointment showed immediately. "You found a way to go back, didn't you?"

Questor nodded. "Last night."

She bit her lip. She looked at Abernathy, brow furrowed. "But you only just got here. Can't you stay another day or so? Maybe I can—"

"No, Elizabeth." Abernathy straightened and met her desperate gaze with kind eyes. "The High Lord needs us. Mistaya needs us. Any further delay is dangerous. We can't stay."

Elizabeth looked down at her cereal and gave it a few stirs with her spoon. "It doesn't seem fair. I don't want to be selfish, and I know it's important you go back. But you just got here." She glanced up, then quickly down. "I've been waiting four years to see you again."

Abernathy couldn't speak. His face was stricken.

There was a momentary silence. "What about Poggwydd?" she asked finally.

Questor cleared his throat. "Poggwydd will go back with us. Abernathy and I will seek his release as soon as we leave here."

"I'll go with you," Elizabeth announced at once.

"No," Abernathy said quickly, thinking it was bad enough that they were going themselves but resigned to the inevitability of it.

"What he means," Questor said, jumping in with both feet, "is that the moment we free Poggwydd, we will be on our way. Poof!" He tried a smile, failed. "If we encounter any trouble, we don't want you involved. Isn't that right, Abernathy?"

"But you might need my help!" Elizabeth didn't wait to hear what Abernathy had to say. "You don't know your way around Seattle! How will you get anywhere? How will you even find Poggwydd?"

"Well, perhaps you *could* help us with that last part," the wizard suggested soothingly.

"Elizabeth." Abernathy folded his hands on the table and sighed. "If we could stay, we would. If we could spend even a little more time with you, we would. You have been our friend. Mine especially. Twice now, not just once. But there are limits to what we can allow you to risk. It will be hard enough explaining us to your father."

"I'm not worried about him! I'm not worried about Mrs. Ambaum or anyone!" She was adamant.

"I know," he replied softly. "You have never let anyone stop you. If you had, I would not be here now." He smiled sadly. "But we worry for you. We worry that something will happen to you, and then we would be responsible. Remember what happened with Michel Ard Rhi? Remember how close you came to being hurt? I was scared to death for you! I cannot take a chance that such a thing might happen again. We have to say good-bye now. Here, at your house, where we know you are safe. Please, Elizabeth."

She took a moment to consider the matter and then nodded. "Okay, Abernathy." Still upset, defensive, angry. "I guess." She sighed. "Well, at least you're a man again, aren't you? At least you're not a dog anymore."

Abernathy smiled bravely. "Yes, at least I'm not a dog."

They finished breakfast in silence.

In an effort to find out what had become of Poggwydd, Elizabeth called the King County police, who referred her

to King County animal control, who in turn referred her to
the King County animal shelter on Elliott. Because no one
had been certain what Poggwydd was and therefore what to
do with him, the G'home Gnome had been passed from hand
to hand like an old shoe. The final result was temporary as
well, she discovered when she spoke with one of the animal
shelter employees. A zoologist from Woodland Park and an
anthropologist from the University of Washington were both
due to pay a visit later that morning. Territorial disputes
would be resolved, and Poggwydd would be sent one place or
the other for further study.

Elizabeth hung up the phone, gave her report, and said,
"You'd better hurry."

A taxi was called to spirit Abernathy and Questor Thews
to their destination at the animal shelter. Elizabeth gave them
money for the fare. She stood with them at the end of the
walk until the cab arrived, giving them final words of caution
and encouragement and providing her phone number in case
things went horribly wrong and it turned out they needed her
after all, secretly hoping they would, hoping they would find
some way to come back but knowing they wouldn't. When
the cab arrived, she hugged them both and wished them a safe
journey. She kissed Abernathy on the cheek and told him that
he was her best friend, even if he was from another world, and
that she would always wait for him because she knew that
someday he would come back. Abernathy said he would try.
He said he would never forget her. She cried in spite of saying
that she wouldn't, and Abernathy had to work hard at not crying with her.

Then Questor and Abernathy were off, speeding down
four- and five-lane highways, zipping around other vehicles,
barely missing all sorts of obstacles and barriers. They crossed
a bridge, turned down a rampway, sped along a two-lane roadway at a slightly slower speed, and wheeled into a parking area

next to a brown brick building with a sign that read "King County Animal Shelter."

They gave Elizabeth's money to the cab driver, stepped back onto solid ground with an unmistakable sense of relief, and headed inside. The walk diverged, and there were entries at either end. They went left through a door to a desk where a bored-looking employee sent them outside again and down the walk to the other door. At the second desk a young woman in a uniform looked up expectantly as they entered.

"Professor Adkins? Mr. Drozkin?" she greeted them.

Questor recognized an opportunity when he saw one. He smiled and nodded.

The young woman looked relieved. "Do you have any idea what this thing is?" she asked. "No one here has ever seen anything like it. It's giving us fits! I've tried everything—we all have—but we can't even get close. After the police brought it in, I removed the restraints and it tried to take my hand off. And it eats everything! Do you know what it is?"

"I have a pretty good idea," Questor Thews said. "Can we have a look?"

"Of course; right this way." She was eager to accommodate them, to rid herself of the burden of Poggwydd. Abernathy understood perfectly.

She brought them around the counter to a heavy metal door, which she unlocked and swung open. From there she led them down a hallway into an area of cages. At the far end was Poggwydd, slumped down at the back of the largest cage. His clothing was torn, and his fur was caked with grime and sweat. Cuts and scratches marked him from head to foot, and his tongue was hanging out. He looked, even for a G'home Gnome, decidedly miserable.

When he saw them, he leapt to his feet and attacked the cage with a vengeance that was astonishing. He shook and rattled and bit at the heavy wire in a frenzy, trying to get at them.

"He's gotten even worse!" the young woman declared in astonishment. "I'd better tranquilize him right now!"

"No, let's wait on that, please," Questor interrupted hurriedly. "I'd like simply to observe him for now. I don't want him sedated. Can you leave us for a few minutes . . . I'm sorry, I don't know your name."

"Beckendall. Lucy Beckendall." She reached out her hand, and he shook it cordially, not bothering with an introduction on his end because he had already forgotten who he was supposed to be.

"A few minutes?" he repeated helpfully. "We can just stand here and have a good long look."

Poggwydd was racing up and down the wire, showing all his teeth, shaking his fist, desperately trying to speak.

"Of course," she agreed. "I'll be right outside. Just call if you need me."

They waited until she went back through the heavy door and closed it securely behind her. Questor looked at Abernathy, then stepped close to the cage.

"Stop that!" he snapped at Poggwydd. "Behave yourself and listen to me! Do you want out of there or not?"

Poggwydd, worn out anyway, dropped to the floor and stood glaring at him. It was very close and antiseptic in the room. Abernathy pictured himself locked away in there for a full day and was suddenly sympathetic toward the Gnome in spite of himself.

"Now, listen!" Questor addressed Poggwydd firmly. "There is no point in leaping about like that! We came for you as soon as we could, as soon as we found out where you were!"

Poggwydd gestured toward his mouth in frustration.

"Oh, of course, you want to say something," Questor furrowed his brow fiercely. "Just keep your voice down when you speak so you can't be heard or I'll silence you again. Understood?"

The G'home Gnome nodded blackly. Questor spoke some words in a low voice, made a gesture, and Poggwydd's voice came back with a gasp.

"You certainly took your time!" he said. "I might have died in here! Those people are animals!"

Questor inclined his head slightly in acknowledgment. "I apologize. But now here we are. We have come to get you out and take you back to Landover."

The Gnome's face scrunched into a mass of angry wrinkles. "Well maybe I don't want to go! Maybe I've had quite enough of you, Questor Thews! And your friend!"

"Don't be ridiculous! You want to stay in there?"

"No, I don't want to stay in here! I want out! But once I'm out, I want to go back on my own. I can find my own way better than you, I'm willing to bet!"

"You couldn't find your way out of an open field, much less another world! Whatever are you talking about?"

"Leave him, Questor Thews!" Abernathy snapped. "We've wasted enough time!"

The three of them began arguing heatedly and were still at it when abruptly the metal door opened and Lucy Beckendall stepped into view. All three went instantly silent. She stared from one to the other, almost certain she had heard the creature in the cage speaking.

"There is some sort of mix-up here," she announced, looking uncomfortable and wary. "I have two gentlemen at the reception desk who had identified themselves as Professor Adkins from the University of Washington and Mr. Drozkin from the Woodland Park Zoo. They have shown me their ID cards. Do you have any identification to offer?"

"Of course," Abernathy declared quickly, smiling and nodding. *Drat!*

He walked quickly down the line of cages, reaching into his pocket, fumbling, and shaking his head. When he reached Lucy Beckendall at the door, he placed his hands firmly on her shoulders, shoved her back through the opening, and yanked the door closed once more. "Questor Thews!" he bawled, bracing himself against the door as pounding immediately began without. "Help!"

The wizard pulled up his sleeves, raised his skinny arms, and sent an electric blue clot of magic zapping into the lock. The lock and handle melted and fused in place.

"There, they won't be getting in that way!" he declared in satisfaction.

"And we won't be getting out, either!" Abernathy stalked back down the walkway. "So you had better know what you are going to do next!"

Questor Thews wheeled on Poggwydd. "There is only one way out, Mr. Poggwydd—with us, back to Landover. If we leave you, they'll have you back in this cage in a matter of minutes. Who will help you then? Now, I'm sorry you're in this mess, but it isn't our fault. And we don't have time to debate the matter." The pounding without had given way to a violent hammering, metal on metal where the lock was fused. Questor's mouth tightened, and his bony finger jutted at the Gnome. "Just think what they'll do to you! Experiments! Tests! Potions of all sorts! What's it to be, Poggwydd? Landover and freedom or a cage for the rest of your life?"

Poggwydd licked his grimy lips, his eyes bright with fear. "Get me out! I'll go with you! I won't make any more trouble, I promise!"

"Good choice," Questor muttered. "Step back from the door."

The G'home Gnome scurried into a back corner. Questor gestured and twisted with his hands, and the door sprang open. "Out!" the wizard snapped.

Poggwydd crawled out meekly and hunkered down like a beaten dog. "Stop that!" Questor ordered. "There's nothing wrong with you! Stand up!"

Poggwydd straightened, his lower lip quivering. "I don't

want to see that little girl again! Or her mud puppy, either! Not ever!"

Questor ignored him, already at work marking a circle on the concrete floor with the heel of his boot. When he was done, he motioned the Gnome and Abernathy inside. They stood close together in the heat and silence as the wizard took a deep breath, closed his eyes, and began to concentrate.

"I hope you know what you are doing," Abernathy said quietly, unable to help himself.

"Hush!" the wizard snapped.

Outside, the hammering had been replaced by a large number of voices. Reinforcements, Abernathy thought dismally. Then something heavy rammed into the door. They were trying to break it down! The frame and hinges shook with the force of the blows. Mortar cracked and sifted downward. Whoever was out there would be inside pretty quickly.

Questor began to speak the words of the spell slowly, clearly, deliberately. He had gone somewhere deep inside himself to concentrate, and he seemed oblivious to the hammering and shouting. Just as well, Abernathy thought. It would be just like the wizard to become distracted and get the spell wrong. What would he end up being then? A radish? He looked at Poggwydd. The G'home Gnome had his head lowered and his eyes shut tight. His arms were clasped about his scrawny body. Well, of course, Abernathy thought. We are all afraid.

Questor droned on, sweat beading his forehead. Abernathy could see the tension in his face. Changing me back again, he thought. And hating every moment of it. Abernathy experienced a sudden urge to cry out, to stop him from what he was doing, to make him do something else. But he suppressed that urge, his decision made, his fate accepted. He looked down at himself, wanting to remember everything about how he looked, not wanting to have to wonder again later. It hadn't been so bad being a dog, really. Not so bad.

Light surged upward about them, filling the circle from

floor to ceiling, encasing them in its bright cylinder. Questor's voice rose, the words snapping like blankets hung in the wind. Poggwydd whimpered. Abernathy thought of Elizabeth. He was glad she wasn't there to see this happen. It was better that she remember him as he was supposed to be.

The light brightened into a blinding radiance. Abernathy felt himself melting away. The feeling was not unexpected. He had experienced it once before, more than twenty years ago.

He closed his eyes and let it happen.

Venom

It took Ben and Willow the better part of two days to reach the Deep Fell. They left at sunrise on the first, accompanied by Bunion and an escort of two dozen King's Guards, and made their way north and east out of the hill country to the edge of the Greensward. From there they turned directly north and followed the line of the forested hills toward the witch's lair. The summer heat continued, sticky and damp against their skin, a shimmer of cellophane in the sun's glare. There was little wind to offer relief. There was little shade. Their pace was slow and steady, and they rested the animals and themselves often. All about, the countryside was sultry and still.

They camped where the waters of the Anhalt emerged from the hill country on the long journey down out of the mountains west. They sat on a low bluff above the river, having crossed before sunset, and watched the fading light turn purple and pink. To the east herons and cranes flew low above the sluggish waters, fishing for dinner.

"We'll be there by tomorrow noon," Ben declared after a long silence, anxious to engage an unusually quiet Willow in some form of conversation. "Then we'll know."

The sylph's voice was a soft, resigned sigh. "I already know. Nightshade has her. I can sense it. She wanted Mistaya from the very beginning, and she finally found a way to get her."

Her shoulder was touching Ben's as they stared off into the approaching dark, but the distance between them was frightening. All day long she had been withdrawing, closing herself away. Now she was someplace where no one could reach her if she did not wish it. Ben had waited patiently for her to work out whatever was disturbing her, hoping it wasn't him.

He cleared his throat. "She probably thinks of Mistaya as her property. Mistaya is payment for the debt she thinks she is owed for what befell her in the Tangle Box."

Willow was silent for a moment. "If it was only a matter of debt or even a claim to property, she would have stolen Mistaya away and been done with it. She would have ransomed her back or killed her, intending to hurt us by doing so. Instead, she concocted this elaborate scheme involving Rydall of Marnhull and his monsters. Mistaya is the prize to be won or lost, but she is something more as well. I think Nightshade has another use for her."

Ben looked at her. "What use?"

She shook her head. "I don't know. Perhaps it has something to do with Mistaya's magic. She was born in the Deep Fell, so perhaps they share something from that. Or maybe it is something darker. Perhaps she seeks to turn Mistaya's thinking so that it mirrors her own."

"No, Mistaya would never let that happen." Ben went cold all the way to his toes. "She is too strong."

"No one is stronger than Nightshade. Her hate drives her."

Ben went silent, a swell of horror rising inside at the prospect of Mistaya becoming like Nightshade. His good sense told him it could never happen. His emotions said otherwise. The two warred within him as he watched the shadows lengthen across the land, darkening the river and the hills.

"She would do that to hurt us, wouldn't she?" he said finally. "She would." He took a deep breath. "But how does that explain the Rydall charade?"

"Rydall gives her time to work on Mistaya. Rydall occupies us, keeps us at a distance and off balance. We don't realize the truth of things until it is too late."

Her eyes were empty and lost when he looked into them. "You've been thinking on this all day, haven't you?" he asked quietly. "That's why you're so far away from me."

She looked at him. Her smile was wan. "No, Ben. I have been preparing myself for tomorrow. There is a good chance I will lose Mistaya. Or you. Or even both. It isn't easy to accept the possibility, but it is there nevertheless."

"You won't lose either of us," he promised, putting his arm about her, drawing her close, knowing even as he did that he had just made a promise he might not be able to keep.

They slept poorly, made restless by anticipation of what lay ahead, of what they might find. They rose at sunrise, ate a quick breakfast, and were under way before the sun had fully crested the horizon in the mountains to the east. This day was steamy and suffocating as well, and they moved through it like swimmers on a sluggish tide. Bunion scouted ahead, keeping a wary eye out for any more of Rydall's monsters. Two remained to be faced, and Nightshade might choose now to unleash them. If indeed the witch was Rydall. Some doubt remained in Ben's mind, even if Willow was convinced. But by now he was doubting everything.

Ahead, the land stretched away in a ragged carpet of burned-out grasses and patchwork forest green, the line between foothills and plains blurred by the heat. He listened to the sounds of leather and traces as the horses plodded ahead resolutely. What would he do when they reached the Deep Fell? Would he go down into the hollow? Would he send the Paladin? How would he confront the witch? How would he learn the truth about Mistaya?

He glanced at Willow, riding beside him in silence. What he read in her face suggested that he had better find his answers soon.

Nightshade knew of their coming long before they were in view. She had known of it almost from the moment they had left Sterling Silver and had kept careful watch over their progress. The confrontation she had envisioned from the beginning was fated at last to take place. Somehow Holiday had figured it out. She did not know how he had done it, but he clearly had. He was coming to the Deep Fell, and he would be doing that only if he knew the truth.

The seeming inevitability of things did not escape her. The Ardsheal had failed her, just as all the other creatures she had sent had failed her. Under Rydall's agreement she had two monsters left to send, but time had run out on that game and only one chance remained for her now. She had enjoyed playing with Holiday, seeing him struggle, watching him suffer as he fought one monster after another in an effort to survive long enough to rescue his beloved daughter. She had enjoyed breaking him down a little at a time, leaving him physically and emotionally drained by forces he did not even begin to understand. How could he know that it was Mistaya's own magic working against him? How could he realize what that would do to him? It had been satisfying, but the greatest satisfaction of all was yet to come.

The anticipation of it kept her anger and frustration in check, for although she would not admit it even to herself, she was disappointed that Holiday was still alive. Her expenditure of time and effort, of magic and power, could not be dismissed out of hand even with the argument that all was as expected. Nightshade hated to lose, hated to be denied anything, even where she could rationalize that it must necessarily be so. She wanted Holiday dead, and postponement of that result, whatever the justification, was difficult to bear.

Still, she had made her plan and believed it to be fool-
proof. Mistaya was hers yet, her unwitting tool, and she would
be put to the use intended before this business was done. It
was better, perhaps, that it happen now, before any more time
passed. Mistaya was growing unmanageable, increasingly reluc-
tant to engage in the practice of magic that Nightshade decreed, suspicious of the role in which she had been cast. It was
bad enough that she had refused to help create another monster after the robot had failed. It was unbearable that she
should dare to leave the hollow. Yet Nightshade had persisted.
One more time she had found a way to use Mistaya, joining
the girl's magic with her own to bring the Ardsheal back from
the dead so that it could be sent against Holiday, but it had required great cunning and subterfuge on the witch's part to
conceal the truth of what she was about. It would be difficult
to deceive Mistaya again.

Yet she would be deceived, Nightshade promised herself.
One final time.

She let Mistaya do what she wished with her magic and
her lessons on the first day of Holiday's journey to the Deep
Fell. She let her practice what she would, encouraging her,
complimenting her, putting her at ease. Only one day remained, Mistaya was told. One—and then she would be going
home. Nightshade prowled the hollow restlessly, barely able to
concentrate on anything but the approach of the event she had
schemed to bring about for two years. She wandered off into
the mists, playing out the moment over and over in her mind,
seeing it happen, anticipating the joy it would give her. Holiday dead. Holiday gone at last. It had become for her the sole
reason for her life, the single purpose for which she existed. It
had become for her as necessary as breathing.

At night she went out in the form of a crow, flying over
the land to where the play-King slept in the company of the
sylph and his Guards. She would have lighted on his face and
pecked out his eyes if she could have done so, so great was her

hatred. But she knew better than to take chances after employing so much care. She would not cheat herself now of the end she had devised for him. She made certain of his distance from the Deep Fell, of the time she would need to prepare, and flew back again to wait.

The following morning she waited until Mistaya had eaten her breakfast before approaching her. Darkly sleek and vaguely menacing, she swept up to the girl with a smile and a light touch of one slender white hand against her cheek.

"Your father comes for you today," she advised in her most compelling voice.

Mistaya looked up expectantly.

"He should arrive by midday. Are you anxious to see him?"

"Yes," the girl answered, and the undisguised anticipation in her voice set the witch's teeth on edge.

"He will take you back to Sterling Silver, back to your home. But you will not forget me, will you?"

"No," the girl said softly.

"We have learned a lot together, you and I." Nightshade looked off into the trees. Mistaya had withdrawn from her since coming back down into the Deep Fell. She had distanced herself as only children could, barely tolerant, clearly marking time. It was a bitter recognition for the witch. She had expected better. "There are still many secrets to learn, Mistaya," she offered, trying to win back something of what she had lost. "I will teach them to you one day if you wish. I will show you everything. You need only ask." She looked back at Mistaya, eyes liquid. "This can be your home, too. One day you may wish to come live here with me. You may decide that this is where you belong. We are very much alike. You must know that. We are different from others. We are witches, and we will always be each other's greatest friend."

She almost meant it. There was enough truth behind the

words to make it so. But fate had decreed long ago that it could never be. Her hatred of Holiday, so obsessive a presence, so monstrous and driving, had determined that it must be otherwise.

Mistaya's eyes dropped hesitantly. "I will come back to visit you. When it is safe to do so."

Nightshade's smile was cool and fixed. "That time may come to pass sooner than you think. I have arranged for Rydall to withdraw his challenge to your father. He will be here when your father arrives. Once he is gone from Landover, there no longer need be any barriers between us. Your father and mother will agree, I am sure."

Mistaya's brow wrinkled. "Rydall will withdraw? For good? He has given up completely?"

"I have persuaded him it is best for all concerned." Nightshade's eyes narrowed. "Magic can accomplish anything. This is what I have tried to teach you."

Mistaya looked down at her clothes and brushed at them while she spoke. "I have learned a lot from you," she whispered.

"You were a good student," Nightshade praised. "You have great talent. Do not forget that I first told you so, that I revealed to you what no one else would, that I helped you discover who you really are. No one else would have done that for you. Only me."

There was a moment of awkward silence. Nightshade could feel a shift in the balance of things. "I have something for you," she said to the girl.

Mistaya's eyes lifted. Nightshade reached down into her robes and brought forth a silver chain and pendant. The pendant was carved in the shape of a rose, the petals carefully detailed, the stem and thorns intricately worked into the metal. She took the chain and pendant and placed them about Mistaya's neck.

"There," she said, stepping back. "A gift to remember me

by. So long as you wear it, you will never forget our time together."

Mistaya lifted the pendant from her breast and held it gently between her fingers. There was surprise and gratitude in her green eyes. Her child's face shone. "It is beautiful, Nightshade. Thank you very much. I shall wear it always, I promise."

A handful of hours will be enough, the witch thought to herself, keeping her smile carefully in place. Long enough to meet your loving father and embrace him one final time. Long enough for the pendant's hidden magic to cause the rose thorns to prick the play-King's skin and for their deadly poison to seep into his body. You can do what you wish with my gift after that. After it has served its purpose.

After you have served yours.

Questor Thews came out of the light of his magic in a wash of dizziness that very nearly toppled him. He staggered momentarily as the brightness faded, trying to gain his balance. Then, finding his feet on solid ground once more, he steadied himself, blinked away the last of his discomfort, and took a quick measure of his surroundings. To his relief he discovered that he was back in Landover. A scattering of pale moons dotted the midday sky, visible through the heavy screen of tree limbs. Stalks of Bonnie Blue poked out of scrub and from between moss-covered trunks. Familiar smells reached out to him. There was no mistaking any of it. But despite being back in Landover, he was no longer in the lake country. The look of things was all wrong for that. He was somewhere else, somewhere farther north . . .

"Jumping junipers, that is just about enough of that!" an irate Poggwydd snapped, grabbing a tight hold of Questor's sleeve. The wizard jumped at the unexpected contact. "I don't know what you did to get us back here, but I believe I'll simply walk next time! Next time, did I say? Bite my tongue!

Next time? Beat me with a switch if there's ever a next time! Hah! Not likely! Not for this fellow!"

Scrunching up his face as if to cause his features to disappear completely, he released Questor and wheeled away in a snit. "Good day to you, sir! Good day, good day!" Then he stopped dead in his tracks. "Gracious me and mercy on us all, what's happened to him?"

He was looking at Abernathy. Landover's scribe sat on the ground next to an aging hickory, staring down at himself. He was a dog once more, a soft-coated Wheaten Terrier, shaggy and unkempt beneath his clothing, fur sticking out everywhere, ears perked, glasses perched awkwardly on his long nose. His liquid brown eyes seemed both startled and sad as he studied his human fingers, all that remained of his old body. Then he shrugged, looked up at Poggwydd, and sighed.

"What seems to be the trouble, Poggwydd? Haven't you ever seen a talking dog before?"

Poggwydd's wrinkled, furry face went through a series of bizarre contortions as he huffed and spit in an effort to speak. "Well, I . . . Well, of course, I . . . Humph! Mumble, mumble! Well, you certainly weren't a dog earlier!"

Abernathy climbed slowly to his feet and brushed himself off. "How much earlier do you mean?"

"Just a little bit ago! Just before we were gobbled up by the wizard's magic! You were a man, confound it!"

Abernathy's smile was rueful even for a dog. "That was just a disguise. This is the real me. Can't you tell?" He sighed again, and his eyes locked on Questor. "Well, you were right, Questor Thews. Congratulations."

Questor gave a quick nod in reply. "Yes, it appears I was, thank you. I must say again that I wish it could be otherwise."

"We all wish things could be otherwise, but this is the real world, isn't it? Or as real as it gets for us." Abernathy looked around in puzzlement. "Where are we, anyway?"

"I was just about to ask our friend," the wizard replied, looking in turn to Poggwydd.

The G'home Gnome seemed startled by the question. He glanced right and left momentarily as if to confirm his suspicions, then cleared his throat officiously. "We're right back where we started, is where we are. Well, back where I started, anyway. This is where that little girl found me, minding my own business, not causing anyone the least amount of . . ." He trailed off quickly as he saw a dark look creep into Questor's eye. "Ahem! What matters to you, I imagine, is that we're just a mile or so from the Deep Fell."

"I don't understand," Abernathy ventured, coming over to stand next to them. "What are we doing here? Why aren't we back in the lake country?"

Questor Thews was rubbing his chin furiously, twisting his whiskers into rat's tails while thinking the matter through. "We're here, old friend, because Mistaya's here—down in the Deep Fell with the witch. This is where Poggwydd saw her last. Nightshade took her back to the Deep Fell, and there's no reason to think she isn't still there. We've been brought here to save her, I believe."

"I don't understand any of this!" the G'home Gnome declared abruptly. "But that's fine, that's just fine, because I don't want to understand any of it! I just want to be on my way. So good-bye to the both of you and good luck!"

Once more he started away, this time heading east, away from the witch's lair.

"Don't you want to know what happens with Nightshade?" Questor Thews called after him.

"I don't want to know another thing about any of this!" The Gnome did not slow his pace. "I already know more than enough! Much more!" He scuffed at the dirt furiously, raising dust with his feet. "Do me a favor, please. If you find that little girl, give her my regards and tell her I never want to see her again. Nothing personal, but that's the way it is." His voice rose dangerously. "I hope she is a King's daughter! I hope she becomes a Queen! I hope if she ever goes for another walk, she does it somewhere else! Good day!"

He disappeared into the trees and was gone, a hunched ragtag figure leaving in his wake a scattering of rude gestures and indecipherable mumbles.

Questor dismissed him instantly and turned to Abernathy, eyes intent. "You know what we have to do, don't you?"

Abernathy looked at him as he might a small child. "I know perfectly well. Probably better than you."

"Then we had better hurry. I have an uneasy feeling about things."

And he did, too. It was hard to describe but impossible to discount. The feeling had been with him in the High Lord's old world: a need for haste, to get back into Landover as quickly as possible so that something could be done to prevent whatever it was that Nightshade intended. Now the feeling was even stronger, a growing certainty that the trap around Holiday and his family was about to close and that only he and Abernathy could prevent it. Perhaps it was a bit conceited and overdramatic to assume responsibility for so much, but Questor Thews needed to believe that there was a reason for Abernathy's sacrifice, that there was a greater good being served. His magic might have cost Abernathy his human identity, but it had gotten them back into Landover, to where Mistaya had last been seen and was probably captive still, and that had to count for something. Nightshade had told them that Rydall was her creature, that she had set in motion a chain of events that would crush Holiday, and that Mistaya would be the instrument of his destruction. Somehow the witch was using the little girl to get at the High Lord. If they could reach her in time, perhaps they could still make a difference.

They hurried away through the shadows and midday heat, off to the rescue. Gnats swarmed around them, drawn by their sweat, stirred by their passing. Questor brushed the gnats away, preoccupied with his thoughts. A horse would have been a welcome sight just about now, but then Abernathy wanted nothing to do with horses, so maybe going on foot was for the best. They crossed a stream and passed through a glade dappled crimson and yellow with wildflowers. Finches darted from cover and sailed off into the blue. Abernathy was breathing hard, but Questor did not let up on the pace. He was in some pain himself. He pushed his old bones harder, ignoring his aching joints. He forced himself to walk more quickly. He gathered up his robes and clambered down slopes and along pathways through the tall grasses and past the thorny scrub.

"Questor Thews, slow down!" he heard Abernathy gasp, for the scribe was trailing steadily farther behind by now.

The wizard never considered it for a moment.

Ahead, the mist and gloom of the Deep Fell were already in view.

Holiday Heart

Mistaya was sitting with Nightshade on a grassy rise at the south edge of the Deep Fell when her father and mother rode into view. Bunion preceded them, edging out of the midday heat like a spider emerging from its hole, crouched down warily against the sun-scorched earth. King's Guards flanked and trailed them, armed with lances and swords, all metal and flash in the brightness. The company slowed as they saw her, reining in the horses, easing to a halt. Mistaya could see the tension etched on her father's face, could see the movement of his eyes as they swept the empty stretch of grasslands separating him from his daughter and came to rest finally on Rydall.

Marnhull's King sat atop his black charger a short distance to her right, concealed in his black armor and cloak, his visor pulled down, motionless in the shadows of a broad-limbed chestnut. He had been waiting there when Nightshade and Mistaya had climbed to the rim of the hollow. He had done nothing to acknowledge them. He had failed to move or speak a word since. He did nothing now. He was as still as stone, facing directly back toward Landover's King.

Nightshade rose, and Mistaya stood up with her. Ben Holiday's eyes flicked back to his daughter instantly. Mistaya wanted to run to him, to call out, to do or say something, anything, but Nightshade had forbidden it. *Let me speak first,* she had warned. *The negotiations between Rydall and your father are in a very delicate state. We must be careful not to disrupt them in any way.* Mistaya understood. She did not want to do anything to endanger her father. She just wanted to go home. She had been thinking about it since she had returned to the Deep Fell after meeting Poggwydd. She had grown steadily more anxious since, excited but a little afraid as well at the prospect of seeing her parents again after so many weeks. Now she felt a surge of emotion rise inside her chest, tightening her throat, bringing tears to her eyes. She had not realized how much she missed them, she guessed. She had not known how badly she would want to go home.

"High Lord!" Nightshade called out suddenly. "Your daughter is here with me, safe and well. She is ready to return home. I have gained King Rydall's promise that she may do so. He has agreed to withdraw from Landover. There will be no more threats, no further attacks. You need only promise that you will seek no retribution against him for anything that has happened."

Mistaya waited expectantly. There was a long silence, as if her father did not know how to answer, as if what he was hearing was entirely unexpected. She saw him look at her mother and her mother speak softly in response. Bunion moved restlessly between them, teeth gleaming, eyes fixed on the witch.

"What about Questor Thews and Abernathy?" Ben Holiday shouted back.

"They will be returned as well!" Nightshade answered.

Abernathy and Questor? Mistaya glanced up at the witch questioningly. What were they talking about? Had something happened to the wizard and the scribe? Weren't they safely back in Sterling Silver? Wasn't that what she had been told?

Nightshade smiled down, her face distant and shrouded within the hood of her black robe. Nothing to worry about, the smile said. Do not concern yourself.

"I will seek no retribution if everyone is well," she heard

her father agree, but she did not miss the troubled tone of his voice. She looked back across the space that separated them, an empty, burned-out stretch of grassland fronting the shadowy depression of the hollow. Her father seemed a long way off.

Nightshade put a slender white hand on her shoulder. "You must go to your father now, Mistaya," she advised. "When I tell you to do so, walk out to meet him. Do not deviate from your path in any way. Go directly to him. No one else. Do you understand?"

Mistaya was aware suddenly that something was happening she did not understand, something hidden and possibly dangerous. She could sense it in Nightshade's words, in the same way she could sense so much about the witch. She hesitated, wondering what she should do. But there was nothing she could do, she knew. Nothing but agree. She nodded silently.

"High Lord!" Nightshade called out once more. "Your daughter is coming to you! Dismount and walk out to meet her. Come alone! That is the agreement I have made."

Again Mistaya could see her father hesitate, thinking it over. He was not sure of this, she could tell. There was something bothering him, something he could not seem to reconcile. She thought perhaps she should try to reassure him, then realized that she wasn't sure of things herself, that she was troubled as well. Her green eyes shifted to find Rydall. Marnhull's King hadn't moved. She looked quickly to Nightshade. The witch was still and expressionless.

Her father dismounted slowly and began to walk forward. Bunion started to go with him, but he sent the kobold back with a wave of his hand.

"Go now!" Nightshade whispered quickly in her ear. "Give him a special hug from me!"

Mistaya moved forward reluctantly, still pondering her confusion, still wondering what was wrong. She shuffled through the dry grasses with small steps, watching her father advance, watching him draw steadily closer. She glanced back at Nightshade, but the witch did not respond, a tall and dark etching against the hollow's steamy mist. Mistaya brushed at her hair where it fell across her face, and her green eyes flicked right and left. Her father came on, steady and watchful. She saw a worried, uncertain smile form on his lips. She could see his eyes clearly. There was relief mirrored there—as if he had not expected to see her again. A rush of confusion swept through her. Why was he looking at her so?

Suddenly she wanted to do as Nightshade had urged. She wanted to hug her father as tightly as she could, to hold him close, to feel the strong press of his body against her own. She wanted him to take her in his arms and give her shelter and reassurance. She needed to tell him how much she had missed him. She needed to be reassured of his love for her.

The day was still and hot, and the breeze that brushed her face was as dry as fly wings. "Father," she breathed softly, and hurried forward.

Then a sudden, desperate shout rose out of the silence. "High Lord! Mistaya! Wait!"

Questor Thews broke from the trees to her left, stumbling out of the shadows and into the sunlight. Disheveled and unkempt, robes trailing in tatters where the bright sashes had come loose and the seams had ripped, he raced toward them with his arms waving, his white hair and beard flying, and his eyes as wild and frightened as those of a creature pursued by hunters. Mistaya and her father both whirled in surprise, watching the ragtag figure come hurtling toward them. From out of the trees behind him, some thirty yards back, Abernathy appeared, huffing and panting and trying futilely to keep up.

Then Mistaya heard Nightshade's gasp of fury. The witch had gone into a crouch, looking like a cat poised to spring, arms extended as if to ward off something terrible. Her eyes locked on Mistaya's, as red as blood. "Go to your father!" she shrieked in rage.

Mistaya started forward in response, barely aware of what she was doing. But Questor Thews was still coming, running doggedly onward through the heat and dust, arms and legs pinwheeling wildly. Again, Mistaya stopped, transfixed.

"Mistaya, don't!" Questor Thews cried out. "It's a trap!"

Suddenly everyone was trying to reach her: her mother surging forward atop her mount with the King's Guards in close pursuit and Bunion racing ahead, Nightshade lifting her arms and spreading her dark robes like some great bird of prey, Rydall fighting to bring his rearing, panic-stricken black horse under control, Abernathy tumbling head over heels through the dry grasses as he lost his footing, and her father breaking into a sudden sprint.

But it was Questor Thews who reached her first, careening wildly across the last bit of space that separated them, snatching her up as if she were a rag doll, and crushing her to his breast.

"Mistaya!" he whispered in relief.

Then wicked green light flared between them, spraying outward from the pendant like shattered glass. Questor Thews grunted in shock, and the blood drained from his face. His grip on Mistaya weakened, and he dropped to his knees, barely able to cling to her.

"Questor!" she shrieked in horror.

She drew back as she realized where the light was coming from and peered quickly down. The thorns on the rose stem had grown impossibly long and jutted from the old man's chest like spikes. There was blood seeping from the wounds. Questor was shaking, and his fingers had tightened into claws. He was gasping for breath. Mistaya yanked the thorns from his body, tore off the pendant, and flung it away. Questor's eyes fixed on her without seeing, and he slumped to the ground and lay still.

"Questor!" Mistaya gasped. "Questor, get up! Please!"

Questor Thews did not move. He had quit breathing.

Mistaya leapt to her feet, sobbing with rage and despair. "Nightshade!" she screamed. "Do something!"

Her father came up quickly and reached for her, but she pushed him away. She rushed to where the pendant lay, looked down at it, then squinted out across the scorched flat. "Nightshade!"

The witch stood frozen in place, her pale, smooth face empty of expression but her eyes filled with terrible fury. Her arms swept downward, casting off the magic they had gathered.

"You gave me that pendant!" Mistaya screamed. "You made this happen!"

Nightshade's hand swept the air before her. "I am not responsible for this! Questor Thews shouldn't have interfered! He was a fool!"

"I trusted you!" Mistaya shrieked.

Now her mother was there as well, dismounting and hurrying over as King's Guards reined to a halt behind them, weapons drawn, and Bunion hissed at Nightshade in warning. "Mistaya, look at me," Willow ordered.

But Mistaya waved her away, picked up the pendant by its chain, and held it out accusingly toward Nightshade. "You intended this for my father, didn't you? You meant this for him!"

"I did not mean—"

"Don't lie to me anymore!"

"Yes!" The witch shrieked. "Yes, I meant it for him! The poison was meant to take his life, not that old fool's!"

Mistaya was shaking with fury. Her small body was as taut as a spear's wooden shaft, all straight and set to fly. Her hands were clenched into fists, and her face was streaked with tears. "I hate you!" she screamed.

She threw down the pendant. Her small hands came up, and fire lanced out of them, shattering it where it lay on the ground, turning the metal to dust. Ben and Willow shrank back in spite of themselves, startled at the power Mistaya possessed.

Abernathy finally reached them, panting heavily, tongue hanging out. He bent hurriedly over Questor Thews, dog's ear to the old man's chest. "There isn't any heartbeat!" he whispered.

Mistaya was stalking toward Nightshade now, all determination and iron will. "You're going to help him or else!" she hissed. "Do you hear me, Nightshade?"

The witch took a step back, then straightened. "Do not presume to threaten me, you little fool! I am still your mistress and your better!"

"You were never anything but a liar and a sneak!" the little girl snapped. "You tricked me! You used me! What else have you made me do? What of those monsters I helped you make? The earth giant and the metal man and the others? To what use did you put them?"

"They were sent to kill your father," she heard her mother say from behind her. "Ask her to deny it."

"Rydall!" Nightshade wheeled on Marnhull's King. "You wanted your chance at Holiday! Well, here it is! Kill him!"

Rydall was still struggling with his charger, barely managing to keep the frightened animal under control. At Nightshade's words, he twisted about to face her, menace radiating from his black armored body. For a moment it seemed he might attack her instead. Then he reached for his sword, shouted in challenge, spurred his charger forward, and came at Holiday. But Bunion was quicker. The kobold rushed at Marnhull's King, teeth bared, a small black blur in the heat, and threw himself into the horse's face. The animal shied, reared, bucked, and threw Rydall from his saddle. Rydall's right foot caught in the stirrup as he fell. Burdened by the weight of his armor, he could not break free. He tumbled to the earth beneath the rearing, stamping horse and was hammered by the iron-shod hooves. The horse bolted, dragging his helpless rider across the flats. Bits and pieces of armor broke free, and blood stained the ground. King's Guards spurred forward to catch the terrified horse, but by the time they had reined him in, Rydall of Marnhull was a ruined, battered husk.

Mistaya continued to advance on Nightshade. "No!" the witch shrieked, clearly shaken. "We are even now! A life for a life! Rydall goes back to where he came from, and you and I do the same, little girl!"

But Mistaya did not slow. Her father and mother were hurrying after her, both of them grim-faced. Bunion came skittering like quicksilver through the brown grasses. King's Guards spread out all about them. Ben Holiday had the medallion out, and he held it up to the light in one hand. A streak of fear crossed Nightshade's face. She crouched to meet these threats, a feral look on her face, bits of green fire rising off her fingers. Instantly Mistaya pointed at her, crying out. Magic lanced from the little girl's hands and knocked Nightshade flying. The witch gasped in shock and tumbled backward. Then she scrambled up in rage.

"No! You cannot touch me! You have no right!" She whirled on Mistaya. Her pale face was contorted and ugly. Her self-control was shattered. "I will show you what magic can really do, little witch! I will send you back where you belong!"

Her hands came up, wicked green flames swirling at her fingertips. Mistaya locked her arms before her in self-defense.

Then, suddenly, Haltwhistle was there, materializing at the edge of the Deep Fell. Frost rose off his hackles and turned into ribbons of steam. Nightshade became aware of him an instant too late. She turned, but the mud puppy's magic lanced out and knocked her legs from beneath her. Flailing wildly, her conjuring out of control, she collapsed in a heap. Down came her magic, falling about her like rain.

Nightshade was engulfed. The strange mix surrounded

and consumed her in the blink of an eye. She had time for a single quick scream, and then she was gone.

For a moment afterward no one moved. They stood rooted in place, half expecting the Witch of the Deep Fell to reappear. But she did not, and then Haltwhistle came up to Mistaya where she stood transfixed before the smoldering bit of earth where the witch had stood. The mud puppy looked up at the little girl with soulful eyes and slowly wagged his tail. Mistaya broke into tears.

Her father came up, knelt, and put his hands on her slender shoulders, bracing her and looking into her eyes. "It's all right, Mistaya," he told her. "It's all right." And then he drew her close and held her against him.

Willow took her then, holding her as well, rocking her, telling her that it was over now, that she was safe. As she did so, Ben rose and walked to where Rydall lay sprawled in a crumpled heap on a patch of barren ground within a ring of King's Guards. He dropped to one knee beside the fallen King, lifted the black visor, and peered down at the face inside. Blood-filled eyes blinked up at him from beneath a shock of red hair.

Ben Holiday shook his head bleakly. "Kallendbor," he whispered.

The Lord of the Greensward coughed weakly. Blood streaked his face and beard and leaked in a steady stream from his mouth. "I should . . . have killed you that first day . . . on the drawbridge. I . . . should never have listened to . . . the witch."

He drew one last breath, sighed, and went still. His eyes stared sightlessly into space. Ben closed the visor once more. Kallendbor had never been able to accept the way things had worked out, it seemed. Only Ben's death would have satisfied him. He must have been desperate indeed to have allied himself with Nightshade. Now Ben knew how the robot had managed to get so close to them at Rhyndweir without being detected. Now he knew how the witch had been able to use her magic to make him think he had lost the medallion. Kallendbor had arranged it all. Nightshade must have told him Ben was coming, and he had laid his trap for Landover's King and waited for him to die. Now the Lord of Rhyndweir himself lay dead, and there would probably never be any real understanding of the madness that had allowed it to happen.

He rose and walked back toward his family, but Mistaya was already crouched over Questor Thews, surrounded by the others, her small face intent with concentration.

"He can't die," she was saying as Ben came up and dropped to his knee beside her. "This is my fault. All my fault. I have to make it right. I have to."

Ben looked at Willow, and she lifted her stricken eyes to meet his. Questor Thews was not breathing. His heart had stopped. There was nothing anyone could do for him.

"Mistaya, he came out of love for you," Abernathy said softly, reaching out to touch her shoulder. "We all did."

But Mistaya was barely listening. She reached down impulsively and seized Questor's limp hand. "I learned something from Nightshade that might help," she murmured fiercely. "She taught me how to heal. Even the dead, sometimes. Maybe I can heal Questor. I can try, anyway. I have to try."

She rocked back on her heels and closed her eyes. Ben, Willow, Abernathy, and Bunion exchanged hesitant, wary glances. Mistaya was calling on the magic Nightshade had revealed, and nothing good had ever come of that. *Don't use it,* Ben wanted to say, but knew he mustn't. The sun beat down on them, and the air was thick and humid with its heat. All about, the grasslands were still, as if nothing lived there or what little did waited as they did to see what would transpire.

Mistaya shuddered, and a bright shimmer ran from her body down her arm and into Questor Thews. The wizard lay motionless and unresponsive. Twice more the shimmer of light passed from Mistaya's body into Questor's. The little girl's eyes fluttered wildly, and her head drooped forward, her hair spilling down around her face. Again Ben thought to intervene, and again he kept himself from doing so. She had a right to do what she could, he told himself. She had a right to try.

Suddenly Questor Thews jerked. The movement startled Mistaya so that she gave a small cry and dropped his hand. For a moment no one moved. Then Abernathy hurriedly bent down over his old friend, listened for a moment, and looked up in astonishment.

"I can hear his heart beating!" he exclaimed. "I can hear him breathe! He's alive!"

"Mistaya!" Ben whispered, and hugged his daughter to him.

"I knew I could do it, Father," she said. She was shaking, and he could feel tremendous heat radiating from her body. "I knew I could. I do have magic."

"You do indeed," Ben agreed, alarmed, and called immediately for cold water and cloths.

The others hugged Mistaya as well, save for Bunion, who merely gave her a toothy grin. The cloths were applied, she was given water to drink, and her temperature fell again. She seemed to recover. But the battle to save Questor was not yet over. His heartbeat was weak, his breathing was shallow, and he remained unconscious. The poison was still in his body, and while Mistaya had managed to negate some of its effects, she had not been able to slow them entirely. Ben sent several of his King's Guards in search of a wagon and had the others build a stretcher in the meantime. They secured Questor in place, tied the stretcher to Jurisdiction, and started slowly home.

Mistaya insisted on riding on the stretcher next to Questor. When a wagon was found, she rode next to him there as well. She held his hand the entire way. She refused to let go.

Specimen

For six days after their return to Sterling Silver Mistaya sat by Questor Thews as he slept. She held his hand almost continually. She left only when necessary and then only for moments at a time. She took her meals on a bedside tray and slept on a pallet on the floor. Now and again Haltwhistle would appear, materializing out of nowhere to let her know he was close before disappearing once more. More than once Ben Holiday slipped into the bedchamber at midnight to cover his daughter with a blanket and smooth her rumpled hair. He thought each time to carry her to her own bed, but she had made it plain that she intended to see the matter through to its end. Questor would recover or die, but in either case she would be there when it happened.

Bit by bit Ben pieced together the story of how Nightshade had tried to destroy him. They elicited from Mistaya the Earth Mother's role in providing Haltwhistle to help disrupt Nightshade's plans and were then able to deduce by themselves how the mud puppy was meant to insure that even when separately deceived they might find a way back to each other and the truth. Abernathy filled in his part, trying to gloss over what the transformation from dog to man and back again had done to him, trying to downplay his role in saving Ben's life. But Ben would not allow it, knowing what it had cost his faithful scribe to give up his human form once again, painfully aware that Abernathy might never be able to return to who he was. They spoke quietly of Questor Thews and his determination to save Mistaya. They worried together what it might mean for the little girl if Questor died.

Willow spent long hours talking candidly with Mistaya of Nightshade and her experience in the Deep Fell, smoothing away some of the hurt and guilt that her daughter felt. It was not Mistaya's fault, she pointed out, that the witch had used her to get at her father. It was not her fault that she had not realized what was being done. She had not intended her father harm or meant to give help of any kind to the witch. In fact, she had used her magic in what she believed to be an effort to save her father's life. Given her position, her mother would have done the same. All of them had been deceived by the witch, and not for the first time. Nightshade's was a pervasive, devious evil that would have destroyed anyone with less character and courage. Mistaya needed to know that. She needed to accept the idea that she had done the best she could.

Her father, speaking to her alone at one point, said, "You must forgive yourself for any blame in this, Mistaya. You made a mistake, and that's part of growing up. Growing up is painful for every child but more so for you. Do you remember what you said the Earth Mother told you?"

Mistaya nodded. She was holding tightly to Questor's hand, one finger on his pulse where it beat softly in his wrist.

"Growing up for you will be harder than for most. Because of who you are and where you come from. Because of your parents. Because of your magic. I wish it could be otherwise. I wish I could make it so. But I cannot. We have to accept who we are in this life and make the best of it. Some things we cannot change. All we can do is try to help each other when we see that help is needed."

"I know," she said softly. "But it doesn't make me feel any better."

"No, I don't suppose it does." He reached over and pulled her gently against him. "You know, Mistaya, I can't afford to think of you as a child anymore. At least not a child of two. You've grown way beyond that, and I guess I'm the only one who didn't see it."

She shook her head and kept her face lowered. "Maybe I'm not so grown up as everyone thinks. I was so sure of myself, but none of this would have happened if I'd been a little more careful."

He gave her a small hug. "If you remember that the next time you decide to use your magic, you'll be grown up enough for me."

Ben sent word to the River Master that his granddaughter was safe and would come to visit soon. He went back to the work of governing Landover, although a part of him was always in the bedchamber with Mistaya, sitting next to Questor Thews. He ate and slept out of necessity and found concentrating difficult. Willow talked with him when they were alone, sharing her own thoughts, her own doubts, and they gave each other what comfort they could.

Several times more Mistaya used her magic to try to strengthen Questor Thews. She told her parents what she intended so that they could be there to lend their support. The magic shimmered down her arm and into the old man's body without apparent effect. Mistaya said she could feel it grappling with the witch's poison, could feel the struggle taking place inside. But there was no change in the wizard's condition. His heartbeat remained slow, his breathing was ragged, and he did not wake. They tried to feed him soup and water, and some small portion of what touched his lips was consumed. But he was skin and bones, all waxy and drawn, a skeleton flattened down against the sheets, barely alive.

Mistaya tried strengthening him with other forms of magic, giving whispers of encouragement, lending deep measures of her love. She refused to give up. She willed him to come awake for her, to open his eyes and speak. She prayed for him to live.

Her parents and Abernathy gradually lost hope. She could see it in their eyes. They wanted to believe, but they understood too well the odds against survival. The depth of their concern did not lessen, but the look in their eyes flattened out into acceptance. They were preparing themselves for what they saw as the inevitable. Abernathy could no longer speak to her in Questor's presence. Each of them was withdrawing, cutting ties, severing feelings, hardening. She began to despair. She began to worry that the old man would lie there like that forever, trapped between waking and sleep.

Then, on the seventh day of her vigil, as she sat with him in the bedchamber in the early morning light, watching the sunrise color the sky through the windows, she felt his hand tighten unexpectedly around her own.

"Mistaya?" he whispered weakly, and his eyes blinked open.

She hardly dared to breathe. "I'm here," she replied, the tears starting. "I won't leave."

She called loudly for her mother and father and, with the old man's frail hand clasped firmly in her own, waited anxiously for them to come.

Vince had completed his shift at the Woodland Park Zoo in Seattle and was on his way to his car when he impulsively changed direction and went back into the aviary for a last look at the crow. The damn thing fascinated him. It was right where he had left it earlier, sitting by itself on a branch near the top of the enclosure. The other birds left it alone, wanting nothing to do with it. You couldn't blame them. It was a mean-looking thing. Vince didn't like it, either. But he couldn't stop wondering about it.

A crow with red eyes. Not another one like it that anyone had ever heard of. Not another anywhere.

It had popped up out of nowhere. Literally. Same day
as that incident at the King County animal shelter when
those two nuts posing as Drozkin and some guy from U
Dub had stolen that monkey or whatever it was. No one
knew what had happened to them. They'd just disappeared
into thin air, if you could believe the lies being spread
around. Then, not two hours later, this bird appeared, right
there in the same cage the monkey disappeared from. What
were the odds of that happening? No one could explain it,
of course. It was like one of those UFO stories, one of those
sightings where weird things happened to the people involved but no one could prove it had really happened.
Vince believed in UFOs. Vince thought there were a lot of
things happening in the world that you couldn't explain, but
that didn't make them any less real. It was like that with this
bird.

Anyway, there's the bird, this crow with the red eyes, lying there in the cage, stunned. The animal shelter people were
no fools. They knew a specimen when they saw it, even if
they didn't know exactly what sort of specimen it was. So they
hobbled it and brought it over for study. An exotic bird, so it
belonged in the zoo. Now it was Woodland Park's job to figure out what it was. No one knew how long that might take.
Months, he guessed. Maybe years.

Vince leaned against the wire, trying to get the bird to
look at him. It didn't. It never looked at anyone. But you always felt it was watching you nevertheless. Out of the corner
of its eye or something. Vince wished he knew its story. He
bet it was a good one. He bet it was better than any UFO
story. There was a lot more to this bird than met the eye.
You could tell that much by the way it conducted itself.
Aloof, disdainful, filled with some inner rage at life. It
wanted out of there. It wanted to go back to where it had

come from. You could see it in those red eyes if you looked long enough.

But Vince didn't like to look into the crow's eyes for too long. When he did, he could almost swear they were human.

About the Author

TERRY BROOKS was born in Illinois in 1944. He received his undergraduate degree from Hamilton College, where he majored in English Literature, and his graduate degree from the School of Law at Washington & Lee University.

A writer since high school, he published his first novel, *The Sword of Shannara*, in 1977. It became the first work of fiction ever to appear on the *New York Times* Trade Paperback Bestseller List, where it remained for over five months. *The Elfstones of Shannara* followed in 1982, and *The Wishsong of Shannara* in 1985. *Magic Kingdom for Sale—Sold!* began a bestselling new series for him in 1986—the most recent book in that series was *The Tangle Box*. **The Heritage of Shannara**, a four-book series begun in 1990 with *Scions of Shannara*, concluded with the publication of *The Talismans of Shannara* in 1993.

The author was a practicing attorney for many years, but now writes full time. He lives with his wife Judine in the Pacific Northwest and Hawaii.